Mary Higgins Clark's bestselling novels have sold more than three million copies in the UK alone. She is the author of thirty-seven suspense novels as well as three collections of short stories and a memoir.

Carol Higgins Clark is the author of the bestselling Regan Reilly mysteries. She is co-author, along with her mother, Mary Higgins Clark, of five novels. Also an actress, Carol Higgins Clark studied at the Beverly Hills Playhouse. She lives in New York City.

The
Christmas
Thief

& Other Stories

Mary Higgins Clark
&
Carol Higgins Clark

SIMON &
SCHUSTER

London · New York · Sydney · Toronto · New Delhi

A CBS COMPANY

The Christmas Thief & other stories bind-up first published in
Great Britain by Simon & Schuster UK Ltd, 2017
A CBS COMPANY

Containing:

The Christmas Thief
First published in Great Britain by Simon & Schuster UK Ltd, 2004
Copyright © Mary Higgins Clark and Carol Higgins Clark, 2004

Dashing Through the Snow
First published in Great Britain by Simon & Schuster UK Ltd, 2008
Copyright © Mary Higgins Clark and Carol Higgins Clark, 2008

Silent Night
First published in Great Britain by Simon & Schuster UK Ltd, 1995
Copyright © Mares Enterprises Inc., 1995

1 3 5 7 9 10 8 6 4 2

Simon & Schuster UK Ltd
1st Floor
222 Gray's Inn Road
London WC1X 8HB

Simon & Schuster Australia, Sydney
Simon & Schuster India, New Delhi

www.simonandschuster.co.uk
www.simonandschuster.com.au
www.simonandschuster.co.in

A CIP catalogue record for this book
is available from the British Library

Paperback ISBN: 978-1-4711-7016-4
eBook ISBN: 978-1-4711-7017-1

Printed and bound by CPI Group (UK) Ltd, Croydon, CR0 4YY

MIX
Paper from
responsible sources
FSC® C020471

Simon & Schuster UK Ltd are committed to sourcing paper
that is made from wood grown in sustainable forests and support the Forest
Stewardship Council, the leading international forest certification organisation.
Our books displaying the FSC logo are printed on FSC certified paper.

The Christmas Thief

by Mary Higgins Clark &
Carol Higgins Clark

I

Packy Noonan carefully placed an **x** on the calendar he had pinned to the wall of his cell in the federal prison located near Philadelphia, the City of Brotherly Love. Packy was overflowing with love for his fellow man. He had been a guest of the United States Government for twelve years, four months, and two days. But because he had served over 85 percent of his sentence and been a model prisoner, the parole board had reluctantly granted Packy his freedom as of November 12, which was only two weeks away.

Packy, whose full name was Patrick Coogan Noonan, was a world-class scam artist whose offense had been to cheat trusting investors out of nearly $100 million in the seemingly legitimate company he had founded. When the house of cards collapsed, after deducting the money he had spent on homes, cars, jewelry, bribes, and shady ladies, most of the rest, nearly $80 million, could not be accounted for.

In the years of his incarceration, Packy's story never changed. He insisted that his two missing associates had run off with the rest of the money and that, like his victims, he, too, had been the victim of his own trusting nature.

Fifty years old, narrow-faced, with a hawklike nose, close-set eyes, thinning brown hair, and a smile that inspired trust, Packy had stoically endured his years of confinement. He knew that when the day of deliverance came, his nest egg of $80 million would sufficiently compensate him for his discomfort.

He was ready to assume a new identity once he picked up his loot; a private plane would whisk him to Brazil, and a skillful plastic surgeon there had already been engaged to rearrange the sharp features that might have served as the blueprint for the working of his brain.

All the arrangements had been made by his missing associates, who were now residing in Brazil and had been living on $10 million of the missing funds. The remaining fortune Packy had managed to hide before he was arrested, which was why he knew he could count on the continued cooperation of his cronies.

The long-standing plan was that upon his release Packy would go to the halfway house in New York, as required by the terms of his parole, dutifully follow regulations for about a day, then shake off anyone following him, meet his partners in crime, and drive to Stowe, Vermont. There they were to have rented a farmhouse, a flatbed trailer, a barn to hide it in, and whatever equipment it took to cut down a very large tree.

"Why Vermont?" Giuseppe Como, better known as Jo-Jo, wanted to know. "You told us you hid the loot in New Jersey. Were you lying to us, Packy?"

"Would I lie to you?" Packy had asked, wounded. "Maybe I don't want you talking in your sleep."

Jo-Jo and Benny, forty-two-year-old fraternal twins, had been in on the scam from the beginning, but both humbly acknowledged that neither one of them had the fertile mind needed to concoct grandiose schemes. They recognized their roles as foot soldiers of Packy and willingly accepted the droppings from his table since, after all, they were lucrative droppings.

"O Christmas tree, *my* Christmas tree," Packy whispered to himself as he contemplated finding the special branch of one particular tree in Vermont and retrieving the flask of priceless diamonds that had been nestling there for over thirteen years.

Even though the mid-November afternoon was brisk, Alvirah and Willy Meehan decided to walk from the meeting of the Lottery Winners Support Group to their Central Park South apartment. Alvirah had started the group when she and Willy won $40 million in the lottery and had heard from a number of people who e-mailed them to warn that they, too, had won pots of money but had gone through it in no time flat. This month they had moved the meeting up a few days because they were leaving for Stowe, Vermont, to spend a long weekend at The Trapp Family Lodge with their good friend, private investigator Regan Reilly, her fiancé, Jack Reilly, head of the Major Case Squad of the NYPD, and Regan's parents, Luke and Nora. Nora was a well-known mystery writer, and Luke was a funeral director. Even though business was brisk, he said no dead body was going to keep *him* away from the vacation.

Married forty years and in their early sixties, Alvirah and Willy had been living in Flushing, Queens, on that fateful evening when the little balls started dropping, one after the other, with a magic number on each of them. They fell in the exact sequence the Meehans had been playing for years, a combination of their birthdays and anniversary. Alvirah had been sitting in the living room, soaking her feet after a hard day of cleaning for her Friday lady, Mrs. O'Keefe, who was a born slob. Willy, a self-employed plumber, had just gotten back from fixing a broken toilet in the old apartment building next to theirs. After that first moment of being absolutely stunned, Alvirah had jumped up, spilling the pail of water. Her bare feet dripping, she had danced around the room with Willy, both of them half-laughing, half-crying.

From day one she and Willy had been sensible. Their sole extravagance was to buy a three-room apartment with a terrace overlooking Central Park. Even in that they were cautious. They kept their apartment in Flushing, just in case New York State went belly up and couldn't afford to continue making the payments to them. They saved half of the money they received each year and invested it wisely.

The color of Alvirah's flaming orange-red hair, now coiffed by Antonio, the hairdresser to the stars, was changed to a golden red shade. Her friend Baroness Min von Schreiber had selected the handsome tweed pantsuit she was wearing. Min begged her never to go shopping alone, pointing out that Alvirah was natural prey for salespeople trying to unload the buyer's mistakes.

Although she had retired her mop and pail, in her newfound life Alvirah was busier than ever. Her penchant for finding trouble and solving problems had turned her into an amateur detective. To aid in catching wrongdoers she had a microphone hidden in her large sunburst lapel pin and turned it on when she sensed someone she was talking to had something to hide. In the three years of being a multi-millionaire, she had solved a dozen crimes and wrote about them for *The New York Globe,* a weekly newspaper. Her adventures were enjoyed so much by the readership that she now had a biweekly column even when she didn't have a crime to report on.

Willy had closed his one-man company but was working harder than ever, devoting his plumbing skills to bettering the lives of the elderly poor on the West Side, under the direction of his eldest sibling, Sister Cordelia, a formidable Dominican nun.

Today the Lottery Winners Support Group had met in a lavish apartment in Trump Tower that had been purchased by Herman Hicks, a recent lottery winner, who, a worried Alvirah now said to Willy, "was going through his money too fast."

They were about to cross Fifth Avenue in front of the Plaza Hotel. "The light's turning yellow," Willy said. "With this traffic I don't want us to get caught in the middle of the street. Somebody'll mow us down."

Alvirah was all set to double the pace. She hated to miss a light, but Willy was cautious. That's the difference between us, she thought indulgently. I'm a risk taker.

"I think Herman will be okay," Willy said reassuringly. "As he said, it always was his dream to live in Trump Tower, and real estate is a good investment. He bought the furniture from the people who were moving; the price seemed fair, and except for buying a wardrobe at Paul Stuart, he hasn't been extravagant."

"Well, a seventy-year-old childless widower with twenty million dollars after taxes is going to have plenty of ladies making tuna casseroles for him," Alvirah noted with concern. "I only wish he'd realize what a wonderful person Opal is."

Opal Fogarty had been a member of the Lottery Winners Support Group since its founding. She had joined after she read about it in Alvirah's column in *The New York Globe* because, as she pointed out, "I'm the lottery winner turned big loser, and I'd like to warn new winners not to get taken in by a glib-talking crook."

Today, because there were two more new members, Opal had told her story about investing in a shipping company whose founder had shipped nothing but money from her bank to his pocket. "I won six million dollars in the lottery," she explained. "After taxes I had just about three million. A guy named Patrick Noonan persuaded me to invest in his phony company. I've always been devoted to Saint Patrick, and I thought that anyone with that name had to be honest. I didn't know then that everyone called that crook Packy. Now he's getting out of prison next week," she explained. "I just wish I could be invisible and follow him around, because I know perfectly well that he's hidden lots of money away."

Opal's blue eyes had welled with tears of frustration at the thought that Packy Noonan would manage to get his hands on the money he had stolen from her.

"Did you lose *all* the money?" Herman had asked solicitously.

It was the kindness in his voice that had set Alvirah's always matchmaking mind on red alert.

"In all they recovered about eight hundred thousand dollars, but the law firm appointed by the court to find the money for us ran up bills of nearly a million dollars, so after they paid themselves, none of us got anything back."

It wasn't unusual for Alvirah to be thinking about something and have Willy comment on it. "Opal's story really made an impression on that young couple who won six hundred thousand on the scratch-a-number," Willy said now. "But that doesn't help her. I mean, she's sixty-seven years old and still working as a waitress in a diner. Those trays are heavy for her to carry."

"She has a vacation coming up soon," Alvirah mused, "but I bet she can't afford to go anywhere. Oh, Willy, we've been so blessed." She gave a quick smile to Willy, thinking for the tenth time that day that he was such a good-looking man. With his shock of white hair, ruddy complexion, keen blue eyes, and big frame, many people commented that

Willy was the image of the late Tip O'Neill, the legendary Speaker of the House of Representatives.

The light turned green. They crossed Fifth Avenue and walked along Central Park South to their apartment just past Seventh Avenue. Alvirah pointed to a young couple who were getting into a horse-drawn carriage for a ride through the park. "I wonder if he's going to propose to her," she commented. "Remember that's where you proposed to me?"

"Sure I remember," Willy said, "and the whole time I was hoping I had enough money to pay for the ride. In the restaurant I meant to tip the headwaiter five bucks, and like a dope I gave him fifty. Didn't realize it until I reached for the ring to put on your finger. Anyhow, I'm glad we decided to go to Vermont with the Reillys. Maybe we'll take a ride on one of the horse-drawn sleighs up there."

"Well, for sure I won't go downhill skiing," Alvirah said. "That's why I hesitated when Regan suggested we go. She and Jack and Nora and Luke are all great skiers. But we can go cross-country skiing, I've got books I want to read, and there are walking paths. One way or another we'll find plenty to do."

Fifteen minutes later, in their comfortable living room with its sweeping view of Central Park, she was opening the package the doorman had given her. "Willy, I don't believe it," she said. "Not even Thanksgiving, yet, and Molloy, McDermott, McFadden, and Markey are sending us a Christmas present." The Four M's, as the brokerage firm was known on Wall Street, was the one Alvirah and Willy had selected to handle the money they allocated to buying government bonds or stock in rock-solid companies.

"What'd they send us?" Willy called from the kitchen as he prepared manhattans, their favorite five o'clock cocktail.

"I haven't opened it yet," Alvirah called back. "You know all that plastic they put on everything. But I think it's a bottle or a jar. The card says 'Happy Holidays.' Boy are they rushing the season. It's not even Thanksgiving yet."

"Whatever it is, don't ruin your nails," Willy warned. "I'll get it for you."

Don't ruin your nails. Alvirah smiled to herself remembering the years when it would have been a waste of time to put even a dab of polish on her nails because all the bleaches and harsh soaps she used cleaning houses would have made short work of it.

Willy came into the living room carrying a tray with two cocktail glasses and a plate of cheese and crackers. Herman's idea of nourishment at the meeting had been Twinkies and instant coffee, both of which Willy and Alvirah had refused.

He put the tray on the coffee table and picked up the bubble-wrapped package. With a firm thrust he pulled apart the adhesive seals and unwound the wrapping. His expression of anticipation changed to surprise and then amazement.

"How much money have we got invested with the Four M's?" he asked.

Alvirah told him.

"Honey, take a look. They sent us a jar of maple syrup. That's their idea of a Christmas present?"

"They've got to be kidding," Alvirah exclaimed, shaking her head as she took the jar from him. Then she read the label. "Willy, look," she exclaimed. "They didn't give us just a jar of syrup. They gave us a *tree!* It says so right here. *'This syrup comes from the tree reserved for Willy and Alvirah Meehan. Please come and tap your tree to refill this jar when it is empty.'* I wonder where the tree is."

Willy began rummaging through the gift-wrapped box that had contained the jar. "Here's a paper. No, it's a map." He studied it and began to laugh. "Honey, here's something else we can do when we're in Stowe. We can look up our tree. From the way it looks here, it's right near the Trapp family property."

The phone rang. It was Regan Reilly calling from Los Angeles. "All set for Vermont?" she asked. "No backing out now, promise?"

"Not a chance, Regan," Alvirah assured her. "I've got business in Stowe. I'm going to look up a tree."

3

"Regan, you must be exhausted," Nora Regan Reilly said with concern, as she looked fondly across the breakfast table at her only child. To others, beautiful raven-haired Regan might be a superb private investigator, but to Nora, her thirty-one-year-old daughter was still the little girl she would give her life to protect.

"She looks okay to me," Luke Reilly observed as he set down his coffee cup with the decisive gesture that said he was on his way. His lanky six-foot-five frame was encased in a midnight blue suit, white shirt, and black tie, one of the half-dozen such outfits in his possession. Luke was the owner of three funeral homes in northern New Jersey, which was the reason for his need for subdued clothing. His handsome head of silver hair complemented his lean face, which could look suitably somber but always broke into a ready smile outside his viewing rooms. Now that smile encompassed both his wife and his daughter.

They were at the breakfast table in the Reilly home in

Summit, New Jersey, the home in which Regan had grown up and where Luke and Nora still lived. It was also the place where Nora Regan Reilly wrote the suspense novels that had made her famous. Now she got up to kiss her husband goodbye. Ever since he'd been kidnapped a year ago, he never walked out the door without her worrying that something might happen to him.

Like Regan, Nora had classic features, blue eyes, and fair skin. Unlike Regan, she was a natural blond. At five feet three, she was four inches shorter than her daughter and towered over by her husband.

"Don't get kidnapped," she said only half-jokingly. "We want to leave for Vermont no later than two o'clock."

"Getting kidnapped once in a lifetime is about average," Regan volunteered. "I looked up the statistics last week."

"And don't forget," Luke reminded Nora for the hundredth time, "if it wasn't for my pain and suffering in that little predicament, Regan would never have met Jack and you wouldn't be planning a wedding."

Jack Reilly, head of the Major Case Squad of the New York Police Department and now Regan's fiancé, had worked on the case when Luke and his young driver vanished. He not only caught the kidnappers and retrieved the ransom, but in the process had captured Regan's heart.

"I can't believe I haven't seen Jack in two weeks," Regan said with a sigh as she buttered a roll. "He wanted to pick me up at Newark Airport this morning, but I told him I'd take a cab. He had to go into the office to wrap up a few things but he'll be here by two." Regan started to yawn. "Those overnight flights make me a little spacey."

"On second thought, I would suggest that your mother is right," Luke said. "You do look as if a couple of hours of sleep would be useful." He returned Nora's kiss, rumpled Regan's hair, and was gone.

Regan laughed. "I swear he still thinks I'm six years old."

"It's because you're getting married soon. He's starting to talk about how he's looking forward to grandchildren."

"Oh, my God. That thought makes me even more tired. I think I will go upstairs and lie down."

Left alone at the table, Nora refilled her own cup and opened *The New York Times*. The car was already packed for the trip. This morning she intended to work at her desk because she wanted to make notes on the new book she was starting. She hadn't quite decided whether Celia, her protagonist, would be an interior designer or a lawyer. Two different kinds of people, she acknowledged, but as an interior designer it was feasible that Celia would have met her first husband in the process of decorating his Manhattan apartment. On the other hand, if she was a lawyer, it gave a different dynamic to the story.

Read the paper, she told herself. First lesson of writing: Put the subconscious on power-save until you start staring at the computer. She glanced out the window. The breakfast room looked out onto the now snow-covered lawn and the garden that led to the pool and tennis court. I love it here, she thought. I get so mad at the people who knock New Jersey. Oh, well, as Dad used to say, "When they know better, they'll do better."

Wrapped in her quilted satin bathrobe, Nora felt warm and content. Instead of chasing crooks in Los Angeles, Regan was home and going away with them. She had gotten engaged in a hot air balloon, of all places, just a few weeks ago. Over Las Vegas. Nora didn't care where or how it happened, she was just thrilled to finally be planning Regan's wedding. And there couldn't be a more perfect man for her than wonderful Jack Reilly.

In a few hours they would be leaving for the beautiful Trapp Family Lodge and would be joined there by their dear friends Alvirah and Willy Meehan. What's not to like? Nora thought as she flipped to the Metro section of the newspaper.

Her eye immediately went to the front-page picture of a handsome woman dressed in a long skirt, blouse, and vest and standing in a forest. The caption was "Rockefeller Center Selects Tree."

The woman in that picture looks familiar, Nora thought as she skimmed the story.

An 80-foot blue spruce in Stowe, Vermont, is about to take its place as the world's most famous Christmas tree this year. It was chosen for its majestic beauty, but as it turned out, it was planted nearly fifty years ago in a forest adjacent to the property owned by the legendary Von Trapp family. Maria von Trapp happened to be walking through the forest when the sapling was planted, and her picture was taken standing next to it. Since the fortieth anniversary of the world's most successful musical film, *The Sound of Music*, is about to occur, and since the film emphasizes family values and courage in the face of adversity, a special reception has been planned for the tree on its arrival in New York.

It will be cut down on Monday morning and then taken on a flatbed to a barge near New Haven and floated down Long Island Sound to Manhattan. Upon its arrival at Rockefeller Center it will be greeted by a choir of hundreds of schoolchildren from all over the city who will sing a medley of songs from *The Sound of Music*.

"Well, for heaven's sake," Nora said aloud. "They'll be cutting down the tree while we're there. What fun it will be to watch." She began to hum: " 'The hills are alive . . . ' "

4

On that same morning a scant hundred miles away, Packy Noonan woke up with a happy smile plastered on his face.

"It's your big day, huh, Packy?" C.R., the racketeer in the next cell, asked sourly.

Packy could understand the reason for his sullen manner. C.R. was in only the second year of a fourteen-year stretch, and he had not yet adjusted to life behind bars.

"It's my big day," Packy agreed amiably as he packed his few possessions: toiletries, underwear, socks, and a picture of his long-dead mother. He always referred to her lovingly and with tears in his eyes when he spoke in the chapel in his role as a counselor to his fellow inmates. He explained to them that she had always seen the good in him even when he had gone astray, and on her deathbed she told him that she knew he'd turn out to be an upstanding citizen.

In fact, he hadn't seen his mother for twenty years before she died. Nor did he see fit to share with his fellow inmates the fact that in her will, after leaving her meager possessions to the Sisters of Charity, she had written, "And to my son, Patrick, unfortunately known as Packy, I leave one dollar and his high chair because the only time he ever gave me any happiness was when he was small enough to sit in it."

Ma had a way with words, Packy thought fondly. I guess I got the gift of gab from her. The woman on the parole board had almost been in tears when he had explained at his hearing that he prayed to his mother every night. Not that it had done him any good. He had served every last day of his minimum sentence plus another two years. The bleeding heart had been overruled by the rest of the board, six to one.

The jacket and slacks he had worn when he arrived at the prison were out of fashion, of course, but it felt great to put them on. And thanks to the money he swindled, they had been custom-made by Armani. As far as he was concerned, he still looked pretty sharp in them—not that they would be in his closet for thirty seconds after he got to Brazil.

His lawyer, Thoris Twinning, was picking him up at ten o'clock to escort him to the halfway house known as The Castle on the Upper West Side in Manhattan. Packy loved the story that in its long history The Castle had twice been an academy for Catholic high school girls. Ma should know that, he thought. She'd think I was defiling the place.

He was scheduled to stay there for two weeks to reintroduce himself to the world where people actually worked for a living. He understood that there would be group sessions in which the rules about signing in and signing out and the importance of reporting to his parole officer would be explained. He was assured that at The Castle they would be able to find him permanent housing. He could predict that it would be in a crummy rooming house in Staten Island or the Bronx. The counselors would also help him get a job immediately.

Packy could hardly wait. He knew that the receiver appointed by the Bureau of Securities to try to find the money lost by the investors would probably have him tailed. There was nothing he looked forward to more than the fun of losing that tail. Unlike thirteen years ago when detectives were swarming all over Manhattan looking for him. He was just leaving for Vermont to retrieve the loot and get out of the country when he was arrested. That wasn't going to happen again.

It had already been explained to him that as of Sunday he would be allowed to leave The Castle in the morning but had to be back and signed in by dinner time. And he had already figured out exactly how he would shake the nincompoop who was supposed to be following him.

At ten-forty on Sunday morning, Benny and Jo-Jo would be waiting on Madison and Fifty-first in a van with a ski rack. Then they'd be on their way to Vermont. Following his instructions, Benny and Jo-Jo had rented a farm near Stowe six months ago. The only virtue of the farm was that it had a large if decrepit barn where a flatbed would be housed.

In the farmhouse the twins had installed an acquaintance, a guy without a record who was incredibly naive and was happy to be paid to house sit for them.

That way, just in case there were any slips, when the cops were searching for a flatbed with a tree on it, they wouldn't start looking in places where people lived. There were enough farms with barns that were owned by out-of-town skiers for them to investigate. The skiers usually didn't arrive until after Thanksgiving.

I wired the flask of diamonds onto the branch thirteen and a half years ago, Packy thought. A spruce grows about one and a half feet a year. The branch I marked was about twenty feet high at the time. I was standing at the top of the twenty foot ladder. Now that branch should be about forty feet high. Trouble is no regular ladder goes that high.

That's why we have to take the whole tree, and if someone with nothing better to do than mind other people's business asks questions, we can say it's going to be decorated for the Christmas pageant in Hackensack, New Jersey. Jo-Jo has a fake permit to cut the tree and a phony letter from the mayor of Hackensack, thanking Pickens for the tree, so that should take care of that.

Packy's agile brain leaped about to find any flaw in his reasoning but came up dry. Satisfied, he continued to review the plan: Then we get the flatbed into the barn, find the branch where the loot is hidden, and then we're off to Brazil, cha, cha, cha.

All of the above was racing through Packy's mind as he ate his final breakfast at the Federal Correctional Institution and, when it was over, bid a fond farewell to his fellow inmates.

"Good luck, Packy," Lightfingered Tom said solemnly.

"Don't give up preaching," a grizzled long-timer urged. "Keep that promise to your mother that you'd set a good example for the young."

Ed, the lawyer who had vacated his clients' trust funds of millions, grinned and gave a lazy wave of his hand. "I give you three months before you're back," he predicted.

Packy didn't show how much that got under his skin. "I'll send you a card, Ed," he said. "From Brazil," he muttered under his breath as he followed the guard to the warden's office where Thoris Twinning, his court-appointed lawyer, was waiting.

Thoris was beaming. "A happy day," he gushed. "A happy, happy day. And I have wonderful news. I've been in touch with your parole officer, and he has a job for you. As of a week from Monday you will be working at the salad bar in the Palace-Plus diner on Broadway and Ninety-seventh Street."

As of a week from Monday a bunch of lackeys will be dropping grapes into my mouth, Packy thought, but he turned on the mesmerizing smile that had enchanted Opal

Fogarty and some two hundred other investors in the Patrick Noonan Shipping and Handling Company. "My mama's prayers have been answered," he said joyfully. His eyes raised to heaven and a blissful expression on his sharp-featured face, he sighed, "An honest job with an honest day's pay. Just what Mama always wanted for me."

5

My, my, this is such a beautiful car," Opal Fogarty commented from the back seat of Alvirah and Willy's Mercedes. "When I was growing up we had a pickup truck. My father said it made him feel like a cowboy. My mother used to tell him it rode like a bucking steer, so she could understand why he felt like a cowboy. He bought it without telling her, and boy was she mad! But I have to say this: It lasted for fourteen years before it stopped dead on the Triborough Bridge during rush hour. Even my father admitted it was time to give up on the truck, and this time my mother went car shopping with him." She laughed. "She got to pick out the car. It was a Dodge. Daddy made her mad by asking the salesman if a taxi meter was an option."

Alvirah turned to look at Opal. "Why did he ask that?"

"Honey, it's because Dodge made so many taxis," Willy explained. "That was funny, Opal."

"Dad *was* pretty funny," Opal agreed. "He never had two nickels to rub together, but he did his best. He inherited two thousand dollars when I was about eight years old, and somebody convinced him to put it in parachute stock. They said that with all the commercial flying people would be doing, all the passengers would have to wear parachutes. I guess being gullible is genetic."

Alvirah was glad to hear Opal laugh. It was two o'clock, and they were on route 91 heading for Vermont. At ten o'clock she and Willy had been packing for the trip and half-watching the television in the bedroom when a news flash caught their attention. It showed Packy Noonan leaving federal prison in his lawyer's car. At the gate he got out of the car and spoke to the reporters. "I regret the harm I have caused the investors in my company," he said. Tears welled in his eyes and his lip trembled as he went on. "I understand that I will be working at the salad bar at the Palace-Plus diner, and I will ask that ten percent of my wages be taken to start to repay the people who lost their savings in the Patrick Noonan Shipping and Handling Company."

"Ten percent of a minimum wage job!" Willy had snorted. "He's got to be kidding."

Alvirah had rushed to the phone and dialed Opal. "Turn on channel twenty-four!" she ordered. Then she was sorry she had made the call because when Opal saw Packy, she began to cry.

"Oh, Alvirah, it just makes me sick to think that terrible cheat is as free as a daisy while I'm sitting here thrilled to get a week's vacation because I'm so tired. Mark my words, he'll end up joining his pals on the Riviera or wherever they are with my money in their pockets."

That was when Alvirah insisted that Opal join them for the long weekend in Vermont. "We have two big bedrooms and baths in our villa," she said, "and it will do you good to get away. You can help us follow the map and find my tree. There won't be any syrup coming from it now, but I packed the jar that the stockbrokers sent me. We have a little kitchen so maybe I'll make pancakes for everyone and see how good the syrup tastes. And I read in the paper that they'll be cutting down the tree for Rockefeller Center right near where we're staying. That would be fun to watch, wouldn't it?"

It didn't take much to persuade Opal. And she was already perking up. On the trip to Vermont she made only one comment about Packy Noonan: "I can just see him working at a salad bar in a diner. He'll probably be sneaking the croutons into his pocket."

6

Sometimes Milo Brosky wished he had never met the Como twins. He had run into them by chance in Greenwich Village twenty years ago when he attended a poets' meeting in the back room of Eddie's Aurora. Benny and Jo-Jo were hanging out in the bar.

I was feeling pretty good, Milo thought as he sipped a beer in the shabby parlor of a rundown farmhouse in Stowe, Vermont. I'd just read my narrative poem about a peach who falls in love with a fruit fly, and our workshop thought it was wonderful. They saw deep meaning and tenderness that never verged on sentimentality in my poem. I felt so good I decided to have a beer on the way home, and that's when I met the twins.

Milo took another sip of beer. I should have bought back my introduction to them, he thought glumly. Not that they weren't good to me. They knew that I hadn't had my big breakthrough as a poet and that I'd take any kind of job to keep a roof over my head. But this roof feels as though it could fall in on me. They're up to something.

Milo frowned. Forty-two years old, with shoulder-length hair and a wispy beard, he could have been an extra in a film about Woodstock '69. His bony arms dangled from his long frame. His guileless gray eyes had a perpetually benevolent expression. His voice with its singsong pitch made his listeners think of adjectives like "kind" and "gentle."

Milo knew that a dozen years ago the Como Brothers had been obliged to skip town in a hurry because of their involvement with the Packy Noonan scam. He hadn't heard from them in years. Then six months ago he had received a phone call from Jo-Jo. He wouldn't say where he was, but he asked Milo if he would be interested in making a lot of money without any risk. All Milo had to do was find a farmhouse for rent in Stowe, Vermont. It had to have a large barn, at least ninety feet long. Until the first of the year Milo was to spend at least long weekends there. He was to get to know the locals, explain that he was a poet and, like J. D. Salinger and Aleksandr Solzhenitsyn, needed a retreat in New England where he could write in solitude.

It had been clear to Milo that Jo-Jo was reading both names and that he had no idea who either Salinger or Solzhenitsyn was, but the offer had come at a perfect time. His part-time jobs were drying up. The lease on his attic apartment was expiring, and his landlady had flatly refused to renew it. She simply couldn't understand why it was imperative for him to write late at night even though he explained that was when his thoughts transcended the everyday world and that rap music played loud gave wings to his poetry.

He quickly found the farmhouse in Stowe and had been living in it full-time. Even though the regular deposits to his checking account had been a lifesaver, they were not enough to support another apartment in New York. The prices were astronomical there, and Milo rued the day he had told his landlady that he needed to keep the music blasting at night so it would drown out her snoring. In short, Milo was not happy. He was sick of the country life and longed for the bustle and activity of Greenwich Village. He liked people, and even though he regularly invited some of the Stowe locals to his poetry readings, after the first couple of evenings no one came back. Jo-Jo had promised that by the end of the year he would receive a $50,000 bonus. But Milo was beginning to suspect that the farmhouse and his presence in it had something to do with Packy Noonan getting out of prison.

"I don't want to get in trouble," he warned Jo-Jo during one of his phone calls.

"Trouble? What are you talking about?" Jo-Jo had asked sadly. "Would I get my good friend in trouble? What'd you do? Rent a farmhouse? That's a crime?"

A pounding on the farmhouse door interrupted Milo's

reverie. He rushed to open it and then stood frozen at the sight of his visitors—two short, portly men in ski outfits standing in front of a flatbed with a couple of straggly-looking evergreen trees on it. At first he didn't recognize them, but then he bellowed, "Jo-Jo! Benny!" Even as he threw his arms around them he was aware of how much they had changed.

Jo-Jo had always been hefty, but he had put on at least twenty pounds and looked like an overweight tomcat, with tanned skin and balding head. Benny was the same height, about five-six, but he'd always been so thin you could slip him under the door. He'd gained weight, too, and although he was only half the size of Jo-Jo, he was starting to look more like him.

Jo-Jo did not waste time. "You got a padlock on the barn door, Milo. That was smart. Open it up."

"Right away, right away." Milo loped into the kitchen where the key to the padlock was hanging on a nail. Jo-Jo had been so specific on the phone about the size of the barn that he had always suspected it was the main reason he had been hired. He hoped they wouldn't mind that the barn had a lot of stalls in it. The owner of the farm had gone broke trying to raise a racehorse that would pay off. Instead, according to local gossip, when he went to claiming races, he invariably managed to select hopeless plugs, all of which ate to the bursting point and sat down at the starting gate.

"Hurry up, Milo," Benny was yelling even though Milo

hadn't taken more than half a minute to get the key. "We don't want no local yokel to come to one of your poetry recitals and see the flatbed."

Why not? Milo wondered, but without taking the time to either grab a coat or answer his own question, he raced outside and down the field to undo the padlock and pull open the wide doors of the barn.

The early evening was very cold, and he shivered. In the fading light Milo could see that there was another vehicle behind the flatbed, a van with a ski rack on the roof. They must have taken up skiing, he thought. Funny, he would never have considered them athletes.

Benny helped him pull back the doors. Milo switched on the light and was able to see the dismay on Jo-Jo's face.

"What's with all the stalls?" Jo-Jo demanded.

"They used to raise horses here." Milo did not know why he was suddenly nervous. I've done everything they want, he reasoned, so what's with the angst? "It's the right size barn," he defended himself, his voice never wavering from its singsong gentleness, "and there aren't many that big."

"Yeah, right. Get out of the way." With an imperious sweep of his arm, Jo-Jo signaled to Benny to drive the flatbed into the barn.

Benny inched the vehicle through the doors, and then a splintering crash confirmed the fact that he had sideswiped the first stall. The sound continued intermittently until the flatbed was fully inside the barn. The space was so tight that Benny could exit only by moving from the driver's seat to the passenger seat, opening the door just enough to squeeze out, and then flattening himself against the walls and gates of the stalls as he inched past them.

His first words when he reached Milo and Jo-Jo at the door were "I need a beer. Maybe two or three beers. You got anything to eat, Milo?"

For lack of something to do when he wasn't writing a poem, Milo had taught himself to cook in his six months of babysitting the farm. Now he was glad that fresh spaghetti sauce was in the refrigerator. He remembered that the Como twins loved pasta.

Fifteen minutes later they were sipping beer around the kitchen table while Milo heated his sauce and boiled water for the pasta. To Milo's dread, listening to the brothers talk as he bustled around the kitchen, he heard the name "Packy" whispered and realized that the farmhouse indeed had something to do with Packy Noonan's release.

But *what?* And where did *he* fit in? He waited until he put the steaming dishes of pasta in front of the twins before he said point-blank: "If this has something to do with Packy Noonan, I'm out of here now."

Jo-Jo smiled. "Be reasonable, Milo. You rented a place for us when you knew we were on the lam. You've been getting money deposited in your bank account for six months. All you have to do is sit here and write poetry, and in a couple of days you get fifty thousand bucks in cash and you're home free."

"In a couple of days?" Milo asked, incredulous, his mind conjuring up the happiness that $50,000 could buy: A decent place to rent in the Village. No worry about part-time jobs for at least a couple of years. No one could make a buck last as long as he could.

Jo-Jo was studying him. Now he nodded with satisfaction. "Like I said, all you need to do is sit here and write poetry. Write a nice poem about a tree."

"What tree?"

"We're just as much in the dark as you are, but we'll all find out real soon."

can't believe I'm sitting here having dinner with not only Alvirah and Willy but Nora Regan Reilly, the famous writer, and her family, Opal thought. This morning after watching that miserable Packy Noonan on television, I felt like turning my face to the wall and never getting out of bed again. Shows how much everything can change.

And they were all so nice to her. Over dinner they had told her about Luke being kidnapped and held hostage on a leaky houseboat in the Hudson River with his driver, who was a single mother with two little boys, and how they would have drowned if Alvirah and Regan hadn't rescued them.

"Alvirah and I make a good team," Regan Reilly said. "I wish we could put our heads together and find your money for you, Opal. You do think that Packy Noonan has it hidden somewhere, don't you?"

"Sure he does," Jack Reilly said emphatically. "That case was in the federal court, so we didn't handle it, but my guess is that guy has a stash somewhere. When you add up what the feds knew Packy spent, there's still between seventy and eighty million dollars missing. He probably has it in a numbered account in Switzerland or in a bank in the Cayman Islands."

Jack was sipping coffee. His left arm was around the back of Regan's chair. The way he kept looking at her made Opal wish that somewhere along the way she had met a special guy. He's so handsome, she thought, and Regan is so pretty. Jack had sandy hair that tended to curl, his hazel eyes were more green than brown, and his even features were enhanced by a strong jaw. When he and Regan walked into the dining room together, they were holding hands. Regan was tall, but Jack was considerably taller and had broad shoulders to match.

Even though it was only the second week in November, an early heavy snowfall had meant there was real powder on the slopes and on the ground. Tomorrow the Reillys were going to downhill ski. It was funny that Jack's name was Reilly too, Opal thought. She and Alvirah and Willy were going to take a walk in the woods and find Alvirah's tree. Then in the afternoon they were going to take lessons in cross-country skiing. Alvirah told her that she and Willy had done cross-country skiing a couple of times, and it wasn't that hard to keep your balance—and it was fun.

Opal wasn't sure how much fun it would be, but she was willing to give it a try. Years ago in school, she had always been a good athlete, and she almost always walked the mile back and forth to work to keep trim.

"You have that blank look in your eyes that says you're doing some deep thinking," Luke observed to Nora.

Nora was sipping a cappuccino. "I'm remembering how much I enjoyed the story of the Von Trapp family. I read Maria's book long before I saw the film. It's so interesting to be here now and realize that a tree she watched being planted has been chosen for Rockefeller Center this year. With all the worries in the world, it's comforting to know that New York schoolchildren will welcome that tree. It makes it so special."

"Well, the tree is only down the road enjoying its last weekend in Vermont," Luke said drily. "Monday morning before we leave, we can all go over, watch it being cut down, and kiss it good-bye."

"On the car radio I heard that they'll take it off the barge in Manhattan on Wednesday morning," Alvirah volunteered. "I think it would be exciting to be there when the tree arrives at Rockefeller Center. I know I'd like to see the choirs of schoolchildren and hear them sing."

But even as the words were coming from her mouth, Alvirah began to have a funny feeling that something would go wrong. She looked around the cozy dining room. People were lingering over dinner, smiling and chatting. Why did a cold certainty fill her that trouble was brewing and Opal would be caught up in it? I shouldn't have asked her to come, Alvirah worried. For some reason she's in danger here.

8

Packy's first night in the halfway house known as The Castle was not much better, in his opinion, than a step up from the federal penitentiary. He was signed in, given a bed, and once again had the rules explained to him. He immediately reconfirmed his ability to leave The Castle on Sunday morning by piously explaining that as a good Catholic he never missed Mass. He threw in for good measure the fact that it was the anniversary of his mother's death. Packy had long since forgotten exactly when his mother died, but the easy tear that rushed to his eye on cue and the roguish smile that accompanied his confession—"God bless her. She never gave up on me"—made the counselor on duty hasten to reassure him that on Sunday he could certainly attend Mass on his own.

The next day and a half passed in a blur. He dutifully sat in on the lectures warning him that he could be sent back to prison to complete his sentence if he did not follow strictly the terms of his parole. He sat at meals visualizing the feasts that he would soon be eating at fine restaurants in Brazil, sporting his new face. On Friday and Saturday night he closed his eyes in the room he was sharing with two other recently released convicts and drifted into sleep, dreaming of Egyptian cotton sheets, silk pajamas, and finally getting his hands on his flask of diamonds.

Sunday morning dawned crisp and clear. The first snowfall had occurred two weeks ago, much earlier than usual, and the forecast was that another one was on the way. It looked as if an old-fashioned winter was looming, and that was fine with Packy. He wasn't planning to share it with his fellow Americans.

Over the years of his incarceration he had managed to keep in contact with the Como twins by paying a number of carefully chosen visitors to other convicts to mail letters from him and then bring the Comos' letters to him. Only last week Jo-Jo had confirmed the arrangement to meet behind Saint Patrick's Cathedral by writing to urge him to attend the 10:15 Mass at the cathedral and then take a walk on Madison Avenue.

So Benny and Jo-Jo would be there. Why wouldn't they? Packy asked himself. At eight o'clock he closed the door of The Castle and stepped out onto the street. He had decided to walk the one hundred blocks, not because he wanted the exercise, but because he knew he would be followed and wanted his pursuer to have a good workout.

He could hear the instructions received by the guy who had been assigned to tail him: "Don't take your eyes off him. Sooner or later he'll lead us to the money he's hidden away."

No, I won't, Packy thought as he walked rapidly down Broadway. Several times, when stopped by a red light, he looked around casually as though enchanted by the world he had been missing for so long. The second time he was able to pick out his pursuer, a beefy guy dressed like a jogger.

Some jogger, Packy thought. He'll be lucky if he hasn't lost me before Saint Pat's.

On Sunday mornings the 10:15 Mass always drew the biggest crowds. That was when the full choir sang, and on many Sundays the Cardinal was the celebrant. Packy knew just where he was going to sit—on the right side, near the front. He would wait until Holy Communion was being given out and get on line with everyone else. Then, just before he received, he would cut across to the left of the altar to the corridor that led to the Madison Avenue townhouse that served as an office for the archdiocese. He remembered that when he was in high school, the kids in his class had assembled in the office and marched into the cathedral from there.

Jo-Jo and Benny would be parked in the van at the Madison Avenue entrance of the townhouse, and before the beefy guy had a chance to follow, they would be gone.

Packy got to the cathedral with time to spare and lit a candle in front of the statue of Saint Anthony. I know if I pray to you when I've lost something, you'll help me find it, he reminded the saint, but the stuff I want is *hidden*, not lost. So I don't need to pray for anything that I want to find. What I want from *you* is a little help in losing Fatso the Jogger.

His hands were cupped in prayer, which enabled him to conceal a small mirror in his palms. With it he was able to keep track of the jogger who was kneeling in a nearby pew.

At 10:15 Packy waited until the processional was about to start from the back of the church. Then he scurried up the aisle and squeezed into an end seat six rows from the front. With the mirror he was able to ascertain that four rows behind him the jogger was unable to get an end seat and had to move past two old ladies before he found space.

Love the old ladies, Packy thought. They always want to sit at the end. Afraid they'll miss something if they move over and make room for someone else.

But the problem was that there was lots of security in the cathedral. He hadn't counted on that. Even a two-year-old could see that some of those guys in wine-colored jackets weren't just ushers. Besides that, there were a few cops in uniform stationed inside. They would be all over him if he set foot on the altar.

Worried for the first time and his confidence shaken, Packy surveyed the scene more carefully. Beads of perspiration dampened his forehead as he realized his options were few. The side door on the right was his best shot. The time to move was when the Gospel was read. Everybody would be standing, and he could slip out without the jogger noticing he was gone. Then he would turn left and run the half block to Madison Avenue and up Madison to the van. "Be there, Jo-Jo. Be there, Benny," he whispered to himself. But if they were not and even if he was followed, it wasn't a parole violation to leave church early.

Packy began to feel better. With the help of the mirror he was able to ascertain that one more person had squeezed into the jogger's pew. True to form, the old ladies had stepped into the aisle to let him in, and now the jogger was cheek by jowl with a muscular kid who would not be easy to push aside.

"Let us reflect on our own lives, what we have done and what we have failed to do," the celebrant, a monsignor, was saying.

That was the last thing Packy wanted to reflect on. The epistle was read. Packy didn't hear it. He was concentrating on making his escape.

"Alleluia," the choir sang.

The congregation got to its feet. Before the last man was standing, Packy was at the side door of the cathedral that opened onto Fiftieth Street. Before the second alleluia was chanted, he was on Madison Avenue. Before the third prolonged al-le-lu-ia, he had spotted the van, opened the door, leaped into it, and it was gone.

Inside the cathedral the husky teenager had become openly belligerent. "Listen, mister," he told the jogger. "I might have knocked over these ladies if I let you shoot past me. Cool it, man."

9

On Sunday afternoon Alvirah said admiringly, "You're a natural on skis, Opal."

Opal's gentle face brightened at the praise. "I really used to be a good athlete in school," she said. "Softball was my specialty. I guess I'm just naturally coordinated or something. When I put on those cross-country skis, I felt as if I was dancing on air right away."

"Well, you certainly left Alvirah and me at the starting gate," Willy observed. "You took off as if you'd been born on skis."

It was five o'clock. The fire was blazing in their rented villa at the Trapp Family Lodge, and they were enjoying a glass of wine. Their plans to find Alvirah's tree had been postponed. Instead, on Saturday, when they learned that the afternoon cross-country lessons were all booked up, they quickly signed up for the morning instructor. Then, following lunch on Saturday, a vacancy had opened in the afternoon group, and Opal had gone off with them.

On Sunday, after Mass at Blessed Sacrament Church and an hour of skiing, Alvirah and Willy had had enough and were happy to go back to their cabin for a cup of tea and a nap. The shadows were lengthening when Opal returned. Alvirah had just started to worry about her when she glided up to the cabin, her cheeks rosy, her light brown eyes sparkling.

"Oh, Alvirah," she sighed as she stepped out of the skis, "I haven't enjoyed myself this much since—" She stopped, and the smile that had been playing around her lips vanished.

Alvirah knew perfectly well what Opal had been about to say: "I haven't had this much fun since the day I won the lottery."

But Opal's smile had been quick to come back. "I've had a wonderful day," she finished. "I can't thank you enough for inviting me to be with you."

The Reillys—Nora, Luke, Regan, and Regan's fiancé, Jack "no relation" Reilly—had spent another long day of downhill skiing. They had arranged with Alvirah to meet at seven for dinner in the main dining room of the lodge. There Regan entertained them with the story of one of her favorite cases: a ninety-three-year-old woman who became engaged to her financial planner and was to marry him three days later. She secretly planned to give $2 million each to her four stepnieces and -nephews if they *all* showed up at the wedding.

"Actually, it was her fifth wedding," Regan explained. "The family got wind of her plan and was dropping everything to be there. Who wouldn't? But one of the nieces is an actress who had taken off on a 'Go with the Flow' weekend. She shut off her cell phone, and nobody knew where she was. It was my job to find her and get her to the wedding so the family could collect their money."

"Brings tears to your eyes, doesn't it?" Luke commented.

"For two million dollars I would have been a brides-maid," Jack said, laughing.

"My mother used to listen to a radio program called 'Mr. Keen, Tracer of Lost Persons,'" Opal recalled. "Sounds like you're the new Mr. Keen, Regan."

"I've located a few missing people in my time," Regan acknowledged.

"And some of them would have been better off if she hadn't tracked them down," Jack said with a smile. "They ended up in the clink."

Once again it was a very pleasant dinner, Opal thought. Nice people, good conversation, beautiful surroundings—and now her newfound sport. She felt a million miles away from the Village Eatery where she had been working for the last twenty years, except for the few months when she had the lottery money in the bank. Not that the Village Eatery was such a bad place to work, she assured herself, and it's kind of an upscale diner because it has a liquor license and a separate bar. But the trays were heavy and the clientele was mostly college students, who claimed to be on tight budgets. That, Opal had come to believe, was nothing but an excuse for leaving cheap tips.

Seeing the way Alvirah and Willy lived since they won the lottery, and the way Herman Hicks had been able to use some of his lottery winnings to buy that beautiful apartment, made Opal realize all the more keenly how foolish she had been to trust that smooth-talking liar, Packy Noonan, and lose her chance for a little ease and luxury. What made it even harder was that Nora was so excited when she talked about the wedding she was planning for Regan and Jack. Opal's niece, her favorite relative, was saving for her wedding.

"I've got to keep it small, Aunt Opal," Kristy had told her. "Teachers don't make much money. Mom and Dad can't afford to help, and you wouldn't believe how much even a small wedding costs."

Kristy, the child of Opal's younger brother, lived in Boston. She had gone through college on a scholarship with the understanding that she would teach in an inner city school for three years after she graduated, and that's what she was doing now. Tim Cavanaugh, the young man she was marrying, was going to school at night for his master's degree in accounting. They were such fine young people and had so many friends. I'd love to plan a beautiful wedding for

them, Opal thought, and help them furnish their first home.
If only . . .

Woulda, shoulda, coulda, hada, oughta, she chided herself. Get over it. Think about something else.

The "something else" that jumped to mind was the fact
that the group of six people she skied with on Saturday afternoon had passed an isolated farmhouse about two miles
away. A man had been standing in the driveway loading skis
on top of a van. She had had only a glimpse of him, but for
some crazy reason he seemed familiar, as if she had run into
him recently. He was short and stocky, but so were half the
people who came into the diner, she reminded herself. He's
a type, nothing more than a type; that's the long and short of
it. That's why I thought I should know who he is. Still, it
haunted her.

"Is that okay with you, Opal?" Willy asked.

Startled, Opal realized that this was the second time
Willy had asked that question. What had he been talking
about? Oh, yes. He had suggested that they have an early
breakfast tomorrow, then head over to watch the Rockefeller
Center tree being cut down. After that they could find
Alvirah's tree, come back to the lodge, have lunch, and pack
for the trip home.

"Fine with me," Opal answered hurriedly. "I want to buy
a camera and take some pictures."

"Opal, I have a camera. I intend to take a picture of

Alvirah's tree and send it to our broker." Nora laughed. "The only thing we ever got from him for Christmas was a fruit-cake."

"A jar of maple syrup and a tree to tap hundreds of miles from where you live isn't what I call splurging," Alvirah exclaimed. "The people whose houses I cleaned used to get big bottles of champagne from their brokers."

"Those days went the way of pull-chain toilets," Willy said with a wave of his hand. "Today you're lucky if someone sends a gift in your name to his favorite charity which (a) you never heard of, and (b) you haven't a clue how much he sent."

"Luckily in my profession people never want to hear from us, especially during the holidays," Luke drawled.

Regan laughed. "This is getting ridiculous. I can't wait to watch the Rockefeller Center tree being cut down. Just think of all the people who are going to see that tree over the Christmas season. After that it would be fun to see how swift we are following the map to Alvirah's tree."

Regan couldn't possibly know that their lighthearted outing would turn deadly serious tomorrow when Opal skied off alone to check out the short, stocky man she had glimpsed at the farmhouse—the farmhouse where Packy Noonan had just arrived.

10

I feel like I'm at the Waltons, Milo thought as he raised the lid of the big pot and sniffed the beef stew that was simmering on the stove. It was early Sunday evening, and the farmhouse actually felt cozy with the aroma of his cooking. Through the window he could see that it had started to snow. Despite the heartwarming scene he couldn't wait for this job to be finished so he could get back to Greenwich Village. He needed the stimulation of attending readings and being around other poets. They listened respectfully to his poems and clapped and sometimes told him how moved they were. Even if they didn't mean it, they were good fakers. They give me the encouragement I need, he thought.

The Como twins had told Milo that they expected to be back at the farmhouse anytime after six on Sunday evening and to be sure to have dinner ready. They had left on Saturday afternoon, and if they'd seemed nervous when they arrived with the flatbed, it didn't compare to how they acted when they took off in the van. He had innocently asked them where they were going, and Jo-Jo had snapped back, "None of your business."

I told him to take a chill pill, Milo remembered, and he almost blew a gasket. Then Jo-Jo screamed at Benny to take the skis off the roof of the van and load them back again properly. He said one ski looked loose, and it would be just like Benny to load a ski that would fall off on the highway and hit a patrol car. "All we need are state troopers on our case, pawing our phony licenses."

Then fifteen minutes later he had yelled at Benny to come back inside because a bunch of cross-country skiers were passing across the field. "One of them skidding around out there could be an eagle-eyed cop," he snapped. "Your picture was on TV when they did the story on Packy, wasn't it? Maybe you want to take his bunk in the pen?"

They're scared out of their minds—that had been Milo's assessment. On the other hand, so was he. It was clear to him that wherever the twins were going involved risk. He worried that if they were arrested and talked about him, he could at the very least be accused of harboring fugitives. He shouldn't be doing business with people on the lam, and he was already sure that their little excursion had to do with Packy Noonan getting out of the can. Would anyone believe that thirteen years ago he didn't know that the twins had disappeared at the exact time Packy was arrested and that he had had nothing to do with them since? Until now, of course, he corrected himself.

No, he decided. No one would believe it.

The twins had eluded capture for years, and from the well fed look of the two of them and their new bright choppers that didn't even look fake, they had been living well. So they certainly had at least *some* of the money that the investors had lost in the scam. Why did they risk coming back? he wondered.

Packy had paid his debt to society, Milo thought, but he's still on parole. But from the way the twins were talking when they didn't think I could overhear them, it's obvious they're all planning to skip the U. S. of A. in the next few days. To where? With what?

Milo forked a chunk of beef from the stew and popped it in his mouth. Jo-Jo and Benny had stayed with him for less than twenty-four hours, but in that short time all the years they hadn't laid eyes on each other melted away. Before Jo-Jo got crabby, they had had a few laughs about the old days. And after Benny had downed a couple of beers, he had even invited him to come visit them in Bra—

At that memory Milo smiled. Benny had started to say "Bra—" and Jo-Jo had shut him up. So instead of saying "Brazil," which he clearly meant to say, Benny had said, "Bra-bra, I mean, Bora-Bora."

Benny had never been all that swift on the uptake, Milo remembered.

He began to set the table. If by chance the twins showed up with Packy Noonan, would Packy enjoy the stew, or had he gotten his fill of stew in prison? Even if he did, it wouldn't be anything like the way *I* make it, Milo assured himself. And, besides, if anyone doesn't like stew, I have plenty of spaghetti sauce. From all the stories he had heard, Packy could get pretty mean when things didn't go exactly his way. I wouldn't mind making his acquaintance, though, he admitted to himself. There is no denying that he has what they call charisma. That is one of the reasons his trial got so much coverage—people can't resist criminals with charisma.

A green salad with slivers of Parmesan cheese, home-made biscuits, and ice cream would complete the meal that would satisfy the queen of England if she happened to show up on her skis, Milo congratulated himself. These mis-matched chipped dishes aren't fit for royalty, he thought, but they didn't matter. God knows it shouldn't matter to the twins. No matter how much money they got their hands on, they'd still be the same goons they always were. As Mama used to say, "Milo, honey, you can't buy class." And, boy, was she right about *that!*

There was nothing more he could do until they returned. He walked to the front door and opened it. He glanced at the barn and once again asked himself the question: What's with the flatbed? If they are headed back to Bra Bra Brazil, they sure can't be traveling there by way of a flatbed. There had been a couple of scrawny-looking spruces on the flatbed when they arrived, but yesterday Benny threw them into one of the stalls.

Maybe I should write a poem about a tree, Milo mused as he closed the door and walked over to the battered old desk in the parlor that the renting agent had the nerve to call an antique. He sat down and closed his eyes.

A scrawny tree that nobody wants, he thought sadly. It gets thrown into a horse stall, and there's a broken-down nag that is headed for the glue factory. They are both scared. The tree knows its next stop is the fireplace.

At first the tree and the nag don't get along, but because misery loves company and they can't avoid each other, they become best friends. The tree tells the nag how he never grew tall, and everyone called him Stumpy. That's why he has been plopped here in the stall. The nag tells how in the one race he could have won he sat down on the track after the first turn because he was tired. Stumpy and the nag comfort each other and plan their escape. The nag grabs Stumpy by a branch, flings him over his back, breaks out of the stall, and races to the forest where they live happily ever after.

With tears in his eyes, Milo shook his head. "Sometimes beautiful poetry comes to me full-blown," he said aloud. He sniffled as he pulled out a sheet of paper and began to write.

II

*F*rom the first moment he spotted the van on Madison Avenue, Packy Noonan realized that in thirteen years the combined brain power of the Como twins had not increased one iota. As he leaped into the backseat and slammed the door behind him, he fumed. "What's with the skis? Why not put up a sign reading Packy's Getaway Car?"

"Huh?" Benny grunted in bewilderment.

Jo-Jo was behind the wheel and stepped on the gas. He was a fraction too late to make the traffic light and decided not to risk it, especially with a cop standing at the corner. Even though the cop wasn't actually facing them, running a light was not a good idea.

"I said you should bring skis so that we could put them on after you picked me up," Packy snapped. "That way if someone noticed me hightailing it down the block, they'd say I got in a van. Then we pull over somewhere and put the skis on top. They're looking for any old van, not a van with skis.

You're so dopey. You might as well plaster "Honk if You Love Jesus" stickers all over the van, for God's sake."

Jo-Jo spun his head. "We risked our necks to get you, Packy. We didn't have to, you know."

"Get moving!" Packy shrieked. "The light's green. You want a special invitation to step on the gas?"

The traffic was heavier than usual for a Sunday morning. The van moved slowly up the long block to Fifty-second Street, and then Jo-Jo turned east. Precisely the moment they were out of view, the man Packy had dubbed Fatso came running up Madison Avenue. "*Help!-Help!* Did anybody see some guy running?" he began to yell.

The cop, who had not noticed Packy either running or getting in the van, hurried over to the jogger, clearly believing he had a nut case on his hands. New Yorkers and tourists, united for the moment in a bit of excitement, stopped to see what was going on.

The jogger raised his voice and shouted, "Anybody see where a guy went who was running around here a minute ago?"

"Keep it down, buddy," the cop ordered. "I could arrest you for disturbing the peace."

A four-year-old who had been standing across the street next to his mother while she answered a call on her cell phone tugged at her skirt. "A man who was running got into a van with skis on it," he said matter of factly.

"Mind your business, Jason," she said crisply. "You don't

need to be a witness to a crime. Whoever they're looking for is probably a pickpocket. Let them find him. That's what they're paid to do." She resumed her conversation as she took his hand and started walking down the street. "Jeannie, you're my sister, and I have your best interests at heart. *Drop that creep.*"

Less than two blocks away the van was moving slowly through the traffic. In the backseat Packy willed the vehicle forward: Park, Lexington, Third, Second, First.

At First Avenue, Jo-Jo put on the turn signal. Ten more blocks to the FDR Drive, Packy fretted. He began to bite his nails, a long-forgotten habit he had overcome when he was nine. I'm not doing anything wrong until I don't show up at The Castle tonight, he reasoned. But if I'm caught with the twins, it's all over. Associating with known felons means instant parole revocation. I should have had them leave the van parked somewhere for me. But even if I was alone and got stopped, how would I explain the van? That I won it in a raffle?

He moaned.

Benny turned his head. "I got a good feeling, Packy," he said soothingly. "We're gonna make it."

But Packy observed that sweat was rolling down Benny's face. And Jo-Jo was driving so slowly that they might as well be walking. I know he doesn't want to get caught in an intersection, but this is nuts! Overhead, a thumping sound indicated that one of the skis was coming loose. "Pull over," Packy screamed. Two minutes later, between First and Second Avenues, he yanked the skis off the roof of the van and tossed them in through the back door. Then he waved Jo-Jo over to the passenger seat. "Is this the way they taught you to drive in Brazil? You, Benny, get in the back."

For the next twenty minutes they sat in dead silence as they traveled north. Benny, easily intimidated, cowered in the backseat. He had forgotten that Packy goes nuts when he's worried. So what's going on? he wondered. In those letters he told us to find somebody we could trust to rent a farmhouse with a big barn in Stowe. We did that. And then he sends word to get a two-handled saw, a hatchet, and rope, and then the flatbed. We did that. He told us to pick him up today. We did that. So what's it all about? Packy swore that he had left the rest of the loot in New Jersey, so why are we going to Vermont? I never heard of going to New Jersey by way of Vermont.

Sitting in the front seat, Jo-Jo was thinking in the same vein. Benny and I had ten million bucks with us when we took off for Brazil. We lived nice there, very, very nice, but not over the top. Packy tells us that he has another seventy or eighty million he can get his hands on once he's out of jail. But he never said how much Benny and me get in the split. If it goes sour, Benny and me could end up with Packy in the slammer. We should've stayed in Brazil and let him slave away for a few weeks at that dumpy diner where they got him a job. Then when we came to rescue him, maybe he'd appreciate us a little more. In fact, he'd be kissing our feet.

When they saw the "Welcome to Connecticut" sign, Packy let go of the wheel and clapped his hands. "One state closer to Vermont," he chortled. With a broad grin he turned to Jo-Jo. "But we're not gonna be there long. We'll take care of business and be on our way to sunny Brazil."

God willing, Jo-Jo thought piously. But something tells me that Benny and I should have made do with ten million bucks. His stomach gurgled as he made a feeble attempt to return Packy's smile.

12

At a quarter of eight Milo heard the sound of a vehicle coming up the driveway. With nervous anticipation he rushed to open the front door. He watched as Jo-Jo got out of the front passenger door of the van and Benny emerged from the door behind him.

So who's driving? he wondered. But then the question was answered as the driver's door opened and a figure appeared. The faint light from the living room window was all Milo needed to confirm his hunch that Packy Noonan was the mystery guest.

Benny and Jo-Jo waited for Packy to precede them up the porch steps. Milo jumped back to open the door as wide as possible. He felt as if he should salute, but Packy extended his hand. "So you're Milo the poet," he said. "Thanks for holding down the fort for me."

If I had known I was holding it down for you, I wouldn't be here, Milo thought, but he found himself smiling back. "It's a pleasure, Mr. Noonan," he said.

"Packy," Packy corrected him gently as his glance darted around the room. He sniffed. "Something smells real good."

"It's my beef stew," Milo told him, the words tumbling from his mouth. "I hope you enjoy beef stew, Mr. — I mean, Packy."

"My favorite. My mama made it for me every Friday — or maybe it was Saturday." Packy was starting to enjoy himself. Milo the poet was as transparent as a teenager. I *do* have a natural way of impressing people, he thought. How else would I have gotten all those dopey investors to keep pouring money into my sinkhole?

Jo-Jo and Benny were coming into the house. Packy decided this was the moment to make sure that Milo joined their team for good. "Jo-Jo, you brought that money like I told you?"

"Yeah, Packy, sure."

"Peel off fifty of the big ones and give them to our friend Milo." Packy put his arm around Milo's shoulders. "Milo," he said, "this isn't what we owe you. This is a bonus for being a swell guy."

Fifty hundred-dollar bills? Milo thought. But he said *the big ones*. He couldn't mean fifty *thousand*, could he? *Another* fifty thousand? Milo's brain couldn't handle the thought of that much money being handed to him in cold, hard cash.

Two minutes later he could not keep his mouth closed as a grumpy-looking Jo-Jo counted out fifty stacks of bills from a large suitcase filled with money. "There are ten C-notes in each of these here piles," he said. "Count them when you're finished writing your next poem."

"By any chance have you got anything smaller?" Milo asked hesitantly. "Hundred-dollar bills are hard to change."

"Chase the Good Humor wagon down the block," Jo-Jo snapped. "What I hear, the driver carries lots of change."

"Milo," Packy said gently. "Hundred-dollar bills aren't hard to change anymore. Now let me explain our plans. We'll be out of here by Tuesday at the latest. Which means all *you* have to do is go about your business and ignore our comings and goings until we leave. And when we leave, you will be given the other fifty thousand dollars. Are you agreeable to that situation?"

"Oh, yes, Mr. Noonan—I mean, Packy. I surely am, sir." Milo could taste and feel Greenwich Village as though he were already there.

"If somebody happened to ring the bell and ask if you'd seen a flatbed around here, you'd forget that there is indeed one on the premises, wouldn't you, Milo?"

Milo nodded.

Packy looked directly into his eyes and was satisfied. "Very good. We understand each other. Now how about some dinner? We hit a lot of traffic, and your stew smells great."

13

They're not hungry, they're *starving*, Milo thought as he refilled Packy's and the twins' plates for the third time. With satisfaction he watched as his biscuits disappeared and his salad vanished. He had done so much tasting and sampling that he had hardly any appetite, which was just as well since he kept getting up and down to open yet another bottle of wine. Packy, Jo-Jo, and Benny seemed to be in a contest to see who could drink the fastest.

But the more they drank, the more they mellowed. The skis wobbling on the roof of the van suddenly seemed hilarious. The fact that four cars had rear-ended one another on route 91, causing a massive traffic jam and forcing them to drive slowly past an army of cops, sparked another round of belly laughs.

By eleven o'clock the twins' eyes were at half-mast. Packy had a buzz on. Milo had limited himself to a couple of glasses of wine. He didn't want to wake up tomorrow and forget anything that had been said. He also intended to stay sober until his money was safely under a mattress in Greenwich Village.

Jo-Jo pushed back his chair, stood up, and yawned. "I'm going to bed. Hey, Milo, that extra fifty thousand means you do the dishes." He started to laugh, but Packy thumped on the table and ordered him to sit back down.

"We're all tired, you idiot. But we have to talk business."

With a burp he didn't try to stifle, Jo-Jo slumped back into his chair. "I beg your pardon," he mumbled.

"If we don't get this right, you may be begging the governor for a pardon," Packy shot across the table.

A nervous tremor ran through Milo's body. He simply didn't know what to expect next.

"Tomorrow we're getting up real early. We'll have some coffee, which Milo will have ready."

Milo nodded.

"Then we back the flatbed out of the barn, drive to a tree a few miles from here that happens to be located on the property of a guy I worked for when I was a kid, and cut down this very special tree."

"Cut down a *tree?*" Milo interrupted. "You're not the only one cutting down a tree tomorrow," he said excitedly. He ran over to the pile of newspapers by the back door. "Here it is, right on top!" he crowed. "Tomorrow at ten A.M. the blue spruce that was selected as this year's Rockefeller Center

Christmas tree is being cut down. They've been preparing it all week! Half the town will be there, and there'll be lots of media—television, radio, you name it!"

"Where's this tree?" Packy asked, his voice dangerously quiet.

"Hmmmm." Milo searched the article. "I could really use a pair of reading glasses," he observed. "Oh, here it is. The tree is on the Pickens property. Guess there's good pickins on the Pickens property." He laughed.

Packy jumped out of his seat. "Give me that!" he yelled. He grabbed the paper out of Milo's hands. When he laid eyes on the picture of the tree—alone and majestic in a clearing—that was about to be sent to New York City, he let out a scream. "That's my tree! *That's my tree!*"

"There are a lot of nice trees around here we could cut down instead," Milo suggested, trying to be helpful.

"*Roll out the flatbed!*" Packy ordered. "*We're cutting down my tree tonight!*"

14

At eleven o'clock, just before she got into bed, Alvirah stood at the window and looked out. Most of the villas were already in darkness. In the distance she could see the silhouette of the mountains. They're so silent and still, she thought, sighing.

Willy was already in bed. "Is anything wrong, honey?"

"No, not at all. It's just that I'm such a New Yorker, it's hard to get used to so much quiet. At home the sounds of traffic and police sirens and trucks rumbling kind of blend into a lullaby."

"Uh-huh. Come to bed, Alvirah."

"But here it's so peaceful," Alvirah continued. "I bet if you walked along any of these paths right now, you wouldn't hear a sound other than a little animal scampering through the snow or a tree rustling or maybe an owl hooting. It's so different, isn't it? In New York right now there's probably a line of cars at Columbus Circle, honking their horns because the light just changed and somebody didn't step on the gas fast enough. In Stowe you don't hear a sound on the road. By midnight all the lights will be out. Everyone will be dreaming. I love it."

A gentle snore from the bed told her that Willy had fallen fast asleep.

"Let's see what's going on in the world," Nora suggested as Luke unlocked the door to their cabin. "I like to catch the news before I go to sleep."

"That's not always the best idea," Luke commented drily. "The bedtime stories on the news aren't always catalysts for sweet dreams."

"If I can't sleep in the middle of the night, I always turn on the news," Regan said. "It helps me fall back asleep—unless, of course, there's something big going on."

Jack picked up the remote and pressed the TV button. The screen filled with the anchor desk of the Flash News Network. The coanchors were not flashing their usual sunny smiles. A tape rolled showing Packy Noonan leaving prison. "Look at this!" Jack exclaimed.

The anchor reported solemnly: "Packy Noonan, recently released from prison after serving twelve and a half years for cheating investors in his fake shipping company, left his halfway house this morning to attend Mass at Saint Patrick's Cathedral. He was being followed by a private investigator hired by the law firm that was appointed to recover the money Packy stole. But Noonan slipped out of the cathedral during the service and was seen running down Madison Avenue. When he did not return to the halfway house this evening, he officially broke his parole. We have been receiving phone calls and e-mails from outraged investors who heard this story earlier on Flash News. They have always believed that Noonan had squirreled away their money and is on his way to collect their fortunes right now. There is a $10,000 reward for information that helps lead to Noonan's capture. If you have any information, please contact the number on your screen below."

"That guy is taking a big risk," Jack said. "He served his time, and now if he's caught he'll be thrown back in jail for breaking parole. He must have that money stashed away somewhere and doesn't want to wait the two or three years he'd spend on parole to get his millions. My guess is that he'll be out of the country in no time flat."

"Poor Opal," Nora sighed. "That's all she needs to hear. She always said the money was hidden somewhere, and if she got her hands on Packy, she'd wring his neck."

Regan shook her head. "It makes me sick to think how many investors like Opal were cheated out of money that really would have made a difference in their lives. At least when Packy was in prison, they knew he was miserable. Now they have to wonder if he's going to be living high on the hog on their dime, just thumbing his nose at them."

"I told you," Luke said. "Now everybody's worked up before it's time to go to sleep."

In spite of the situation, they all laughed. "You're terrible," Nora chided. "I just hope Opal didn't watch the news tonight. She'd never close an eye."

A few doors down, in the villa she shared with Alvirah and Willy, Opal had fallen into a dead sleep as soon as her head hit the pillow. Even though she had not heard the news about Packy's disappearance, when she began to dream, it was of him. The gates of a dreary stone prison were bursting open. Packy came running out clutching fat pillowcases in his arms. She knew they were stuffed with money—*her* money. Her lottery money. She began to chase him, but her legs wouldn't move. In her dream she became increasingly agitated. "Why won't my legs move?" she thought frantically. "I have to catch up with him." Packy disappeared down the road. Gasping for breath as she struggled to move forward, Opal woke with a start.

"Oh, my God," she thought as she felt her heart pounding. Another nightmare about that stupid Packy Noonan. As she calmed down, she thought there was something more that her subconscious was working to bring to the surface. It's going to come to me, she thought as she closed her eyes again. I know it is.

ll my plans," Packy moaned. "Twelve and a half stinking years doing time, and every single minute I'm dreaming of getting my hands on my tree. Now this!"

From the backseat Benny leaned forward. He stuck his head between Packy and Jo-Jo. "What's so special about getting your hands on that tree?" he asked. "Are you supposed to make a wish or something?"

It was pitch dark. The van was the only vehicle on the quiet country road. Packy, Jo-Jo, and Benny were on their way to case the situation on the Pickens property. As Packy had exclaimed bitterly, "For all we know the Rockefeller Center people left a guard overnight watching the tree. Before we go lumbering over there in the flatbed, we gotta see what's going on."

"Benny, figure it out," Jo-Jo snarled. "Packy must've hid something in the tree and is worried he won't be able to get it out. It has to be our money stuck in there, Packy. Right?"

"Bingo," Packy snapped. "You should apply to be a member of the Mensa Society. You'd be a shoo-in."

"What's the Mensa Society?" Benny asked.

"It's a kind of club. You take a test. If you pass, you get to go to meetings with other people who passed, and you congratulate one another on how smart you all are. One of them was in my cell block. He was so smart that when he passed a note to the bank teller to fork over money, he wrote it on his own deposit slip."

Packy knew he was ranting as though he was out of his mind. Sometimes it was like that when he got rattled. Get your cool back, he told himself. Breathe deep. Think beautiful thoughts. He thought about money.

Outside the temperature was dropping. He could feel the slight slip of the tires as the van hit a patch of ice.

"So answer me, Packy," Jo-Jo insisted. "Our money's in that tree. You were in the can over twelve years. So why didn't you stash it in a numbered account in Switzerland or in a safe deposit box? What turned you into a squirrel?"

Packy could not prevent his voice from becoming shrill. "Let me explain. And listen real good so I don't have to repeat 'cause we're almost there." He floored the brake as he spotted a deer emerging from the bushes at the side of the road. "Get lost, Bambi," he muttered. As though it had heard him, the deer turned and disappeared.

The road was bending sharply to the right. Packy picked

up speed again but more cautiously. Suppose the tree was being guarded? What then?

"So, Packy, I wanna know what's going on," Jo-Jo said impatiently.

Jo-Jo and Benny had a right to know what they were up against, Packy admitted to himself. "You two were in on the shipping scam up to your necks. The difference is that you got away with big bucks and got to spend the last twelve years in Brazil while I shared a cell with a whacko."

"We only got ten million," Benny corrected, sounding injured. "You held on to at least seventy million."

"It didn't do me any good when I was in jail. The whole time the lamebrains were giving us money to invest I was buying diamonds, unset stones, some of them worth two million each."

"Why didn't you ask us to mind them while you were in jail?" Benny asked.

"Because I'd still be waiting on Madison Avenue for you to pick me up."

"That's not nice," Benny said, shaking his head. "So I guess the diamonds are in your tree somewhere, huh? Good thing Milo mentioned the tree's going to be cut down tomorrow morning. To think we could have been a day late and a dollar short."

"You're not helping matters, Benny," Jo-Jo interrupted his brother. "Now, Packy, why did you pick this tree way up here in Vermont? You know, Jersey has a lot of nice trees, and it's much closer to the City."

"I used to work for the people who owned this property!" Packy snapped at them. "When I was sixteen, my dear old Ma got the court to send me up here on some kind of 'save-the-troubled-kid' experiment."

"What kind of job did you have up here?" Jo-Jo asked.

"Cutting down trees, mostly for the Christmas market. I was pretty good at it. I even learned how to use a crane to get the big ones that were bought for the centers of towns all over the country. Anyway, when I was afraid that the auditors were catching on to us, I took the diamonds from the safe deposit box, put them in a metal flask, and stowed them up here. I didn't think it would be thirteen years before I'd be back for them. The people who own this property planted the tree on their wedding day fifty years ago. They swore they'd never cut it down."

"That would have been bad," Benny agreed. "With all the developments these days, it just could have happened. Ya know, in our old neighborhood, the ball field —"

"I don't want to hear about your old neighborhood!" Packy shouted. "Now here's the turn into the clearing. Keep your fingers crossed. I'll pull over, and we'll walk the rest of the way."

"Suppose there's a guard there."

"Maybe he'll have to spend the rest of the night watching us cut down a tree. Jo-Jo, give me the flashlight."

Packy opened the door of the van and got out. His blood was racing so rapidly through his veins that he didn't notice the sharp difference between the cold night air and the warmth of the van. Keeping to the side of the path, he was ready to merge into the shadows if he caught sight of anyone near the tree. Slowly he edged around the final turn, the twins following. He couldn't believe what he saw. The light snowfall allowed enough visibility to vaguely outline the scene. Packy turned on the flashlight and kept it pointed at the ground.

Next to the tree, his tree, was a flatbed. A crane was already in place, its cables looped near the top to guide the tree onto the flatbed after it was cut down. There didn't seem to be anyone around guarding it.

Jo-Jo and Benny knew enough not to say a word.

Slowly, tentatively, Packy approached the cab of the flatbed and peered inside. There was no one there. He tried the handle of the driver's door, but it was locked. Under the bumper, he thought. Nine out of ten truck drivers leave another set of keys under the bumper.

He found them and began to laugh. "This is a gift," he told the twins. "The flatbed and the crane just *waiting* for us. We're on our way to a flask full of millions of dollars' worth of diamonds, hidden somewhere in that tree. But we have to go back to the farmhouse to get the two-handled saw. Too bad one of you imbeciles didn't think to throw it in the back of the van."

"There's a power saw on the flatbed," Benny pointed out. "Why can't we use that?"

"Are you crazy? That thing would wake the dead. You guys can cut down the tree in no time while I handle the crane."

"I've got a bad back," Benny protested.

"Listen!" Packy exploded. "Your share of eighty million dollars will pay for plenty of chiropractors and masseuses. Come on, we're wasting time!"

16

Two hundred acres away, in the eighteenth-century farmhouse in the center of his property, Lemuel Pickens was finding it hard to get to sleep. Normally he and his wife, Vidya, got into bed promptly at nine-thirty and passed out. But tonight, because of the tree, they had been reminiscing about the old days, and then they dug out the album and looked at the picture of the two of them planting the tree the day they were married, fifty years ago.

We weren't spring chickens, either. Lemuel chuckled to himself. Vidya was thirty-two, and I was thirty-five. That was old in our day. But as she always said, "Lemmy, we had responsibilities. I had my mother to take care of, and you had your father. When we'd see each other in church on Sundays, I could tell you were sweet on me, and I liked that." Then Viddy's mother died. Two weeks later Pa was feeling poorly, and before you could say "Jiminy Cricket," he had passed over, too, Lemuel remembered as he gave Viddy a poke. That woman can sure snore up a storm, he thought as she turned on her side and the rumbling stopped.

We never were blessed with children, but that tree has been almost like a child to us. Lemuel's eyes moistened. Watching it grow, the branches always so even and perfect, and the touch of blue that comes out in the sunlight. It sure is the prettiest tree I've ever seen. Even the way it stands alone in the clearing. We never wanted to plant anything near it. Over the years we've put mulch around it. Babied it. It's been fun.

He turned on his side. When those people rang the door and asked if we'd let them cut down the tree for Rockefeller Center, I almost took a gun to them. But then I heard that after I turned them down they hightailed over to Wayne Covel's place and were considering his big blue spruce. Boy, did that get my goat.

Viddy and I took about two minutes to talk it over. We're not going to be here much longer to take care of our tree. Even if we have it in our will that no one can cut it down, it won't be the same after we're gone. It won't be special to anyone, but if it goes to Rockefeller Center, it will make thousands and thousands of people happy. And when it gets to New York, the schoolkids and those cute Rockettes will greet our tree and sing the songs from Maria von Trapp's movie. Funny that she came along just as we were planting it. She knew it was our wedding day, and she sang an Austrian wedding song for us and took our picture next to the tree. Then we took her picture standing in the same spot.

Lemuel sighed. Viddy is looking forward so much to going to New York City and seeing our tree come ablaze with lights. It'll be on television all over the country, and everyone will know it's our fiftieth anniversary. They even want to interview us on the *Today Show.* Viddy's so excited, she's planning to have her hair washed and set at one of those fancy salons in New York. When I heard how much it was gonna cost, I almost dropped my teeth. But as Viddy reminded me, she's only had it done twice in all these years.

I just wish I could see the expression on Wayne Covel's face when we're on the TV talking to Katie or Matt. He's as sour as a wet hen because when we went running over and said we'd let them have our tree, they dropped *his* like a hot potato.

Lemuel gave Vidya another poke. She makes more noise than a tree crashing in the forest, he thought.

17

Twenty feet up, Wayne Covel could not believe his ears. He had been standing on the ladder behind Lemuel Pickens's prize blue spruce, machete in hand, about to start hacking off branches. His intention was to make such a mess of the tree that the men sent by Rockefeller Center would come running back to him. He still hadn't decided whether or not to play hard to get, but in the end he would let them have his beautiful tree.

The *Today Show* here I come, he thought.

But then from the other side of the tree he heard footsteps approaching and realized that subconsciously he had been aware of the faint sound of a car engine a few minutes earlier. It was too late for him to climb down the ladder and escape, so he did the only thing possible: He jammed the machete into the tool belt around his waist and stood perfectly still. Maybe they'll go away quickly, he hoped. Please don't let it be guards who'll stay here all night.

What do I do? he wondered frantically. I'm a trespasser.

Lem Pickens would know exactly what I was up to. My goose would be cooked.

Wayne could hear several men walking around, then moving on the far side of the tree. They were talking about diamonds hidden in the tree—millions of dollars' worth of diamonds! He almost fell off the ladder, he was concentrating so hard in his attempt to make out every word they were saying.

They had to be kidding! But they weren't—he knew it. There were diamonds hidden in a metal flask somewhere in the tree, and these guys were going to steal the tree to find the jewels.

Wayne was terrified. These weren't good guys, obviously. Could he get out of here without them seeing him? If they discovered him, they'd know he heard what they were saying. Then what? He didn't want to think about the possibilities.

"We have to go back to the farmhouse to get the two-handled saw," one of them was saying in a grouchy tone. "Too bad one of you imbeciles didn't think to throw it in the back of the van."

Thank you, God! Wayne wanted to shout. They're leaving. That'll give me time to climb down and call the cops. Maybe there'll be a reward! I'll be a hero. These guys wouldn't have hid diamonds in the tree if they got them honestly, that much he knew for sure.

He waited until he could no longer hear the sound of their car, then reached into his belt, pulled out his flashlight, and turned it on. Where could they have hidden a flask of diamonds? It had to be attached to a branch or to the trunk. The branches weren't thick enough to hold a flask inside. And if anyone had drilled a hole in the trunk, the nutrients wouldn't get through, and the tree would die.

Wayne leaned forward, lifted a few of the branches with his thick protective gloves, and shined the flashlight all around. What a joke, he thought. Talk about a needle in a haystack. But maybe I'll get lucky and spot the flask. Sure—and maybe Boston will finally win the World Series.

Even so, he descended the ladder one step at a time, carefully parting the branches and shining the flashlight between them. Three steps down, the beam of light caught on something resting on a branch above, about halfway between the trunk and the ladder.

It couldn't be—or could it?

Wayne grabbed the machete from his belt and leaned into the tree. The needles scratched his face and became embedded in his handlebar mustache, but he didn't feel them. He couldn't reach the machete far enough to cut the branch off past the object, or could he?

Wayne was on his tiptoes leaning into the tree when, with one strike, he cut the branch in half, pulled off the severed end, and scampered down the ladder. At the bottom his flashlight revealed a metal flask held tight to the branch with the kind of thin wire used in electric fences. Wayne's whole body quivered with excitement.

With a sweep of the machete Wayne cut the branch again so that the section holding the flask was only a foot long. He stifled the impulse to let out a whoop of triumph, as he did whenever the Red Sox scored a run against the Yankees, and began to run. In his haste he did not realize that the machete with his name on the handle had slid out of his belt and fallen to the ground.

All thoughts of calling the cops had vanished.

God works in strange ways, he thought as he ran around the perimeter of Lem Pickens's property. If my tree had been picked, I would have had my fifteen minutes of fame, but then it would have been over. This way, if this flask really is full of diamonds, I'm rich—and that pain in the neck Lem misses his chance to be a star.

He only wished he had the nerve to show up the next morning and see Lem's face when he visits his tree for the last time and finds nothing but a stump. Wayne was delirious with joy. And how about seeing the faces on the guys when they discover that the branch with the flask is half gone? But he wished them luck. They were doing his job for him. If they really succeeded at cutting down Lem's tree, then his might be on its way to Rockefeller Center.

Wayne ran faster through the night. I should check my horoscope, he thought. My planets must be all lined up. They just gotta be.

18

Back at the farmhouse Milo was roused from his nap on the couch and ordered into the kitchen for a briefing from Packy.

"I don't want to get in this any deeper," Milo protested.

"You're in it up to your neck," Packy barked. "Now we've got to get this right. We can't fit two flatbeds in the barn, and we can't leave one out in sight."

"There are plenty of lonely roads around here," Benny noted. "Why don't we leave ours on one of them? Although it's a shame—it was a good buy. Right after you sent word from prison to buy an old flatbed, Jo-Jo and I came across that one at an auction. Paid cash for it, too. We were so proud of ourselves."

"Benny, please!" Packy yelled. "When we get back here with my tree, you'll pull our flatbed out of the barn, drive north on route 100 for about ten miles, and lose it somewhere. No. Wait a minute! Milo, you drive the flatbed. They know you around here. There's no law against driving a flatbed. Benny, you follow in the van and drive him back."

This is more than I bargained for, Milo thought. I don't think I'll ever get to spend that money. But he decided not to protest. He was already in too deep, and he had never felt more miserable in his life.

"Okay, that's decided," Packy said briskly. "Milo, don't look so worried. We'll be out of your life soon enough." He glanced at the twins. "Come on, you two. We don't have that much time."

When they got back to the site, the light snowfall had ended and a few stars were visible through the clouds. In a way Packy was glad to see them. It meant that he didn't need more than the lowest setting of the flashlight to guide Jo-Jo and Benny when they were sawing the tree.

The Rockefeller Center crane was in place to receive the tree when it fell. The cables of the crane were already attached to the tree to keep it from falling away from the flatbed.

I was nuts to think I could cut anything this big and count on its landing on our flatbed, Packy admitted to himself. I was nuts to forget that the bottom branches of a tree this big had to be wrapped. Let's face it, I was nuts to hide the diamonds in a tree in the first place. But the boys hired by Rockefeller Center took care of everything for me, he consoled himself. What pals.

Jo-Jo and Benny took their places on either side of the tree. They were each holding one end of the saw.

"All right," Packy directed. "This is the way you do it. Benny, you push while Jo-Jo pulls. Then, Jo-Jo, you push while Benny pulls."

"Then I push while Jo-Jo pulls," Benny confirmed. "And Jo-Jo pushes and I pull. Is that right, Packy?"

Packy wanted to scream. "Yes, that's right. Just start. Do it! Hurry up!"

Even though it was a manual saw, the sound seemed to reverberate through the woods. Seated on the crane, Packy pointed the beam of the flashlight on the base of the tree. For an instant he pointed it at the tree's back where he knew that somewhere the flask was hidden. He could see a ladder that hadn't been visible to him before and then noticed that a length of branch was lying on the ground. An uneasy feeling stirred inside him. He pointed the light back at the twins pushing and pulling.

Ten minutes passed. Fifteen.

"Hurry up," Packy urged them. "Hurry up."

"We're pushing and pulling as fast as we can," Benny panted. "We're almost done. We're almost—Timber!" he yelled.

They had severed the tree at the base of the trunk. For a moment it wavered and then, guided by Packy at the crane, the large tree was held in the air by cables and lowered in a straight line onto the flatbed. Sweat was pouring down

Packy's face. How did I ever remember to do that right? he wondered. He released the cables, scrambled down from the crane, and rushed into the driver's seat of the cab of the flatbed. "Benny, you get in with me. Jo-Jo, follow in the van, like you're escorting us. Now if our luck holds . . ."

With agonizing slowness he drove the flatbed out of the clearing and onto the dirt road. He passed the east side of Lem Pickens's property, pulled on to route 108, and finally drove up Mountain Road.

A few cars passed them on 108, their occupants hopefully too tired or too indifferent to wonder what was going on. "Sometimes they transport big trees like this at night to avoid causing a traffic jam," Packy explained, more to himself than to Benny. "That's what these birds probably think we're doing if they think at all."

There was more that he was worried about than getting back to the barn undetected—that branch lying on the ground, right below the area where the flask was hidden. That side of the tree was now exposed on the top of the flatbed. He couldn't wait to start looking for his flask.

It was exactly 3 A.M. when they reached the farmhouse. Benny jumped out, ran to the barn, and opened the door. He backed out their flatbed, making an ear-splitting racket as the remaining horse stalls broke into splinters. Milo came rushing out of the house and took over the driver's seat of the flatbed from Benny. As Benny drove the van past Packy, he waved, smiled, and gave a light tap of the horn. Packy grunted while driving the stolen flatbed into the barn. As he climbed out, Jo-Jo was shutting the barn door.

"Now I look for the red line I painted around the trunk at the spot where the branch with the flask is, and we're halfway to Brazil. The way I figure it, now it should be about forty feet up."

Jo-Jo pulled out the tape measure Packy had ordered him to bring, and together they started to measure the tree from its base. Packy's throat went dry when he saw a broken branch about twenty feet up. Could this be where that piece of branch on the ground came from? he wondered. Ignoring the sharpness of the needles, he pulled the remaining branch back and then yelled as a piece of jagged wire cut his finger. His flashlight was pointed at the trunk and the red circle around the base of the broken branch.

There was no sign of a flask, only the remnants of the wire with which he had so carefully secured his treasure.

"What?" he screamed. "I don't get it! I thought my branch would be higher by now. We've got to go back! That flask must be stuck to the branch I saw lying on the ground by the ladder."

"We can't drive the flatbed out again! We gotta wait till Benny and Milo get back with the van," Jo-Jo pointed out.

"What about Milo's heap?" Packy screamed.

"He keeps those keys in his coat pocket," Jo-Jo answered. I should have stayed in Brazil and let Packy make salads at that dumpy diner, he thought for the third time that day.

19

Lem Pickens kept waking up. He was having bad dreams. He didn't know why, but he kept worrying that something would go wrong, that maybe he had made a mistake after all about giving up the tree.

Just natural, he told himself. Just natural. He had read in a book somewhere that any cataclysmic event in our lives brings fear and anxiety. It certainly doesn't seem to bother Viddy, he thought as she continued to make the depth of her slumber known to him. Right now the noise she's making is somewhere between a jackhammer and a chainsaw.

Lem tried thinking pleasant thoughts to ease his anxiety. Think of when they flip the switch and our tree is lit up in Rockefeller Center with over thirty thousand colored lights on it. Just think about *that!*

He knew why he was worried. It would be hard to watch the tree actually being cut down. He wondered if the tree was scared. At that moment he made a decision: I'll wake up Viddy extra early, and after we have a cup of coffee, we'll walk over and sit by our tree and say a proper good-bye to it.

That settled, and feeling somewhat content, Lem closed his eyes and drifted back to sleep. A few minutes later the racket from his side of the bed was still no competition for Viddy, an Olympic snorer if there ever was one.

As they slept, a tearful Packy Noonan was sitting on the stump of their beloved tree holding a machete in his hand, the beam of his flashlight pointing to the name visible on the handle: *Wayne Covel.*

20

Wayne Covel was panting when he reached his back door, the piece of Lem's branch with the crooks' flask wired to it clutched in his hand. He laid the branch on the table in his messy kitchen, poured a tall glass of whiskey to calm his nerves, and then dug the wire cutters out of his tool belt. With trembling fingers he cut the wire that held the flask to the branch and freed it.

Flasks hold only good things, he thought as he took a sip of the whiskey. This one had been just about sealed shut, there was so much sediment around it, and he tried to un-screw it. He walked over to the sink and turned on the faucet. A groaning sound was followed by a slight trickle of water that eventually turned hot. He held the flask under it until most of the sediment was washed off. It still took three pow-erful twists with his hands before the cap loosened.

He grabbed a greasy dish towel and rushed over to spread it on the table. He sat down and slowly, reverently, began to shake the contents of the flask onto the crowing rooster that marked the center of the raggy towel. His eyes bugged at the sight of the treasure unfolding in front of him. They weren't kidding—diamonds as big as an owl's eye, some of them the prettiest golden color, some of them with a bluish tint, one he'd swear was as big as a robin's egg. That one he had to give an extra shake to get through the mouth of the flask. His heart was beating so fast, he needed another long swig of whiskey. It was hard to believe this was happening.

I'm lucky Lorna dumped me last year, he thought. She said eight years of me was enough. Well, eight years of her was enough. Nag, nag, nag. I was just too nice to kick her butt out. She moved forty-five minutes away to Burlington. He heard she was doing some of that Internet dating. Good luck at finding that sensitive man you're after, honey, he thought.

He picked up a handful of diamonds, still not believing his luck. Maybe when I figure out how to unload some of this fancy stuff, I'll take a first-class trip and send Lorna a postcard telling her what a good time I'm having—and that I don't wish she was there.

Pleased at the thought of one-upping Lorna, Wayne got down to the business at hand. The minute Lem finds out that tree is gone, he'll be yelling that I was behind it. I know my face got scratched, so I have to figure out an excuse for how that happened. I could always say I was pruning one of my trees and lost my balance, he decided. The one thing he did well was take care of the trees on the property that he hadn't yet sold off.

The next problem was where to hide the diamonds. He began to put them back in the flask. I'm going to be under suspicion for cutting down the tree, so I gotta be real careful. I can't keep them in the house. If the cops decide to search the place, with my luck they'll find the flask.

Why don't I just do what those crooks out by the tree did? he thought. Why not hide it in one of my own trees until everything blows over and I can make a trip to the big city?

Wayne wrapped the flask with brown masking tape and then fished around in one after another of the cluttered kitchen drawers until he found the picture-hanging wire Lorna had bought in a forlorn attempt to beautify the house. Five minutes later he was climbing the old elm tree in his front yard and, using the crooks' fine example, he returned the flask of diamonds to the protection of Mother Nature.

21

After her nightmare about Packy, Opal could barely sleep. She woke up again and again during the night, glancing at the clock at 2:00 A.M., at 3:30, and then an hour later.

The nightmare had really been upsetting and had brought to the surface all the anger and resentment she felt toward Packy Noonan and his accomplices. She had tried to make a joke of it, but it was just so *insulting* for Packy to say that he would give 10 percent of his earnings in the diner to pay back his victims!

He's making fools of us again, she thought.

The television coverage of his release kept running through her mind. On one of the stations they had done a quick review of the scam and showed Packy with those idiots Benjamin and Giuseppe Como, better known as Benny and Jo-Jo, at their indictments. Opal remembered sitting across a conference table from the three of them when they were urging her to invest more money. Benny had gotten up to help himself to more coffee. He moved like such a shlump—as though he had a load in his pants, as my mother used to say.

That was it! Opal thought. She quickly sat up in bed and turned on the light. She had suddenly realized that the man she had spotted putting skis on the rack of the van in front of a farmhouse when she was cross-country skiing the other day reminded her of Benny.

The group of skiers she was with on Saturday afternoon had been following the instructor, but the trail they were on had such a large group of slowpokes ahead of them that the instructor had said, "Let's try going around them this way." They ended up skiing through the woods near a shabby old farmhouse.

My shoelace broke, Opal remembered, so I sat on a rock, still in the woods but closer to the house. In front of it a man was putting skis on top of a van. He seemed familiar, but then somebody called him and he moved away. Even though he was hurrying, he seemed to shlump back into the house.

He was short and stocky. He shlumped. I'd swear now it was Benny Como!

But that's impossible, Opal told herself, her mind racing. What would he be doing up here? The district attorney who was going to prosecute the Comos at their trial said he was sure that Benny and Jo-Jo had skipped the country when they were out on bail. Why would Benny be in Vermont?

There was no staying in bed. Opal got up, put on her

robe, and went downstairs. The great room was one open space with a beamed ceiling, stone fireplace, and large windows that looked out on the mountains. The kitchen area was two steps up from the rest of the room and defined by a breakfast bar. Opal made a pot of coffee, poured herself a cup, and stood at the window sipping the special Vermont brew. But she barely tasted it. As she looked out at the beautiful landscape, she wondered if Benny could possibly still be out there at that farmhouse.

Alvirah and Willy won't be up for a couple of hours, she thought. I could ski over to the farmhouse now. If that van is outside, I'll copy down the license plate number. I'm sure Jack Reilly could check it out for me.

Otherwise we'll just go watch the Rockefeller Center tree being cut down, visit Alvirah's maple syrup tree, and then go home. And I'll always wonder if that man was Benny and I missed a chance to get him locked up.

I'm not going to let that happen, Opal decided. She went upstairs and dressed quickly, putting on a heavy sweater under the ski jacket she had bought at the gift shop in the lodge. When she stepped outside, she saw that the sky was overcast and felt a damp chill in the air. More snow on the way, she thought—all the diehard skiers must be in seventh heaven to have snow this early in the season.

I have a pretty good sense of direction, she told herself as she stepped into her skis and mentally reviewed the way to the farmhouse. I won't have any trouble finding it.

She pushed off with her poles and began to ski across the field. It's so quiet and peaceful, she thought. Even though she had barely slept, Opal felt awake and alert. This might be crazy, she admitted to herself, but I need to feel as if I haven't overlooked a chance to catch those thieves and see them in handcuffs.

Leg irons, too, she added. That would be a sight to behold.

She was moving uphill at a steady pace. I'm pretty darn good on these, she thought proudly. Wait till we're having breakfast and I tell Alvirah what I was doing this morning! She'll be mad as heck at me for not waking her up.

Half an hour later Opal was in the wooded area across from the farmhouse. I have to be careful. People get up early in the country, she reminded herself—not like some of her neighbors in the city whose drawn shades were never snapped up before the crack of noon.

But there was no activity at all around the farmhouse. The van was parked directly at the front door. Any closer, and whoever was driving would have gotten out in the living room, Opal thought. She waited for twenty minutes. There wasn't a sign of anyone getting up to milk cows or feed chickens. I wonder if they have animals in the barn, she thought. It really is big. It looks as if it would hold all the animals on Noah's ark.

She skied to the left to try to get a look at the license plate on the van. It was a Vermont plate, but from where she was standing, it was impossible to make out the numbers on it. It would be taking a risk, but she had to get closer.

Opal took a deep breath, skied out of the woods and into the clearing, and didn't stop until she was a few feet from the van. I've got to make this fast and get out of here, she thought. Now very nervous, she whispered the numbers on the green and white plate. "BEM 360. BEM 360," she repeated. "I'll write it down when I'm out of sight."

Inside the farmhouse, at the very table where only hours before conviviality had reigned, three hungover, tired, and angry crooks were trying to figure out how to recover the flask of diamonds that had been their ticket to lifelong easy living. The machete with Wayne Covel's name engraved on the handle was in the center of the table. The local phone book was open to the page where Covel's name and phone number had been circled by Packy. Covel's address was not listed.

Milo had already made two pots of coffee and two batches of pancakes with bacon and sausage. Packy and the twins had devoured the breakfast but now ignored his cheerful suggestion: "One more batch of pancakes for growing boys?"

All three were casting malevolent stares at Covel's machete.

Might as well rustle them up, Milo thought, as he began to spoon batter into the pan. Their bad fortune had obviously not affected their appetites.

"Milo, forget the Magic Chef routine," Packy ordered. "Sit down. I've got plans for you."

Milo obeyed. Intending to turn off the pancakes, he instead flipped the flame under the frying pan that was brimming with bacon grease.

"You're sure you know where this crook Covel lives?" Packy asked accusingly.

"Yes, I do," Milo confirmed proudly. "It's in the second page of that article I showed you about the tree. It said how unusual it was to find two trees worthy of Rockefeller Center in the same state, never mind on neighboring property. Everybody knows where Lem Pickens lives, and Covel's right next door."

Benny wrinkled his nose. "What's burning?"

They all looked over at the stove. Flames and smoke were rising from the ancient cast-iron frying pan full of grease. Next to it the pancakes were rapidly turning black.

"You trying to kill us?" Packy screamed. "This place stinks!" He jumped up. "I get asthma from smoke!" He ran to the front door, yanked it open, and hurried out onto the front porch.

Standing only a few feet away, a woman on cross-country skis was staring at the license plate on the back of the van.

Her head jerked around, and their eyes locked. Even though over twelve years had passed, there was instant recognition on both their parts.

Opal turned and in a futile effort to escape pushed down

hard on her poles, but in her haste she slipped and fell. Instantly, Packy was on her, his hand firmly covering her mouth, his knee on her back, holding her down. A moment later, dazed and terrified, she felt other hands grab her roughly and drag her into the house.

lvirah awakened at 7:15 with a sense of anticipation. "It feels like the beginning of the holiday season, doesn't it, Willy?" she asked. "I mean, to be seeing the Rockefeller Center Christmas tree here in its natural setting, before it's all lit up in New York."

After forty years of marriage, Willy had long since become used to Alvirah's early-morning observances and had learned to grunt approval of them even as he savored the last few minutes of drowsy near sleep.

Alvirah studied him. His eyes were closed, and his head was buried in the pillow. "Willy, the world has just come to an end, and you and I are dead," she said.

"Uh-huh," Willy agreed. "That's great."

No use rousing him yet, Alvirah decided.

She showered and dressed in dark gray wool slacks and a gray and white cardigan sweater set, another of Baroness Min's selections for her. She checked her appearance in the full-length mirror on the closet door. I look okay, she decided matter-of-factly. In the old days I'd be wearing purple slacks and an orange and green sweatshirt. Inside, I'm still wearing them, I guess. Willy and I haven't changed. We both like to help out other folks. He does it by fixing leaky pipes for people who can't afford plumbers. I do it by trying to straighten out situations when people are overwhelmed with problems.

She walked over to the dresser and picked up her sunburst pin with the microphone in the center and clasped it on her sweater. I want to record what people have to say when the tree is cut down, she decided. It will make a nice little story for my column.

"Honey."

Alvirah turned. Willy was sitting up in bed. "Did you say something about the end of the world?"

"Yes, and I told you we were both dead. But don't worry. We're still alive, and they called off the end of the world."

Willy grinned sheepishly. "I'm awake now, honey."

"I'll start packing while you shower and dress," Alvirah said. "We're meeting the others in the dining room for breakfast at eight-thirty. Funny, I haven't heard a sound from Opal's room. I'd better wake her up."

She and Willy were in the master bedroom suite on the main floor of the villa; Opal was upstairs in another large bedroom. Alvirah walked into the great room, caught the aroma of coffee, and spotted Opal's note on the breakfast bar.

Why would Opal be up and out already? she wondered as she hurried to read the note.

Dear Alvirah and Willy,

I left early to do some cross-country skiing. There's something I have to check out. I'll meet you for breakfast at the lodge at 8:30.

Love,
Opal

With growing concern, Alvirah reread the note. Opal's a good cross-country skier, but she doesn't know all these trails, she told herself. They can go into pretty remote areas. She shouldn't be out there alone. What was so important that she had to leave so early to check it out? she wondered.

Alvirah went over to the coffeepot and poured herself a cup. It had a slightly bitter taste, like coffee that had been sitting on the burner for a couple of hours. She must have left *very* early, Alvirah thought.

While she waited for Willy to dress, she found herself staring out at the mountains. Heavy clouds were forming. It was a gray day. There are so many trails out there, she thought. It would be so easy for Opal to get lost.

It was a quarter after eight. Opal had promised to meet

them at eight-thirty. It's silly to worry, Alvirah decided. We'll all be eating a nice breakfast together in a few minutes.

Willy emerged from the bedroom wearing one of the Austrian sweaters he had bought at the gift shop. "Do you think I should learn how to yodel?" he asked, then looked around. "Where's Opal?"

"We're meeting her at the lodge," Alvirah answered. I only hope we are, she thought.

23

Regan, Jack, Nora, and Luke left their cabin at 8:20 and headed toward the lodge.

"This is so lovely," Nora sighed. "Why is it that just when you really start to relax it's time to go home?"

"Well, if you didn't agree to speak at so many luncheons, you could be as relaxed as my dearly departed clients," Luke observed drily.

"I can't believe you said that," Regan protested. "But then again, I can."

"It's hard to say no when I can help raise money for a charity," Nora defended herself. "The event tomorrow is particularly worthwhile."

"Of course it is, dear."

Jack had listened to the exchange with amusement. Luke and Nora have so much fun together, he thought. This is the way Regan and I will be when we've been married a long time. As he put his arm around her, she smiled up at him and rolled her eyes. "This is an ongoing dialogue," she commented.

"Let's see what you two end up talking about in thirty years," Luke said. "I guarantee you it won't be fascinating. Couples do tend to return to the same few favorite topics of conversation."

"We'll do our best to keep it interesting, Luke," Jack promised with a smile. "But I hardly think that there's anything dull about the two of you."

"Sometimes dull is preferable," Nora commented as Luke opened the door of the lodge. "Especially when I know that Regan is in potential danger because of the case she's working on."

"It's a concern I very much share," Jack said.

"That's why I'm so glad you're getting married," Nora said. "Even when you're not together, I have the feeling that you're watching out for her."

"You bet I am," Jack answered.

"Thanks, guys," Regan said. "It's nice to know I have a team of worriers behind me."

They walked through the lobby and into the dining room. A breakfast buffet was set up on a long table at one end of the room.

The hostess greeted them cheerfully. "I have your table ready. Your friends aren't here yet." She picked up menus and led them to the table. As they sat down, she said, "I understand you're leaving us today."

"Unfortunately, yes," Nora said, "but first we're going over to watch the Rockefeller Center tree being cut down."

"Too late."

"What?"

"You're too late."

"Did they do it earlier than expected?" Nora asked.

"I'll say. Lem Pickens went over to say good-bye to his tree at six o'clock this morning, and *he* was too late. It was gone. Someone cut it down in the middle of the night, and they even stole the flatbed that was supposed to take the tree to New York. Everybody's talking about it. One of the guests just said she was watching Imus on MSNBC, and he's onto the story."

"I can only imagine what Imus has to say about this," Regan commented.

"Imus said it must have been done by a bunch of drunks," the hostess reported as she handed out the menus. "He wondered who else would bother."

"It's the sort of stunt kids would pull," Jack said.

"What are they going to do now?" Nora asked the hostess.

"If they can't find the tree today, they'll probably go back to the guy who lives next door to Pickens. His tree was their second choice."

"*There's* a motive," Jack suggested, only partly in jest.

"You better believe it," the hostess replied, her eyes wide with excitement. "Lem Pickens was already on the local news this morning, screaming that he thought his neighbor was responsible."

"He could get sued for that," Regan noted.

"I don't think he cares. Oh, look, here are your friends."

Alvirah and Willy had spotted them and were heading toward the table. Regan had the immediate impression that even though Alvirah was smiling, she seemed anxious. That feeling was confirmed when, after a quick "good morning," Alvirah asked, "Isn't Opal here yet?"

"No, Alvirah," Regan answered. "Wasn't she with you?"

"She left this morning to go cross-country skiing and said she'd meet us at breakfast."

"Alvirah, sit down. I'm sure she'll be along in a few minutes," Nora said comfortingly. "Besides, you wouldn't believe the news around here."

"What news?" Alvirah asked eagerly.

As Alvirah and Willy sat down, Regan could see that Alvirah perked up with the prospect of hearing some dirt.

"Someone cut down the Rockefeller Center tree in the middle of the night and disappeared with it."

"*What?*"

"Nobody took Alvirah's tree, did they?" Willy asked. "Then they'd really be in trouble."

Alvirah ignored him. "Why on earth would anyone go to all that trouble to steal a tree? And where could they possibly take it?"

Quickly Regan filled them in on the fact that not only were the tree and the flatbed missing, but the owner of the tree, Lem Pickens, was accusing his neighbor of theft.

"As soon as we eat breakfast, I want to get over there and see for myself what's going on," Alvirah announced. She glanced at the doorway of the dining room. "I do wish Opal would hurry up and get here," she said.

Jack took a sip of the coffee that the waitress had just poured for him. "Do you know if Opal heard the news about Packy Noonan?"

"What news?" Alvirah and Willy asked in unison.

"He didn't go back to his halfway house last night, which means he's already broken his parole."

"Opal has always sworn that he had plenty of money hidden somewhere. He's probably on his way out of the country with that loot right now." Alvirah shook her head. "It's disgusting." She reached for the bread basket, examined it carefully, and decided on an apple strudel. "I shouldn't," she murmured, "but they're so good."

Alvirah's purse was on the floor beside her feet. The sudden ring of her cell phone made her jump. "I forgot to turn this off before I came into the dining room," she noted as she dove for her purse and fumbled for the phone. "Men have it so much easier. They just hook these things onto their belt and answer on the first ring—unless, of course, they're up to no good. . . . Hello . . . oh, hi, Charley."

"It's Charley Evans, her editor at *The New York Globe*," Willy informed the others. "Dollars to doughnuts he knows about the missing tree. He's always on top of everything before it happens."

"Yes, we've heard about the tree," Alvirah was saying. "As soon as I finish breakfast, I'm going to run right over there, Charley. It's good human interest to talk to the locals. It has turned into a crime story, hasn't it?" She laughed. "I sure wish I could solve it. Yes, Willy and I can stay for an extra day or two to see what happens. I'll report back to you in a few hours. Oh! By the way, what's the latest on Packy Noonan? I just heard a minute ago that he didn't show up at his halfway house last night. My friend who lost money in his scam is up here with me."

As the others watched, Alvirah's expression became incredulous. "He was seen getting into a van with Vermont license plates on Madison Avenue?"

The others looked at each other. "Vermont license plates!" Regan repeated.

"Maybe he's the one who cut down the tree," Luke suggested. "Either it was Packy Noonan or George Washington." His voice deepened. "Father, I cannot tell a lie. I did chop down the cherry tree."

"Our local historian strikes again," Regan said to Jack. "The difference between Packy Noonan and George Washington is that Packy wouldn't admit it even if he was caught with the ax in his hand."

"George Washington never said that anyhow," Nora protested. "Those silly stories were made up about him after he died."

"Well, I bet whoever cut down that tree will never become president of the United States," Willy remarked.

"Don't count on it," Luke mumbled.

Alvirah snapped closed her cell phone. "I'll turn the ringer off and put it on vibrate. Maybe Opal will call if she's running late." Placing the phone on the table, she continued, "A priest at Saint Patrick's noticed a van with Vermont license plates standing in front of the rectory on Madison Avenue. Then a mother called in and said her little boy claimed he saw a man run up the block and get into that van. Of course Packy had just been at Mass at Saint Patrick's. The detective who was following him said he even lit a candle in front of the statue of Saint Anthony."

"Maybe the detective should light a candle there himself to help him find Packy," Willy suggested. "My mother was always praying to Saint Anthony. She was always losing her glasses, and my father could never find the car keys."

"Saint Anthony would have made a great detective," Regan commented in the same dry tone that was Luke's trademark. "I should have a picture of him in my office."

"We'd better eat," Nora suggested.

All through breakfast Alvirah kept glancing at the door, but there was no sign of Opal. The phone vibrated in Alvirah's hand as they were walking out of the dining room. It was her editor again.

"Alvirah, we just dug up some background on Packy Noonan. When he was about sixteen, he worked in a troubled youth program in Stowe, Vermont, cutting down Christmas trees for Lem Pickens. There might be no connection, but as I just told you, he *was* seen leaving New York in a van with Vermont plates. I can't imagine why he'd be bothered cutting down a tree, but keep this in mind when you're talking to people."

Alvirah's heart sank. Opal was an hour late, and there was a chance that Packy Noonan was in the area. Opal had gone to check something out. The sixth sense Alvirah could always rely on told her that there was a connection.

And it wasn't a good one.

arlier that morning, as the sun was coming over the mountain, Lem and Viddy, hand in hand, were trudging across their property in their snowshoes in anticipation of one last look at their beloved tree before it belonged to the world.

"I know it's hard, Viddy," Lem said. As he spoke, his breath was visible in the early morning chill. "But let's just think of all the fun we're going to have in New York. And the tree isn't gone forever, Viddy. I hear that after they take it down, they sometimes use these trees to make chips for the Appalachian Trail."

As Viddy teetered along, she replied with tears in her voice, "Well, that's nice, Lem, but I'm not up for a hike on the Appalachian Trail. Those days are long since gone."

"Sometimes they use the tree trunks to make horse jumps for the U.S. Equestrian Center."

"I don't want any horses jumping over my tree. Where is the Equestrian Center, anyway?"

"Someplace in New Jersey."

"Forget it. This trip to New York will be the last time I pack a suitcase. When we get back from New York, you can give my bags to Goodwill and take a deduction."

They turned the bend into the clearing, and their mouths dropped. Where their beloved tree had been growing and thriving for fifty years, there was only a ragged foot-high stump. The ladder the workmen had used in preparing the tree for the trip to New York City was lying on its side, and the angle of the crane was different from the night before.

"They sneaked in early and cut down our tree," Lem raged. "Wait till I get my hands on those New York people. It was our tree until ten A.M. this morning. They didn't have the right to cut it down a minute before."

Viddy, always the quicker of the two to process information, pointed to the crane. "But, Lemmy, why would they do this when they knew there were going to be a lot of reporters and television cameras? Everybody in New York loves publicity. Remember we read about that?" Shocked out of her earlier sentimental state, she declared, "This just doesn't make sense."

As they moved closer to the stump, they heard the sound of a vehicle approaching.

"Maybe they're coming back for the crane," Lem said as they stood protectively on either side of the stump. "I'm going to give those folks a piece of my mind."

A man in his thirties whom Lem had met yesterday when they were tying up the bottom branches of the tree was coming toward them. Phil something was his name, Lem remembered. They watched as a shocked expression came over his face. *"What happened to the tree?"* he yelled.

"You don't *know?!*" Lem exploded.

"Of course I don't know! I woke up early and decided to come on over. The others will be here by eight o'clock. And where's our flatbed?"

Viddy exclaimed, "Lem, I told you it didn't make sense for those Rockefeller Center people to cut our tree down early. But who else would have done it?"

Next to her, her husband straightened up to his full height, which had shrunk to six feet one, pointed through the woods with an accusatory finger, and bellowed, "That no good skunk Wayne Covel did this!"

Almost four hours later, when the Meehans and the Reillys arrived on the scene, Lem was still sputtering that accusation for all the world to hear. Because word had already gone out that somebody had managed to make off with a three-ton tree, the expected crowd of one hundred had grown to three hundred and counting. The woods were swarming with reporters, television cameras, and stringers from the major networks. To the delight of the assembled media, what had begun as a feel-good piece of Americana had turned into a major news story.

The Meehans and Reillys made their way to the police captain at what appeared to be the command post at the edge of the clearing. Alvirah was scanning the crowd in the hope that Opal might have gone directly there if she was running late.

Jack introduced himself and the others and told the captain that Alvirah was writing a story for a New York newspaper. "Can you bring us up to date, Chief?"

"Well, this tree that was supposed to end up in your neck of the woods got swiped. We found a flatbed abandoned on route 100, near Morristown, which I think may have been involved in the crime. They're tracing the registration. The Rockefeller Center people have offered a $10,000 reward for the tree if it's still in good condition. With all this coverage," he pointed to the cameras, "you're going to have a lot of people on the lookout for that tree."

"Do you think it might be kids who did this?" Alvirah asked.

"They would have to be darn smart kids," the Chief said skeptically. "You don't just go and chop down a tree that size. Cut it at the wrong angle, and it could fall on you. But who knows? It could turn up on a college campus full of tinsel, I suppose. I doubt it, though."

Lem Pickens was finally calming down. He had not left the spot for nearly four hours, except for his rushed trip with the police to bang on Wayne Covel's door at twenty of seven. Even Lem's righteous wrath could not keep him warm any longer. Viddy had gone back and forth to the house a couple of times to get a cup of coffee and warm up. Now, as they walked past the police chief, they stopped.

"Chief, has anyone spoken to that low-down tree-napper Wayne Covel again?"

"Lem," the Chief began wearily, "you know that there's nothing to ask him now. We routed him out of bed this morning. He denies knowing anything. Just because you think he's responsible doesn't *make* him responsible."

"Well, who else would do this?" Lem demanded. By now it was a rhetorical question.

Alvirah seized the moment. "Mr. Pickens, I'm a reporter for *The New York Globe*. Could I possibly ask you about someone who worked for you years ago?"

Lem and Viddy turned and focused on the group.

"Who did you say you were?" he asked.

"We're all from New York, and you'd be interested to know that between us all, we've solved a lot of crimes." Alvirah introduced the group to the Pickenses.

"I read your books, Nora!" Viddy exclaimed. "Why don't you all come up to the house for a cup of hot chocolate, and we'll talk."

Wonderful, Alvirah thought. We'll be able to ask about Packy Noonan without interruption.

"Yeah, come on," Lem said gruffly, confirming the invitation with a wave of his sinewy hand.

Alvirah turned to the police chief. "My friend went out

cross-country skiing early this morning and was supposed to meet us for breakfast. I'm getting concerned."

Willy interrupted. "Honey, I'm sure she's fine. I'll wait here. She's bound to come along. We'll catch up with you or meet you back here."

"Do you mind?"

"No. There's a lot of action going on around here. Maybe you should give me your pin to wear."

Alvirah smiled. "That'll be the day." She fell in step with the others as they followed the Pickenses to the family homestead.

25

Opal had fainted as she was dragged into the house. The men laid her on a lumpy couch in the living room. She came to immediately, then realized it was better to act as if she was still unconscious until she could figure out what to do. The house smelled of burning grease, the windows and doors were open in an obvious attempt to get rid of the odor, and a cold draft made Opal shiver. Through narrowed eyes she could see that Benny and Jo-Jo must have been the ones to help Packy drag her inside.

Those three crooks all together again! Moe, Larry, and Curly, she thought disdainfully. God didn't bless those twins with good looks, that's for sure, she thought. I remembered Benny shlumped, and now here I am. I should have told Alvirah where I was going and why. And then she had a chillier thought: What are they going to do to me?

"You can close the windows now," Packy barked. "It's freezing in here." He came over to the couch and looked down at Opal. He started to pat her on the face. "Come on, come on. You're all right."

Repulsed by his touch, Opal's eyes flew open. "Get your hands off me, Packy Noonan! You miserable thief!"

"It seems like you've come to your senses," Packy grunted. "Jo-Jo, Benny, bring her into the kitchen and tie her to a chair. I don't want her making a dash for it."

Opal's cross-country skis were on the floor. The twins hustled her into the kitchen, where a nervous Milo was making another pot of coffee and wondering what the penalty for kidnapping was. The windows in the kitchen were still open. The smell of bacon grease and charred pancakes combined with the cold air made everything seem so much worse to Opal.

She looked at Milo. "Are you the short-order cook around here? If so, it looks as if you could use a few lessons."

"I'm a poet," Milo answered unhappily.

Benny and Jo-Jo wrapped a rope around Opal's legs and torso.

"Leave my hands free," she snapped. "You might want me to write another check. And I'd like a cup of coffee."

"She's a stand-up comedienne," Jo-Jo grunted.

"No, Jo-Jo," Benny smiled. "She's a sit-down comedienne." He started to laugh.

"Shut up, Benny," Packy ordered as he came into the kitchen. "I don't see anybody else out there. She must have come alone." He sat down across the table from Opal. "How did you know we were here?"

"Give me my coffee first." Shock and then anger had been Opal's initial reactions to what had happened. She read the desperation in Packy's face and realized that he was supposed to be at the halfway house in New York. She was sure he didn't get a weekend pass to Vermont. Was he up here to get his hands on the money she had always suspected he had hidden, and then get out of the country fast? Was the money up here somewhere? Why else would he and the Como twins have come to Vermont? Certainly not to ski.

"Milk and sugar in your coffee?" Milo asked politely. "We have two percent or skim."

"Skim and no sugar." She looked at the twins. "It wouldn't hurt you two to take your coffee that way." In a crazy way Opal was beginning to feel a sense of satisfaction at getting the chance to hurl insults at these men who had caused her so much misery. I should be more afraid, she thought. But I feel as if they've already done the worst to me.

"I've been trying to diet," Benny said, "but it's hard when you're under stress."

"You've been under stress for four days. Try twelve and a half years in the can," Packy shot back.

Milo placed a mug of coffee in front of Opal. "Enjoy," he whispered kindly.

"Now talk, Opal," Packy demanded.

Opal had been silently debating how much information she should give him. If she told him that someone would surely come looking here for her, would they leave her or take her with them? She decided to stay close to the truth. "When I was cross-country skiing the other day, I saw a man in the yard here putting skis on the roof of the van. He seemed familiar. I couldn't get it off my mind, and this morning I realized he reminded me of Benny so I decided to check the license plate. That's it."

"Benny strikes again," Packy growled. "Who'd you tell?"

"No one. But the people I'm with are going to start wondering why I haven't come back." She decided not to say that the friends she was with included the head of the NYPD's Major Case Squad, a licensed private investigator, and the best amateur detective on this side of the Atlantic.

Packy stared at her. "Turn on the television, Benny," he ordered. There was a ten-inch set on the kitchen counter. "Let's see if they've discovered the stump in the woods yet."

His timing was perfect. The camera zoomed in on an agitated and furious Lem Pickens pointing at the stump on the ground and swearing that his neighbor Wayne Covel had done this to him. Packy picked up the machete on the table with Wayne's name on it.

"Yup. He's our guy," Packy said flatly. "Benny, Jo-Jo, I need to speak to you inside." He jerked his head toward Milo. "Keep an eye on her. Recite a poem or something."

"Someone cut down the Rockefeller Center tree!" Opal exclaimed as the three of them filed into the living room and huddled in the corner, out of earshot.

Milo pointed to the living room. "*They* did. Can you believe it?"

"Jo-Jo," Packy said, "did you get the sleeping pills for the flight back to Brazil?"

"Sure, Packy."

"Where are they?"

"In my bag."

"Bring me the bottle right now."

Benny looked bothered. "Packy, I know we didn't get any sleep last night. I know you're nervous and upset. But I don't think you should take a pill right now."

"*You* are an idiot," Packy said through clenched teeth.

Jo-Jo hurried upstairs and returned a moment later with the bottle of sleeping pills in his hand. He looked at Packy questioningly as he handed it to him.

"We gotta somehow get into Wayne Covel's place and find the diamonds. Even if we tie her up, there's a chance she could get away. Or if someone finds her here, she could talk. We gotta make sure she's out of it until we board the plane and are well on our way. A couple of these will keep her quiet for at least eighteen hours."

"I thought Milo was going to stay here."

"He is. He'll be sleeping right next to her." Packy shook four pills out of the bottle.

"How are you going to make them swallow those babies?" Benny whispered.

"You pour Milo a fresh cup of coffee. Drop two of these into it and stir. He'll drink it. I'm surprised he can sit still long enough to write a poem with all the coffee he inhales. I'll be nice and fix another cup for Miss Moneybags. If she doesn't drink it, we'll move to Plan B."

"What's Plan B?"

"Shove it down her throat."

Wordlessly, they all went back into the kitchen where Opal was giving Milo a laundry list of all the people who had lost money in the scam.

"One couple invested their retirement money," she said. "And they had to sell their sweet little house in Florida. Now they're supplementing their Social Security doing odd jobs. And then there was the woman who—"

"The woman who blah, blah, blah," Packy interrupted. "It's not my fault you were all so stupid. I'd like another cup of coffee."

Milo jumped up.

"Don't bother, Milo. I'll pour it," Benny offered.

"Oh, look at this!" Packy said, pointing to the television as he took Opal's cup and walked over to the stove.

On the screen they could see the chief of police and Lem Pickens knocking at the door of a rundown farmhouse. A reporter's voice was informing the viewers that about an hour ago the police chief insisted on accompanying an outraged Lem Pickens to Wayne Covel's home. "Pickens has been feuding on and off over the years with Covel, and Covel's prized tree was almost picked for Rockefeller Center," the reporter explained.

"I remember seeing that dump when I was a kid," Packy said as he put Opal's cup back down next to her. "It looks even worse now."

The door opened, and a rumpled-looking man wearing a red nightshirt appeared. A heated dialogue ensued between him and Lem. Wayne Covel's face appeared in closeup. It was not a pretty sight.

"Take a look at those scratches," Packy snarled. "They're fresh. He got them from poking around the tree and stealing our flask."

"I hear you cut down that tree," Opal accused Packy. "What did you have hidden in it? Anything of mine?"

Packy looked her straight in the eye. "*Diamonds*," he said with a sneer. "A flask of diamonds worth a fortune. One of them is worth three million bucks. That's the one I named after you." He pointed to the television. "Scratchy stole them. But we're getting them back. I'll think of you when we're living it up on your money."

"You'll never pull this off," Opal spat.

"Yes, we will." He looked at her half-empty coffee cup and smiled. He looked over at Milo's, which was still three-quarters full. He sat down. "Now everyone be quiet. I want to watch the news."

They sat through several commercials, then the local weather report came on.

"It's gray and cold out there. It looks like more storm clouds will be moving in on us today," the weatherman warned.

Packy and Jo-Jo looked at each other. They had called their pilot in the middle of the night and told him to get to the airstrip just outside Stowe and wait. Now with a possible storm coming, their getaway could be delayed. Packy was about to jump out of his skin, but he knew he had to sit still until the sleeping pills started to do their magic. He could feel the window of opportunity for his escape to Brazil rapidly closing on him.

When the weatherman finished his report, there was more rehashing about the stolen tree. Finally, a new segment was being introduced. "Packy Noonan, a convicted scam artist who broke parole, was seen yesterday getting into a van in Manhattan. The van had skis on the roof and Vermont license plates." Packy's mug shot flashed on the screen. "So maybe he's heading our way," the anchor suggested.

"Let's hope not," his coanchor trilled. "It's amazing that he conned so many people. He doesn't look that smart."

"He isn't," Opal said drowsily.

Packy ignored her as he jumped up to lower the volume. "Great. We can't use the van, and now my mug has been seen by people all over town."

"And nobody forgets a pretty face," Opal said. Her eyes felt so heavy.

Benny began to yawn. He looked down at the mug of coffee he was holding in his hand, and a horrified look came over his face. He turned and saw that Packy and Jo-Jo were staring at him, equally horrified. Even Benny knew better than to say anything.

Jo-Jo mouthed the words "You dope" and hurried upstairs to fetch two more sleeping pills. He came down and refilled Milo's cup.

Within twenty minutes there were three comatose figures in the farmhouse kitchen. All their heads were resting on the old wooden table.

"I'm sorry my brother Benny got distracted by the news story," Jo-Jo apologized. "Sometimes it's hard for him to focus on more than one thing at a time."

"I *know* what happened," Packy snarled. "Let's drag the poet and the mouth upstairs and tie them to the beds. Benny we'll stick in the trunk of Milo's car. As soon as we get those diamonds, we're out of town fast."

"Maybe we should leave Benny a note and come back and pick him up," Jo-Jo suggested.

"I'm not running a car pool! He'll be fine in the trunk. I just hope we don't have to carry him onto the plane. Now let's move it!"

26

The four Reillys and Alvirah sat in the parlor of Lem and Viddy's farmhouse. Over the fireplace, in identical frames, were a picture of Lem and Viddy on their wedding day planting the now missing blue spruce and another of a smiling Maria von Trapp pointing to the sapling.

Lem carried in a tray laden with cups of steaming hot chocolate. Viddy was following with a platter of homemade cookies in the shape of Christmas trees. "I just learned how to make these. I was going to give them out today when they cut the tree down, and if they went over big, I was going to make a batch to bring to New York." She frowned. "Now I can just throw away the recipe."

"Hold your horses, Viddy," Lem ordered. "We're getting that tree back even if I have to shoot Wayne Covel in the toes, one by one, until he tells us where he hid it."

Oh, boy, Regan thought. This guy means business.

Lem began to pass around the cups to the guests. Then he sat down on the high-backed old rocker across from the couch. That rocker looks as though it's part of him, Regan thought. She accepted one of the cookies from Viddy with a murmured thanks. Clearly Lem was ready to get down to business.

"Now, Alvirah, is that what you said your name was?"

"Yes."

"Where'd you get a name like that?"

"Same place you got a name like Lemuel."

"Fair enough. Now who did you want to ask me about?" He took a sip of his hot chocolate which was followed by a "hahhhhhhh." He looked around. "You'd better blow before you take a taste. It'll burn your tongue off."

Alvirah laughed. "My mother had a friend who used to pour her hot tea into a saucer. Her husband used to ask, 'Why not fan it with your hat?' "

"I have to admit that would have bugged me."

Alvirah laughed. "I guess he got used to it. They were married for sixty-two years. Now what I needed to ask you," she continued, "is if you remember someone named Packy Noonan who worked up here years ago in the late fall in a troubled youth program."

"Packy Noonan!" Viddy exclaimed. "He's the only one from that group who ever came back to pay a visit. The rest were a bunch of ingrates. Although, to be honest, for years I wondered if he'd been the kid who swiped the cameo pin off my dresser."

"We never had children of our own," Lem explained, "so

we used to take part in that program during the busy season when people were coming up here and selecting their own trees. It did a lot of those troubled kids good. Made them feel good about themselves. Helped straighten them out."

"It didn't work for Packy Noonan," Alvirah said flatly.

"What do you mean?"

"He just got out of prison after serving more than twelve years for scamming people out of a lot of money. He broke his parole yesterday in New York City and was seen getting into a van with Vermont license plates. I was just wondering if you'd had any contact with him at all over these years."

"He went to prison twelve years ago?" Lem exclaimed.

"I can't believe it!" Viddy said. "Maybe he *did* take my pin! But he was so nice when he came back to say hello. I was thinking how well he had turned out. He was all spiffed up. When he was a kid he looked like a bum, but that day he looked like a million dollars."

"Somebody else's million," Luke said under his breath.

"Viddy, when was it that he knocked on our door?" Lem asked.

Viddy closed her eyes. "Now let me see. My memory is not as good as it used to be, but it's still pretty darn good."

They all waited.

Her eyes still shut, Viddy fumbled for her cup of hot chocolate, picked it up, blew on it, and took a dainty sip. "I remember it was springtime, and I was making pies for the bake sale we were having at church to raise money for the senior citizens center after the basement flooded. All the bingo cards were ruined. I can tell you that that was exactly thirteen and a half years ago. It was right after the big Mother's Day storm. Everyone got drenched coming out of church, and their corsages were ruined. Anyway, that week Packy showed up at the door. I invited him in, and he was so charming. He had a piece of my pie and a glass of milk. He said it reminded him of sitting with his mother, and he told me how much he missed her. He even had tears in his eyes. I asked what he was doing with himself, and he said he was in finance."

"I'll say he was in finance," Alvirah exclaimed. "Did you see him that day, Lem?"

"Lem was back in the woods doing some tree trimming," Viddy answered. "I blew the whistle I keep by the back door, and Lem came in 'cause he knew I never blow it unless it's important."

"I got down off the ladder and came in. Boy, was I surprised to see Packy."

"Why did he say he was here?" Alvirah asked.

"He told us he was passing through on business and wanted to come over and just thank us for all we had done for him. Then he saw the picture of the tree over the fireplace and asked if it was still our baby. I said, 'You betcha. Come out back with me and take a look.' And he did. He said it looked great. Then he helped me carry the ladder back to the barn. I invited him to stay for supper. He said he had to get going but would be in touch. Never heard from him again. Now I know why. The only calls you can make from prison are collect."

"I hope he doesn't pay us another visit. Next time I'll slam the door in his face," Viddy promised.

Regan and Alvirah exchanged glances.

"And that was thirteen and a half years ago?" Alvirah asked.

"Yes, it was," Viddy confirmed, her eyes now wide open.

"I can't understand why Packy Noonan would come back here," Lem wondered aloud. "What happened to the money he stole?"

"Nobody knows," Regan said. "But everyone seems to think that wherever he is right now, he's headed for the money he managed to hide."

"He didn't hit you up to invest in his phony shipping company that day?" Alvirah asked. "That was at the very time when his scam was operating at full steam."

"He didn't ask us for one red cent," Lem exclaimed. "He knew better than to try and pull one over on Lemuel Pickens!"

Alvirah shook her head. "He pulled one over on a lot of smart people. I have a friend who lost money in his scam at that very time. Even up to the day before Packy was arrested he was trying to get her to suggest some of her friends who might want to make an investment. It's surprising that he didn't try to get you to write a check. He must have been up here for something else. This friend I mentioned was supposed to meet us for breakfast this morning and never showed up. Just the thought of Packy possibly coming to Vermont and maybe even to this area has me terribly nervous."

"The only criminal you have to worry about around here," Lem bellowed, "is the one who lives next store. Wayne Covel. He cut down my tree, and he's going to pay for it!"

"Lem, hush," Viddy scolded. "Alvirah is worried about her friend."

"Would this Wayne Covel know Packy from when Packy was up here years ago?" Alvirah asked.

Lem shrugged. "Maybe. They're about the same age."

"Maybe I'll see if he'll talk to me."

"He won't talk to me!" Lem cried.

Viddy felt the need to change the subject. When Lem got worked up, it took a lot to calm him down. "Nora," she said quickly. "I just love to read. I even tried writing poetry. There's a new fellow in town here who got a few people together for poetry readings at the old farmhouse where he's staying. But he was dreadful, so I never went back. He read one of his old poems about a peach that falls in love with a fruit fly. Can you imagine?"

"He's Milo, that really weird guy with the long hair and short beard, right, Viddy?" Lem asked.

"Honey, he's not that weird."

"Yes, he is. He comes up to Vermont. Doesn't ski. Doesn't

ice skate. Sits in that junky old farmhouse all day writing poetry. There's something weird there. Right, Nora?"

"Oh, well," Nora began, "sometimes it's good for a writer
to get away and work in peace and quiet."

"Work? Writing about peaches and fruit flies is not work!
I don't know how long he can keep that up. How does he pay
the bills?"

Alvirah felt restless. She wanted to get out and see if there
was any sign of Opal. "As you know, I'm working on a story
for my paper about your tree. Is it all right if I call you later?
Maybe by then the police will have some leads. I can't believe that an eighty-foot Christmas tree could vanish into
thin air."

"Neither can I," Lem said. "And I'm going to organize a
posse to find it!"

"More hot chocolate anyone?" Viddy asked.

27

Wayne Covel tried to get some sleep after he hid the flask of diamonds in the elm tree in his front yard.

But it was no use. He realized that hiding the diamonds in the tree was a dumb idea. If those Rockefeller Center people came swarming onto his property begging him to let them have his blue spruce, who knew what might happen? The tree in which he had hidden the flask wasn't far from it. Suppose some photographer got the notion to climb the elm and get a good picture of them cutting it down?

Having the flask out of his sight gave Wayne the willies.

Just before dawn he opened the door, went outside, climbed the elm, and retrieved the flask. He brought it back to bed with him, unscrewed the cap, took a quick peek at the diamonds, and then drifted off to sleep, cuddling the flask like a baby with a bottle.

When Lem Pickens came banging on the door with the police chief, Wayne jumped up and the flask went flying out of his hands. The cap went sailing through the air as the flask hit the uneven wooden floor with a thud. Diamonds scattered randomly around the atrociously untidy room and settled among the piles of dirty clothes on the floor.

Wayne answered the door in his red nightshirt and was appalled to find an array of television cameras waiting for him. His first thought was the terrifying possibility that the police chief had that search warrant he was worried about. When he realized they had only come a-calling so Lem could scream at him, Wayne screamed back and slammed the door in their faces. A man's home is his castle, he told himself. He didn't have to take that guff from anyone. He bolted the door and raced back to his room to retrieve the diamonds. After he had sorted through his dirty clothes and was satisfied that he had all the diamonds back in the flask, he was uncharacteristically motivated to do a wash. I wish I'd thought to count my diamonds last night, but the flask looks full, he mused.

Grabbing one of the heaps of laundry, he walked to the door in the kitchen that led to the basement, pulled it open, flicked on the light, and made his way down the creaky steps, carefully avoiding the bottom step that was broken. No wonder I don't come down here much, he thought as he breathed the dank sour smell of the musty cellar. I should get around to cleaning up this place someday, he thought, but now I can *hire* somebody to do it. First thing I ought to do is get rid of that coal bin. Pop switched to oil heat after World War II, but he never got around to getting rid of it. He just closed it off, put a door on it, and made it into a little workroom he never used.

I sure haven't used it either, Wayne thought. It would probably be easier to burn this place down and start from scratch than to clean it up. He dropped the pile of clothes on the floor in front of the washing machine, reached up to the shelf, grabbed the nearly empty box of detergent, and shook its remains into the machine. He scooped up half of the clothes, dropped them around the agitator, closed the lid, turned the dial, and went back upstairs.

His television set was on the kitchen counter next to his laptop computer. He put on a pot of coffee, flipped on the TV, and moved his computer to the table. For the rest of the morning he kept the television on, nervously flipping among the news stations, all of which seemed to be covering the story of the missing tree. He also heard over and over that Packy Noonan, a swindler who had just been paroled, had been seen getting into a van with Vermont plates and had worked in Stowe in a troubled youth program.

Packy Noonan, Wayne thought. Packy Noonan. It sounds familiar. I kind of remember that name.

At the same time Wayne was trying to educate himself on what was going on in the diamond world by visiting different Web sites. I've got to figure out where I can sell these, he thought. He came across a number of ads for appraisals. "We buy at the highest prices and sell at the lowest" seemed to be the slogan for most of the places that traded and sold diamonds. Yeah, right, Wayne thought. And yeah, I know diamonds are forever. They're a girl's best friend. They show you care. Give me a break! He smiled. Lorna would be salivating if she were here right now and got a look at these babies.

As if he had ESP or, better yet, she had ESP, he heard the click that meant a new e-mail had popped up in his box. Expecting it might be from someone who wanted him to do an odd job, he was surprised to see it was from the ex instead.

Wayne

I see you still haven't gotten rid of that red nightshirt and you're still feuding with Lem Pickens. And I hear that if they can't find his tree, yours might be cut down for Rockefeller Center. I know you'd never steal his tree—it would be too much work! Maybe you'd take that machete I gave you for Christmas and hack off a branch or two, but that would be it. If they pick your tree and you want some company to go with you to New York, give me a call.

xoxo
Lorna

P.S. What's with the scratches on your face? It looks as though you have a lively new girlfriend—or maybe you were poking around that tree!

Wayne stared at the e-mail with disgust. Xoxo, hugs and kisses, he thought disdainfully—she's just looking for a free trip to New York. Wants to get in on the act. If she only knew what the really big news was around the Covel household, she'd come flying back on her broom.

It gave him a laugh that she made a point of reminding him about the machete she gave him for Christmas. When he had opened it, she made a big deal about getting his name engraved on it. You'd have thought it was a hunk of gold. Then, slowly but surely, a troubling possibility occurred to him.

Machete.

His tool belt had felt light when he strapped it on this morning to get the flask. When he took it off, he had tossed it on the other kitchen chair. Now he dove for it and, hoping against hope, held it up.

The machete was missing!

Did I drop it near Lem's tree last night? I was out of my bird when I found the flask, so I might not have noticed if I dropped it. What did she have to put my name on it for?

Lem couldn't have found it yet, or he would have been waving it at me this morning.

Those crooks who cut the tree—maybe *they* found it. Maybe they're on the way here. Maybe they'll kill me for taking the loot.

I don't want to be here all by myself, he thought. On the other hand, if I just take off, everyone will think I cut down the tree.

The phone rang. Eager to hear the sound of another voice, Wayne grabbed it. "Hello."

Whoever was at the other end of the phone said nothing.

"Hello," Wayne repeated nervously. "Is anybody there?"

The response was a click in his ear.

28

He definitely has the flask," Packy reported as he closed his cell phone.

"How do you know?" Jo-Jo asked.

"I just know. Call it criminal instinct."

"It takes one to know one, huh, Packy?"

They were getting a late start. It was 10 A.M., and Packy and Jo-Jo were sitting in the decrepit brown sedan that the owner of the farm had originally kept around for his handyman and then had willingly sold to Milo. Fifteen years old, with dents in all the fenders, a rear bumper held on by ropes, and replacement parts that had been salvaged from a junkyard, it was a spectacular example of a vehicle that only a person as blissfully impractical as Milo would buy.

Between them Packy and Jo-Jo had hauled Milo and Opal to the upstairs bedrooms and tied them to the bedposts. They had tried to revive Benny by dunking and dunking his head in a sink full of cold water. Finally, they gave up, dragged Benny outside, and hoisted him into the trunk of the car. In a burst of brotherly love, Jo-Jo ran back inside and grabbed a pillow to place under Benny's head and a quilt to cover him. Then he closed Benny's hand over a flashlight and pinned a note to his jacket just in case he woke up and wondered what was going on.

"I wrote that he should stay put and keep quiet until we got back," Jo-Jo explained.

"Why don't you read him a bedtime story?" Packy growled.

Packy knew there was no way they could use the van even though Jo-Jo warned him that Milo complained the car wasn't too reliable.

"Maybe you can't hear what they're saying on television," Packy yelled. "They're all talking about me getting in a van with a ski rack and Vermont plates. They're saying I worked up here in Stowe when I was a kid. Every cop in Vermont, especially in this area, is taking a long, hard look at a van with ski racks. We go out in the van, and we might as well turn ourselves in and collect the reward for finding me."

"We go out in that heap, and we're lucky if we get as far as the barn," Jo-Jo retorted.

"Maybe we should go in the flatbed with the tree on it."

Packy and Jo-Jo glared at each other. Then Packy said, "Jo-Jo, we've got to get our diamonds. That guy Covel has to have them. Nobody's looking for us in this heap. Let's go."

Packy was behind the wheel. He put on his dark glasses. "Give me one of the ski hats," he snapped.

"Do you want the blue with the orange stripe or the green with the—"

"Just give me a hat!"

Packy turned on the ignition. It sputtered and died. He pumped the gas. "Come on! Come on!"

"Maybe I should put a hat on Benny," Jo-Jo suggested. "There's no heat in the trunk. His hair is still damp."

"What's the matter with you?" Packy screamed. "The minute Benny falls asleep, you act dopier than Benny when Benny's at his dopiest."

Jo-Jo had the door open. "I'm putting his hat on," he said stubbornly. "Besides, his blood is thin after being in Brazil so long."

In an effort to preserve his sanity, Packy began to consider his problems and his options. Nobody will pay attention to this car, he assured himself. The poet's been tooling around in it long enough. We have to take the chance that it won't break down. At least we know Covel is home. We have to get inside that dump he lives in and make him give us the flask. It's only ten miles to the airstrip, and the pilot is waiting for us there.

Jo-Jo got back in the car.

"Hurry up," Packy barked. "We've gotta get out of here before somebody shows up looking for Sherlock Holmes."

"Who's Sherlock Holmes?" Jo-Jo asked.

"Opal Fogarty, you idiot! *The investor!*"

"Oh, *her*. That one has a temper. I don't want to be around when she wakes up and finds herself hog-tied."

Packy did not dignify that observation with a comment. He stepped on the gas and with a roar the car took off with its three occupants, two of whom were determined to recover their diamonds and the third who, if awake, would have shared that determination.

Inside the securely locked farmhouse, the burner that Jo-Jo thought he had completely turned off under the coffeepot was flickering slightly. Before the car had left the yard, the flame went out. A moment later a noxious odor slowly began to drift from the stove, an odor that warned of escaping gas.

29

The minute Alvirah saw Willy standing off by himself near the stump of Lem and Viddy's tree, her heart sank. She charged through the crowd of gawking onlookers and rushed to him. "No Opal?" she asked.

Knowing how upset Alvirah was becoming, Willy hedged. "Well, she's not here, honey, but I bet anything she's back at our villa right now, probably packing to go home and fretting about missing us at breakfast."

"She would have called my cell phone. I left a message at the villa for her. Willy, we both know that something's happened to her."

The Reillys caught up with them. From the look on Alvirah's face, Regan could tell that Opal was still among the missing. "Why don't we head to your place?" Regan suggested. "Maybe Opal got lost when she was cross-country skiing and is just getting back to the lodge."

Alvirah nodded. "Oh, how I wish. Let's keep our fingers crossed."

They walked rapidly from the clearing, which was still filled with television cameras and reporters. Before they reached the area where they had parked their cars, Alvirah's cell phone rang. Everyone held their breath while Alvirah pulled the phone out quickly to answer it.

It was Charley Evans, Alvirah's editor. "Alvirah, the story's getting bigger by the minute. It's on every one of the cable news stations. People from all over the country are sending in e-mails expressing their disgust at whoever stole the tree. The viewers say the tree represents a piece of Americana, and they want it back."

"That's good," Alvirah said halfheartedly. All she could think about was Opal. But Charley's next statement sent chills through her.

"And as for Packy Noonan, wait till you hear this. One of his roommates at the halfway house was watching the news about the tree stolen from Stowe and Packy being seen getting into a van with Vermont plates. He called the cops and told them that Packy was talking in his sleep the other night. First he kept mumbling, 'Gotta get the flask.' "

" 'Gotta get the flask,' " Alvirah repeated. "Well, I guess he hasn't had a drink in thirteen years. He's probably been dreaming of a cocktail or two all this time."

"But it's what else he was mumbling that is really interesting," Charley continued.

"What was that?"

"He kept saying 'Stowe.' The roommate didn't think of the town until he connected Stowe with the Vermont plates this morning."

"Oh, my God," Alvirah cried. "The friend I told you about who lost money in his scam and who came up here with us is missing."

"She's *missing!*"

Alvirah could tell that Charley's antennae for a good news story had just shot up. "She never came back this morning after an early cross-country ski run. She was supposed to meet us hours ago."

"If she ran into Packy Noonan, would she recognize him?" Charley asked.

"Like the nose on her face."

"I can tell how worried you are, Alvirah. I hope she turns up soon," Charley said. "But keep me posted," he added hastily.

Alvirah told the others about Packy's nocturnal mumblings.

" 'Gotta get the flask'?" Regan questioned. "If he wanted a drink, he didn't need to use a flask. It has to mean something else."

"A lot of people use flasks to hide their liquor," Nora suggested, "so they can have a quick nip when no one is looking."

"Remember, your uncle Terry used to do that, Nora,"

Luke said. "No one was better at sneaking a slug than he was."

"Dad, could you wait until after I'm married to share those heartwarming family stories?" Regan asked.

"Wait till you meet the rest of my relatives," Jack said to Regan with a smile. Then he turned serious. "I do wonder what would make Packy Noonan dream about a flask."

"I'd love to know the significance of the flask for Packy," Alvirah said quickly, "but right now what really concerns me is that he was talking about *Stowe* in his sleep."

Opal was not at the villa, nor had she been there to pack her bags. Everything was the same as when Alvirah and Willy had left hours before. Alvirah's note to Opal was still on the counter.

They hurried to the lodge and inquired at the desk.

"Our friend Opal Fogarty seems to be missing," Alvirah said. "Have there been any reports of anyone injured out on the cross-country trails?"

The girl at the desk looked concerned. She shook her head. "No, but I can assure you we patrol the trails all the time. I'll notify the people at the Sports Shop to go out and start looking for Miss Fogarty. How long has she been gone?"

"She left our villa early this morning and had planned to meet us for breakfast at eight-thirty. That was almost three hours ago," Alvirah said anxiously.

"They'll get the snowmobiles out right away. If she doesn't show up soon, we'll call the Stowe Rescue Center."

Stowe Rescue Center. The very name sounded ominous to Alvirah. "Opal went out cross-country skiing the last couple of days," she told the clerk. "Would you know if the instructors she was with on Saturday afternoon and Sunday afternoon are around? We only skied with her in the morning."

"Let me find out for you." The clerk picked up the phone, called the Sports Shop, and began to ask questions. A few moments later she hung up. "The instructor Miss Fogarty skied with yesterday said nothing unusual happened when they were on the trails. The instructor from Saturday afternoon is off today, but she certainly didn't make any reports of trouble on the trails when they came in."

"Thank you," Alvirah said. She gave her cell phone number to the clerk and asked her to please call immediately if she received any word about Opal. Then she turned to the group, all of whom were wearing somber expressions. "I certainly have no interest in visiting my maple syrup tree at this point, and I know you all have to get going. So go ahead. I'll call you as soon as Willy and I hear anything."

Regan looked at Jack. "I don't have to get back. I'll stay and help Alvirah and Willy look for Opal."

"I'm staying, too," Jack said decisively.

Nora looked frustrated. "I wish we could stay, but I have

to catch a plane first thing in the morning." She shook her head. "I can't back out of this luncheon."

"Nora, don't worry," Alvirah said. "And, Regan, you and Jack don't have to stay."

"We're staying," Regan said with finality.

"Don't look so worried, honey," Willy said to Alvirah. "It's going to be all right."

"But, Willy," she cried, "there is a chance that Packy Noonan is around here somewhere. He's broken parole, and Opal is missing. If Opal and Packy crossed paths, I don't know what he'd do to her. He knows she hates his guts and would be happy to see him back in jail. By breaking parole that's just where he'd end up."

"Alvirah, do you have a picture of Opal with you?" Regan asked.

"I don't even have a picture of Willy."

"Was Opal's picture in the newspaper when she won the lottery?" Regan asked.

"Yes. That's how that idiot Packy Noonan found out she had money and decided to go after her."

"We can get her picture off the computer then and make copies to show people and ask if they've seen her," Regan said.

"Regan and I will take care of that," Jack volunteered. "Luke and Nora, I know you have to pack up and go. Alvirah and Willy, why don't we meet you back at your villa in half an hour? Then we'll start spreading Opal's face around town."

"I have such a bad feeling," Alvirah confided. "I blame myself for inviting her up here. From the minute we arrived I had a feeling something would go wrong."

It was almost as if she could smell the gas that was already seeping through the farmhouse where Opal and Milo were lying in a drug-induced sleep.

30

fter the Reillys and Alvirah left the farmhouse, Viddy began to collect the empty hot chocolate cups. Lem helped her carry them to the kitchen, and it was there that the reality of what had happened hit Viddy full blast. The shock at finding her tree gone hadn't really sunk in when the police and the media were swarming around. Being on television with Lem had been exciting, and then meeting up with those nice people, the Meehans and the Reillys, had been a good distraction—particularly since Nora Regan Reilly was her favorite mystery writer.

But now all she could think about was her tree, how she and Lem had planted it on their wedding day and how Maria von Trapp had happened to come walking along the footpath, stopped to congratulate them, and agreed to have her picture taken. And then I had the nerve to ask her if she would sing that beautiful Austrian wedding song that I had heard her sing at the lodge. She was so kind, and the song was magical. I remember thinking that we'd never plant any other tree too close so that our children would be able to play in the clearing around our wedding tree.

Viddy's eyes were welling with tears as she put the cups she was holding in the sink. We were never blessed with children, and maybe it's foolish, but how we babied that tree! We measured its height every year even though somebody else had to do it for us for the last ten years because I wouldn't let Lem get up that high on the ladder anymore.

When her unexpected company came to the house, Viddy had rushed to the breakfront and taken out the cups and saucers from her cherished set of good china. She never used them except on Thanksgiving and Christmas, and then she had her heart in her mouth for fear someone would break something. Lem's nephew's wife, Sandy, was a good enough soul, but she piled dishes one on top of the other helter-skelter when she helped to clear the table. In spite of that unwanted assistance, Viddy had somehow managed to keep her china intact all these years. A few chips here and there, but nothing to get too upset about.

Knowing Viddy's feelings about her china, Lem carefully placed the cups he was carrying on top of the drainboard. Viddy went to pick them up and put them in the sink, but suddenly her eyes flooded with tears. In an involuntary gesture to brush them away, she dropped one of the cups. But before it fell into the sink where it would certainly have landed on another cup, Lem's big hand swooped under it and saved it.

"I got it, Viddy," Lem exulted. "You still have all your fancy china."

Viddy's response was to run from the kitchen into the bedroom. Then she hurried back into the parlor with their photo album. "I don't even care about my china anymore," she cried. "I know perfectly well that the minute I close my eyes for good and Sandy gets my china, she'll use it when she makes bologna sandwiches for the kids."

With trembling fingers Viddy opened the photo album and pointed to the last picture they had taken of the tree. "Our tree! Oh, Lem, I just wanted to see the expressions on people's faces when they saw it in New York City all ablaze with lights. I wanted the tree to be like a work of art with everybody admiring it and oohing and aahing over it. I wanted to have a great big beautiful picture to put right between them."

She gestured to the two photos over the fireplace. "I wanted to have a recording of the schoolchildren singing songs when our tree arrived at Rockefeller Center. Lem, we're old now. Each year when spring comes around, I wonder if I'll see another one. I know we're not going to go out in any burst of glory, but our tree was somehow going to do it for us. It was going to make us special."

"There, there, Viddy," Lem said awkwardly. "Calm down now."

Viddy ignored him, pulled a tissue out of her housedress, blew her nose, and continued. "At Rockefeller Center they keep a history of all the trees—how tall they were and how wide they were and how old they were and who donated them and whatever was special about them. A few years ago the tree was given by a convent, and they have a picture of the nun who planted it, and another picture of her fifty years later, on the day it was cut down. That's history, Lem. Our history with our tree was going to always be there for people to read about. And now our tree has probably been thrown in the woods somewhere where it will begin to rot, and *I CAN'T BEAR IT!*"

With a wail Viddy threw down the album, collapsed onto the couch, and buried her face in her hands.

Lem stared at her, dumbfounded. In fifty years he had never heard quiet, retiring Viddy say so much or show so much emotion. I never realized how deep she is, he thought. I can't say I like it.

Forget the posse.

He leaned down and took her face in his hands.

"Leave me alone, Lem. Just leave me alone."

"I'll leave you alone, Viddy, but first I'm going to tell you something. Listen to me. You listening?"

She nodded.

He looked into her eyes. "You stop that crying right now because I'm making you a promise. I saved your cup, didn't I?"

Sniffling, she nodded.

"Alrighty. I say that snake Covel cut down our tree. But you heard the Rockefeller Center people say that whoever took it must have used the crane to get it onto their flatbed. So that means it should be in good shape. Now maybe that skunk managed to take the tree, but he couldn't have gotten far with it. He was still in his nightshirt early this morning when I banged on his door. He could have hidden a tree by dumping it in the woods, but he can't hide no flatbed. Our tree is around here somewhere, and I'm going to find it. I'm going to cover every inch of this town. I'm going to walk across any property that has a big backyard and peek in every barn that's big enough to hold a flatbed, and *I'm going to find our tree!*"

Lem straightened up. "As sure as my name is Lemuel Abner Pickens, I'm not coming back till I come back with our tree. Do you believe me, Vidya?"

Viddy scrunched up her face. She looked unconvinced.

"Do you believe me, Vidya?" Lem asked again, sternly.

"I want to. Just don't get yourself arrested trespassing on other people's property."

But Lem was already out the door.

"Or get yourself shot," she called after him.

Lem did not hear her.

Like Don Quixote, he was a man with a mission.

31

Will you look at all these cars?" Jo-Jo snarled. "You'd think they were giving away diamonds."

"Why do you always know just the right thing to say?" Packy snapped. "They're all here gawking at that stump we left in the ground."

There was a solid line of traffic both coming and going on the road to Lem Pickens's farm. People were pulling over, parking their cars on the rough shoulder, and walking the rest of the way into the forest. It had the feeling of opening day of football season.

"I'm surprised they're not tailgating," Packy growled. "What's the big deal about that tree anyway? If they knew the real story behind it . . ."

"If they knew the real story behind it, there'd be a lot more traffic," Jo-Jo said practically.

The road was gradually curving. As they got closer to the turnoff at the dirt road, cars were parked in a solid line.

"This may be a break for us," Packy muttered as they passed the spot where they had pulled in last night.

The road continued to curve as they went another thousand feet to a wire fence that defined the property line between Lem Pickens's and Wayne Covel's acreage. A television truck was in the driveway of the ramshackle house they had seen on television when Lem Pickens had so rudely banged on Wayne Covel's door and begun shouting accusations. A group of reporters was standing around a huge tree in Covel's front yard.

"That must be the runner-up in the beauty contest," Packy stated. "If I had time, I'd chop it down."

"Too bad it didn't win," Jo-Jo said. "Then Covel wouldn't have been nosing around our tree. Look, there he is."

The front door had opened, and Wayne Covel was standing there, grinning as the cameras were turned on him.

"This works for us," Packy said quickly. "Everyone seems to be out front. We'll go in the back way."

He drove around the bend. There were a few more cars parked there. He chose a space between two cars and parallel-parked Milo's heap where it would be less noticeable than if it stood alone.

Pulling his ski hat down over his forehead as far as it would go, Packy opened the door and got out of the car. He leaned back in and picked up the paper bag that contained Wayne Covel's engraved machete. Thank God for engravers, he thought, or else we'd be whistling in the dark for the crook who made off with our flask. But why would you bother to get a machete engraved? What a loser.

With a nervous glance in the direction of the trunk, Jo-Jo got out of the car and fell in step behind Packy who darted into the woods. They made their way to the back of Wayne's farmhouse. Peering out from the protection of the trees, they could see a small barn. The door was open, and a pickup truck was parked inside it.

"What now, Packy?" Jo-Jo whispered. "You think we can get in those cellar doors?" He pointed to the rusty metal doors that slanted up from the ground and obviously led to the basement.

"First I want to disable his car in case he decides to take off before we get the diamonds. I'm gonna yank a couple of wires in that truck."

"That's a good idea, Packy," Jo-Jo said admiringly. "It's like what the nuns did in *The Sound of Music*. Remember when the nuns said to the mother superior that they had sinned?"

"Shut up, Jo-Jo. Wait here. I'll signal you when I'm finished, and we'll cut across to the basement doors."

Packy ran across the twenty feet of open field to the barn, praying to his dead mother the whole time that no one would see him. Within two minutes he had pulled up the hood, cut a few wires with Covel's machete, and closed the hood with the intense satisfaction that Covel's machete was working for him now. That thought was followed by the realization that the last time the machete had been used was to free his flask from the branch where it had been hidden for over thirteen years. He waited at the door of the barn until he was as sure as he could be that the coast was clear. He raced diagonally across the open field to the cellar doors. A padlock that looked as though it had been in place for many years came apart easily with one blow of the machete. Holding his breath, Packy leaned over and lifted one of the doors. The creak of the rusty hinges made his blood freeze. He pulled it up enough to allow him to lower himself onto the steps. Then he signaled to Jo-Jo to make a run for it.

As Packy watched in agony, Jo-Jo lumbered across the yard. Packy held the door up as Jo-Jo began to step down, but then Jo-Jo stopped. "Should I pick up the padlock?" he asked in what to him was a whisper. "I mean, if someone takes a walk around the back and sees it, they might say to themselves, 'Hey! What's this all about?' "

"Grab it and get in here!"

Packy lowered the door above Jo-Jo, and for a moment they couldn't see anything.

"This place stinks," Jo-Jo said.

"No worse than a gym, which you obviously haven't seen the inside of lately."

"I like the beach."

When their eyes adjusted, they could see one window thick with grime that offered the only light. Packy flicked on his flashlight and looked around as he carefully navigated his way across the cluttered cement floor. The washing machine was clattering.

"Who does wash at a time like this?" Jo-Jo asked. "Maybe he's cleaning the clothes he wore when he cut off the branch. Destroying the evidence, you know, Packy? That's what they do in the movies."

"I didn't know you were such a film buff," Packy snapped.

Next to the washing machine was a crudely put together walled-off section with a door. Packy opened the door and looked inside. "Here's where we hide until we're sure Covel is alone." The tiny room had a workbench and some tools lying around.

The door from upstairs opened, and a lightbulb hanging from a wire over the stairs was flicked on. Packy and Jo-Jo practically dove into the workroom as a load of dirty clothes came flying down the steps. The light flicked off, and the door was slammed shut.

Jo-Jo peered out at the laundry all over the basement floor. "That guy is some slob. And he didn't need to scare us like that."

Packy's heart was thumping. "This isn't going to be easy. We've gotta figure out whether he's alone."

They stepped out of the work area, and Packy ran the

flashlight over the new load of dirty clothes that were scattered around the base of the stairs. The washing machine began to spin with the force of a tornado.

"That thing sounds like it's going to take off," Jo-Jo noted in amazement.

The door from the upstairs opened again, shocking them both. This time in their haste to get back to the protection of the workroom, Jo-Jo tripped over one of Wayne Covel's tattered flannel shirts. He threw out his palms to soften the impact of his contact with the rough cement floor. His right hand grazed what felt like a sharp stone. With a stifled yelp he yanked up his hand and glanced down. The stone glittered. He grabbed it and, holding it tightly, scampered on his hands and knees into the workroom.

Another load of laundry had come flying down the stairs, and the door was once again slammed shut.

"I scraped my hands," Jo-Jo complained, trying to catch his breath. "But I think it might have been worth it." He opened his hand and held it up. "Take a look." Packy leaned over and shined the flashlight on Jo-Jo's chubby palm.

Packy picked up the uncut diamond he hadn't laid eyes on in nearly thirteen years and kissed it. "I'm back," Packy mumbled.

"You sure that's one of yours?" Jo-Jo asked. "I mean *ours*."

"Yes, I'm sure! It's one of the yellow ones. You might not realize it, but you're looking at two million bucks. But what did that nut case do with the rest of them?"

"Maybe we should go through the laundry," Jo-Jo suggested. "As distasteful as I find that task, it might be worth it."

"Good idea. Get started," Packy ordered. He picked up the machete. "I'll sneak up the stairs to see what I can hear. If he's alone, we're going for him now."

32

rmed with photocopies of Opal's radiantly happy face as she held up her lottery check, Regan and Jack went back to Alvirah and Willy's villa. Under Opal's picture they had printed the information that she was missing and requested anyone who had seen her or had any leads to call either Alvirah's number or the local police.

"We posted a few of these at the lodge," Regan said. "Jack and I found out what trails her group went on yesterday. We're going to walk those trails and put up her picture on trees along the way, and where there are homes nearby, we'll ring doorbells."

"And we'll be looking out for a white van with a ski rack," Jack said. "I called my office and asked them to keep me updated on anything they learn about Packy Noonan or any breaks in that case. They can't believe I was up here when the Rockefeller Center tree was stolen. I told one of my guys to keep an eye on that case as well and to keep me posted."

They were sitting in the living room of the villa, which had somehow lost its cheery warmth. Alvirah's sense that Opal was in imminent danger strengthened with every passing minute. "Opal could be anywhere," she said, the tension in her voice obvious. "She could have been forced into a car with someone. She left so early that not many people would have been outside. Willy and I will go into town and post some pictures and show them to people. We've got to get moving before it's too late. I know I said it before, but I have a feeling that Opal is in real danger and that every second counts."

"Let's check in with each other in an hour," Regan suggested. "Jack and I both have our cell phones, and you have yours."

They left the villa together. Willy and Alvirah got into their car. Jack and Regan walked to the trail where Opal had skied with her Sunday group and followed it into the woods. Today there was no one in sight. As they walked along, Regan asked, "Jack, what do you think the chances are that Opal ran into Packy Noonan?"

"She went to check something out this morning and never came back. If she saw something suspicious and Packy Noonan is in this area . . ." He raised his hands. "Who knows, Regan?"

The snow crunched under their feet as they walked side by side, shoulders touching. Their eyes darted in and out of the woods on either side of them.

"Maybe he has a friend in this area who is hiding him," Regan said. "But why? He just spent over twelve years in prison. He's paid his debt to society for that swindle. As you said last night, he's risking a lot by breaking parole. You know, Jack, it really is odd that Packy Noonan worked for Lem Pickens and Lem's tree was cut down less than twenty-four hours after Packy broke parole and was seen getting into a van with Vermont plates. I don't know why he'd bother cutting down a tree, but it really is a little *too* coincidental, don't you think?"

Jack nodded. Deep in thought, they continued to walk along the trail, and every thousand feet or so they posted Opal's likeness on a tree. They knocked at the doors of the occasional farmhouse they passed along the way. No one recognized Opal's picture or had seen any unusual occurrence. Anyone who was home had the television on and was watching the news about Lem Pickens's missing tree.

"Those two never did get along," one woman crisply observed. "But if you want to know my opinion, Wayne Covel would never have the energy to cut down that tree then haul it out of there. Forget it! I hired him once to do some odd jobs here, and it took forever and a day for him to get them done." She invited them in for coffee, but Regan and Jack declined.

As they walked down her path and back to the cross-country trail, Regan said, "It's been just about an hour. I'll give Alvirah a call." But from Alvirah's discouraged tone it was clear even before she told them that she and Willy were having no success in finding anyone who could help.

Regan had barely closed her phone when Jack's began to ring. It was his office. Regan watched his expression change as he listened. When he closed his cell phone, he looked at Regan. "They traced the registration on the flatbed that was abandoned. It was registered to a guy who knew nothing about the tree, but it turns out his cousins, Benny and Jo-Jo Como, were part of Packy Noonan's shipping scam. And here's the kicker: They lifted Benny's fingerprints from the steering wheel."

"Oh, my God," Regan said quietly. "Maybe Opal had a run-in with him."

"Everyone thought those guys had fled the country," Jack said. "Maybe not."

"Maybe Benny's the one who picked up Packy in the van," Regan speculated. "But a flatbed? Could Packy Noonan really have been involved in the theft of the tree? Why?"

"He paid a visit to the Pickens house less than a year before he was arrested. Maybe he was looking for a hiding place for his loot. As we both know, a lot of crooks don't trust the banks or safe deposit boxes or even accounts in places like the Cayman Islands."

"He made off with millions and millions of dollars," Regan said. "It can't all be in cash. That's a lot of cash to try to hide."

"Thieves put their money in other things such as jewelry

and precious stones," Jack stated. "They can be harder to trace."

"But if he hid jewelry in Lem Pickens's tree, why would he have to go to all the trouble to cut the tree down to get it?" Regan asked. "It doesn't make sense. Well, we'd better let Alvirah know. I'm sure it will be all over the news in a few minutes. Maybe her editor has called her already." Regan re-dialed Alvirah's number.

Alvirah had just heard the news from Charley. "Regan, we're going back to the lodge," she said. "I feel as though we're wasting our time in town. I want to talk to the desk clerk again and find out who was actually in Opal's ski group. I just hope they all aren't gone by now. And I want to try again to reach the ski instructor who's off today."

"We'll meet you back there. We're just about at the end of this trail."

A dead-end trail, Regan thought as she hung up the phone.

33

em jumped in his pickup truck and roared down the driveway. The only comfort he felt was in knowing that there was a reward for his tree, which meant that a lot of people were looking for it. He didn't care if somebody else found it first and ended up with $10,000 of Rockefeller Center's money. All he wanted was his and Viddy's tree, still pretty as a picture, on its way to its glory time in New York City. He could just see the look on Viddy's face when they pulled the switch at the big ceremony and its branches lit up with thousands of lights.

Lem turned at the end of his driveway and stepped on the gas. His plan was to drive first past Wayne Covel's house and see what was going on. From there he would go from one barn to another and up some of the dead-end roads on the outskirts of town, where skiers had built homes. A lot of those people didn't start coming around until after Thanksgiving. Covel could have driven the Rockefeller Center flatbed up any one of those roads and just left it there. No one would see it for days unless they were looking for it.

He flipped on the radio. The local station was buzzing with the news about the tree.

"If I were Wayne Covel and I had nothing to do with the disappearance of that tree, I'd sue Lem Pickens for everything he's worth—every tree he has left on his property, every chicken in his barn, all the gold in his teeth," the host was saying. "In this country you can't publicly slander people and expect to get away with it. Now we have our legal expert here—"

Faintly uneasy, Lem shut off the radio. "You people don't know anything about justice," he said, spitting out the words. "Sometimes a man just has to take things into his own hands. Viddy needs her tree. I can't be bothered waiting around for the cops to find it. And they'd probably need something stupid like a search warrant just to take a peek in somebody's barn."

He drove slowly past Wayne Covel's house. The sight of Wayne's big tree made his blood boil. If that tree ends up in Rockefeller Center instead of mine, it'll do Viddy in, he thought. Reporters were camped on Covel's driveway. He noticed that many of the people he knew from town were standing around, admiring Covel's tree. He knew some of them couldn't stand Covel but just wanted to get their faces on TV. It was a disgrace.

Around the bend he spotted the poet's car. You couldn't

miss it, with that bumper tied on. He had a mind to take the air out of the tires. How dare he waste an evening of Viddy's life boring her to death with his god-awful poems? He'd even had the nerve to hand out copies of his poem about the fruit fly. Viddy said he likes to share it with anyone and everyone.

Lem kept driving. Maybe I'll go to the outskirts of town first, he decided. Even Covel wouldn't be dumb enough to leave the tree too close to his house.

For the next hour and a half Lem trespassed on property all over Stowe. He wandered into barns, opened doors, and climbed up and looked into windows if that was the only way he could check out a structure large enough to contain a flatbed. He was chased away by clucking chickens, neighing horses, and a barnyard dog that yapped at his heels as he made his escape.

By now Lem had worked up an appetite but couldn't go home. He did not want to face Viddy until he returned with the tree. He got back in his truck and turned on the radio to see if there were any updates about its whereabouts. That was when he got the news about Benny Como's fingerprints in the flatbed. He hit the steering wheel with his hand.

"Packy Noonan did this!" he cried. I knew in my gut he was up to no good when he happened to stop by thirteen years ago, he thought. But I wanted to believe that he had mended his ways. Huh! And Viddy always said she thought he swiped her cameo pin. I just hope Packy's in on this with Wayne Covel. If Covel's innocent, I'm in big trouble. Not only will Viddy be without her tree, but she won't have a roof over her head. He decided not to let himself think about it.

Lem abandoned his plan to stop for a quick lunch at the diner. I've just got to find my tree, he thought frantically.

First things first.

34

Packy crouched near the top of the basement steps, fully aware that at any moment Wayne Covel might have a third burst of domesticity and send another load of wash flying into the basement. Which means I catch it in the face, Packy thought. But we can't wait much longer, he decided.

His knees and back were aching. He had already been there forty minutes.

First Dennis Dolan, a reporter from some town in Vermont, had rung the bell and been invited by Wayne to come in and have a cup of coffee or a beer. Dolan explained that he wanted to do a human interest story on Wayne in case his tree ended up in Rockefeller Center.

Packy had had to endure the story of Wayne's life, including the fact that his last girlfriend, Lorna, had sent him an e-mail just this morning.

When Dolan had finally asked his last inane question and departed, Wayne went back to the kitchen and turned up the sound of the television. Machete in hand and Jo-Jo behind him armed with masking tape and rope, Packy had been about to throw open the door and pounce on Covel when a sharp rap at the front door torpedoed that plan. Covel left the kitchen to answer it, then heartily greeted someone. From the conversation, it was a drinking buddy, Jake, who had stopped by to offer moral support to him about Lem Pickens's accusation. With the door from the basement to the kitchen open a slit, Packy was privileged to hear their exchange.

"Wayne, old boy, I told those reporters that Lem's out of his bird. He just doesn't like you no how and never did. Couldn't wait to lay something like this on you, could he? I get the idea if his tree don't show up, they'll be begging you for yours. Just a little tip. In case they ask you to be on television standing next to it when it's cut down, maybe you better run off to the barber and get a haircut. I'm on my way to him now. How about you jump in the car with me?"

At that suggestion Packy almost cried in frustration. But Wayne refused the friendly overture.

"Maybe you'll skip the haircut, but if I were you, I'd trim your mustache and get a nice close shave, though with all those scratches on your face, that might get a little messy," Jake continued. "Well, I'll be on my way."

The mention of the scratches on Wayne's face made Packy tighten his grip on the machete. You got them stealing my flask, he thought.

Wayne opened the front door as he thanked his buddy for stopping by. Then, to his despair, Packy heard another voice.

"Mr. Covel, may I introduce myself? I am Trooper Keddle, an attorney specializing in litigation. May I come in?"

No, Packy agonized. No!

He felt a tug on his leg. Jo-Jo whispered, "We can't wait around here like wallflowers hoping someone will ask us for a dance, Packy. You can't see much out of that window, but I can see enough to tell that it's getting real cloudy."

"I don't need the weather report," Packy snapped. "Shut up."

The lawyer was following Wayne into the kitchen. "Sit down," Covel told him. "Get out your notebook and write this down. If you think Lem Pickens can send you over to scare me, you're nuts, and he is, too. I didn't take his tree, and he's not suing me, neither. Got that, Troopy?"

"No, no, no, no, no, Mr. Covel," Keddle soothed. "We're talking about *you* suing *him*. He's made slanderous accusations. You see, he didn't use the word *alleged*. In the legal world you can accuse somebody of just about any crime as long as you say you *allege* that someone did something. In no uncertain terms and on national television Mr. Pickens has accused you of committing a crime. Oh, dear Mr. Covel, it is the ambition of our legal firm to see you fully compensated for this insult to your integrity. You *deserve* that, Mr. Covel. Your family deserves that."

"I'm not married, and I don't like my cousins," Wayne responded. "But are you telling me that what I heard them say on the radio is right? You mean I can sue Lem for badmouthing me?" At the thought he leaned back in his chair and laughed heartily.

"You can sue him for damaging your reputation, for causing grievous pain and emotional suffering that will undoubtedly diminish your ability to adhere to your normal work schedule, for throwing your back out when you rushed out of bed to respond to his hammering at your door, for—"

"I get the picture," Wayne said. "Sounds good to me."

"Not one penny do you have to lay out. My firm first and foremost cares about justice. 'Justice for the Victim' is inscribed over the desk of all our associates."

"How many people you got in your place, Troopy?"

"Two. My mother and myself."

I never once carried a gun, Packy thought. I never had to. I'm a white-collar crook. But I'd give anything to have one now. Still, Jo-Jo's a powerhouse. He can hold Covel down. I'll swing this machete around like I'm going to use it on him, and we'll have our diamonds in two seconds flat. Covel won't take the chance that I don't mean it. But we can't take on the ambulance chaser, too. From what I can see, he's pretty hefty, and there may still be some people in the front yard. If someone hears one yell, we're cooked.

Jo-Jo was tugging on his pants again. "You say the diamond

we found is worth two million?" he whispered. "Maybe we oughta settle for that."

Packy shook his head so violently that he banged it on the door.

"That door to the basement sure creaks," Wayne explained to Trooper Keddle as he pocketed Keddle's business card and got up. "Maybe with Lem's money I can get me a new one." The suggestion elicited another guffaw, which Keddle did his best to match.

But at last Keddle, with a final sales pitch about his ability to redress the wrong Wayne had suffered, was gone.

This is it, Packy thought. No more delays. He nodded to Jo-Jo. A moment later, as Wayne passed the door to the basement on his way back to the table, it flew open, and before he could do more than grunt, he was on the floor. Packy slapped tape over his mouth, and Jo-Jo yanked first his arms and then his legs back and tied them together.

"Pull down the shades in the front room, Jo-Jo," Packy ordered. "Lock the front door. Let anyone still out there get the idea that this guy's had enough company." He laid the machete down on the floor an inch from Covel's face. "You recognize it?" he asked. "I bet you do. Maybe it'll help you remember what you did with my diamonds."

He tapped Wayne on the head. "Don't even think of trying to make a noise, or you'll be eating your name off the handle. Get it?"

Wayne nodded and kept nodding.

Packy got up and hurried to the kitchen window. Standing to the side he pulled down the shade, which ended up draped over his arm. It had been tied to the roller with twine. Some handyman, he thought, and with a contemptuous glance at Wayne, he grabbed the masking tape, pulled a chair over to the window, stood on it, and began to wrap the shade around the roller with one hand and tape it with the other.

Jo-Jo had better luck pulling down the shades in the bedroom and living room, but as he was heading for the front door to lock it, the handle turned and it opened. "Wayneeeeee, sweeteeeee," Lorna trilled as she stepped inside. "Surprise! Surprise!"

35

O pal felt the way she had when she was under the anesthesia during her appendix operation. She remembered hearing someone say, "She's coming out of it, give her more."

Someone else said: "She's had enough to knock out an elephant."

She felt the way then that she did now—as if she were in a fog or under water and trying to swim to the surface. Way back when, during the appendix operation, she remembered trying to tell them, "I'm tough. You can't knock me out easily."

That's what she was thinking *now*. When she went to the dentist, it took practically a tank of nitrous oxide to get through having her wisdom teeth extracted. She kept telling Dr. Ajong to turn up the dial, that she was still as sober as a judge.

Where do I get such high tolerance? she asked herself,

vaguely aware that for some reason she couldn't move her arms. I guess they strap you down when they're operating on you, she thought as she fell back asleep.

Some time later she began to swim up to the surface again. What the heck's the matter with me? she asked herself. You'd think I'd downed five vodkas. Why do I feel this way? The possibility came to her that she was at her cousin Ruby's wedding again. The wine they had served had been so cheap that after only a couple of glasses she ended up with a hangover.

My cousin's Ruby. . . . I'm Opal. . . . Ruby's daughter is Jade. . . . All jewels, she thought drowsily. I don't feel like an opal. Right now I feel like a pebble. The Flintstones. Somebody won a prize for suggesting they call the baby Pebbles. When I told Daddy I thought Opal was a dumb name, he said, "Talk to your mother; it was her idea." Mama said that Grandpa was the one who called us his jewels and suggested the names. *Jewels.*

Opal fell asleep again.

When she opened her eyes again, she tried to move her arms and immediately knew something was wrong. Where am I? she thought. Why can't I move? I know—Packy Noonan! He saw me looking at the license plate. Those other two. They tied me up. I was sitting at the kitchen table. They bought diamonds with the money they stole from me. They stole the Christmas tree. But they don't *have* the diamonds, not yet.

The man on TV, the one with the scratches on his face, has them. What was his name? Wayne . . . I was sitting at the kitchen table. What happened? The coffee tasted funny. I didn't finish it. She fell back to sleep.

Just before she woke again, she slipped into a dream in which she had forgotten to turn off a jet on the stove. In the dream she was smelling gas. As she woke, she whispered aloud, "It's not a dream. I *am* smelling gas."

36

lvirah and Willy reached the lodge before Regan and Jack.

"The ski patrol has covered all the trails at least once," the clerk at the front desk told them. "There is no sign of her, but everyone is on the alert."

Opal's picture was prominently displayed on top of the desk. "Have a lot of people been checking out?" Alvirah asked.

"Oh, yes," the clerk said. "As you can understand, we get a lot of weekend guests. We've pointed out the picture to everyone, but unfortunately nobody so far has had any information. A few people said they remember seeing Miss Fogarty in the dining room, but that's about it."

Regan and Jack came into the lobby.

"Oh, Regan," Alvirah said. "I just *know* that Packy Noonan and Benny Como have their hands on Opal. I called the police to see if anyone reported anything, but of course no one has. They certainly would have contacted me."

Willy voiced the thought that was on all their minds. "What next?"

Alvirah turned to the clerk. "I know you left a message for the ski instructor who was working Saturday afternoon. Could you try her again?"

"Of course I can. We left several messages, on her home phone and on her cell phone, but I'll try her again. I know she's a late sleeper on her days off. Or she could be out downhill skiing. I don't think she has her cell phone with her all the time."

"Late sleeper?" Alvirah exclaimed. "It's past noon."

"She's only twenty," the clerk said with a slight smile and began to dial.

As the clerk once again started to leave a message, Alvirah commented, "I guess we're not having any luck there."

"You mentioned trying to talk to the people who were in Opal's ski group on Saturday," Jack said. "They probably have a list of those names somewhere in the computer."

"We do. I can pull that up," the clerk told him. "Give me a minute." She darted into the office around the corner from the desk.

They stood together silently as they waited. When the clerk came back out, she was holding a list with six names on it. "I know I checked out some of these people this morning, but let me look in the computer to see if any of the rest of them are still here."

The lobby door was fired open. A redheaded boy who

looked to be about ten years old charged into the lobby. His remarks to his weary-looking parents who were right behind him could not be missed by anyone on the first floor of the hotel.

"I can't *believe* someone cut down that tree! I mean, how did they *do* it? Mom, can we have the pictures developed today so I can show the kids at school tomorrow? Wait until they see that stump! I want to go to New York to see whatever tree they get with all the lights on it. Can we go there during Christmas vacation? I want to take a picture of it so I can put it next to the picture of the stump."

He only stopped talking when he noticed the picture of Opal posted by the front desk. "There's that lady who was in my cross-country ski group Saturday afternoon!" Bursting with energy, he was bouncing around as he looked at the picture.

"You know this lady?" Alvirah asked. "You went skiing with her?"

"I did. She was really cool. She told me her name was Opal, and this was her first time on skis. She was really good—a lot better than another old lady who kept crossing the tips of her skis."

Alvirah decided to ignore the "old lady" remark.

"Bobby, I *told* you," the boy's father said. "Say 'elderly woman,' not 'old lady.' "

"But what's wrong with 'old lady'?" Bobby asked. "That's what that lead singer Screwy Louie calls his wife."

"When did you ski with Opal?" Alvirah asked quickly.

"Saturday afternoon."

Alvirah turned to the parents. "Were you in that group?"

They both looked embarrassed. "No," the mother said. "I'm Janice Granger. My husband, Bill, and I skied all morning with Bobby. After lunch he wanted to go out again. The instructor knows him very well and was keeping an eye on him."

"Keeping an eye on me? I was keeping an eye on Opal." He pointed to her picture.

"What do you mean, keeping an eye on her?" Alvirah asked.

"The instructor had taken us on a different trail because there was a bunch of really slow skiers ahead of us driving us all crazy. Opal had to stop and sit down to fix her shoelace because it broke. I waited for her. I had to tell her to hurry up because she kept staring at a farmhouse."

"She was staring at a farmhouse?"

"Well, some guy was putting skis on the rack on top of his van. She was watching him. I asked her if she knew him. She said no, but he seemed familiar."

"What color was the van?" Alvirah asked quickly.

He raised his eyes, bit his lip, and looked around. "I'm pretty sure it was white."

Regan, Jack, Willy, and Alvirah, now absolutely sure that the person Opal had seen was either Packy Noonan or Benny Como, were all fearing the worst.

"Where was this farmhouse?" Jack asked quickly.

"Has somebody got a map around here?" Bobby asked.

"I've got one right here," the clerk answered.

"We've been coming up here since Bobby was born," the boy's father said. "He knows his way around here better than anybody."

The clerk placed the map of the trails on the front desk. Bobby studied it. He pointed to one trail. "This is a really cool place to ski," he said.

"The farmhouse?" Alvirah asked. "Bobby, where is that farmhouse?"

He pointed to a spot on the map. "This is where the slow-pokes were. We kind of looped around them this way. And right over here is where the elderly woman, Opal, stopped to knot the lace on her shoe."

"And the farmhouse was right there?" Regan asked him.

"Yeah. And there's a really big barn on the side of it."

"I have an idea where that is," Bill Granger volunteered.

"Can you show us the way?" Jack asked. "We can't waste any time. This is an emergency."

"Of course."

"I'm coming, too," Bobby said emphatically, his eyes wide with excitement.

"No, you're not," Janice Granger said.

"No fair! I'm the only one who knows what the farm-house looks like for sure," Bobby insisted.

"He's absolutely right," Alvirah said firmly.

"I don't want Bobby near any trouble," Janice said.

"Could you all just lead us there then?" Jack asked. "Please. This is terribly urgent."

Bobby's parents exchanged glances. "Our car's right outside," his father said.

"Yipppeeee," Bobby cried as he ran out the lobby door ahead of them.

They all raced out to the parking lot. Jack got behind the wheel of Alvirah and Willy's car. They followed the Grangers down The Trapp Family Lodge's long winding hill on their way to the gas-filled farmhouse where a sleepy Opal was struggling to regain consciousness.

37

Resolve was one thing. Success was something else. Lem was racing everywhere but getting nowhere. His promise to Viddy to recapture their tree was looking to be as much a possibility as jumping over the moon.

Lem was now driving down Main Street. When he saw the sign for his favorite diner, he hesitated and then pulled over. His stomach was growling so loud, he couldn't think straight. A man can't think when he's hungry, Lem quickly decided. He justified his sabbatical from his quest by reminding himself that he hadn't even had breakfast. I never got back to the house till we went there with those city folk, and, good as it is, Viddy's hot chocolate can sustain a man just so far.

He got out of the truck, and a picture of a woman tacked to a lamppost caught his eye. Lem took a quick moment to study the photo of a lady holding up her winning lottery ticket. It reminded him of the time that he could have won

the Vermont lottery but forgot to buy a ticket. The numbers
he and Viddy always played came up that week.

Viddy was mighty cool to me for a spell, he remembered.
Thank goodness it wasn't one of those real big wins. I told
Viddy the taxes they take out would knock your socks off,
and then the phony salesmen would start coming around
bugging us about buying things we didn't need, like land in
Florida that is probably nothing but a swamp filled with alli-
gators.

There was something mulish in Viddy's makeup. She
just didn't agree.

Lem's eyes narrowed. The numbers you were supposed
to call if you knew anything about that Opal woman were either the police or Alvirah Meehan's.

Alvirah was at the house today. Fancy that. We're both
looking for something real important to us.

Lem went into the diner and sat at the counter. Danny
was working the day shift. "Lem, sorry about your tree."

"Thanks. I've got to make this fast. I'm gonna find that
tree if it kills me."

"What'll you have?"

"Ham, bacon, two fried eggs, hash browns, O.J., and two
slices of white toast. No butter. I'm staying away from butter."

Danny poured him a cup of coffee. Over his head and to
the right, the television set was on, but the volume was low.

Lem glanced at it. A reporter was pointing to a flatbed.

Lem's hearing was starting to fail him a bit. Like in the morning, if Viddy asked if he wanted more orange juice, he was likely to answer her by asking her, "What's loose?"

"Turn that sound up, Danny," Lem yelped.

Danny grabbed the remote control and hit the volume button.

"—the abandoned flatbed where the prints of Benny Como were found was a mess. But our inside sources tell us that among the potato chip bags, gum wrappers, and fast-food boxes, investigators found something quite odd, considering who was driving that truck."

Lem leaned forward.

"A copy of a poem entitled 'Ode to a Fruit Fly' was found above the visor. The poet is unknown. His signature is impossible to decipher."

Lem jumped up as though he had touched an electric wire. "That's Milo's poem!" he cried. "And it stinks! I am some dope!" He ran out of the diner and rushed across the street to his truck.

As he started the car and jerked out of the parking space, he got madder and madder at himself. I'm a dope! he thought again. It was as plain as the nose on my face, but did I see it? No. The guy that owns the dump Milo rents made his barn bigger years ago. Thought those mules he calls racehorses would win the Kentucky Derby. But the *barn! It's big enough to hold my tree!*

here is my flask?" Packy asked quietly. "Where are my diamonds?"

It was a question impossible to answer since Wayne's mouth was taped shut. Wayne and Lorna were sitting on the kitchen chairs. Like Wayne, Lorna's hands and legs were tied. After Packy warned her that one squeal would be her last, he had not bothered to tape her mouth. He figured that she was too frightened to yell, and he was right. He also figured, in case Wayne the crook started playing games, that she might know where he was likely to have hidden the diamonds.

"Wayne," Packy said, "you took the flask out of Pickens's tree. That wasn't nice. It was my flask, not yours. I'm going to take that tape off your mouth, and if you start to yell, I'm not going to be very happy. Understand?"

Wayne nodded.

"He understands," Lorna quavered. "He really does. He

may not look smart, but he really is. I always say he could have amounted to a lot if he wasn't so lazy."

"I've heard his life story," Packy interrupted. "He told it to a reporter. He even mentioned you."

Lorna spun her head. "What did you say?" she asked Wayne.

"Packy, we've got to hurry," Jo-Jo urged.

Packy glared at Jo-Jo. He had seen the fear begin to fade from Covel's eyes. The girlfriend was right. Covel wasn't dumb. Right now the brains inside his skull were working overtime, trying to figure out how to keep the diamonds. With a quick movement Packy ripped the tape off Wayne's mouth, bringing with it some of the longer hairs of his mustache.

"Ewwwwwww," Wayne moaned.

"Don't be such a baby. Millions of women pay to get that done every month. It's called waxing." Packy leaned across the table. "The flask. The diamonds. Now."

"He hasn't any diamonds," Lorna protested. "In fact, he doesn't have two nickels to rub together. If you don't believe me, look in that cigar box next to the sink. It's full of bills. Most of them are marked 'overdue.' "

"Lady," Packy said, "shut up! Covel, we want the diamonds."

"I don't have—"

"Yes, you do!" Packy growled. From his pocket he pulled out the yellow diamond they had found on the basement floor. He waved it under Covel's nose and placed it on the kitchen table.

"This was mixed up with the dirty rags you threw downstairs."

"Somebody must have dropped it. There were a lot of people in and out of here today." Covel's voice was high-pitched.

"That diamond is gorgeous!" Lorna squealed.

He's scared, but not scared enough yet not to waste our time, Packy thought. He leaned across the table until his face was only an inch from Wayne's.

"I could let Jo-Jo get rough with you. And if he does, you'll talk. But I'm kind. I'm fair." He picked up the diamond and dropped it in the chest pocket of Wayne's shirt. "That little number next to your heart is worth two million dollars. It's yours if you give us the flask with the rest of them right now."

"I'm telling you, I don't know anything about them."

He's playing for time, Packy thought. Maybe he knows someone is coming back here. He picked up the machete and looked at it thoughtfully. "I guess we're out of patience, right, Jo-Jo?"

"We're out of patience," Jo-Jo confirmed grimly.

Packy raised the machete over his head and aimed it at the kitchen table. With a loud thwack it embedded itself in the wood of the table. He pulled it free.

"That's the nice machete I gave you for Christmas, Wayne," Lorna yelled accusingly.

"That's what got us into this mess," Wayne snarled. He turned to Packy. "All right, all right, I'll tell you. But only if you give me one more diamond—the one that looks like a robin's egg. You still have plenty more."

"If you have a lot of diamonds, I'd like one, too," Lorna said. "It could be a small one."

"There are no small ones," Packy snapped. "Covel, you want the robin's egg, and your lady friend wants a little one. You two ought to stick together. You're a real team. *Where's the flask?*"

"Have we got a deal?" Wayne asked. "I get the two diamonds. Don't worry about her."

"The flask?"

"But you still haven't promised."

"I promise! I cross my heart and hope to die!"

Wayne hesitated, shut his eyes, and opened them slowly. "I'm going to trust you. The flask is in the bottom drawer of the stove, inside a big pot with a missing handle."

In an instant Jo-Jo was on his knees, yanking open the drawer and tossing out pots, pans, and a rusty cookie sheet. The big pot was wedged in the drawer. Jo-Jo yanked at it so hard that the whole drawer came clattering out, sending him back on his heels. The big pot remained clutched in his hands. He opened it, looked inside, and reached in.

"This is it, huh, Packy?" He held up the flask.

Packy grabbed it from him, unscrewed the top, peeked inside, shook some of the diamonds into his hand, and cradled them lovingly as he sighed with relief. "Okay, it looks pretty full. Guess the one we found was the only one missing."

"The robin's egg?" Wayne reminded him.

"Oh, yeah, right." Carefully, Packy shook out more diamonds. "There it is — so big it can hardly get out. But that doesn't matter." He poured the diamonds back into the flask. Then he turned and his hand shot out. As he scooped the yellow diamond from Wayne's pocket, Wayne bit his finger.

"Ow!" Packy cried. "I'd better not get rabies."

"Wayne, I knew you shouldn't trust him!" Lorna cried. "You never get anything right."

An instant later Jo-Jo had taped their mouths. Packy dangled the flask in front of Covel's eyes. "You think you're smart," he said. "Your girlfriend thinks she's smart. Too bad I don't have time to sell you both the Brooklyn Bridge. Anyone who believes a crook keeps his word shouldn't take up room in this world."

He and Jo-Jo started for the back door.

39

The Grangers turned down the dirt road marked "Dead End" and were forced to drive carefully because of the snow-covered ruts and crevices they were encountering. Behind them, Alvirah, Willy, Regan, and Jack agonized at the need to slow down. But then the Grangers stopped in front of a farmhouse, and their back door flew open.

"There it is!" Bobby cried, pointing.

"Get back in the car!" his mother ordered.

Jack pulled the Meehans' car onto the field in front of the house and stopped.

"This place looks deserted," Willy said as he looked from the house to the big barn.

They walked rapidly toward the house. "Look," Jack said, pointing to the side of the barn. "There's a white van with a ski rack."

Alvirah and Regan rushed to the porch and began peering in the windows. Alvirah grabbed Regan's arm. "There are cross-country skis on the floor there."

"Alvirah, they could be anybody's," Regan said.

"They're not anybody's," Alvirah said emphatically. "That's Opal's hat on the floor next to them! We've got to go in!"

"You're right, Alvirah," Willy agreed. He tried the front door and found it was locked. He picked up a chair on the porch and tossed it through the window. At their surprised reaction he said, "If we're wrong, I'll pay for the window, but I trust Alvirah's instincts."

The overpowering smell of gas hit them.

"Oh, my God," Alvirah cried. "If Opal's in there somewhere . . ."

In a moment Jack kicked out the rest of the glass, climbed in, and opened the door. His eyes were already watering from the effect of the gas.

"Opal!" Alvirah started screaming.

They ran through the downstairs floor, but there was no sign of anyone. In the kitchen Willy hurried to the stove and turned off a burner. "This is where the gas is coming from!"

Regan and Jack raced upstairs, Alvirah behind them. There were three bedrooms. The doors of all of them were closed.

"The gas isn't as strong up here," Regan said, coughing.

The first bedroom was empty. In the second one they could see a man tied to the bed. Alvirah threw open the third bedroom door and gasped. Opal was lying motionless, also tied to the bed.

"Oh, no!" Alvirah whispered. She ran to the bed, leaned down, and saw that Opal's lips were moving and her eyes were fluttering. "She's alive!"

Jack was next to her, quickly cutting the ropes with his pocket knife. Regan was putting one arm under Opal and lifting her up.

"If the bedroom doors hadn't been closed, these two would be dead by now," Jack said grimly. "Can you two handle Opal?"

"You bet we can," Alvirah said.

As Jack hurried into the other room, Regan and Alvirah draped Opal's arms over their shoulders and rushed her down the hall.

Jack and Willy were behind them, carrying a totally comatose long-haired man.

Within seconds they were out the front door, off the porch, and hurrying to get a safe distance from the house.

"If we had rung that bell, we might have blown the whole place up," Jack said. "The way that downstairs was filled with gas, the electric discharge could have set off an explosion."

As they crossed the field, they heard a vehicle approaching. A pickup truck was barreling onto the property. Before the thought could even occur to them that it might be Opal's abductors returning, they saw Lem Pickens at the wheel. Without appearing to notice them, he whizzed past and came to a screeching halt next to the barn. As they watched, he raced to the doors, flung them open, and began to jump up and down.

"Our tree!" he yelled. "Our tree! I found our tree!" He rushed inside the barn to examine it.

"Their tree is here!" Regan exclaimed.

Opal was still draped over her and Alvirah's shoulders.

"Packy," Opal mumbled. "Diamonds. My money."

"Do you know where Packy is?" Alvirah asked her.

Lem came running out of the barn and raced over to them. "Our tree's fine. Just one branch broken!" He finally noticed what was going on in front of him. "What's the matter with these two?" he asked.

"They must have been drugged," Alvirah said. "And Packy Noonan is behind this."

"And so is this so-called poet," Lem declared, pointing at the sleeping Milo, still being supported by Willy and Jack.

"Wayne . . . has . . . diamonds. . . . Packy went there," Opal was mumbling.

"Where?" Regan asked her.

"Wayne's house. . . ."

"I knew Wayne Covel was in on this up to his ears!" Lem cried gleefully.

Regan turned to him. "Lem, you know the way to Wayne Covel's house. Ride with us there. Please! We can't waste a minute!"

Jack was on his cell phone, alerting the local police.

Lem looked back at the barn. "No way!" he shouted. "I can't let our tree out of my sight!"

Bobby Granger had escaped from his parents and came running toward them. "I'll mind your tree, mister," he called. "I won't let anybody touch it!"

"The police are on their way here and to Covel's house. Your tree will be fine," Jack said crisply. "Mr. Pickens, we really need your help. You know your way around this town."

The Grangers had caught up with their son. "We'll guard your tree," Bill Granger assured Lem.

"Well, all right," Lem said. "But tell them I have the keys to the flatbed in my pocket. I'm the one who'll drive it home to Viddy. But I'm not getting in any car with that poet."

"We'll mind him, too," Bill Granger said.

Alvirah got into the backseat of the Meehans' car. Then Jack lifted Opal in. Willy followed, to prop her up. Regan, Jack, and Lem jumped into the front seat. Jack turned on the ignition and drove as fast as he dared off the property and onto the bumpy dirt road.

"Turn left up here," Lem ordered. "I knew Wayne Covel, Packy Noonan, and that so-called poet were all tarred with the same brush. If you're looking for stolen goods, I wouldn't be surprised at all to find the loot in Wayne Covel's house. Now turn right."

Milo's beat-up car was on the other side of the road, heading in the opposite direction.

"There's the poet's car!" Lem cried. "But we know he's not driving!"

As it passed them, Alvirah shrieked, "It's Packy Noonan driving!"

Jack did a U-turn and was caught behind a delivery truck. The road was too narrow and winding for him to pass. "Come on!" he said. "Come on!"

When they came to an intersection, Milo's battered heap was no longer in sight.

"They went thataway!" Lem pointed to the left.

"How do you know?" Jack asked.

"Look! The bumper is in the middle of the road there. It finally fell off that heap."

Regan had dialed the local police. She told them rapidly that they had spotted Packy Noonan and described the car to them and the direction it was headed. Next to her, Opal was mumbling, "Get him. Please. . . . All my money."

"We will, Opal," Regan promised. "Too bad you're not wide awake for this."

Around a bend they caught up with Milo's car, which was chugging along. Smiling broadly, Jack followed the old jalopy, speeding up when necessary to prevent another car from getting in between. In the distance they could see a police car speeding toward them, its lights flashing. Jack stopped to allow the police car to make a U-turn and get right behind Packy. A moment later the sound of a policeman's voice on the bullhorn could be heard even through the closed windows.

"Pull over, Packy. Don't get in any more trouble than you're in already."

A second police car went past Jack, and two more were coming from the opposite direction. Inside Milo's heap, Packy picked up the flask and handed it to Jo-Jo. "Get rid of it!" he ordered.

Jo-Jo opened the window, lowered his hand, and tossed it. The flask of diamonds rolled down the embankment.

"All that work swindling those dopey investors down the drain," Packy lamented wryly as he watched the flask disappear. He stopped the car and turned off the ignition.

"Come out with your hands up" came the command over the bullhorn as policemen poured from several patrol cars.

Jack stopped the car, and they all jumped out, except for Opal who slumped down on the backseat. Regan ran to the side of the road and backtracked about one hundred feet. Then, sliding and slipping, she made her way down the embankment. In the snow a metal flask was resting beneath a large evergreen tree. Regan picked it up, shook it, and heard a faint rattle. Smiling, she opened the cap. "My God," she murmured as she caught the first glimpse of the contents. She poured a few of the diamonds into her hand. "These have to be worth a fortune," she said to herself. "Wait till Opal sees this."

With infinite care she dropped the diamonds back into the flask and climbed up the embankment. She ran up to Packy Noonan who was now in handcuffs. "Is this the flask in your dreams, Packy?" she asked sarcastically. "The people who lost all their money in your shipping company are going to be mighty happy to see it."

A banging from the trunk of Milo's car startled them all. Guns drawn, two policemen threw the catch and stood back as the trunk swung up. Benny sat up, Jo-Jo's note still pinned to his jacket, and took in the whole scene. "I knew we shouldn't have gotten greedy," he said yawning. "Wake me up when we get to the police station." He lay back down and closed his eyes.

Regan turned to Alvirah. "Before we have to turn these over, let's show them to Opal."

They hurried back to their car, propped Opal into a sitting position, and wrapped her hands around the flask. "Opal, honey, look," Alvirah urged. "Stay awake long enough to look."

Regan unscrewed the cap.

"What?" Opal asked drowsily.

"These diamonds represent your lottery money. Now you'll get at least some of it back," Alvirah told her.

Drowsy as Opal was, the meaning of Alvirah's words penetrated her drugged brain, and she began to cry.

An hour later Lem Pickens was driving the flatbed through town, honking the horn incessantly. Beside him, Bobby Granger was waving to the cheering crowd that had gathered along the way. Finally, they were heading up the hill to Lem's home.

Alvirah, Willy, Regan, Jack, the Grangers, and a now more alert Opal were standing with Viddy on the Pickenses' front porch. The word of the recovered tree had spread like wildfire. Media crews had hastily set up in the front yard to capture the moment when, still honking the horn, Lem Pickens triumphantly drove the Rockefeller Center flatbed onto his property. The look on Viddy's face when she saw her beloved blue spruce reminded Alvirah of the dazed joy she had seen on Opal's face, and like Opal, Viddy began to cry.

Epilogue

By the time the day of the Christmas tree lighting arrived, Lem and Viddy were practically seasoned New Yorkers. Two days after Lem recovered their tree, they were in Rockefeller Center watching its ceremonious arrival and listening to the choir of schoolchildren sing a medley of songs as the tree was raised into place. The selections from *The Sound of Music* especially delighted Viddy.

Edelweiss, she thought. Our blue spruce is my edelweiss.

They had been invited back for the party that Opal's fellow investors in the Patrick Noonan Shipping and Handling Company had thrown for her. The diamonds were valued at over seventy million dollars, so the investors would all recover at least two-thirds of their lost money.

Packy Noonan, Jo-Jo, and Benny were in prison awaiting trial and wouldn't set foot on a beach in Brazil or anywhere else for a long, long time. Milo had escaped with a slap on the wrist because of all the incriminating evidence he promised to offer and Opal's strong testimony that he had clearly been an unwilling participant who became entangled in a criminal web of deceit. Milo was now back in Greenwich Village, writing poems about betrayal. The $50,000 bonus the police found at the farmhouse was counterfeit. But he'd already won an award for a poem he wrote about a flatbed.

When the police had found Wayne Covel and his girl-friend Lorna tied up, Wayne tried to pretend he had no idea why Packy Noonan had done that to him. His testimony was shot down by the combined stories of Opal, Milo, Packy, Jo-Jo, and Benny. But as Wayne Covel then put it, "If it weren't for me, Packy Noonan would be in Brazil now with all the investors' money." He pleaded guilty to destroying the branch of the tree and claimed that he was trying to figure out how to return the diamonds without admitting how he got them. That story raised a few eyebrows, but in his plea bargain he was sentenced to only twelve hours of community service. Some community service they'll get out of that one, Viddy thought. His ex-girlfriend was back in Burlington, once again computer dating and looking for a kind and sensitive man. Lots of luck, Viddy thought.

The hardest pill Packy had to swallow was that he didn't know blue spruces grew from the top. He needn't have cut down the tree. His flask was the same distance from the ground as it had been when he tied it there. If he had known that, he and the twins could have just gone around to the back of the tree, found Wayne standing on the ladder, forced him off it, and cut the branch that held the flask.

Now Lem and Viddy were in the reserved section waiting for the tree to be lighted. Alvirah, Willy, Regan, Jack, Nora, Luke, Opal, Opal's friend Herman Hicks, who Alvirah had told her was a recent lottery winner, and the three Grangers were with them. They'd all be heading back to Herman's apartment after the ceremony. It was a beautiful cool night. Rockefeller Center was overflowing with people, and the streets surrounding it were all blocked off.

"Viddy, you and Lem did a great job on the *Today Show* this morning," Regan said. "You're both naturals."

"You think so, Regan? Did my hair look all right?"

"It better have looked all right, with what it cost!" Lem observed.

"I loved having my makeup done," Viddy admitted. "I told Lem I want to have it done again when we come back for your wedding."

"Lord, help me," Lem mumbled.

Opal and Bobby were sitting next to each other. He turned to her. "I'm really glad I was in that ski group with you," he said.

"I am, too," Opal said.

"'Cause otherwise I wouldn't be here."

Opal laughed. "I wouldn't be here or anywhere else!"

Herman took her hand. "Please don't say that, Opal."

"This is so beautiful," Alvirah sighed as she admired the whole spectacle.

Willy nodded and smiled. "Something tells me we'll be stopping by every night for the next month."

"Alvirah, we never did get a look at your maple syrup tree," Nora reminded her.

"Honey, we missed a lot of the excitement," Luke drawled.

"I don't need any more of that kind of excitement!" Opal protestd. "And believe me, from now on my money stays in a piggy bank. No more Packy Noonans in my life—the creep."

Christmas carols were being sung. It was one minute to the moment.

It's magical, Regan thought. Jack put his arm around her. That's magical, too, she thought with a smile.

The crowd started the countdown. "Ten, nine, eight . . ."

Lem and Viddy held their breaths and entwined their hands. They watched as in a brilliant and breathtaking moment the tree they had loved for fifty years was suddenly ablaze with thousands of colored lights, and everyone in the gathered throng began to cheer.

Dashing Through
the Snow

by Mary Higgins Clark &
Carol Higgins Clark

1

Thursday, December 11th

In the picturesque town of Branscombe, in the heart of the Granite State of New Hampshire, lights and banners were being strung to herald the first, and many hoped annual, Festival of Joy. It was the second week of December, and the town was buzzing. Volunteers, their faces glowing with good will, were helping to transform the village green into a holiday wonderland. The weather was even cooperating. As if on cue, a light snow was falling. The pond was frozen solid, ready for the ice-skating events planned for the weekend. Most everyone in Branscombe grew up on ice skates.

Learning of the Festival and its purpose to promote the wholesome lifestyle of a small town and the true meaning of the holiday season, a major cable network, BUZ, had decided to cover the event. They had big plans for a warmhearted special that would air on Christmas Eve.

Muffy Patton, the thirty-year-old wife of the newly elected mayor, had suggested the concept of the Festival at a summer meeting of the town council. "It's time for us to do something special for this town. Other towns in our state are famous for their sled races and bike weeks. Branscombe has been ignored for too long. We should celebrate the fact that Branscombe is a simple hamlet, full of people with good old-fashioned values. There's no better place to raise a family."

Her husband, Steve, had agreed heartily. The third-generation owner of a real estate business, he was all for promoting the land values in the area. His firm had houses listed for sale that would be perfect as a country retreat for people living in Boston. A persuasive and spirited idea man, Steve had helped Muffy generate rousing enthusiasm for the Festival.

"In so many places the spirit of Christmas isn't what it used to be," he opined. "It's all about shopping days and sales. Artificial Christmas trees jamming the stores before the Halloween pumpkins have disappeared. My city friends tell me they all get short-tempered and sulky with the stress of the season. Let's have ourselves a down-home weekend, with caroling in the town square, a new set of lights for the big tree, and lots of fun stuff to do all weekend. We'll set the example that Christmas 'tis the season to be jolly and joyful."

"What about food?" one of the council members asked practically.

"We'll get Conklin's to cater the whole works. We'll price

tickets just to cover our costs. We're so lucky to have a family-owned store like that in this town—it's an institution."

They had all nodded, thinking of how soothing it felt to just walk into Conklin's. The scents of roasting turkeys, baking hams, simmering pasta sauces, and bubbling chocolate chip cookies were a treat to inhale. Food fit for a king, and a few aisles down you'd find wrenches and garden hoses and even clothespins. People in Branscombe liked their sheets and towels to smell of fresh, cold air.

By the end of the meeting, the enthusiasm had spread to a fever pitch. Now, three months later, the Festival would begin the next day. The opening ceremony was scheduled for Friday at 5 P.M. in the town square. Branscombe's huge Christmas tree had already been lit. All the other trees along Main Street and around the Bowling Green would go on at exactly the same moment as Santa arrived on his horse-drawn sleigh. Candles were to be distributed, and the church choir would lead the crowd in singing Christmas carols. A buffet supper in the church basement would be followed by the first of many screenings of *It's a Wonderful Life*.

On Saturday, Nora Regan Reilly, whose son-in-law was a close college friend of the mayor, would be signing her just-published book during the holiday bazaar. She had also agreed to hold a story hour with the children. Outside, there would be hay rides and sleigh rides, and ice skaters would be serenaded by recordings of Bing Crosby and Frank Sinatra singing everyone's favorite Christmas music. Saturday night another buffet supper would be followed by a staging of "A Christmas Carol," performed by the amateur Branscombe thespian group. Sunday morning the festivities would wrap up with a pancake breakfast, yet another meal to be held in the church basement.

So far all the plans were running smoothly.

Over at Conklin's Market, the employees were working nonstop to prepare for the weekend. The Festival had been a great idea for the town and for Conklin's business, but the workers were worn out. The holiday season, from Thanksgiving through New Year's Day, was always busy, but this year things were crazed. And thanks to the television coverage, more and more people from the surrounding towns were expected to join in the activities. The workers at Conklin's had to be ready to supply extra food at a moment's notice. They knew they wouldn't be able to enjoy a single minute of the festivities themselves, but they were sure that Mr. Conklin would reward them with a bigger bonus than usual, a bonus that traditionally had been handed out by now. Some of the staff had even been grumbling that they hadn't received it yet.

Tonight the 8:00 closing hour couldn't come fast

enough for any of them. At ten of eight, Glenda, the head cashier, was locking up one of the registers when the front door flew open and Mr. Conklin's bossy new wife, Rhoda, marched in, followed by her increasingly sheepish husband, Sam, whom she now referred to as Samuel. In her late fifties, Rhoda and old man Conklin had met at a senior singles dance in Boston, when he was visiting his son for the weekend. It didn't take Rhoda long to realize that Sam was ripe for the picking. A recent widower, he didn't know what hit him until one day he found himself in his best blue suit, a flower in his lapel, and the sight of Rhoda in a glittery cocktail dress, marching down the aisle toward him. Since then life at Conklin's Market had not been the same. Rhoda was trying to put her stamp on a forty-year-old business that had run just fine without her.

She told Ralph the butcher, whose roasted turkeys were legendary, that he was using too much butter when he basted them. Her attempt to convince the sweet-faced, seventy-five-year-old Marion, who had run the bakery department since Day One, to use canned fillers for her cakes and pies, was not well received. Tommy, a burly, ruggedly handsome young man in his twenties, who had a magical way with salads and sandwiches, was told to cut down on the generous portions of cold cuts he allotted to the submarine sandwiches. Duncan, the head of produce, was mortally offended when Rhoda retrieved a bruised apple he'd tossed out and put it back in the bin.

And then there was Glenda. Glenda knew, because she handled the cold, hard cash, that whenever Rhoda was around she was being watched like a hawk. This offended Glenda to the core. She had worked at Conklin's since high school, and in the sixteen years following there'd never been a dime missing on her watch, nor would there ever be. Now the sight of the new Mrs. Conklin made Glenda's stomach churn. While the employees had all been working themselves to death, Rhoda had obviously been out having her hair done. The broad white streak that ran from her forehead to the back of her midnight black hair looked freshly oiled. Thanks to Glenda's referring to that dye job as "reskunked," Rhoda was now known to the employees of Conklin's as "The Skunk."

Rhoda darted over to Glenda. "Wait till you see the surprise we have for our five key employees! Samuel and I would like you, Ralph, Marion, Duncan, and Tommy to come to the office as soon as you're finished closing up."

"Sure," Glenda answered, as she suspiciously eyed the two heavy shopping bags with the logo of the local frame shop that Mr. Conklin was carrying. What could be in them?

Ten minutes later she found out. The group stood together as Rhoda made her little speech about how the Festival of Joy was really bringing home the true meaning of the holidays. "Samuel and I are so pleased that the town of Branscombe is being celebrated for its emphasis on people, rather than things. Spirituality. Good neighbors. That's why we've decided, in lieu of a cash bonus, which is so mercenary, to give you something else." Diving into the bags, she began to hand each of them a gift-wrapped package. "Open them all at once so it doesn't ruin the surprise for any of you."

A dead silence fell over the room as the senior employees of Conklin's, after yanking the string and paper off the boxes, found themselves staring at the group picture of the five of them taken with the bride and groom six months ago on the porch of the Branscombe Inn. The frames were engraved with the words, "In appreciation of your long and faithful service. Joyous holidays to you! Samuel and Rhoda Conklin."

Glenda was appalled. Every one of us needs a cash bonus and was counting on it, she thought angrily. Duncan had gotten so thrifty he didn't even go in our group lottery tickets today. She was planning to use her bonus to pay off the cash advance she'd taken on her credit card. She'd needed the money to reimburse her ex-husband, Harvey, for his clothes that were "maliciously ruined" when she left them out in two garbage bags on the driveway, just as an unexpected storm made its appearance. Violent winds had blown the bags into the street just as a delivery truck rumbled through. Five minutes late, Harvey found his clothes scattered all over the street, soaked and squashed.

"If I hadn't left them out at the appointed time," Glenda

had protested, "he'd be complaining I was in contempt of court."

The judge didn't buy it and ordered her to pay the replacement value of the tacky getups Harvey favored. The bonus would have meant she could have paid him off and be rid of him and his cheating ways forever.

"You don't have to thank us," Rhoda chirped, as they all held the pictures in their hands. "Come along, Samuel. We need to get a good night's rest. It's going to be a busy weekend."

Mr. Conklin followed her out the door without making eye contact with any of his workers.

Glenda saw that Marion was blinking back tears. "I promised my grandson a nice wedding present," she said. "But after paying for the flight to California, now I don't know what I'll be able to afford . . ."

Ralph moaned, "Judy and I were planning to take a cruise this winter to give ourselves a break. With both girls in college, we're always stretched to the limit. Even tonight Judy is babysitting to pick up some extra cash."

Tommy looked as though steam was about to come out of his ears. Glenda knew that he still lived with his elderly parents because they needed his help financially. A good skier, he'd been planning to take a long overdue trip out west with some of his pals.

Tall, thin, quiet Duncan, who at almost thirty-two was just a couple of years younger than Glenda, grabbed his coat and thrust his arms into it. As he pulled up the hood, his sandy hair fell forward on his forehead. His face was flushed. Glenda had always had an almost maternal feeling for him. He was so methodical, so orderly, his produce section of Conklin's was always so inviting, that it was out of character for him to be visibly upset. "I'm out of here," he said, his voice shaking.

Glenda caught his arm. "Wait a minute," she urged. "Why don't we all go down to Salty's Tavern and get a bite to eat?"

Duncan looked at her as though she was nuts. "And spend more money that we don't have?" he asked, his voice rising with every word. "The financial planning course I've been taking emphasizes that eating out when you can just as easily fix something at home is one of the primary reasons so many people are in debt."

"Then go home and make yourself a peanut butter sandwich," Glenda snapped. "Don't you think we're all upset? Sometimes after a blow like this it's good to get out with friends and relax."

But Duncan was gone before she could finish.

"*Some* misery loves company," Ralph shrugged with an attempt at a smile. "Let's go."

"I'm with you," Marion cried. "I almost never touch the stuff, but right now I could use a stiff drink."

*   *   *

Two hours later, Glenda, Tommy, Ralph, and Marion, feeling somewhat better, and even able to joke about The Skunk, were about to leave Salty's Tavern when Tommy pointed to the television over the bar.

They all watched as the local announcer, his voice excited, cried, "There are two winners in the mega-mega multistate lottery tonight. Two winners who will share 360 million dollars, and what is so incredible is that both tickets were bought within ten miles of one another in New Hampshire!"

As one, their bodies froze. Could they even dare hope that their group could possibly have one of the winning tickets? For every drawing, they each threw in a dollar and purchased five tickets. They played the same five numbers on each ticket and the same separate Powerball numbers on four of them, but the fifth Powerball number they took turns choosing.

The announcer read the first five numbers. "They're ours!" Marion shrieked.

"And the Powerball number is . . . 32!"

Tommy and Ralph pounded the table. "No!" they cried. "32 isn't one of our regular Powerball numbers."

"What about the extra number this week?" Marion cried. "It was Duncan's turn, but he decided not to play."

Glenda was digging in her purse. Her hands were trembling. Sweat popped out on her forehead. She pulled out her wallet and unzipped the special compartment where she kept the tickets.

"Duncan told me the Powerball number he had chosen. He was about to hand me his dollar, then put it back in his wallet. I was so used to buying five tickets that when I got to the convenience store and pulled out a five dollar bill, I thought what the heck? I bought the extra ticket and used Duncan's Powerball number . . . I'm sure it was in the 30s."

"I can't take it," Marion cried. "What was it? Hurry up Glenda!" she croaked.

Glenda dealt out the tickets like a deck of cards. "Let's all take a look."

In the dim light of the votive candle, the tickets were hard to read. Marion bent over, straining to decipher the Powerball number on the ticket in front of her. An other-worldly grunting sound emanated from the depths of her being. "Oh, my God!" she finally screamed as she jumped up, waving the ticket. "WE WON! WE WON!"

"Are you SURE it's 32?" Glenda shouted.

Marion's hand was shaking so much the ticket fluttered to the floor. Tommy reached down and grabbed it. "It's got the number 32!" he boomed. "It's 32!"

By now, everyone in the tavern was on his feet.

"The four of us get to split 180 million bucks!" he shouted as he lifted the diminutive Marion off her feet and spun her around.

Wait till Harvey hears about this, Glenda thought wildly as she and Ralph hugged.

"How about one of those group hugs?" Marion cried as the four of them put their arms around each other, laughing, crying, and still not believing.

This can't be true, Glenda thought. How can it possibly be true? Our lives have changed forever.

"Drinks for everyone," the bartender cried. "But you guys are paying!"

The foursome fell back into their chairs and just looked at each other.

"Are you thinking what I'm thinking?" Marion asked as she wiped the tears from her eyes.

Glenda nodded. "Duncan."

"It was his Powerball number," Ralph said.

"Yes, it was," Glenda confirmed. "I would never have picked 32. But I decided to throw in the extra dollar. So you all owe me a quarter!"

"I'll even pay you interest," Tommy promised.

They all laughed, but immediately their expressions turned serious. "We should share this with Duncan," Glenda said. "The poor guy. He wouldn't even treat himself to a burger tonight. And without his number, we wouldn't have won."

"And we wouldn't have won if you hadn't thrown in that extra dollar," Marion said. "How can we all ever thank you?"

Glenda smiled. "We've been in this together for years,

and now we've been blessed. Let's start our own Festival of Joy. I can't wait to hear Duncan's reaction." She pulled out her cell phone. Duncan's numbers were in her list of contacts. She tried his home phone and his cell, but he didn't pick up either one. She left a message for him to call immediately, no matter what time it was. "That's strange," she said when she hung up. "He certainly sounded as if he were going straight home. I wonder if he knows yet that our numbers won and thinks he's not part of it."

"He might think that you just played our four dollars and we lost out," Tommy said.

At that moment the bartender came over, uncorked a bottle of champagne, and started to pour it into four glasses. "Time to celebrate. I'm sure none of you are planning to go to work in the morning."

"You bet we're not," Marion said. "This is the new Mrs. Conklin's big chance to run the whole show. Let her try and bake a cake as good as mine. Good luck, honey!"

They clinked glasses as they nodded in rapturous agreement at the thought of the expression on The Skunk's face when she heard of their good fortune.

But Glenda couldn't put the nagging worry about Duncan out of her mind. He had been so upset about not getting a bonus, and now he wasn't answering his phone.

Could anything have happened to him?

2

Alvirah and Willy Meehan were leaving the Pierre Hotel in New York City where they'd just attended a fundraising dinner for one of Alvirah's favorite charities. Alvirah had been so busy talking to everyone who stopped by the table to say hello, she barely had a bite of food. Willy, who had ended up eating both their meals, was more than ready to go home. It was nearly eleven o'clock and the cocktail hour had started at six. Even the emcee of the event, by the time he finished reading the raffle numbers, seemed a tad weary as he thanked everyone for coming.

It wasn't a long walk to their apartment, but Willy hailed a cab. The night was cold, and Alvirah was wearing high heels. They were also getting up early to drive to a Christmas festival in New Hampshire with their close friends, the private investigator Regan Reilly, her husband, Jack, head of the NYPD Major Case Squad, and Regan's parents, suspense writer Nora Regan Reilly and her husband, Luke, a funeral director. As Willy started to speak to the driver, Alvirah tugged his arm. He knew exactly what that meant. She was hungry. Always agreeable, instead of saying 211 Central Park South, he gave the address of the all-night diner they favored at times like this. "Leo's, 45th and Broadway."

Alvirah sighed contentedly. "Oh, Willy. I know how tired you are. But I'm starving. I'll just get a bowl of Leo's delicious minestrone and a grilled cheese sandwich, then I'll sleep like a baby."

It was not in Willy's nature to say that Alvirah always slept like a baby, no matter what she had or hadn't eaten before bed. But he certainly knew she'd barely had a chance to swallow a morsel tonight. Sometimes he thought she worked harder now than when she was cleaning houses and he was repairing leaky pipes. A few years ago, when they were in their early sixties, they'd won 40 million dollars in the lottery. These days Alvirah wrote a column for the New York *Globe*, involved herself in numerous charities, was the founder of the Lottery Winners Support Group, but most of all had perfected her nose for sniffing out other people's troubles. That he could have done without.

Because of her work as an amateur detective, Alvirah had been injected with poison, had almost been asphyxiated, and had jumped off a cruise ship to escape gunshots.

It's a miracle she doesn't suffer from Post-Traumatic Stress Disorder, Willy thought, as the cab pulled up to Leo's.

"We'll make this quick, honey," Alvirah promised as Willy paid the fare. "We can sit at the counter."

Inside Leo's they were almost knocked out by the odor of a strong cleaning solution that was being sloshed around the floor by a bored looking worker. A yellow sign warned, "Caution. Wet Floor."

"Oh boy," Alvirah groaned. She turned to Willy as they were about to sit down. "I didn't think they used that kind of eye-stinging junk anymore. There aren't many things in this world that can kill my appetite, but the smell of that stuff is one of them. Let's get out of here."

Willy was thrilled. He couldn't wait to get home. He could just visualize getting under the covers and leaning back into his pillow on their big comfortable bed. At that moment, Leo came out from the kitchen. Willy waved at him. "We're not staying."

"Leo, what kind of insecticide are you using in that bucket?" Alvirah asked.

"It's pretty awful," Leo agreed. "The new supplier talked me into it. It's supposed to kill every germ known to man."

"I've got news, Leo. It's killing *me,*" Alvirah said, as she started toward the exit. But she hadn't taken three steps when she started to slip on the wet tile. In a futile gesture, Willy lunged to steady her. Alvirah managed to break her fall by grabbing a stool, but her upper body snapped forward, and she hit her head on the Formica countertop.

An hour later they were in the emergency room of St. Luke's Hospital, waiting for a plastic surgeon to close up the cut above her left eyebrow.

"Mrs. Meehan, you're one tough lady," a young intern had said admiringly after he read her X-ray. "You don't have a concussion, and your blood pressure is fine. The plastic surgeon will be here any minute, and you'll be good as new."

"I want his references," Alvirah said, raising her good eyebrow. "Just tonight I saw enough blank faces to know there's at least one lousy plastic surgeon on the loose in this city."

"Don't worry. Dr. Freize is the best."

Dr. Freize might have been the best, but his words that were meant to be caring, rubbed Alvirah the wrong way. As he finished stitching her wound, he said softly, "Now I want you to go home and rest very quietly over the weekend."

Alvirah's eyes flew open. "We're going to New Hampshire in the morning for a Festival of Joy. I don't want to miss it."

"I'm sure you don't," Dr. Freize agreed. "But you must consider your age."

Alvirah bristled.

"I keep reminding Alvirah we're not spring chickens," Willy tried to joke.

"You're not," the doctor confirmed. "You must take my advice. Stay home."

3

Agitated and heartsick, Duncan drove home to his tiny rented house on Huckleberry Lane. Twenty minutes from Conklin's Market, his abode was located at the far end of a heavily wooded dead-end street.

"No bonus!" he kept exclaiming as he gripped the wheel of his "previously owned" eleven-year-old SUV. "No bonus! How am I going to pay for Flower's ring?" He'd spotted the ring in the window of Pettie's Fine Jewelry last June, and even though he and Flower had just met once, after having found each other online, he already knew she was the one. The setting of the ring was shaped like a flower with a little diamond in the center and semiprecious stones in the surrounding petals. Mr. Pettie had begrudgingly agreed to accept a modest down payment and set it aside until Christmas.

Now what was he going to do? He could put the ring on his credit card, but everyone knew that if you didn't pay the balance in full at the end of the month, you were socked with sky-high interest charges that just kept on accumulating.

Last month a pair of investment experts had come to town to conduct a weekly seminar on financial planning that would wrap up before Christmas. Duncan, already planning for his future with Flower, had eagerly signed up for the course. After last Wednesday night's class, the experts, Edmund and Woodrow Winthrop, cousins in their early fifties, had called him aside. "We have been given the opportunity to buy shares in an oil drilling company that promises to return ten times our investment within the year. It's a home run," Edmund whispered.

"A grand slam!" Woodrow corrected.

"There is room for only one more person to invest $5,000. From the financial statement you filled out for us, we see that you have $5,000 in your savings account. Having it sit in the bank like that, Duncan, you're losing money. We like you. You're a hard working, conscientious young man, and you deserve an incredible opportunity like this . . ."

"I . . . I . . . I . . . don't know," Duncan stammered.

"Your concern is understandable," Edmund said soothingly. "We're each putting in a hundred thousand. That's as much as the company officers will let us invest."

"A hundred thousand each!" Duncan had been awed.

"I wish they'd let us put in more," Edmund said. "But that's the law. Duncan, if you want to get in on this, the offer closes tomorrow at noon . . ."

The next morning Duncan was at the bank when it opened, switched all the money from his savings to his checking account, then drove to the house where the Winthrops were living and conducting the seminar. With mixed emotions of anticipation and anxiety, he handed them the check. It was the first time Duncan had been late for work in years.

Now he had no bonus, no savings, and Flower's ring was still sitting in the safe at Pettie's. She was flying in from California late next week, and he planned to propose to her on Christmas Eve.

As he got closer to home, the light snowfall was becoming thicker, but Duncan barely noticed. When he pulled into his driveway and turned off the engine, it made a sputtering noise that was new to the car's various creaks and groans. Another worry, Duncan thought, as he got out, slammed the door behind him, and made a dash up the slippery path.

Inside the chilly house, which Duncan now kept at a thrifty 64 degrees, he shrugged off his coat and threw it on the couch. The first thing he spotted were all the notes he had taken at the financial planning course. They were on the dining room table where he pored over them after every session. Edmund and Woodrow's lecture last night had been about how people waste their hard-earned money. He recalled every word.

"Do you know how much money you spend a year on

those cups of coffee you buy every day? Make a Thermos of coffee and bring it to work or keep it in your car," Edmund had counseled, his thin face set in a worried frown. He'd taken off his glasses and, twirling them for emphasis, intoned, "Every time you walk out of your house without a Thermos, you're cheating yourself of money that will add to the comfort of your retirement."

Woodrow, his beefy face always wreathed in smiles, interrupted his cousin. "Excuse me, Eddie," he said, "but I have a question for our guests." He pointed at the seventeen Branscombe townspeople attending the seminar. "How many of you rinse out those plastic bags in the refrigerator and reuse them?"

No one had raised a hand.

"Just what I thought!" he boomed, then spotted one hand timidly ascending into the air. "Mrs. Potters, I'm so proud of you." He got up from his chair, hurried over, and reached for the elderly former school teacher's hand. She beamed as he raised it to his lips.

"What I was going to say," she said sweetly, "is that I did start saving plastic bags and reusing them, but I found it didn't always work out that well. I put my late husband's leftover birthday cake, the last birthday cake he ever had on earth, in a bag that had been used for Roquefort cheese, and let me tell you, it was the first time I ever heard him use a swear word." She smiled up at Woodrow, who had dropped her hand.

"Thank you for sharing that with us, Mrs. Potters," he said. "But the occasional little glitch on our path to financial wisdom is to be expected."

Mrs. Potters nodded briefly. "I suppose."

Woodrow hurried back to the front of the room. "Folks, we'll wind up with some final useful hints that you can take home, mull over, and hopefully act on. Buy washable clothes! Dry cleaning is expensive. And for goodness sake, and most important, don't waste your money on lottery tickets. You may just as well take a match to your money and burn it. Good night, everyone. We'll see you next week. Drive safely. Remember, walk whenever possible. It's good exercise and it saves gas."

Duncan, because of their kindness in letting him in on their investment, and feeling something akin to being the teacher's pet, had gone up to them after class. "Hey, guys, I love your advice, but I can't agree with you about the lottery. A group of us at work buy tickets together. We all throw in a dollar twice a week and like the ad on the commercial says, 'Hey, you never know!' "

Edmund and Woodrow had shaken their heads with amused disdain. "Duncan, that's 104 dollars a year that you could invest in something that promises a real return."

But Duncan was happy and in love and looking forward to seeing his Flower. "I have to play just one more time," he said. "I just feel lucky. We play the same numbers always but take turns on selecting the Powerball on our last ticket. Tomorrow is my day to choose. My birthday is next week and I'm turning thirty-two, so that's what I'm going to play."

"32 huh?" Woodrow said with a grin.

"32!" Duncan crowed. He recited the rest of the numbers slowly, as if he were chanting, "5, 15, 23, 44, and 52. We've been playing them for years."

"5, 15, 23, 44 and 52," Edmund repeated slowly. "I suppose they stand for birthdays and anniversaries and street addresses."

"Or the day someone's tooth fell out," Woodrow laughed heartily.

"No, not that," Duncan laughed with him. "But the numbers 5, 15, 23, 44, and 52 do mean something to each of us."

"So what," Woodrow said. "We still think you're wasting your money. I hope when we see you next time, you'll be able to tell us that you resisted temptation." He slapped Duncan on the back.

Now, standing alone in his little house, Duncan was anxious to talk to Flower but decided he should wait until he had calmed down. She was so sweet and kind, and so sensitive to his feelings that she would know right away by the tone of his voice that he was upset about something. And what could he tell her? That he didn't get the bonus he expected, had invested all his savings, and now didn't have the money to pay for her engagement ring?

Disgusted with himself, he threw down his cell phone, went into the kitchen, opened the refrigerator, and pulled out a bottle of beer. He took it into the living room, plopped down on his La-Z-Boy, leaned back, and sighed as the footrest rose and snapped in place. From here he had a perfect view of the picture of Flower he had taken on their first date at a restaurant on the wharf in San Francisco. When he walked in, she had been sitting with her hands folded on the table, looking out at the water. She heard him approach the table, turned, and smiled, a small sweet smile that lit up her face and Duncan's heart.

They had started talking and never seemed to stop. With so much in common, including hippy parents, they had traded stories of falling asleep at protests, eating organic food, and changing schools numerous times when they were growing up. Flower had been named Flower because her parents worked for a landscaper. "It could be worse," Flower had laughed. "My father wanted to name me Shrub."

"Mom and Dad named me Duncan because they met at Dunkin' Donuts, waiting in line for takeout coffee," he told her. It was unbelievable to him that after such a nomadic childhood his parents were now living in an over-55 community in Florida, and enjoying bingo nights.

Duncan and Flower had talked about their need for roots. He was delighted when he heard that several times a year she took a bus trip to Lake Tahoe from her apartment in San Francisco. She, like him, loved snow. She loved her job at a day care center for pre-school children, even though it didn't pay very well. But most important, now she loves me, he thought, as he flipped on the television and leaned back further.

I have to count my blessings. Money isn't everything. We have our health. We're better off than 99.9 percent of the people in the world. So cheer up, he scolded himself, it's only money. Maybe Mr. Pettie will let me have the ring now, and I'll arrange to pay it off in monthly installments. He has to know I'm good for it.

Duncan drank his beer as he watched the last thirty minutes of a crime program about a woman con artist who had married four men and cleaned them out of every cent they had. They must have been some dopes he thought as his eyes began to close.

An hour later, the sound of a strident voice filled with phony excitement jolted him awake. When Duncan realized what the announcer was saying, that there were two winners who bought lottery tickets ten miles apart in New Hampshire, he bolted forward, his chair moving with him. He wanted to cover his ears when the announcer started to read the winning numbers, but he didn't.

By the time the third number was read, his heart was pounding. *Our* numbers! he thought frantically. The next two were also their numbers. It can't be, he thought. But when the announcer said, with a big smile, that the Powerball number was 32, Duncan jumped up like a shot.

"I didn't play!" he screamed. "I didn't play! We could have won!" He froze. Could Glenda have used his Powerball number anyway? If she did, and they have one of the winning tickets, I'm not in on it, thanks to those Winthrop idiots!

The uneasy feeling that he'd been trying to ignore about investing his savings in an oil well exploded inside him. Suddenly the whole idea seemed ridiculous.

I want my money back right now!

He grabbed his coat and ran out the door. They've ruined my life, he thought wildly as he got into his car, pumped the pedal, and turned the key in the ignition.

He was rewarded for his efforts by dead silence.

"Come on!" he cried impatiently, as he kept turning the key. He didn't want to even think about the fact that if he had played the lottery he could go out and buy any car he wanted. Even a Rolls-Royce!

"Come *on!*" he cried again, angry tears glistening in his eyes. Finally he pounded the steering wheel and got out.

Half-crazed, he began to run down the darkened street, ignoring the snow that pelted his face and hair. With the speed of an arrow shot from a bow, he raced toward the house the financial wizards had rented for their one-month stay in Branscombe.

Twenty minutes later, huffing and puffing, he was running up the Winthrops' driveway, heading for the side door, which was the entrance for the classes. It opened onto the rec room where the chairs and blackboard were set up. As he was about to ring the bell, he heard shouts from within the house. What's going on? he wondered. It sounds like something's wrong.

With an instinctive gesture, he turned the handle of the door. It was unlocked. He pushed it open and could hear the Winthrops' loud, almost hysterically pitched voices, coming from the kitchen. The kitchen, living, and dining rooms were a half level above the makeshift classroom. The door at the top of the staircase to the kitchen was closed. Duncan moved swiftly across the tired brown carpet, stopped at the bottom of the staircase, and listened. What he heard next confirmed his worst fears.

"Hey, Edmund, do you think any of the dopes in this town would buy the Brooklyn Bridge if we tried to sell it to them?"

Edmund laughed heartily. "I know who'd buy it."

"Duncan Donuts!"

They both guffawed. One of them was obviously pounding a table.

"Duncan's as dumb as the guy in Arizona who invested in windmills in Alaska last year. If he only knew . . ."

"Can you just see the look on his face if he ever found out that we used his lottery numbers and have a winning ticket?"

"I want a front row seat for that."

They were guffawing again.

"Do you think there's any chance he didn't follow our

sage advice and went in on the ticket anyhow with his Power-ball number?"

"Nah. I think we bowled him over too well with our wis-dom. But the other winning ticket *was* sold in this town. Can you imagine if his coworkers won with his Powerball num-ber? Wouldn't that be a scream?"

Duncan's head felt as though it would burst open.

This is a living nightmare, he thought. They're phonies, they're crooks—they stole my money *and* they stole my lot-tery numbers. After they told me not to play! Tears that he'd held back on his run through the streets flowed down his frozen cheeks. I know what I'll do, he thought. I'll call the FBI! I'll make sure those two creeps spend the rest of their lives in orange jumpsuits. Jumpsuits you don't have to dry clean, he thought bitterly.

Just then, he heard movement in his direction and thought he saw the kitchen doorknob start to turn. Pan-icked, he knew he didn't have time to get out of the house without being seen. He darted to the left, opened the door that led to the basement, and disappeared behind it. As he pulled the door closed, his wet shoe slipped on the top step, and he tumbled down the stairs.

He landed hard on the cement floor. The pain that shot through his right leg caused beads of sweat to form on his forehead. Did they hear me? he wondered fearfully. If they ever thought that I overheard what they were saying, my goose is cooked. I'd never see my little Flower again.

"Edmund, what was that noise?"

"Oh no," Duncan whispered.

"Must be the old furnace. This place is the pits. Give me another beer."

"Should we check and make sure?"

"Why bother?"

Thank you, God, Duncan thought as the boisterous activities overhead continued. Through the heating grates he could clearly hear them ridiculing the stupidity of the various suckers they had cheated and their hilarity about having legitimately won the mega-mega millions with "Duncan Donut's" numbers.

They're dangerous, he thought. Sheer panic made his heart race. He tried to move his body, but the pain in his leg made him feel dizzy.

How am I ever going to make it out of here? he wondered as he lay there in the dark, dank basement. An incongruous thought raced through his head. I wish I had taken Glenda up on her suggestion to make myself a peanut butter sandwich.

4

None of the winners wanted to be out of the immediate vicinity of the lottery ticket. Not that they didn't love and trust each other, but they'd done the arithmetic. They knew enough about lottery jackpots to know what they could expect from a 180 million dollar share of the pot. They agreed to take the lump sum payment, which would probably be about 88 million. After taxes, it would leave them with, more or less, 60 million. Divided by five, they'd walk away from The Skunk with twelve million dollars each in their pockets.

"Let's have our picture taken when we accept the big check and send it to her!" Marion crowed.

They all decided to spend the night at Ralph's house. He had a big family room with a couple of lounging couches and some overstuffed chairs. Not that any of them expected to get much sleep. But at least they could put their feet up. As they sipped champagne, they called their families.

Ralph's wife, Judy, screeched at the news and was thrilled to host the sleepover.

"I'll make a pot of coffee," she cried. "I can't believe I babysat those brats all night for a lousy thirty bucks! TWELVE MILLION DOLLARS! Ralph, we're finally out of the hole!"

Ralph, a heavyset redhead, who could look a little scary when he had a big carving knife in his hand, started to cry. "We'll call the girls together, honey. I can't wait to hear their reactions."

"I love you, Ralph!" Judy was crying, too.

Tommy called his parents, who were overwhelmed, then as usual his mother managed to worry about something. "Tommy don't get yourself too excited," she cautioned. "You might make yourself sick. Maybe you should come home now."

"Mom, I'm fine! I'm more than fine. I'll call Gina and tell her to get first-class airline tickets for her and Don and the kids to fly in next week. We haven't had Christmas together in a couple of years."

"Oh, Tommy, that would be so wonderful!"

Marion phoned her son in California. "Tell T. J. that his granny is going to give him a wedding present that will knock his socks off! Come to think of it, he'd better get himself a prenuptial agreement!"

Glenda reached her widowed father in Florida. "Dad, I have something I want you to do tomorrow morning," she said exuberantly.

"What's that, honey?" her father asked in a sleepy voice, never reprimanding her for calling so late. How she could have married a creep like Harvey when her father was such a decent human being would take years of therapy to figure out.

"Dad, go out and buy yourself a powerboat like your friend Walter has. No, buy an even bigger one!" She started laughing.

"Glenda, you sound a little tipsy, dear. I hope you're not depressed about that jerk Harvey. . . ."

"I'm not depressed at all, Dad. And I'm not tipsy . . ." It took Glenda a solid three minutes to convince her father that the unbelievable had happened.

As they were leaving the tavern, several of the patrons asked them to pose for pictures.

"We're famous," Marion sighed. "I can't believe we're famous. I wish I'd worn my new pink blouse. The saleslady said the ruffles around the collar were very flattering."

Glenda, who had seen the pink blouse, didn't necessarily agree. I'll go shopping with Marion and help her find an outfit for her grandson's wedding. I have to do some shopping, too, she thought, as she remembered the remark Harvey had made to her outside the courtroom.

"I really wish you the best, Glenda," he'd said. "And I hope you meet someone who loves you just the way you are," he'd added with a snicker.

She knew what he was saying. She needed to lose some

weight and fix herself up but after years of living with his constant little digs she'd given up even trying to look good. That was about to change. And won't Harvey be sorry to miss all the trips I'll be taking, Glenda thought gleefully. I'll start with a makeover at a spa, just like that lottery winner Alvirah Meehan who is supposed to come to the Festival this weekend with her friend Nora Regan Reilly. If Alvirah does show up, I'd love to get the chance to talk to her.

Ralph's house was fifteen minutes away. Charley, a sixty-ish chauffeur who had the only stretch limo in town, had just walked into the tavern after driving an accounting firm's employees home from their company Christmas party. During the month of December he was hired for a lot of those jobs, advertising himself as "Your Designated Driver." Now he insisted on escorting the brand new millionaires to Ralph's in grand style.

"Leave your cars in the lot here. I'd be honored to give this group their first ride together in a stretch limo." Then he added ruefully, "I knew I should have taken a job at Conklin's years ago. I might be sharing this with you. Oh well."

Climbing into the limo, in deference to the weather they started to sing: "Dashing through the snow . . ." When they reached Ralph's driveway, the front door of his house flew open. Judy half-ran, half-skidded down the path, pulled open the back door of the limo, and dove in, throwing her arms around Ralph. "We're rich!" she screamed. "I never thought I'd utter those two words in this lifetime, honey, but we're rich! A reporter from that network covering the Festival has called three times. He heard from somebody at the tavern about the winning ticket. BUZ wants an interview with all of you."

"Do you think we should be like Paris Hilton and hire bodyguards?" Marion asked in a worried tone. "After all, we have a little piece of paper that's worth millions."

"I've got it right here, Marion," Glenda said reassuringly, patting her purse.

Inside the modest but warmly decorated home, they gathered at the dining room table, which Judy had set with her good china cups and dessert plates. A Christmas tree was twinkling in the living room. It was obvious that Judy loved to decorate for the holidays. There wasn't a square inch of space—on the walls or table tops—that didn't contain a Christmasy knickknack. Lighted Christmas candles glowed on the sideboard and table.

Judy began to pour the coffee, but her hands were trembling. It was all she could do to avoid slopping it into the saucers. As though thinking aloud, she said, "I'm fifty years old and I've hardly ever been out of New Hampshire. Ralph and I have been together since high school." She looked at her husband. "After we take that cruise, I want to go to London and Paris and Rome." Then she glanced down at her well-worn sweater and jeans. "And I want new clothes." She shook her head. "I still can't believe this is real. Can I see the ticket?"

Glenda carefully took the ticket out of her wallet and handed it to her.

"Don't get too close to any of the candles!" Marion warned.

Over coffee and cupcakes they talked about how it would feel when they walked into the convenience store as it opened at seven and had their ticket confirmed. And how they'd feel when they didn't report to work.

Marion showed Judy the framed photo that had been their Christmas bonus.

"That's disgraceful," Judy said as she read the inscription. "The Skunk deserves what she gets and so does he. Old Man Conklin certainly knows that you guys depend, or should I say depended, on that bonus. They're going to have some job catering the Festival of Joy without you."

"I would have gone in to help out if it weren't for that so-called Christmas gift," Glenda said.

The phone rang. This time it was the producer from BUZ. They arranged to meet him and his crew at the convenience store at seven.

As Ralph and Judy called their daughters, Glenda phoned Duncan again. But he didn't answer. "I just hope he decided to turn off his phone and go to sleep," she said, trying to sound cheerful.

"I'm sure he's fine," Tommy reassured her. "When Charley picks us up in the morning we can swing by Duncan's house and collect him. He's bound to be up, getting ready for work. We'll tell him that we voted him in on the winning ticket." Tommy whooped, "I can't wait to see the look on his face!"

5

Friday, December 12th

It was nearly 2 A.M. when Willy and the somewhat battered Alvirah finally arrived home to 211 Central Park South. As they climbed into bed, Willy turned off the alarm clock that had been set for an early start to New Hampshire.

"I was really looking forward to the Festival," Alvirah sighed. "It sounded like so much fun." Regretfully she glanced at their already packed bags. "We've all been so busy that we haven't seen that much of the Reillys, and I miss them."

"We'll go next year," Willy promised. "While you were changing, I sent an e-mail to Regan and Jack and explained what happened. I said you were fine, but we wouldn't be able to join them this weekend and we'd call them later." Then as he turned off the light, he said, "Be sure to wake me up if you don't feel well. That was some whack you got."

When he received no response, he realized Alvirah was already asleep. What a surprise, he thought as he cuddled up to her.

Seven hours later, when Alvirah opened her eyes, she felt completely refreshed. Instinctively she raised her hand and applied tentative pressure to the bandage on her forehead. It's sore but no big deal, she thought. Willy insisted on serving her breakfast in bed. Fifteen minutes later, propped up on three pillows, she quickly dispatched the scrambled eggs he had carefully prepared.

Swallowing her final bite of toast, Alvirah daintily dabbed her mouth with an apricot-colored cloth napkin that had been bought to coordinate with the breakfast tray. "Willy I really feel fine," she said. "Let's go to the Festival."

"Alvirah, you heard what the doctor said. We'll make it next year. Just relax." He picked up the tray. "Let me get you another cup of tea."

"Why not?" Alvirah grumbled. "I've certainly got nothing else to do." She reached for the remote control and flicked on the television. "Let's see what's going on in the rest of the world." She pressed the number of the BUZ network. Immediately the face of Cliff Bailey, the handsome anchorman who had interviewed her about the pitfalls of being a lottery winner, filled the screen. Alvirah remembered telling him there shouldn't be any pitfalls but unfortunately some people went crazy when they got their hands on so much cash.

"And now an unbelievable story," Bailey said breathlessly, "coming out of the town of Branscombe, New Hampshire, where a group of four coworkers at the local market won half the 360 million dollar mega-mega lottery last night."

"Alvirah, would you like another piece of toast?" Willy called from the kitchen.

"Shhhhh" Alvirah ordered as she turned up the volume and shouted, "Willy, get in here!"

Not knowing what to expect, Willy hurried into the bedroom.

". . . the other winning ticket was bought in Red Oak, a town ten miles away from Branscombe. In the history of the lottery, lightning has never struck twice in towns so close to each other. The owner of the second winning ticket has not yet come forward. In Branscombe, however, there is both concern and speculation. A fifth coworker, Duncan Graham, who had been playing the group lottery for years, decided only yesterday to no longer participate. Even so, his friends intend to share the pot with him as it was his choice of the Powerball number that clinched the prize. But he has disappeared without a trace. Duncan hasn't been seen since he left the market last night. Some skeptics think he might have played the numbers on his own, now holds the other winning ticket, and is embarrassed to face his coworkers who immediately after winning left him a message promising to cut him in. Here's a shot of the four coworkers as they validated their lottery ticket this morning."

Alvirah quickly studied the expressions on the faces of the two men and two women. Their smiles seemed somewhat forced. They looked bewildered rather than exuberant. "I can't believe we're not there yet," Alvirah cried as she threw back the covers. Willy took one look at her. He knew there was no use arguing. "I'll do the dishes and make the bed while you take a shower."

"Call the garage and tell them to get the car out pronto. At least we didn't unpack our suitcases. I could wring that doctor's neck for ordering me to stay home. He's never met me before in his life—what does he know about my constitution? In the old days, if I'd gotten three stitches over my eye, I wouldn't have dreamed of calling Mrs. O'Keefe and telling her I couldn't show up to clean her messy house. I would have been out of a job. Willy, get Regan on the phone and tell her we're on the way."

The bathroom door snapped shut behind Alvirah.

"I knew we'd end up at that Festival," Willy muttered as he began to make the bed.

6

Regan and Jack Reilly left their Tribeca loft at 7 A.M. in the large SUV they had rented for the weekend. The plan had been to pick up Regan's parents and Alvirah and Willy Meehan from their neighboring apartments on Central Park South, then they'd all ride together to New Hampshire. The disappointing e-mail from Willy that he and Alvirah would not be able to join them had made the larger vehicle not only unnecessary, but also a continuing reminder of Alvirah and Willy's absence.

Regan's mother, Nora Regan Reilly, chic even at this early hour, glanced wistfully up at Alvirah's building as she got into the car. A casual bystander would have known immediately that Regan was bone of her bone and flesh of her flesh. They shared fair skin, startling blue eyes, and classic features. Where they differed was in hair color and height. Nora was a petite blonde, while Regan had inherited raven black hair from her father's side of the family, and at 5'7" also carried the tall genes of the Reillys. Her father, Luke, was a lanky, silver-haired 6'5".

"I hope Alvirah is going to be all right," Nora worried as she settled in the car.

Luke tossed their suitcases in the back and climbed in beside her. "My bet's on Alvirah," he said. "I feel sorry for the counter."

"That was exactly my thought, but I was afraid Regan would get mad if I said it," Jack agreed. His hazel eyes twinkled as he glanced back over his shoulder at Luke. Jack Reilly had a very special affection for his father-in-law. It was because Luke had been kidnapped by the disgruntled relative of a man he had buried from one of his funeral homes that Jack had first met Regan. As head of the NYPD Major Case Squad, Jack had been called in. Sandy-haired and handsome, with a commanding presence, at thirty-four years old Jack was one of the rising stars of New York's finest. A Boston College graduate, he had elected not to go into the family investment firm, but instead chose the career path of his paternal grandfather. During Regan and Jack's courtship, he became known as Jack "no relation" Reilly.

Two hours later, after fighting the usual Friday morning traffic, the Reillys were well into the state of Connecticut when Jack's cell phone rang. He fished it from his pocket, glanced at the caller ID, and handed it to Regan. "It's Mayor Steve," he said. "Tell him I'm driving. You know me, I'm a law-abiding citizen."

"That's why I married you," Regan said with a smile as she took the phone. "Hello, Steve . . ." she began, then listened as a torrent of information filled her ear. "You're kidding!" she finally managed to interject. "We've been listening to music and traffic reports. I guess we should have turned on the news."

Bursting with curiousity, Nora bolted forward, her body straining the seat belt. Beside her, Luke leaned back, "Tell me if they need my services," he drawled.

Regan tried to ignore the fact that Nora was making gestures for her to hold out the phone. "Yes, Steve, we should definitely be at the Inn by twelve for the press conference."

"Press conference!" Nora exclaimed.

"At ease, sweetie," Luke said mildly, raising his eyebrows as he caught Jack's amused glance in the rear view mirror.

"Okay, Steve, try not to worry too much. The Festival will be a success, I'm sure. We'll see you at the Inn." Regan snapped the cell phone closed. She leaned back. "I'm so tired, I think I'll just close my eyes for a few minutes."

Nora was appalled. "Regan!"

Jack poked his bride in the ribs. "Spit it out."

"Wellllll, if you insist," Regan began. "As you know the Festival of Joy starts this afternoon. Last night a group of employees from the local market that will be catering the Festival won half the mega-mega 360 million dollar lottery."

"There go the bologna sandwiches," Luke muttered.

"And the potato salad," Jack added.

"Will you two please be quiet so Regan can talk?" Nora asked, trying not to laugh. "Regan, go on."

"In a nutshell, there were five workers who always went in on the lottery. This time one of them, at the last minute, decided not to play."

"Poor devil," Luke sighed.

"The others intended to share the lottery with him because he had picked the Powerball number. But he hasn't been seen since he left work last night. They can tell he went home—his car is still in the driveway—but he's not there and doesn't answer his cell phone. They're afraid something happened to him."

"What a shame," Nora said. "Do they think that if he realized he had lost out on the lottery . . ." She stopped not wanting to voice the possibility that was occurring to all of them.

"It gets more complicated," Regan continued. "Another winning ticket was sold a couple of towns away. Some people suspect that after refusing to throw in his dollar with the others, this guy Duncan bought his own ticket and is embarrassed to admit it."

"Oh, well, that's a different story," Luke said. "I started to feel sorry for him, but I bet you anything he's recovering from his shame on a tropical beach with a piña colada in one hand and the winning ticket in the other."

"I guess that would be the best outcome," Nora said, her mystery writer's mind considering the possibilities.

"Apparently the whole town is talking about the lottery instead of the Festival, and the television producer cancelled Steve and Muffy's interview this morning. He's too busy following the lottery story."

"No interview for Muffy?" Luke exclaimed. "Jack, you'd better step on it."

"Dad, don't be mean," Regan protested. "Steve sounds very upset."

"I think he hoped this Festival would help raise his profile in New Hampshire," Jack explained.

"Sounds like it's working," Luke drawled.

"From what I can tell," Jack observed, "Steve wants to go places in politics, and Muffy sees herself as the next Jackie Kennedy. In college Steve was always organizing everything. We called him Mayor Steve back then."

Regan gasped. "I just had a thought. Can you imagine Alvirah's reaction when she finds out what she's missing?" At that moment her cell phone rang.

"No need to check your caller ID, Regan," Luke said. "Dollars to donuts, Alvirah just got wind of what's happening in Branscombe."

"No doubt," Jack agreed. "And we'll be seeing her before the sun goes down."

7

Where am I? Duncan asked himself as he opened his eyes. What happened? Then it all came back to him: He had fallen down the stairs and was lying on the cold cement floor in the basement of the house those idiot crooks were inhabiting. Faint light was coming through the gritty windows, and he could see that it was snowing lightly. He remembered that he had been awake for hours, hungry and in pain, forced to listen to the Winthrops celebrating their good fortune. When they finally went to bed, he must have dozed off. It was the smell of coffee wafting through the grates that woke him. The same grates that had allowed the bragging voices of the cheats to insult his ears.

Every bone in Duncan's body ached, but it was his right leg that was really sore. He wondered if he had broken it. Last night, after the shock of the fall, it had hurt too much to move it.

"Coffee, Eddie?" he heard from above.

Here we go, Duncan thought. Plato and Aristotle are ready to take on the day. I've got to get out of here. But how?

"I could use some," Edmund answered. "And a couple of aspirin. How many beers did we have last night?"

"Who knows? Who cares? I don't even know what time we went to bed."

"With all our money we should be in a palace, having a butler serve us coffee instead of drinking from chipped mugs in this crummy dump."

"It won't be long," Woodrow crowed. "Can you imagine if Grandpa saw us now? He always said neither one of us would amount to anything."

Grandpa was right, Duncan thought as he turned on his side, sat up, and brushed his hair back from his forehead. I want some of that coffee. He licked his lips. His mouth was so dry. What I'd really love is a tall glass of fresh orange juice. And bacon and eggs and bagels. But I can't think about food now. If those guys ever decide to come down here, I'm dead.

Woodrow wouldn't shut up. "I wish we could just blow this town today. But if we skip the final class next week, people who paid for our great advice will start comparing notes. Once they realize almost all of them were in on the oil well investment, we'll have the cops on our tail."

Duncan felt as if he'd been slapped in the face. He knew it was stupid, but he felt betrayed yet again. I never was meant to be the teacher's pet, he thought forlornly. I've been such a fool.

"We can't leave for good, but why don't we drive down to Boston for the day and celebrate? I might even buy my ex-wife a present. That would really be the Christmas spirit," Edmund said, laughing heartily.

"I'm not buying anything for mine. I still can't believe she never once visited me in the clink," Woodrow said, not sounding the least bit upset.

"She did the first time we were in," Edmund reminded his cousin.

"Yes, but all she did was complain. Some visit."

I may be forced to kill myself, Duncan thought.

"Who cares about them?" Edmund said. "With the kind of money we'll have falling out of our pockets, we'll have no trouble meeting girls. Speaking of our future millions, if we go to Boston today, what should we do with the ticket? Do you think it's safe to carry it?"

"With all those pickpockets out during the holiday season? No way. We'd better leave the ticket here," Woodrow said emphatically.

"Where? What if the house burns down while we're gone?"

"We'll leave it in the freezer."

Duncan's eyes widened, and his heart began to race. He held his breath as he waited for Edmund's response. Come on Edmund, he thought. Go for the freezer!

"The freezer?" Edmund asked doubtfully. "I don't know . . . maybe we better just take the ticket with us."

"No," Duncan moaned. He thought of the audiences at

game shows who yelled advice to contestants. "No, Eddie, no! Go for the freezer!" Duncan wanted to yell.

"It's the safest place," Woodrow insisted. "We'll put it in a plastic bag. I've heard stories of people losing their lottery tickets because they were carrying them around. Can you imagine how we'd feel if that happened?"

"It's too awful to think about," Edmund said with a shudder. "There'd be no living with you."

"Me? Look who's talking!"

They both laughed.

"Okay, we'll leave it in the freezer," Edmund finally agreed. "What a joke that we broke parole again by spending a buck on a lottery ticket. Next week when we finish up here, we'll figure where to cash it in and who can front for us. We have a year to decide."

"A year?" Woodrow yelled. "Are you nuts? I'm not waiting a year. You call yourself a financial expert? Every day we wait we're losing interest."

"Of course we're not going to wait a year. We just have to figure it all out . . . Hey, it's almost eleven o'clock. Let's get showered and get out of here. This place gets on my nerves. No wonder they were willing to rent it for a month."

By the time they returned to the kitchen half an hour later, Duncan had come up with a plan, that if successful, would give him infinite pleasure for the rest of his life.

"Woodrow, don't leave it in plain sight," Edmund was saying, his voice clearly annoyed. "Put the bag under that box of frozen peas."

Frozen peas? Duncan thought. My fresh ones taste so much better.

"Okay. There. Are you happy? It's under the peas."

Duncan heard the slam of the front door followed by the sound of their car starting up. They're gone! he thought. All was silent except for the groan of the furnace. I'm alone in a house with a lottery ticket worth 180 million dollars, he thought. Who needs more motivation than that to drag himself off the floor? He reached for the bannister and strained to pull himself up, resting all his weight on his left leg. Gingerly he touched his right foot to the floor and winced. Mind over matter, he told himself. Leaning heavily on the wobbly bannister he hopped slowly up the stairs, opened the door, and continued to hop the few steps to the staircase that led to the kitchen.

The sound of a car passing in front of the house made Duncan hold his breath. But the car didn't stop. That could have been them coming back, he thought. I've got to hurry.

Despite the fact that he was supporting his entire weight on one leg, he made it up the steps and across the small kitchen in record time. No wonder the owner can't sell this place, Duncan thought. Everything here looks as though it's falling apart. Who cares? he asked himself as he reached the aging refrigerator and opened the freezer door. With quivering fingers he grabbed the carton of peas. This brand went out of business ten years ago, he realized with disgust, then feasted his eyes on the plastic bag containing the lottery ticket. Plucking it from the shelf he turned around, hopped over to the wooden kitchen table, and removed the ticket from the bag. He took a split second to verify the winning numbers—his numbers—and then pulled out his wallet. He tucked the ticket inside, then tenderly reached into another compartment for the lottery ticket he and Flower had bought on their first date. Even though she didn't care much about the lottery, they had enjoyed choosing the numbers together.

"We didn't win that day," Duncan said aloud, "but I knew this ticket would come to some good." Holding it to his lips, he kissed it once, twice, three times, then placed it in the plastic bag. A few seconds later he was returning the bag to where the Winthrops had left it, under the carton of expired peas.

At the sound of a car turning into the driveway, adrenaline shot through his body. It was too late to go back to the basement. With the swiftness of Peter Rabbit, he hopped across the kitchen, into the living room, and ducked behind a large, dilapidated chair.

I'm toast, he thought. If they decided against their road trip to Bean Town and don't leave the house, there's no way they won't discover me.

The door was opening. "All right!" Woodrow snapped

impatiently. "You've said it one hundred times. It's not a good idea to leave the lottery ticket behind."

Duncan could hear him opening the freezer door. His heart stopped.

"You see, it's right here!" Woodrow said. "I'm putting it in my wallet. Or you can put it in your wallet. Tell me what you want."

"I'll take it," Edmund said testily.

Once again, they were on their way.

It's a miracle, Duncan thought. They didn't check the numbers. I've got to get out of here, get home, then figure out what to do. I want the Winthrops to be brought to justice, but I can't blow the whistle on them yet. If I do, they'll either disappear or come back and kill me. And if they disappear, I'll be looking over my shoulder for the rest of my life. I could end up in the Witness Protection Program! Flower and I want to spend our lives in Branscombe.

Deciding the cousins weren't coming back immediately, Duncan pushed himself up. As he was passing the closet by the front door, a thought occurred to him. Maybe there was an umbrella or a cane or something he could lean on inside it. As luck would have it, an old broom crashed to the floor when he opened the door. Leaning down, he unscrewed the pole of the broom from its bristly base. This should help a little, he thought.

Back out in the bracing New Hampshire air, with a 180

million dollar lottery ticket in his wallet, Duncan half hopped, half hobbled down the quiet country road. I just hope I can make it home, he thought. But after he had gone three blocks, he could hear a vehicle pulling over behind him. Nervously he turned around.

It was Enoch Hippogriff, a weather-beaten old-timer who regularly shopped at the market. "Duncan?" he called. "What are you doing here? The whole town is looking for you."

Bewildered but relieved, Duncan dragged himself into Enoch's truck. "Why are they looking for me?" he asked. He wondered if Flower had alerted the authorities when he didn't call her before going to bed, as he always did.

"Don't give me that," Enoch said. "You know why."

"I really don't," Duncan said.

Enoch Hippogriff glanced at him sideways. "You don't, do you? I can tell a man's face. You're a sight, hopping around with that stick in your hand. Duncan, your coworkers won the lottery last night."

"They did!" Duncan exclaimed, mixed emotions charging through his head. "I guess they used the Powerball number I chose after all."

"They used it all right. And even though you didn't throw in a buck, they're cutting you in on it. I don't know if I'd be that good-natured."

Duncan blinked back tears. "They did? Wow! I can't believe how wonderful they are. They really care about me. I want to see them. I don't suppose they went to work . . . I wonder where they all are now."

"They're down at the Branscombe Inn. That's the headquarters for your search party. Wait till they hear they can call it off!"

"Would you take me there now?" Duncan asked, wondering how he could explain his lost evening.

"Sure," Enoch said, then slapped him on the arm. "The ride will cost you a thousand bucks." His laughter at his own joke led to a fit of coughing. "Yup," he finally said. "It'll be a mere grand. I should charge you more than that! Some people think you disappeared because you're holding the other winning lottery ticket! Isn't that crazy? Just look at you!"

Duncan stared straight ahead as Enoch's old truck rumbled down the road.

So this is how it feels to win the lottery, he thought.

8

Horace Pettie and his assistant, Luella, were putting the final touches on the window display that they had created to cash in on the Festival of Joy. Business at Pettie's Fine Jewelry had been slow, and it certainly wasn't being helped by all the emphasis the town was now putting on having a simple, homespun Christmas.

"The message of the Festival is all well and good," Horace said. "But a man has to make a living."

"That's right, Mr. Pettie," Luella chimed in. "It was brilliant of you to create a charm commemorating this weekend. Trust me, it's going to sell like hot cakes," she assured him.

"I think it's really pretty if I say so myself," Pettie admitted, holding up one of the charms. The design was a gold holly wreath with the words "Branscombe's Festival of Joy" engraved around the border. He hadn't wanted to put either a date or the word "First" on the charms in case they didn't sell out. If there happened to be another Festival next year, he could dust off the leftovers.

A small, balding man of sixty-eight, Horace Pettie was another lifetime resident of Branscombe and the sole jeweler in town, as his father had been before him. Luella Cobb, a solid blond woman in her mid-fifties, had been working for him for twenty years, ever since her youngest child started high school. It was the only job she had ever wanted. Ever since Luella had been given a box of play jewelry when she was four years old, she had never been without a bauble or two attached to her body. Her enthusiasm for jewelry made her a splendid saleswoman for Horace Pettie. "Jewelry does not have to be terribly expensive, just tasteful," she would whisper to prospective clients. Then, as surely as night follows day, she'd pull out a more expensive item, breathlessly declaring it "stunning," "gorgeous," and finally exulting, "It's so you!"

Horace laid the last of the little gold holly wreaths on a tiny sled in the window, then he and Luella stepped out onto the sidewalk to view the display. The scene was that of a winter wonderland with Festival charms dangling from red ribbons.

Pettie sighed. "We did a lot of work on this. I hope it brings people into the store."

Luella put her hands on her ample hips. A thoughtful expression crossed her heavily made-up face. It was cold, but they were used to standing outside studying their various displays, so neither one noticed. "Mr. Pettie, I have an idea," Luella said slowly, excitement building in her voice. "I know what we can add to our wonderland that will attract attention."

"What's that, Luella?" Pettie asked, like a mouse snapping at a piece of cheese.

She tapped the window with her manicured finger. "Duncan's ring! Let's place it on the middle of the sled."

"I can't sell Duncan's ring!" Horace protested.

"Not sell it!" Luella said impatiently. "We'll make a sign saying, DUNCAN, COME HOME SOON. WE MISS YOU. YOUR RING IS WAITING."

Horace Pettie's eyes widened. "Duncan is the talk of the town. But don't you think it might seem a little insensitive?"

"Not in the least!" Luella declared. "It's a human interest story. Besides, sensitivity doesn't pay the bills." She turned and went back in the store.

Horace trailed after her, always amazed at Luella's creativity in drumming up business.

"You get the ring out of the safe," Luella ordered.

Horace hesitated.

"Mr. Pettie, don't worry about it. My bet is that Duncan is fine and has that other winning ticket, in which case he'll never come back for the ring."

Horace's ears reddened. "After I held it for him all these months!"

"Exactly!" Luella said. She waved her hand. "If that happens you'll end up selling the ring for twice the price. I'd buy it myself, but I think my husband would kill me."

Horace hurried to the back of the store.

"I'll make up the sign, then get on the phone," Luella called after him. "After I tell Tishie Thornton how bad we feel about poor Duncan, there won't be a living soul within a hundred miles who won't know about that ring in our window. With any luck, a news crew will be here before lunch."

9

This is probably the most impulsive thing I've done in my life, Flower thought as she stared out of the window of the bus she had boarded in Concord, New Hampshire. She had been counting the days until she flew in to spend Christmas with Duncan. They had both wished she could be there for the Festival of Joy, even though Duncan would be working, but they knew it didn't make sense. She'd be in for the holidays a week later, and the flights were so expensive. But then the other day, out of the blue, Mrs. Kane had quietly presented her with a check for two thousand dollars.

"Jimmy loves coming to day care, thanks to you," she had whispered to Flower about her three-year-old. "He's always been so terribly shy. You've brought him out of his shell. Please accept this gift, and treat yourself to something very special."

It didn't take Flower long to figure out what that something special would be—a chance to surprise Duncan by showing up in Branscombe for the Festival of Joy. She hoped she'd be allowed to lend a hand with the events Conklin's was catering, so that she could be near Duncan all weekend and get to know the coworkers he always talked about. For the past few months, he'd been hinting he'd bought her something special for Christmas. She hoped against hope that it was an engagement ring.

Flower had been able to get Friday off from work. Before she left for the airport Thursday evening, she had called Duncan, but he didn't pick up on either his cell phone or his home phone. Unlike her, he had a land line. He's probably working late, she thought. She hated to tell even a tiny lie, but she had to if she wanted to surprise him.

"I'm out Christmas shopping," she had said. "My cell phone battery is almost dead. By the time I get home, you'll be asleep. Talk to you in the morning." And then she closed by saying, "I love you, Duncan."

She knew he wouldn't be able to reach her when she was in the air and didn't want him to worry.

On the flight Flower was far too excited to close her eyes, just thinking that every second she was getting closer to Duncan and would finally see Branscombe for the first time. When she landed at Logan Airport at 6 A.M., and switched her cell phone back on, she was disappointed and surprised that Duncan hadn't left her a message. He left her messages all the time, even when he knew she wouldn't be able to pick up.

An hour and a half later, while she was waiting to board

the first bus to New Hampshire, she called him. He still didn't answer. Her heart began to sink. But he could be in the shower, she thought. She left a message to call her back. "I know you must think I'm crazy," she tried to joke. "It's 4:30 in the morning in California, but I'm wide awake. It just felt so strange not to talk to you last night. I'm going back to sleep, but if you get this, leave me a message." She turned off her phone. She knew she couldn't speak to him when she was on the bus, in case someone seated near her started to talk.

She had climbed aboard the bus to Concord, and once there, switched to the local bus to Branscombe. Now that she was approaching Duncan's town, she was starting to feel uneasy. She kept checking her messages, but he *still* hadn't tried to call her back.

Don't borrow trouble, she told herself. But what if Duncan didn't *want* to be surprised like this? He was so orderly and methodical. For her to just show up, when he's the type who would want everything to be perfect for her first visit, might not have been such a good idea after all.

As the bus passed miles of snow-covered countryside, Flower convinced herself that all would be well. Finally they passed a sign reading ENTERING BRANSCOMBE. I know I'm going to love it here, she thought. At the depot, she was the first one off the bus. She switched on her phone again. No messages. Her heart quickening, she went straight to the ladies' room to freshen up.

No wonder they call that flight the red-eye, she thought ruefully as she noticed how tired her eyes looked. She brushed her teeth, splashed water on her face, reapplied light makeup, and ran a comb through her hair. I certainly don't look my best, but I don't care, and I don't think Duncan will either.

She had gotten the address of Conklin's Market online and printed out the directions from the bus depot. The store was only a few blocks away. As she stepped out onto the street, she turned right. She knew that Main Street was in that direction. She began walking, enjoying the sound of the crusty snow as it crunched beneath her sneakers. At the corner, she paused. Main Street's quaint charm was everything she had imagined it would be. Old-fashioned street lamps, the row of tidy stores, and the small decorated Christmas trees lining the curb could have been on a postcard. Duncan had told her the trees would light up as Santa drove through town at the opening of the Festival. As she turned left, she smiled at the sight of a young woman lifting a baby from a stroller into a car seat. That's what I want to be doing before too long, Flower thought. She passed a drug store, a real estate agency, and then, across the street, she saw a man and a woman standing in front of a jewelry store, examining the display window. They must work there, she thought— neither one of them has a coat on. As she watched, they hurried back into the store. If Duncan *did* buy me a ring for

Christmas, is that where he got it? she wondered, and then again the nagging thought hit her—Why hasn't he called me?

Finally she reached Duncan's workplace. A little bigger than she had expected, it still had the look of a nineteenth-century general store. The exterior was painted red with black trim. A sign read CONKLIN'S MARKET—A WELCOME AWAITS YOU.

But when Flower walked through the door, the atmosphere was anything but welcoming. To her right, there were long lines at the registers, with cashiers yelling for price checks. It seemed to her that everyone in her line of vision was scowling.

Duncan had told her that produce aisles were always located on one side of a store or the other. There were no fruits or vegetables in the vicinity of the front door, so Flower started making her way past the rows of aisles to the far wall on the other side. I'll just say a quick hello and get the key to his house, she thought nervously. But when she turned the corner to the produce section, there was no sign of Duncan. A woman with a white stripe in her hair was yelling at a young kid who couldn't have been more than twenty. Apples were scattered all over the floor, some still rolling off in different directions.

"What happened here?" the woman screeched.

"I guess I piled the apples too high."

"I guess so! Pick them up, put them back, and unpack

the bananas. Look at those grapes! I told you to spray them, not drown them."

Oh, my goodness, Flower thought. She must be the owner's wife, the one they call The Skunk. But where was Duncan? Something had to be wrong.

The woman started to hurry past Flower.

"Excuse me," Flower said quickly. "Is Duncan Graham here?"

Her eyes shooting darts, the woman snarled, "You've got to be kidding. Where have you been, under a rock? He won millions in the lottery last night along with four other jokers who worked here. He'll never be back. Talk about ungrateful!"

In a huff, she was off.

Feeling as if she'd been punched in the stomach, Flower lowered her head as she felt tears flooding her eyes. Why didn't he call me? she asked herself frantically. The first thing I would have done if I had won the lottery, if I even played it, would be to call him. No matter what time it was, I would have called him. We phoned each other all the time over the silliest little things . . . And even if he thought my cell phone was dead, he knew it would have taken a message.

A stark realization hit her. He didn't call me because after he won the lottery, he probably thought he'd find someone better. My mother was right. She's laid-back about most things in life, but she warned me to take it slow with a man I met online who lives three thousand miles away . . .

"Flower," her mother had cautioned, "you haven't met his friends or family or visited his home yet. Just be careful."

The words of her late grandmother also echoed in her ears: "You should know someone for a year before getting serious."

She and Duncan had met only seven months ago.

I've made a fool of myself, Flower thought, as she squeezed past the shopping carts that were clustered around the cash registers. But I thought I knew him. He told me the other night that he wasn't going to play the lottery anymore. His financial advisers said it was a waste of money. What made him change his mind?

It was a relief to get out of the store. Flower knew if anyone looked at her closely, they'd see she was crying. I'm so tired, she realized as she shifted her knapsack on her shoulders and started walking toward the bus station. I may have to wait hours for a bus back to the airport. She noticed that an older woman eyed her sympathetically as they passed each other. I bet she's going to turn around and ask me if something's wrong, Flower thought. I've got to get off this Main Street. Ducking down an alley, she walked past a parking lot and found herself on a quiet country lane.

Across the street she could see a rambling white house with a sign that read THE HIDEAWAY — BED AND BREAKFAST. That's perfect, she thought. Just what I need. I can't get back on a bus yet. I need to just collapse and be alone.

She bit her lip, wiped her eyes, and hurried across the

road. Instructions on the front door said to ring the bell and walk in. I just hope they're not booked up, she thought, as she poked her finger on the bell, opened the door, and stepped into a small foyer. On the registration desk, an electrical smiling Santa was waving his arms and bowing. To the left, she could see a parlor with a large fireplace, comfortable looking couches, a crotcheted rug, and a huge Christmas tree, decorated with lights and ornaments and tinsel. The only sound was the ticking of a grandfather clock. Then she heard footsteps hurrying down the hall and a voice calling, "I'll get it, Jed."

A matronly looking woman, her graying hair pulled into a loose bun, was wiping her hands on an apron as she greeted Flower warmly. "Hello, honey. Here for the Festival?"

"Uhhhhh, yes. But I can only stay tonight."

"We happen to have one room left. It's nice and quiet and in the back. I have to warn you though. We have no television, radio, or Internet connection." She laughed. "Are you still interested?"

"More than ever," Flower said, managing a smile.

After handing over her credit card and driver's license, Flower detected the usual reaction to her name. "So you're from California," the woman said, not sounding surprised. She took an imprint of the credit card on an old machine, the likes of which Flower hadn't seen in years. "I'm Betty Elkins. My husband, Jed, and I are the owners here. Anything at all we can do to make you comfortable, please let us know. One of us is here all the time. We serve tea in the parlor at three o'clock with homemade scones and clotted cream." She paused. "You heard about our Festival all the way in California?"

"I did," Flower answered, thinking sadly of her conversations with Duncan. She could tell Betty Elkins was anxious to hear more, but thankfully a man appeared who was obviously Betty's husband. The sleeves of his green flannel shirt were rolled up, revealing muscular arms. He wore suspenders and a knotted bandana around his neck.

Betty glanced at him. "We've got a full house, honey," she said cheerfully, then turned back to Flower. "May I call you Flower?" she asked.

"Of course."

"Flower, this is my husband, Jed."

The gray-haired, thick eyebrowed Jed shook her hand. "I'm here to carry the luggage, but it looks like you don't have much except that knapsack."

"That's it," Flower said with a shrug as he matter-of-factly took the bag from her.

"Show her to the room, Jed. I've got to check on my Christmas cookies. They must be about ready."

Jed led Flower up the stairs and down the hall to a cozy room with yellow flowered wallpaper, a four-poster bed with a jonquil-patterned yellow quilt, a rocking chair, a night table, and a dresser. "This room is perfect for a girl with your name," he commented as he put the knapsack on the chair. "Hope you'll be comfortable."

"I know I will. Thank you." When Flower closed the door behind him, she turned the lock, took off her coat, sat down on the bed, and kicked off her sneakers.

I've never felt so alone, she thought. I truly believed Duncan loved me. But if he still wanted to be with me after winning all that money, he certainly would have called by now. She turned off her cell phone, leaned back onto the fluffy pillows, and immediately fell into a deep, dark sleep.

10

It was quarter of twelve when the four Reillys pulled into the driveway of the quaint, century-old Branscombe Inn. A half dozen television trucks were already lined up near the entrance.

"Looks like this press conference really drew the media," Nora commented.

"It sure does," Regan agreed. Her attention was riveted on a fortyish man, with a red face and balding head, dressed in jeans, boots, and a heavy parka, who was scowling and gesturing as he spoke on-camera to a reporter. "Look at that guy. I wonder what's on his mind. He certainly can't be one of the lottery winners."

"Maybe he is and just found out how much Uncle Sam is going to share in his winnings," Luke suggested.

Jack stopped the car at the front door. "I'll grab a luggage cart. Let's unload the bags and get inside. I know Steve and Muffy will be looking for us."

The Reillys had barely stepped into the noisy lobby when

they spotted their hosts across the room. "Such an attractive couple," Nora murmured. "That will certainly help on the campaign trail."

"You made it!" Muffy cried as she rushed over to them. Her shoulder-length blond hair was perfectly streaked and held back by a red-and-green striped headband. A whimsical sleigh-shaped pin was fastened to the lapel of her emerald-green suit.

Dark-haired, brown-eyed, Steve was right behind her, dressed in a pinstripe business suit, crisp white shirt, and a tie with the same pattern as Muffy's headband. "Hey, buddy, good to see you," he said to Jack, giving him an affectionate hug. His smile was quickly replaced by a worried frown, but he greeted the rest of the Reillys with genuine pleasure. "Hope you all had a good trip."

"Me, too," Muffy added quickly, getting the niceties out of the way. "Nora," she wailed, "you've *got* to help us get this Festival back on track. All anyone cares about is that stupid lottery. And that horrible producer Gary Walker not only cancelled our interview, but now he's trying to make the Festival and this town look foolish."

"We saw a man being interviewed outside who looked very upset," Nora began. "He had on a parka and jeans . . ."

"That's Harvey! His ex-wife, Glenda, is one of the winners. They were divorced about three months ago," Muffy explained.

"His ex-wife is now a multimillionaire?" Jack asked. "No

wonder he's not happy. I bet he wishes they had kissed and made up."

"Glenda doesn't," Steve said. "The guy's a jerk."

"What happened to the poor fellow who's missing?" Nora asked.

"Duncan Graham is still unaccounted for," Steve said. "Folks have been out looking for him all morning. But that producer is pushing the theory that Duncan was the one who bought the other winning ticket, then hightailed it out of here. Everyone in town is arguing about it and taking bets. The latest development is that the local jeweler is displaying a ring Duncan put a deposit on six months ago and was expected to pick up before Christmas. People are guessing that a girlfriend collected him, and they took off."

"Can you believe this happened just at the start of our Festival of Joy?" Muffy asked, her blue eyes widening. "I can't," she answered herself.

She is obviously going with the girlfriend theory, Regan thought.

"Listen," Steve said, looking around and lowering his voice. "There were so many reporters swarming into town this morning when word about the lottery broke that I thought it would be a good idea to call a press conference and let them get their pictures and stories all at once."

I'll bet it was Muffy's idea, Regan thought. One way or the other, she's going to get herself in front of the camera. She's not about to let those coordinating outfits go to waste.

"I'll open with a few remarks," Steve continued, "introduce the lottery winners, then, after they take questions, I'll switch the focus to the Festival and the fact that we have lots of wonderful things going on this weekend, like Nora Regan Reilly here to sign books."

The press is only interested in the lottery winners, Regan thought. Wait till Steve and Muffy find out they ended up on the cutting room floor.

"So, Nora, if you don't mind, after the reporters interview the lottery winners, I'll introduce you, then maybe you could say a few words about the Festival," Steve suggested.

"Of course," Nora said obligingly.

Steve beckoned to a clerk behind the desk. "These people are our guests—the Reillys," he said quickly. "Send their luggage up to their rooms please." He took Muffy's hand, and the Reillys followed him to a large parlor off the main lobby.

"Be careful of the wires," Steve warned as they entered the room. "They're all over the place."

Furniture had been pushed against the back wall. Rows of folding chairs were nearly filled. Cameras were directed at a table at the end of the room where two men and two women were seated. A fifth chair in the middle was empty.

"There are our winners," Steve said.

They look more exhausted than exhilarated, Regan thought as she observed them. She could see from the thin black wires on their lapels that they had already been miked.

The two men, one in his twenties and the other middle-aged, were whispering to each other. An older woman was trying to squash down the ruffles of a pink blouse that climbed halfway up her chin. But it was the obvious distress on the other woman's face that caught Regan's eye. She's *really* worried, Regan thought.

Steve brought the Reillys over to the table and quickly introduced them to the winners. Marion brightened immediately when she met Nora.

"Nora Regan Reilly. I *love* your books. You should write our story . . ."

Regan turned to Glenda. "I know you must be upset about your friend."

"I am," Glenda said.

"I'm a private investigator," Regan told her. "And my husband is the head of the Major Case Squad for the NYPD. We'd love to do whatever we can to help find him."

Glenda's eyes brightened. "Thank you. We were searching for Duncan all morning. Then we had to get ready for this press conference. We promised the mayor we'd be here."

"When did you first realize that he was missing?" Regan asked, wondering if Glenda knew her ex-husband was in the middle of a heart-to-heart interview with a reporter outside.

"I tried to call Duncan last night as soon as we won, but I couldn't reach him. This morning we stopped by his house at quarter of seven on our way to register the ticket, but he didn't answer the door. We thought he might have had a few too many beers and was sleeping it off. Last night we got stiffed on our Christmas bonus, and he was very upset when he left work. After we validated the ticket at the convenience store, we went back to his place and he *still* didn't answer the door. We kept ringing the bell and knocking on the windows. Finally, Tommy noticed the key ring in the ignition of his car. We decided to use his house key to go inside, just in case something happened to him. I felt funny just barging in there . . ."

"I would have done the same thing if I was concerned about a friend," Regan said. "The fact that the keys were in his car would have really worried me."

"That's the way I felt!" Glenda cleared her throat. "The television was on, the lights were on, his bed didn't look as though it had been slept in, there was no sign that he had taken a shower and gone out early . . ." Her voice trailed off. "Then we tried to start his car, but it was dead. I think that last night he must have realized our lottery numbers won. He was probably so frustrated that he hadn't played, he decided to go out, but his car wouldn't start. I think Duncan might have started walking and had an accident or a heart attack. I know he didn't buy that other lottery ticket!" she said, her eyes flashing. "But Tommy and Ralph think he's fine and would have been at work today if he hadn't come into money. They're furious with me because we announced his name as one of the winners of our ticket. If it ever turns out that Duncan cashes in the other winning ticket, I think they'll kill me. I'm the one who initially suggested cutting him in on the ticket, even though he was too cheap and stubborn to throw in a lousy dollar."

Oh boy, Regan thought. Alvirah better get here soon. She has at least four new candidates for the Lottery Winners Support Group.

Steve looked at his watch. "It's noon. We should get started." He gestured for the Reillys to take the seats he'd reserved for them in the front row, then went to the podium and pulled out a folded sheet of paper from his pocket. With Muffy at his side, he tapped on the microphone for silence.

"Welcome everyone, to Branscombe's first annual Festival of Joy. I am Mayor Steve Patton, and this is my wife, Muffy."

"Hi, everyone." Muffy giggled, leaning toward the mike. "I can't tell you what an honor and a pleasure and a delight it is for me to be the First Lady of Branscombe. Branscombe is such a special, special town. For those folks who don't live here, we want to welcome you, and we hope all of you are staying for the entire Festival of Joy. We promise you a wonderful, heartwarming experience . . ."

"Thank you, Muffy," Steve interrupted.

Muffy raised her index finger. "One more thing, honey. Tickets are still available for the community supper tomorrow night and the pancake breakfast Sunday morning. With the ticket you get a pass to see *It's a Wonderful Life,* which will be shown continually in the church auditorium. Don't you just love that movie? I cry every time I see it . . ."

Regan was amused by Steve's ability to keep smiling as he struggled to regain control of the microphone.

"I just love that movie, too," Steve said. "And now I want to introduce our lottery winners, who proved that Branscombe is not only a happy town, but a *lucky* town, a town where people care about each other and cheer each other's good fortune. That fifth seat is reserved for Duncan Graham, the coworker these folks so generously decided would share in that great big pot of money, even though, thanks to advice from his financial advisers, he decided not to play this week." Steve laughed. "I'd love to know what other kind of advice those guys are giving!"

"What are their names?" a reporter called out.

"Not sure," Steve answered. "We'll get you that information later. Now let me introduce the four recent employees of Conklin's Market, which, incidentally, will be catering the Festival."

As their names were called, the winners stood and waved. When they were all seated again, Steve turned to the audience. "I'd like to open up the floor to your questions."

Hands shot up. Steve pointed to a young woman in the second row.

"Is it true you left the framed photos that the Conklins gave you for Christmas outside the store this morning, tied together with a note saying, 'We Quit!'?" the woman asked, clutching her notebook.

"Yes, we did!" Marion said proudly. "That was my idea!"

"Did you think that was a nice way to start off the Festival of Joy?" another reporter called out. "We understand you are, or should I say were, their key employees. Wouldn't it have shown cooperation and good fellowship to work at Conklin's this weekend when they certainly must need your help catering the Festival?"

"It would have shown good fellowship to give us the Christmas bonus we had every right to expect," Ralph said hotly. "I can tell you one thing. We'd all be right there right now, millionaires or not, if they had treated us fairly."

Oh boy, Regan thought. The Festival of Joy is off to a great start.

Another reporter stood. "We understand your missing coworker made a down payment on a ring at Pettie's Fine Jewelry here in Branscombe six months ago. Do any of you know if he has a girlfriend?"

They all shook their heads.

"I see," the reporter said. "I must ask you. Do any of you think your coworker, or perhaps the intended recipient of this ring, bought the other winning lottery ticket?"

Ralph and Tommy both looked at each other, then raised their hands. "We do now," they said in unison.

Marion looked perplexed. She bit her lip, then fluttered her hands, indicating she couldn't make up her mind.

Glenda jumped to her feet. "No!" she said vehemently. "He wouldn't have betrayed us like that. I'm terribly afraid something happened to him."

"Something did!" Duncan cried from the back of the room.

The crowd gasped and turned to see a disheveled, unshaven Duncan hobbling toward the microphone, his right hand wrapped around a splintery-looking wooden pole. "I am outraged that anyone, especially Tommy and Ralph, would think that I would go out and buy a ticket behind my friends' backs!" he shouted. "I did NOT buy that other ticket! I swear on my life I didn't!" His voice was quivering as he reached the podium and turned to face the crowd.

"I knew it, Duncan!" Glenda cried.

"And even worse! That special moment in a man's life when he pops the question to his girlfriend has been ruined for me! I find it disgusting that the jeweler in this town would invade my privacy for his own profit!"

With that ringing statement, Duncan, weakened by fatigue, hunger, and pain, collapsed into the arms of Mayor Steve.

11

An hour into their drive to Boston, Edmund and Woodrow were still bursting with excitement at their incredible stroke of luck.

Woodrow was at the wheel of their rented sedan. "Dark gray, nothing flashy," they had told the agent at Budget Rent A Car. Each of them owned a top of the line Mercedes, but that was not the image of economy and thrift they wanted to convey to their clients.

They took turns coming up with new ways to describe their winnings.

"180 million beans!" Woodrow said.

"180 million big ones!" Edmund countered.

"180 million smackers!" Woodrow chortled.

From time to time ever-cautious Edmund would remind Woodrow to slow down. "We could hit an ice patch and get in an accident. We have too much to live for."

"I have a perfect driving record," Woodrow insisted.

"Too bad you have another record," Edmund said dryly.

Woodrow laughed. "Talk about the pot calling the kettle black. Yours is just as long as mine. Thank God, we can be squeaky-clean from now on. But I'm going to *miss* cheating people."

"Me, too. But it's not worth it. That judge threatened to lock us up and throw away the key if we ever got caught in another swindle."

"I wish we didn't have to go back to Branscombe for the final session."

"You think it's my idea of a good time? But if we're not there for the class, our students might start comparing notes. This way we'll say our individual good-byes to them and promise a weekly report on the oil well until we cash the ticket and disappear."

Woodrow was silent for a moment, then said, "Edmund, I have an idea."

"I'm listening."

"We paid our dues for the other scams. Why not wipe the slate clean? Why don't we return the money to the people in Branscombe next week? We don't need it now. We'll tell them the oil well is not as secure as we were led to believe but promise to keep in touch about future investments we think are worth considering. That way we won't have to worry ever again about having the Feds on our tail."

Edmund frowned. "Give people back their money? How

unnatural." He pretended to shiver. "It goes against my every instinct. Besides, we worked hard convincing them to cough up that dough."

"Eddie, it's chump change now. Sixteen of our seventeen students invested in the greasy driveway we called an oil well. How much did we collect? Seventy-one thousand dollars? I'll tell you one person who will be thrilled to get his money back—Mr. Duncan Donuts. Maybe he'll go back to buying lottery tickets."

"He must be really out of his mind mad at us right now," Edmund laughed.

"I hope he doesn't show up for class next week," Woodrow said. "He might kill us."

"I thought you wanted to pay him back."

"We can send him a check."

Edmund's eyes twinkled. "Woodrow, what are we going to do with ourselves when we collect all that money?"

"Have fun, that's what we're going to do."

"Together, right."

"Of course, together. We're a winning team. We'll always stick together."

Edmund shifted nervously in his seat. "So you think Aunt Millie is the right person to cash in our ticket?"

"She's perfect," Woodrow answered. "She's the one person in our family who always loved us unconditionally, no matter how much trouble we got in. She has no heirs but us, thank God, so she won't have anyone telling her to keep all our money. We'll give her a million bucks to make the trip to lottery headquarters." He laughed. "You know her. She'll love the excitement."

"I just hope she doesn't have a criminal record she hasn't told us about," Edmund joked.

Woodrow laughed. "Can you imagine that? Aunt Millie forbidden to gamble?"

"If that's the case, she's broken parole at least a thousand times. She turns into a demon when she sits in front of those slot machines in Atlantic City. Can you believe how mad she got when they started computerizing those one-armed bandits? She said half the fun is hearing the sound of quarters tumbling into her bucket. Clink, clink."

"We sure take after her more than either one of our mothers," Woodrow said. "I just hope we can trust her to do right by us." He paused. "That wasn't nice. I know we can. We'll pay her a surprise visit next week after we leave Branscombe in the dust."

Edmund leaned forward to turn up the heat. "It must be getting colder out," he observed. "But at least it's not snowing." He pushed the power button on the radio.

"This is station WXY in Boston. We have breaking news from our reporter in Branscombe, New Hampshire, covering the incredible lottery story. What have you got for us, Ginger?"

"Bob, we *do* have quite a story going on up here. The missing man, Duncan Graham, who was cut in on the lottery winnings by his generous coworkers even though he decided not to play last night . . ."

Woodrow whistled. "Way to go, Duncan! But he's missing?" He leaned over and turned up the volume.

". . . arrived just moments ago at the Branscombe Inn, where a press conference with his coworkers is taking place. He looks as if he's been through the ringer. He was angry and upset when he heard that two of his coworkers thought he had bought the other winning ticket behind their backs."

"He didn't," Woodrow and Edmund said in unison.

"He must have had some sort of accident because he limped to the podium, grabbing an old pole for support, a pole that looked as if he had fished it out of a Dumpster. He vehemently denied buying the other winning ticket, but, incredibly, he seemed more furious about the fact that the whole town knows about the engagement ring he bought for his girlfriend. He was so overwhelmed that he literally fainted at the podium!"

"He fainted?" Bob answered with appropriate concern in his voice. "Is he all right?"

"They're just carrying him out now. I'll keep you posted."

"Does he realize that his coworkers have cut him in on the winning ticket and that he's now worth twelve million dollars?"

"Hard to say."

"If he doesn't know, it'll be a nice surprise for him when he wakes up. Thanks, Ginger. And now to the weather . . ."

Woodrow and Edmund looked at each other.

"That gets us off the hook with Duncan," Edmund laughed. "He didn't lose out by following our advice. His coworkers must be crazy. They're cutting him in on millions. We'd never do that."

"We certainly wouldn't," Woodrow agreed.

"But what a shame we're out of the business of scamming people. We could have found some more oil wells for him."

Woodrow slapped his thigh and laughed. "You're right, Edmund. We would have ended up with at least eleven of his twelve million." He tapped on the brake. Construction ahead was reducing the traffic to a crawl.

Edmund shook his head. "Speaking about that ticket makes me want to feast my eyes on it again," he said as he retrieved his wallet from the breast pocket of his suit jacket. Smiling with anticipation, he pulled out the plastic bag and reached inside for the ticket.

Woodrow glanced over. "That sweet little piece of paper is worth 180 million bucks."

"That's right," Edmund said as he unfolded the ticket and looked at the numbers. A feeling of sheer panic raced through his system, a feeling he had never experienced before, not even when he was sentenced to eight years in prison. A moan escaped his lips.

"What's the matter?" Woodrow snapped.

"These numbers . . . they don't look right. I thought . . . I thought the Powerball number was 32."

"What?" Woodrow demanded.

"Wasn't the Powerball number 32?"

"Yes it was!"

"This Powerball number is 18 . . ."

"What are you talking about?" Woodrow screamed.

A bloodcurdling, anguished howl escaped Edmund's lips. "The date on this is June twelfth!" he screamed. "This is an old ticket! This is not our winning ticket! Oh, God, no!"

Woodrow grabbed it from him. "Are you trying to pull something on me?"

"How dare you say that? How dare you? We checked the numbers when we put it in the freezer. But we didn't check them when we went back for it. Someone must have switched the tickets! You're an idiot! I knew we shouldn't have left the ticket behind! I knew it!"

"Who could have come in the house? We made sure it was all locked up! And we weren't gone for that long!"

"Remember last night we thought we heard a noise in the basement but didn't bother to check? We were too busy celebrating and thought it was the old furnace . . ."

Woodrow's eyes were bulging out of his head. "We heard that thumping noise. I wanted to check but you said not to bother." He pointed at the radio. "They said Duncan was missing last night. He just turned up, and he's limping. That stupid side door our students use was always unlocked." He looked back at Edmund. "I bet he came over to yell at us when he realized the numbers he didn't play won! He must have heard us celebrating! He spied on us!" He must have heard us talking about the oil well scam!

"It's *got* to be him!" Edmund screamed. "Who else could it be?"

His temples throbbing, his face beet red, Woodrow gunned the car across the grassy median and made a highly illegal U-turn. "We're going to get that ticket back!"

"What if he already called the cops on us?"

"I don't care!" Woodrow exploded.

Edmund slumped in his seat. "It amazes me that you have a perfect driving record."

12

Up in the clouds above New Hampshire, Willy glanced out the window of the twin-engine jet he and Alvirah had chartered at Westchester Airport. This is the last thing I expected to be doing today, he thought, then looked across the aisle at Alvirah, who was smiling gleefully. She reached out her hand to him.

"When we heard about that oil spill on the Connecticut Turnpike, wasn't it an inspiration for me to call Rent A Jet?"

"Expensive inspiration," Willy commented. "We save a few hours on the road, and it costs us three thousand bucks."

"All that driving would have been too much for you."

"Alvirah, I love to drive."

Dramatically, she touched the bandage on her forehead. "When I was little and I got hurt, my mother always gave me a present. After I broke my arm running down a slide, she bought me a new Dy-dee doll, with two matching outfits. It made me feel so much better. She wasn't even mad at me for being so stupid. This plane ride is my get-well present to my-self. Besides, it's okay to splurge on ourselves once in a while."

"You're right, Alvirah."

"And something else. I'm worried about those lottery winners. They look as if they need my help. If we were in the car, we wouldn't get there until tonight."

It was now 12:15, and they were beginning their descent into the small local airport, ten miles from Branscombe.

Alvirah finished the last of the tiny twist pretzels she had been munching on during the flight. "They were stale," she whispered to Willy as she crumbled the bag. "But I was hungry."

The pilot had called ahead and arranged for a car service to pick them up and take them to the Branscombe Inn. When they landed, a white stretch limo was waiting on the tarmac.

"I'm Charley," the driver said as he loaded their bags into his trunk. "Welcome to the Festival of Joy."

"Have they found the guy who's missing?" Alvirah asked eagerly.

"Oh, you know about him?"

"She knows about *everything,*" Willy explained.

Charley closed the trunk. "He just limped into a press conference a few minutes ago, denied he bought the other winning ticket, then keeled over. I guess he'll be okay, but he had some kind of wild night, that's for sure."

Alvirah's eyes widened. "Do you think he bought that other ticket?"

"Who knows? As a matter of fact, I just passed the place where it was sold."

"Where?"

"A little convenience store down the road."

"The pretzels on the plane made me thirsty. Let's stop there for water."

"Don't worry. I have plenty of bottled water in the car for my guests," Charley said as he opened the door for them.

Alvirah shivered as she climbed into the back of the limo. "You know something? I'm cold. What I really need is a cup of coffee."

"There's a coffee shop along the way that serves the best . . ." Charley began.

"Don't waste your breath," Willy interrupted. "Nothing is going to stop my wife from checking out that convenience store."

"Gotcha," Charley said as he closed the door behind them.

13

"Someone call an ambulance!" Mayor Steve shouted, as he lowered Duncan to the floor and unzipped his parka.

"I know what to do!" Muffy cried. "I was a lifeguard!" Dropping to her knees, she grabbed Duncan's wrist and felt for his pulse. "His heart is still beating!" she announced dramatically.

Regan and Jack had been the first to spring from their chairs. "Muffy, see if he has a medical alert card in his wallet," Regan suggested.

Duncan's eyes flew open. "I'm okay!" he insisted. "I have no medical conditions. None whatsoever." Cameras clicked nonstop as he tried to sit up. "Please! I'm fine. My leg hurts, that's all."

Glenda rushed to his side as photographers and reporters jostled for a good vantage point to catch the action. "Please stand back," she urged, then looked at Steve. "Let's get Duncan out of here."

Jack and Steve lifted Duncan onto a chair, picked it up, and hurried him out of the parlor.

The hotel manager led the way to a guest room down the hall. "When the ambulance comes, I'll send the paramedics in," he said.

"I'll be all right," Duncan insisted. "My leg might need to be X-rayed. I'm thirsty and hungry and I want to call my girl-friend. Glenda, can I borrow your cell phone? I left mine home," he said as Jack and Steve set down the chair and eased him onto the bed.

"I have it right here, Duncan. What's her number?"

Duncan rattled it off then grabbed the phone from Glenda's hand and held it to his ear. "Her voice mail is pick-ing up," he said, his tone frustrated and disappointed, then he dropped his voice. "Flower, I love you. I need to talk to you. I don't have my cell phone with me . . ."

"Tell her to call mine," Glenda said quickly, then gave him her number.

Duncan repeated it into the phone. "I'll try you at work, Flower. I can't wait to talk to you." He hung up. "Glenda, do you mind if I call information? There's a charge for it."

Glenda smiled. "Don't you realize I'm now a multi-millionaire? And you are, too, Duncan."

"Must be nice," Mayor Steve said as he handed Duncan the glass of water he'd hurried to fill.

"I heard. No one ever had a better friend than you,

Glenda," Duncan said humbly. He then gulped every drop in the glass. "You're the best."

"That's for sure," Jack said with a laugh. "I doubt if I'll ever make friends with someone who's willing to share their millions with me."

Duncan reached the day care center but frowned when he was told by Flower's boss that she had taken the day off. "She *did*? I'm surprised she didn't tell me. Okay then, I'll wait to hear back from her."

He hung up and then called and picked up the voice messages on his home and cell phones, smiling as he listened. "Aw, she couldn't sleep last night," he said softly. "I hope she calls me back soon." He then dialed his parents and left a message. As he gave Glenda back her phone, he looked at Jack and Steve. "Thanks, guys. Please don't let me hold you up. I'll be fine here until the ambulance comes."

"How did you hurt that leg?" Jack asked.

"I fell," Duncan said quickly. "I'll be okay. Thanks again for your help. If you don't mind, I'd just like to have a word with Glenda."

"I'm going to the hospital with you," Glenda said firmly. "You shouldn't be alone."

"Glenda, I can't believe that Tommy and Ralph would think . . ." A look of distress came over Duncan's face.

"We'll step outside and let you two talk," Jack said. He and Steve went out into the hallway where the other Reillys were waiting.

"Glenda!" Duncan whispered when they were alone. "I need to tell you something!"

An alarmed look crossed Glenda's face. "Duncan, please don't say you bought that other ticket."

"No! I didn't. But my life could be in danger . . ."

"What are you *talking* about?"

Duncan quickly recounted the events of the previous evening. ". . . so take a look at this," he said hoarsely. He reached into the side pocket of his parka and pulled out his wallet.

Glenda looked dumbfounded as she took the lottery ticket from his hand and checked the numbers. "You *stole* this out of their freezer?"

"Yes! I can never cash it in, but I don't want them to have it. All I care about is getting those two arrested for swindling innocent people out of their hard-earned money. If I ever cashed this, they'd know it was me who stole it, and I'd never be able to sleep at night without worrying they'd someday climb in my bedroom window and kill me. Besides, people around here would always think I might have intended to double-cross you, even though I'd split the winnings."

"You know if you hadn't told those guys our numbers in the first place, we'd be sharing the whole pot," she said wryly.

"I'm sorry! Don't forget it was my Powerball number that won."

"I was joking, Duncan."

"You know, Glenda, the more I think about it, the more I

believe they're not just swindlers—they're dangerous!" From outside they could hear the wail of an approaching ambulance. "What should I do now?"

Glenda pointed in the direction of the hallway. "That guy who just carried you in with the Mayor? He's the head of the NYPD Major Case Squad, and his wife's a private investigator. Before you showed up, she offered their help in looking for you. Why don't you talk to them?"

"You think they can be trusted to keep quiet about the ticket and get those crooks arrested?"

"Yes, I do, Duncan."

Muffy, the former lifeguard, came barging in the room with a breakfast tray, a camera crew close on her heels. "Duncan, our wonderful volunteer ambulance workers are right behind me. But have a few bites of a delicious, homemade waffle before you go."

Glenda had instinctively closed her hand around the lottery ticket. Now she looked at Duncan, her eyes questioning.

"Glenda," he said, gesturing toward her hand. "Why don't you follow up on that, then meet me at the hospital with my cell phone?"

"Follow up on what?" Muffy asked brightly as two men in white uniforms, the seal of Branscombe over their hearts, wheeled a stretcher into the room.

14

Charley drove his limo past the solitary gas pump in front of Ethan's Convenience Store and stopped. A banner in the window proclaimed: A MEGA-MEGA LOTTERY TICKET WORTH $180 MILLION WAS SOLD HERE!

Alvirah, Willy close behind, was inside the store before Charley could even think about opening the door for them. A cameraman and a young male reporter came rushing toward them.

"I'm Jonathan Tuttle from the BUZ network," the reporter said excitedly. "I bet you two have the winning lottery ticket. Showing up in a limo and all . . ."

"Sorry to disappoint you," Alvirah said. As the cameraman snapped off his light and the reporter lowered his mike, she added breezily, "But we did win 40 million dollars in the lottery several years ago."

"Turn the camera back on," Tuttle ordered, then focused on Alvirah and Willy with renewed interest. "Wait a minute. Haven't you been interviewed on our network?"

"Yes, I'm Alvirah Meehan, and this is my husband, Willy. Your anchor Cliff Bailey has had me on whenever there are new lottery winners making headlines."

"Of course," Tuttle said. "What brings you up here?"

"We just flew in for Branscombe's Festival of Joy."

"Our network is doing a special on the Festival."

"I saw that this morning."

"Are you aware that two winning mega-mega lottery tickets were sold in this area, one here in Red Oak and one in Branscombe?"

"Yes we are. I hope to meet the winners in Branscombe and congratulate them personally."

"Do you have any advice for them?"

"Tell them to turn off their phones," Willy grunted.

Alvirah laughed. "What he means is that they'll hear from an awful lot of people with crazy ideas about how they should spend their money."

"I can imagine," Tuttle said. "Thank you Mrs. Meehan."

Alvirah glanced around the store. On the back wall hung a cardboard cutout of Santa and his reindeer landing on a rooftop. Bright red ornaments hung from a fake tree perched atop a table in the corner. Blinking Christmas lights framed the dairy section.

A peppy octogenarian in a plaid shirt and red bow tie was

behind the counter by the cash register. "What can I do for you folks?" he asked.

"We'll have two large black coffees to go, please," Alvirah said.

"You got it."

"Are you Ethan?" she asked.

"Sure am."

"How exciting that you sold one of the winning lottery tickets," Alvirah commented as he poured the coffee.

"Sure is. It's the first time! I get a check, too, because it was bought here. That'll be a nice piece of change for me. But before you ask, I'll answer the questions everyone's been calling me with all morning. I don't know who bought it and I don't have security cameras so there are no tapes to play over and over. As far as that guy they think might have bought it, I have no idea. I don't know what he looks like, and even if I *did* see a picture of him, it wouldn't make any difference. If he's not one of my regular customers, I won't remember."

Alvirah nodded her head. "That answers all my questions."

Ethan laughed as he emphatically secured caps onto the cardboard coffee cups. "Maybe it's my age, but after a while all the people in and out of here become a blur. Yesterday it seemed that everyone who bought gas splurged on a ticket. I was busier than a one-armed paper hanger."

"When the pot gets that big," Willy said, "people want to get in on the dream. Winning the lottery certainly changed our life. Alvirah, do you want anything else besides the coffee?"

"I wouldn't mind something to munch on," Alvirah answered as she looked around the countertop that was cluttered with packages of gum, candy, and donuts. Her eyes stopped at a basket of Christmas caramels, individually wrapped in red and green striped tin foil.

"Are these caramels any good?" Alvirah asked Ethan.

"For a dollar a piece, they'd better be. I just got them in the other day." He shrugged. "I had a couple myself. They're delicious. But more people with an extra buck spent it on a lottery ticket than one of those."

"We'll take a dozen," Willy said, then looked at Alvirah. "They're my get-well present to you."

15

Flower awoke with a start. She had been dreaming that she was hanging from a ledge, trying to pull herself up. Her fingers were slipping, and she was trying to call for help, but no sound would come out of her mouth. She quickly opened her eyes and saw the unfamiliar pattern of the flowered wallpaper. Where am I? she asked herself. Still frightened by the dream, she was grateful to be awake, then the crushing realization of where she was and why she was there set in.

With a heavy heart she glanced at her watch. It was ten after one. I've only been asleep for a few hours, she realized. But I'm hungry, and I'm getting a headache. Betty and Jed had said to let them know if I wanted anything. Maybe I can grab a sandwich and a cup of tea, then I'll call and see if I can catch a flight back tonight. Her cell phone was on the dresser. I don't want to turn it on yet, she thought. Even if there was a message from Duncan, I don't want to listen to his lame excuses or a suggestion that we'd be better off just being friends.

She went into the small bathroom and splashed water on

her face. If things were different, I wouldn't have minded taking a long soak in that claw-foot tub, she thought, envisioning her mother at home, lolling in her bath with layers of seaweed floating around her.

"It's so soothing, Flower," her mother would say, as she sniffed the aroma of the lavender candles that inevitably were part of the ritual. "I can't believe you're not into this."

From the time I was a little kid, I was more than content with hot water and plain soap, Flower thought. Just like Nana, who said the only place seaweed belonged was on the beach, not clogging the drains. She sighed. It had been six years, and she still missed Nana so much.

Enough reminiscing Flower decided, suddenly restless. I want to get something to eat, take a quick shower, and get out of here.

When she left the room there was no sound in the hallway except the creaking of the floorboards under her feet. Betty had said they had a full house, but it didn't seem as if there was anyone around now. She walked downstairs to the first floor.

There was no one at the desk in the foyer, and she could see that the parlor was empty. But the air was filled with the enticing smell of baking—chocolate cake. Betty's last name should be Crocker, Flower thought, as she walked to the back of the house and knocked on the kitchen door.

"Yooooouu hooooo!" Betty called. "Whoever you are, come on in!"

"It's me," Flower said as she pushed the swinging door open and stepped into a large, old-fashioned kitchen. At the far end a fire was blazing in the hearth, two inviting looking club chairs in front of it. Shiny copper pots and pans hung from the ceiling. Checkered curtains framed the large windows on either side of the back door. Through them Flower could see a small red building that looked like an old barn.

Betty was leaning over the oven, examining the toothpick in her right hand. The look on her face was one of intense concentration. "Be right with you, Flower," she said cheerily. "I like my cakes to come out just perfectly. A minute more and this one would start to be a teeny weeny bit dry. I always say, timing is everything." She lifted the baking pan out of the oven and set it on a rack on the side of the stove.

"If it tastes as good as it smells, I'm sure it's perfect," Flower said softly.

Betty turned to her with a big smile. "I'm my own best customer," she said, wiping her broad hands on her apron. "That's why I'll never be a Skinny Minnie. Hey, I'm surprised to see you. You looked so tired when you came in, I was sure you'd sleep for hours."

"I thought I would too, but I guess I woke up because I'm hungry. Would it be possible to get a little something to eat?"

"Of course, honey. Jed and I just had some of my fresh vegetable soup for lunch. Would you like a bowl of that with a nice warm biscuit?"

"I'd love it."

"Okay, then. Would you like to have it right here or perhaps you'd prefer to take it up to your room?"

Betty's friendliness made Flower feel less alone. "Right here, if I won't be in your way."

"You won't be in my way. I love it when our guests drop into the kitchen and we get a chance to visit. You look a little peaked. Why don't you sit down?" she asked, indicating the somewhat battered wooden table.

Five minutes later, Flower was gratefully sipping the soup, and Betty, a cup of tea in hand, had settled in the chair across from her.

"This soup is delicious," Flower said quietly.

"Makes me feel good to see people enjoy my cooking," Betty replied amiably, then sipped her tea. "So the Festival of Joy is finally here. Everyone's been talking about it for months. We have TV people covering the Festival staying here. Are you going to the candlelight ceremony tonight, dear?"

Flower burst into tears.

"I didn't think so," Betty said sympathetically, her motherly face benevolent. "Is this about a man?"

"Yes," Flower said, wiping her eyes. She felt her nose begin to run.

Betty reached in her pocket and took out a packet of tissues. "Oh, my dear," she clucked as she handed them to Flower.

"I'm sorry," Flower apologized as she dabbed at her eyes and blew her nose.

"No need to be sorry. You're such a sweet, pretty girl. Whoever is making you cry is not worth even one of those tears." She reached across the table and enveloped Flower's small hand in hers. "Would it help to talk about it?"

Flower nodded and put down her spoon. "My boyfriend, or I should say my *ex*-boyfriend, lives in Branscombe. I flew in to surprise him for the weekend. This morning I went over to Conklin's Market where he works and found out that he and a group of coworkers had won . . . won . . . won the lottery last night!" She started crying even harder, gasping for breath as she said, "He didn't even call me to tell me. Since last June we spoke at least twice a day and always at night. Last night he didn't call. I left him messages, and he never called me back, not even this morning. I know it means that now that he has money, he wants to be able to live it up without me!"

"Well for land's sake," Betty exclaimed. "He sounds *awful*." She leaned forward. "Some of the workers at Conklin's won the lottery?"

Flower hiccupped. "Yes."

"Who's your boyfriend?"

"Duncan Graham. He runs the produce section."

"Duncan? I'm so surprised, I thought he was a lovely fellow."

A fresh torrent of tears flowed from Flower's eyes, and she began to sob.

"I'm so sorry," Betty said as she got up, went around the table, and pulled Flower's head to her generous bosom. "That was a stupid thing for me to say. If he treated you like that, you're well rid of him. Who did you talk to at the store?"

"I think . . . I think . . . it was Mr. Conklin's wife. She wasn't very nice."

"She's a horrible woman! Nasty as they come." Betty soothingly patted Flower's head.

"I just want to go home," Flower said, weeping. "I'll get a bus to Boston today."

"Are you sure you don't want to spend the night? You can have dinner with me and Jed. Then you can get a fresh start in the morning."

"I don't know," Flower answered uncertainly. "I think I'm better off just leaving here as fast as I can." She looked up into Betty's eyes. "The thing is that Duncan's been taking a financial course with two guys who came to Branscombe last month. He told me they advised him to stop playing the lottery, and he agreed it wasn't a good idea anymore. He obviously didn't listen to them. I wish he had!"

"No you don't!" Betty cried. "He's shown his true colors. If you ask me, you dodged a bullet, honey. Even if he had all the money in the world, he doesn't deserve you."

"Those two financial advisers will really come in handy now. They can tell him what to do with all his winnings," Flower said, sounding forlorn. "Have you heard anything about them? Woodrow and Edmund Winthrop. They're cousins."

"Not a thing," Betty said quickly. "And if I had, I wouldn't have been interested. Money is the ruination of so many people. As they say, it can't buy you happiness. You're going to go back to California and find someone wonderful, I just know it. Jed and I will come to your wedding out there."

"I never met anyone kinder than you," Flower said, trying to smile.

A sharp rapping at the back door made them both jump. "I don't know who that could be," Betty murmured as she released Flower and hurried to answer it. She gasped when she saw who was on the porch. "It's not a good time to stop in," Betty said, her tone firm. Her hand was on the door. She started to close it.

From where Flower was sitting she couldn't see who the unwelcome visitor was.

"What are you talking about, Betty?" a man's voice asked angrily. "We've got a big problem, and we need to stay here. The cops may be looking for us at our place."

"You're always making jokes," Betty said nervously as she struggled to push the door closed.

Flower jumped up.

"Listen, Betty, Woodrow and I were there for you when

you and Jed needed to disappear," another man's voice snapped, his tone low but fiercely angry. "Where is he now? Out in the back duplicating keys of the poor dopes staying here so he can break into their homes?"

A second later Betty stumbled back as the door was shoved open and two men burst into the room. I've got to get out of here, Flower thought, as the intruders caught sight of her, their expressions shocked. Betty's head spun toward her, the look on her once-kindly face now terrifying. Flower turned and started to run out of the kitchen. Before she could reach the door, a heavy arm snapped around her waist, a firm hand covered her mouth, and she felt herself being swung around.

"Now what?" Betty asked Woodrow and Edmund bitterly, as she maintained a smothering grip over Flower's mouth.

16

The Reillys watched as Duncan was wheeled out of the room. The lottery winners had joined them in the hallway.

"Good luck, Duncan," Marion said, briefly touching his hand. "You have to be up and around by Monday so you can ride with us to Lottery Headquarters and officially turn in the ticket. Charley's driving us—we're going to make a day of it."

"Thanks, Marion," Duncan replied wanly.

Tommy and Ralph patted him on the shoulder but said nothing.

They're still not sure about him, Glenda thought. I can only imagine what they'd think if they knew I had the other ticket in my pocket. I can't believe I have both tickets on me right now.

The hotel manager came over to the group. "We're setting up a table in one of our private dining rooms. Please be our guests for a luncheon—relax and enjoy each other."

"That sounds delightful," Marion said. "Right now we'd be on our lunch break at Conklin's!" She turned to Nora. "You will join us, won't you?"

"We'd love to," Nora answered as she and Marion fell in step together.

Glenda tapped Regan's arm as the group moved down the hallway. "I need to speak to you for a moment. It's terribly important."

Regan nodded and stopped. Jack was walking ahead with Mayor Steve and Luke. Muffy had accompanied the stretcher out to the ambulance with the camera crew following. "Of course. What's wrong?"

Glenda looked around to be sure there was no one in earshot. "Duncan's in trouble . . ."

Regan listened as Glenda filled her in.

". . . so Duncan took a big risk by stealing their ticket. But he really wants them to be punished for what they've done to so many people. We need to get those two crooks behind bars as soon as possible."

"We need evidence of their scam before they can be arrested," Regan explained. "Do you know if they gave Duncan any paperwork when he made that investment?"

"I don't know. But I told him I'd go to his house to get his cell phone. This morning I noticed his notes from the financial course were on the dining room table."

"That's a start," Regan said. "I'll get Jack and the three of us will go over to Duncan's right away."

"I'm so lucky you're here, Regan. Thank you. But what excuse can we give for leaving now? We're supposed to stay for lunch."

"You want to deliver Duncan his cell phone. He hasn't been able to talk to his fiancée yet, and he's upset. He might be in the hospital for hours so he asked you to pick up his ring before the jeweler closes." Regan paused. "I hate to ask you this, Glenda, but did you know your ex was outside talking to the press?"

"It doesn't surprise me," Glenda said stoically.

Regan smiled. "It's actually good for us. He looked pretty upset. That gives Jack and me the perfect excuse for going with you. You shouldn't be alone."

Glenda smiled. "Great! If Harvey knew he was doing me a favor by mouthing off to reporters, he'd drop dead."

They walked into the dining room where their group was about to take seats at the table. Regan spoke quietly to Jack while Glenda talked to the others. Tommy's parents had joined the group and so had Ralph's wife, Judy.

"I wish you didn't have to leave!" Marion said. "But I understand about poor Duncan. Glenda, what about us all going to the bank to put our ticket in a safe deposit box for the weekend?"

"You guys go ahead and do that this afternoon. I trust you" she said, giving a look to Ralph and Tommy.

"Trust us?" Ralph joked. "Glenda, tell us. What happened to Duncan last night? How did he get hurt?"

"He fell," Glenda answered. "As you can imagine, he was pretty upset when he heard the winning numbers and he hadn't played. His car wouldn't start, he went for a walk and slipped. He never dreamt we'd be generous enough to share the money with him. I'm sure you've heard about the poor guy who always played the lottery with his friends at work. One day he was out sick and wasn't there to throw in his share. They won and didn't cut him in."

"That's so mean!" Marion exclaimed, then added, "Where was Duncan going? Does his girlfriend live in town?"

"No, she lives in California."

"I can't *wait* to meet her," Marion said. "Maybe she lives near my grandson. What's her name?"

"Flower."

"What?" Marion asked, squinting.

"Flower."

"How does she spell it?" Luke murmured to Nora.

"I see," Marion said. "I hope she likes the ring."

"I'm sure she will. Regan and Jack Reilly are nice enough to offer to come with me. They saw Harvey outside, looking pretty angry." She then joked, "Marion, you said we might need bodyguards. I've got two of them."

Two waiters came in the room, pads in hand, ready to take orders.

"Get going then," Marion chirped. "But don't forget to leave us that ticket."

Which one, Glenda thought wryly, as the whole room

watched her retrieve their winning ticket from her wallet and hand it over to Ralph. She could almost feel Duncan's ticket in her right pocket. I'm going to have a heart attack, she thought.

Regan could tell that her mother's antenna was up. She knows there's something else going on. It's going to kill her, but she'll have to wait until later to find out.

"I'll pull the car up while you two wait inside," Jack offered as he, Regan, and Glenda walked out of the dining room toward the reception area. "Glenda, if your ex is still hanging around, hopefully we can avoid him."

"Regan! Jack! There you are!" Alvirah's voice carried across the lobby. She and Willy were checking in at the front desk.

"Hi, Alvirah!" Regan called, waving her hand. "You got here fast!"

"Is that Alvirah Meehan?" Glenda whispered to Regan.

"Yes," Regan said. "My poor mother was wondering why we were leaving before lunch and was dying to find out. Trying to get out of here without Alvirah realizing that something's up will be a real challenge. She'll definitely want to come with us."

Glenda paused. "I've read about the cases she's solved. And she has always been so caring about her fellow lottery winners who've fallen into trouble. I trust her, and I'm sure Duncan would. If she wants to join us, let's bring her along."

"Believe me," Regan said. "I know Alvirah. She'll want to."

17

Sam Conklin rushed into his small office in the back of the store and slammed the door behind him. At that precise moment the phone rang. It was Richard, his only son, whom he had hoped would go into the family business. Instead, the smell of the greasepaint and the roar of the crowd had been an irresistible draw, and at forty-two, Richard was an established actor. He had just finished a nine-month run of a play in Boston and would soon be heading back to his apartment in New York.

"Dad, what's going on up there? It's all over the news about the lottery winners from Conklin's. They must have gotten the story wrong that you didn't give bonuses. That can't be true. You've always given bonuses and were always more than generous."

Sam sank into a chair and leaned his head on his hand. "It's true," he admitted miserably. "Rhoda talked me into it."

"Why doesn't that surprise me?" Richard asked quietly. "I can't stand that woman."

"Neither can I," Sam admitted.

"That's music to my ears," Richard said, his voice suddenly cheerful. "She's been nothing but trouble since Day One. When you think of how sweet Mom was . . ."

"I know, I know," Sam interrupted. "This morning has been a public relations nightmare. I've worked hard in this store for more than forty years and as you just said have always been generous to my employees. I'm so ashamed that I let her talk me into giving pictures of that godforsaken wedding instead of the bonuses my workers earned. You should have seen the looks on their faces last night. I'll never forget it as long as I live. I'll never feel good about myself again . . ."

"Dad, take it easy."

"Richard, everyone's calling me for interviews. Everyone's calling me cheap. I'm ashamed to walk around the store today. My oldest customers are disgusted with me, I can tell. Not to mention that without my key people, this place is falling apart. And we're catering the Festival . . ."

"I don't have to be in New York until Monday. I'll jump in the car and ride on up. I worked often enough at the store to know what I'm doing."

"Richard, I hate to make you do that. Your play just ended and you have a few days off."

"Forget it, Dad. I'll see you in a couple of hours."

Sam was choked up. It would be so nice to see a friendly face. "Thank you, son," he said. "You don't know what this means to me."

Feeling somewhat better, Sam hung up the phone. I'll have a cup of coffee, he thought, then get back out there to face the firing squad. He walked over to the coffeepot he always kept in his office. He was reaching for his mug when the door burst open. Without turning, he knew who it was. Everyone else in the store would have knocked before coming in. Everyone but his bride of six months. Sam braced himself.

"I just fired that kid in produce!" Rhoda snapped. "He's useless!"

Sam spun around. "You fired him! When we need all the help we can get, you fired him! Ten to one he's outside giving an interview right now."

"He was rude to me when I tried to show him how to stack tomatoes. Then he actually said it was no wonder everyone calls me The Skunk!"

Sam blinked. "The Skunk?"

"*The Skunk.* Behind my back, that's what they call me."

That's pretty good Sam thought as he stared at the white stripe in Rhoda's jet black hair. He was amused and embarrassed at the same time. The folks around here have her number, and they must think I'm an idiot for marrying her. "You had no right to fire that boy," he said angrily. "Zach tries hard and he's a good kid. I'm going to go out and try and catch him."

"And go against my wishes?" Rhoda asked, appalled. "With all I'm doing to keep this place going today?"

Sam pointed his finger at her. "I can tell you one thing right now. I wouldn't have even *needed* your help around here if you hadn't tortured me into giving those stupid pictures to my five key workers. We were like family until you came along. Millionaires or not, they would have been here first thing this morning to help us get through the Festival, and we would have had ourselves a blast!"

"How *dare* you?" Rhoda asked, her eyes blazing.

"How dare *you?*"

"I'm packing my bags and heading to Boston for the weekend. Thank God my apartment hasn't sold yet." She rushed past him, hurrying back into the store. "Enjoy the Festival!" she screamed over her shoulder.

"I will now!" he called after her, as customers stopped pushing their carts to hear the exchange. "And do me a favor," he added, unable to contain himself, "take your la-dee-dah apartment off the market!"

As one, the customers burst into applause.

18

That's where he was all night! On the basement floor, listening to crooks make fun of him and all the other people they swindled!" Alvirah exclaimed, as she, Regan, Jack, and Glenda drove to Duncan's house.

"Yes!" Glenda answered.

"I'm sure glad he got his hands on their ticket. You mean to say that he gave it to you to hold?"

"He didn't know what else to do. I think he's in shock."

"Must be," Alvirah murmured. "Can I see it?"

"Sure. I'm scared to death to be carrying this ticket. I keep feeling in my pocket to make sure it's still there." Glenda pulled it out. "Here it is."

Reverently, Alvirah took the ticket, studied it, shook her head, and leaned forward. "Have a look for yourself, Regan. I doubt if you'll hold anything worth that much again."

Jack had been listening intently. "You know, Glenda," he began, "Duncan may not want those crooks to get the money. But we're going to have to hand the ticket over to the police. I can assure you that if those guys have been swindling people, there won't be any payment to them until all their victims have been compensated."

"Duncan would hate to see them collect on this ticket, but what he's most concerned about is having them locked up." Glenda paused. "Could Duncan be in trouble for taking the ticket?" she asked anxiously. "Would it be considered stolen property?"

"That's the last thing I'd worry about. I doubt those two will be in any position to press charges against him."

The farther they drove out of town, the more rural the landscape became. The houses were farther apart, and it seemed as though all of them had Christmas decorations. One farmhouse had a real sleigh with a life-sized Santa on the roof.

"We're getting close," Glenda noted. "It's this next street up here on the right. The road curves a little, and Duncan's house is the last one at the end of the lane."

A moment later, she murmured, "Oh, look, there's someone parked in front."

As they approached, a van with the BUZ logo began to move and drove past them.

"They're doing the 'before' shots for the lifestyles of the rich and famous," Alvirah commented.

"Wait till they see *my* house," Glenda said as Jack pulled into Duncan's driveway. "I'll get the keys out of Duncan's ignition. I put them back this morning. I didn't know what else to do with them."

When they entered the house, they heard the phone ringing. "I may as well answer it," Glenda said and hurried to pick it up. "Hello."

"Hello," a woman chirped. "Is Mr. Duncan Graham there?"

"No, he's not. Would you like to leave a message?"

"Yes indeed. We're raising money for People Against Government in Any Way, Shape, or Form. We'd like to schedule a meeting with him to get his input into . . ."

Glenda dropped the phone back into the cradle. "A crazy who wants to relieve Duncan of his money before he even collects it," she said.

"Brace yourself," Alvirah advised. "You're all going to be hearing from a lot of them. People say they come out of the woodwork. I say they come from Mars."

Glenda pointed to the stacks of papers on the small dining room table. "Regan, those are the notes on the financial course I told you about."

"Let's take a quick look and see if there's any paperwork on the oil well investment."

They divided the pages and flipped through them.

"They sound like geniuses," Alvirah said, holding up one page. "Turn off the lights when you leave a room. Decide what you want before you open the refrigerator door. Holding it open wastes money." She put the paper down. "You mean to tell me Duncan *paid* for this kind of advice?"

"I never know what I want to eat until I've looked inside the refrigerator to see what appeals to me," Jack said.

"I don't think there's anything here about an oil well," Alvirah grumbled. "Unless it was written in disappearing ink."

"There's nothing here," Regan confirmed. "But they must have given him some kind of receipt for his five thousand dollars."

"Unless we find some proof of a scam, our hands are tied," Jack said.

"I don't think Duncan would mind if I took a quick look around," Glenda said. "He asked me to help him with this."

"I know you think I'm kidding, but check under his mattress," Alvirah suggested.

"You *are* kidding," Glenda said. "Or are you?"

"I'm not. I had five different cleaning jobs every week. At two of them people kept money and important papers under the mattress. One of the others thought it was a good hiding spot for her diary. I'm proud to say I never read a word of it." Alvirah paused. "Not that I wasn't tempted. That lady was something else."

Glenda headed for the bedroom. A moment later, her voice triumphant, she called, "Alvirah! I can't believe it! You were right!" She came rushing back into the living room, opening a legal-sized envelope with the logo of a gushing oil well, and handed it to Jack.

"Oh, boy," Jack muttered. "Those guys are shameless. Let's see what's inside." He extricated a document from the envelope, holding it carefully by the edge. "This may be valuable for fingerprints," he explained as the others read it with him.

"They sure tried to make this look official, but I can tell you right now that seal is a joke." Alvirah sighed. "Some of the people in my support groups who were scammed had documents that looked just like this one."

"I'll call my office and have them run a check on this company," Jack said. "As soon as they verify it's not legit, we'll contact the district attorney's office. They'll obtain warrants to arrest those crooks."

"Poor Duncan," Glenda said. "He worked hard for every penny he turned over to those jerks, and all he ends up with is this Mickey Mouse certificate. It's so sad."

"Twelve million bucks should cheer him up, Glenda," Jack said with a half smile as he reached for his cell phone.

Regan turned to Glenda. "Duncan shouldn't stay here tonight. For that matter, you shouldn't be alone in your house either."

"With Harvey running around town, I don't want to be," Glenda said emphatically. "I'll pack a bag for Duncan. We'd both be better off staying at the Inn with all of you."

"Good idea. Now, where did he say to look for his cell phone?"

"It's probably somewhere around the easy chair."

"I'll look." Alvirah walked over to the chair. "Not on the seat, not on the armrest . . . here it is, it had started to slip down the side . . ." She had no sooner picked up the phone than it began to ring. She looked at the caller ID. "It says 'Mom and Dad.' Isn't that sweet?"

"Let me have it," Glenda said. "Duncan left a message for his parents when he was waiting for the ambulance." She raised the phone to her ear. "Hello, this is Duncan's friend Glenda," she began then waited. "He's fine, Mrs. Graham, don't worry. Yes, he *has* won twelve million dollars. . . . you slept late? . . . uh huh. . . . I don't think you need to charter a plane to be with him. . . . He's at the hospital getting his leg checked out. . . . I'm bringing his cell phone to him, and I'll make sure he calls you. Bye."

She slipped the phone in her purse. "Duncan's parents are what you call night owls. They just woke up. The first they heard of all this was the message Duncan left for them."

"They must have clear consciences," Alvirah said.

"That's for sure," Regan agreed. "But they were spared a lot of worry."

While Glenda was packing for Duncan, Alvirah and Regan studied the framed pictures on the mantel. One of them was of a young woman with shoulder-length light brown hair. "This must be Flower," Regan said. "If Duncan's going to stay at the Inn, I bet he'd be glad to have her photo with him."

Fifteen minutes later they were driving down a crowded Main Street, heading toward the hospital.

"It's only a few hours until the Festival begins," Glenda said. "What's that up ahead? Oh, I don't believe it!"

A reporter, with a cameraman behind him, was talking to a crowd gathered in front of the window of Pettie's jewelry store. "They must all be gawking at Duncan's ring. Let's stop for a minute," Glenda said heatedly. "Regan, that was a good idea you had for me to tell the others I was picking up the ring as an excuse for leaving the luncheon. And that's just what I'm going to do. Jack, there's a parking spot over there. Could you grab it?"

"Sure."

"Do you think the jeweler will let you have the ring?" Regan asked. "He's getting a lot of publicity, which is exactly what he wants."

"He'd better."

"We'll go in with you," Jack volunteered. "We'll make sure he hands it over." He parked the car, and they all got out.

As they passed the reporter, they heard him ask, "I want all of you who think Duncan Graham should spring for a better ring for his girlfriend to raise your hands."

Glenda shot the reporter a look of contempt as she, Jack, and Regan hurried into the jewelry store. Before following them, Alvirah glanced into the display window, then stopped dead in her tracks. With a murmured apology, she maneuvered her way through the crowd to get a better look. Her eyes widened as she stared at the ring with its center diamond surrounded by petal-like semiprecious stones. Then she opened the top buttons of her coat, reached inside, and flicked on the hidden microphone of the sunburst pin that she had fastened to her lapel that morning. Whenever she was on a case and interviewing a person of interest, she always backed up her memory with recorded conversations.

As Alvirah entered the store, the jeweler was reaching into the display window for the ring, a disgruntled look on his face. He grew even more disgruntled as the crowd roared in protest.

"He's not happy, but he agreed to let us have the ring," Regan told Alvirah.

"What's more important is where he got it," Alvirah whispered. "Unless I've lost my mind, which I haven't, this ring was missing after Kitty Whelan, the best friend of Mrs. O'Keefe, my Friday cleaning job, was found dead on the floor."

19

Betty, what are you doing?" Edmund asked desperately. "Are you crazy?"

"Not too crazy to know that this girl has ears," she said angrily as she easily held a struggling Flower in her powerful arms. She looked down. "Flower, meet your boyfriend's financial advisers. They're real geniuses."

"What are you talking about?" Woodrow asked.

"Her boyfriend won the lottery last night."

"Which one is her boyfriend?"

"Duncan."

"Duncan!" both men cried at once.

"Yes. Lucky for him he didn't listen to your advice."

"He *did* follow our advice," Edmund said. "He didn't play, but his friends are cutting him in."

"We didn't follow our own advice," Woodrow said. "We bought the other winning ticket, but we think Duncan stole it from us."

"What? How did you manage that?" Betty asked derisively.

Sputtering, Edmund began to explain. "Someone was in our house last night. We heard a sound like something falling on the basement stairs, and like fools we didn't investigate. But whoever was down there would have heard us talking and knew we hid our ticket in the freezer. We're pretty sure it was Duncan."

"Why?"

"We heard on the radio that he was missing all night, then he showed up an hour ago, hobbling as though he took a spill somewhere." Edmund paused then added, "And we did use the numbers he told us he was planning to play."

Terrified as she was, Flower felt a wave of pure joy go through her. She was sure Duncan hadn't abandoned her after all. How could I ever have lost faith in my Duncan Donuts? she wondered.

"This makes it all easy," Woodrow said. "Duncan gives us our ticket, we give him back his girlfriend."

"He dumped her," Betty hissed. "He hasn't called her since he won. He might not be so willing . . ."

Flower, her faith restored in Duncan, tried to bite Betty's hand.

"Down, girl," Betty said, "or I'll turn you back into a pile of mush." She looked at the cousins. "If you do get that ticket, you're going to split the money four ways with me and Jed."

"That's a little excessive, Betty," Edmund moaned.

"Excessive? Jed and I can't stay here now and neither can

we stand around here with her all day," she said impatiently. "We've got a full house. Some of the others will be back for tea."

"I'm sure they will," Woodrow said sarcastically. "Your scones are delicious."

Betty looked as if she wanted to kill him. "Grab one of those dish towels. There's twine over there in the drawer by the stove . . ."

What are they going to do to me? Flower wondered. Especially Betty. She's evil. Flower felt Betty's hand loosen its grip, but before she could even try to scream, Woodrow stuffed a dish towel in her mouth and tied it tightly. Edmund twisted twine around her feet. Betty yanked her arms behind her and held them for Edmund to secure.

"Let's bring her back to the shed," Betty ordered. "Woodrow, grab the tablecloth in that chest by the hearth. We'll cover her with it."

Woodrow did as he was told. "I'll carry her," he offered, the cloth in his hand.

"No, you've done enough damage by showing up here today. You'll probably drop her on her head." Betty threw Flower over her shoulder with one quick motion and waited impatiently as Woodrow fumbled to shake open the cloth and wrap it around their captive. "Jed's going to have a fit when he sees this," Betty grumbled. "Come on."

Flower's instinct was to kick, but she knew it was useless. She felt a blast of cold air as she was rushed from the house.

Edmund ran ahead and opened the door to the shed. Once inside, Betty dropped Flower down on an old lawn chair and roughly pulled off the tablecloth. Her eyes adjusting to the light, Flower took in the gloomy surroundings. A work bench was cluttered with rusty paint cans; shovels and rakes hung haphazardly from the walls; a snow blower with a flat tire was just inches from her legs. She gasped as a section of the back wall slid open and Jed, the kindly proprietor who had carried her bags, appeared. Behind him, Flower could see a large computer screen and an orderly work space with high-tech equipment.

Looking furious, Jed barked, "I knew it would be trouble for us when you two came to town!"

"This is thanks to your wife's rudeness," Edmund shouted, his voice agitated and trembling. "If she had just been polite and let us in . . ."

"Jed, get out of the way," Betty ordered. "We've got to keep her hidden in your office."

"What?" Jed protested. "Betty, we don't want her to see what's in there . . ."

"It doesn't matter now," Betty said. "We'll be on the run as long as this little Flower keeps blooming."

20

"**Y**ou broke the tibia bone near the ankle." Dr. Rusch, an older man with salt-and-pepper hair and rimless glasses, held up the X-rays as he spoke. "How did you manage that?"

"I fell down a flight of stairs," Duncan replied.

"Lucky you didn't do further damage by hobbling on that leg." He patted Duncan's arm. "You're going to be in a plaster cast for about six weeks." He smiled. "But I gather you don't have to worry about missing work."

"I guess not," Duncan said weakly.

"Does it feel pretty sore now?"

"Kind of," Duncan admitted.

"I'm going to give you something to dull the pain. It might make you a little drowsy."

"Doctor, I don't have my cell phone. I hate to ask, but would you mind lending me yours? I need to talk to my girlfriend for a minute."

This is a first, Rusch thought with amusement. No patient has ever asked to borrow my phone. I guess having boatloads of money does change one's mindset. "Duncan, I'm afraid you're not allowed to use a cell phone in here. How's this? Give me the number. I'll have the receptionist call and give her your message."

Trying not to sound too disappointed, Duncan said, "If she could just tell my girlfriend I'll call later. Thank you."

Ten minutes later the doctor came back to the cubicle in the emergency room . "She must be a popular lady. Her mailbox is full."

There's something wrong, Duncan thought. I *know* there's something wrong.

A nurse came up to his bedside. She handed him a tablet and a glass of water. "This will make you feel better. It's going to be a little while before we can take you in for the cast. We have a couple of skiers ahead of you. Why don't you just try and take a nap?"

Duncan swallowed the pill, leaned back, and closed his eyes. A sense of foreboding drove away his ability to relax and drift into sleep. Flower's voice kept running through his head. "I'm scared, Duncan," she was whispering. "Help me. I'm scared."

21

Horace Pettie threw the WE MISS YOU sign in the back of the store, then plopped the ring down on a velvet pad on the counter. "I held this for Duncan, on a fifty-dollar deposit, for six months," he said sourly. "I don't know any other jeweler who'd have done that. Displaying the ring in the window these last few hours has helped sell my Festival of Joy charms. Now Duncan gets all upset because people get a look at his ring? Too bad about him."

"That's right," Luella agreed quickly, as she tied a red bow on a gift-wrapped package and handed it to the only other customer now in the store. "I've worked for Mr. Pettie for twenty years. He's never been anything but the soul of kindness to the people of Branscombe. It just goes to show, no good deed goes unpunished. Isn't that right Mrs. Graney?"

The spry septuagenarian nodded. "Mmmm hmmmm. It seems to me that Duncan Graham doesn't have to care about anybody now that he has twelve million dollars. Merry Christmas everyone," she trilled as she left the store.

Alvirah watched the door close behind her. "Now we can talk. Excuse me, sir, but I need to know where you got that ring."

Horace Pettie looked startled. "Why are you asking?"

"Because it was probably stolen," Alvirah said, checking again to be sure the microphone in her sunburst pin was on.

Pettie's lips tightened. "If you're implying I obtained this ring in some underhanded way, you're mighty wrong, and I'd appreciate you leaving my store this minute."

"I'm not accusing you of anything, and I certainly don't mean to upset you," Alvirah replied hastily. "But I can tell you that ring disappeared from the home of a woman who died under suspicious circumstances eight years ago in New York City."

"What?" Glenda asked, her eyes widening.

Jack pointed to it. "This ring, Alvirah?"

Alvirah nodded. "That ring. I'm sure of it."

The bracelets on Luella's right arm jangled as she slapped her hand on the counter. "How can you be so sure it's the same ring?" she asked angrily.

"The lady who owned it, Kitty Whelan, loved to garden. Her husband had the ring made for her for their fiftieth anniversary with the diamond in the center and the petals the color of her favorite flowers." Alvirah pointed. "Look— white for lilies, red for roses, yellow for daffodils, and purple for pansies. Kitty just *loved* that ring. After her husband died she wore it every day. I worked for a woman named Bridget O'Keefe who was a good friend of Kitty's. I was only there on Fridays, but before Kitty had a heart attack, she often dropped by. I saw this ring many times. Kitty always boasted that it was one of a kind, made only for her. But when Kitty's nephew found her dead at the foot of her staircase, she didn't have the ring on. He never found it when he cleared out the house."

"Maybe she had a special hiding place for the ring when she wasn't wearing it," Luella said. "You know how many times we've heard about jewelry that has turned up in the most unlikely places? After years and years?"

"You're right about that," Alvirah agreed. "But there's more to this story. Kitty's nephew discovered that her savings account had been almost cleaned out, most likely by a companion who had worked for Kitty the last few months before she died. This of course raised the question if the fall down the stairs that killed her was accidental. But by this time the companion had disappeared into thin air, never to be seen again."

"Those stories disgust me." Luella sighed. "A lady in my sister's town was robbed blind by a so-called"—she paused and held up her fingers, making invisible quotation marks midair—" 'helper.' Turns out the 'helper' was doing all the food shopping for her own family and friends and charging it to the old lady's credit card. Thousands of dollars spent on food, and the woman weighed ninety pounds! Why the accountant didn't call it to somebody's attention is beyond me. It took a suspicious cashier who knew the dear old soul had not only gone into the hospital, but was also allergic to seafood, to raise a red flag. When the 'helper' tried to charge fifteen lobsters and three cases of beer, the cashier reported it to his boss. Turns out it was the 'helper's' boyfriend's birthday. She was throwing a party for him and his thuggish friends." Luella dropped her hands. "It was a disgrace."

I just wasted precious tape on that story, Alvirah thought. "So you understand what I'm talking about?"

"*I* do," Pettie said. Obviously relieved he was not being accused of wrongdoing, he was enjoying the drama surrounding Duncan's ring. "I understand completely. As a matter of fact, I've got a story about my wife's cousin who . . ." The door opened, and new customers walked in. Pettie quickly cut himself off. "But I won't bore you with that now," he said hurriedly. "To answer your question, this ring was found on the street by a man who's lived in Branscombe all his life. His name is Rufus Blackstone. He left it with me on consignment, and, let me tell you, he wasn't as nice as I was about letting Duncan put it on hold for so long. He's a crusty old codger. I'll go in the back and look up his number for you. Glenda, you said you're paying for this on your credit card?"

"Let me pay for it," Alvirah said. "The ring should go

back to Kitty's nephew. And Kitty had said she wanted Mrs. O'Keefe to have it if she died first. She was adamant about that."

"Poor Duncan," Glenda said. "I'm sure he wouldn't want it now, but he told me he thought this ring would be perfect for his girlfriend because her name is Flower."

"If he wants, I can make him a copy with real stones," Pettie volunteered, his face brightening. "It will be *gorgeous*!"

"We'll pass that on to him," Glenda said wryly.

Pettie hurried away with Alvirah's credit card. Luella was just beginning her sales pitch to three giggling young girls wearing Branscombe High School cheerleader jackets. "You all should have one of these charms. You'll love it! And what better way to always remember the Festival of Joy?"

Jack turned to Regan and mumbled. "I don't think we'll need a charm to remember this Festival."

"I don't think so," Regan agreed. "Alvirah, did you ever meet Kitty's companion?"

"Just once for a minute. She and Kitty were getting out of a cab when I was leaving. I wish I'd taken a better look at her, but I was carrying out two big bags of garbage. Mrs. O'Keefe seemed to manufacture pounds of junk on a weekly basis."

Pettie reappeared with a small gift bag, an index card, and a receipt for Alvirah. "Could I get your John Hancock on this, Mrs. Meehan?" he asked.

"Sure."

"And here's Rufus Blackstone's number. I just rang him up, but he's not home and he doesn't have an answering machine. I thought it would be a good idea to let him know that you'd be calling and also to give him the good news that he can pick up a check from me. If I get a chance, I'll try him again."

"Thanks," Alvirah said. "We'll catch up with him later. I just have to find out where this ring has been for the last eight years."

"Wait till Duncan hears this," Glenda said as they started out the door.

"Don't forget to tell him I can make up a beautiful ring for him in no time flat!" Pettie called after them.

The crowd outside the window had dispersed.

22

After making sure that Flower was securely tied, gagged, and immobilized, Betty, Jed, Woodrow, and Edmund left Jed's secret office and went back into the house.

Woodrow walked to the stove where the freshly baked cake was sitting on the rack. He broke a piece off and crammed it in his mouth. "Not bad," he pronounced.

Betty grabbed the baking pan. "Keep your mitts off my cake!" she snapped.

"The only thing I've had to eat today was a couple of pieces of candy," Woodrow complained. "We were on our way to a nice lunch in Boston when we found out we were victims of a terrible crime."

"Jed, fix them something to eat," Betty ordered. "Then you two have to stay out of sight. People are going to be coming here soon for tea. I'll get Flower's gear out of her room now."

"Out of sight? Where should we go?" Edmund asked. "Don't say the shed. It's cold."

"There's only one place you *can* go. The basement. I can't have you sitting here if somebody comes through that swinging door."

"The basement?" Woodrow complained. "You've got to be kidding."

"You're not exactly honored guests," Betty snapped. "I'll be right back."

At the reception desk she reached in the drawer for Flower's credit card receipt and tore it into shreds. Thank God Jed hadn't validated the card yet, she thought. Then a terrible thought occurred to Betty. Had Flower spoken to anyone since she checked in?

Betty hurried upstairs to Flower's room. A cell phone was on the bed. Betty turned it on, held her breath, and pressed "dialed calls." The last call Flower had made was early this morning. Betty exhaled slowly then pressed "received calls." There hadn't been any today, which meant that Flower hadn't answered the phone after she checked in. Betty could see there were messages but would need Flower's passcode to listen to them. If I want it, she'll give it to me, Betty thought darkly, as she turned off the phone and dropped it in the pocket of her apron.

It was clear that Flower hadn't gotten under the bed covers. Betty smoothed the spread and fluffed up the pillows. In the bathroom, she tossed Flower's toiletries into her knapsack, wiped out the sink with a towel, and walked back into the bedroom. She took a quick look around for anything she might have missed, then grabbed Flower's coat from the chair.

In the hallway, she tossed the towel down the laundry chute and momentarily stuffed Flower's things in the linen closet. To be certain that no one had returned while they were in the shed, Betty knocked on, then opened the doors of the other five guest rooms with the master key. Satisfied that the second floor was empty, she retrieved the knapsack and coat, hurried down the stairs, and locked the front door. Now anyone who shows up will be forced to ring the bell, she thought. I can't take a chance on someone else having big ears like Flower.

In the kitchen, Edmund and Woodrow were slurping vegetable soup. Flower's nearly full bowl was still on the table. I should have told her we don't serve lunch, Betty thought angrily. This is what I get for being too nice.

She sat down at the seat Flower had never excused herself from, threw Flower's coat on a chair, and started rummaging through her knapsack. "Nothing," she said dismissively. Then, from a zippered compartment, she fished out Flower's wallet. When she opened it, the first thing she saw was a picture of Flower and Duncan, their heads close together, smiling blissfully. She held it up. "Get a load of this."

"Romeo and Juliet," Woodrow grunted as he scraped the bottom of the soup bowl with his spoon.

"What a pair. They both ended up dead," Edmund commented.

"We all know how it ended, Edmund," Woodrow said impatiently. "You always like to act as though you're smarter than me."

"No need for acting," Edmund shot back. "You're the one who wanted to leave the ticket in the freezer. At least I knew that was a stupid idea. If we had taken the ticket, we'd be having a big juicy steak in Boston right now."

"Stop it!" Jed growled savagely. "There's no way this is going to end well for me and Betty! We want out!"

There was a moment of silence in the kitchen as the impact of what he was saying sank in on the Winthrop cousins.

"I like our life here in Branscombe," Jed continued heatedly. "I don't want to leave." He turned to Betty. "Do you?"

"Not really." Betty agreed. "Traveling is very stressful these days, never mind being on the run. Jed hasn't been feeling that well. He likes to stay home at night watching television. We've turned into homebodies. And it's not so bad. Whatever it takes, no more running."

Jed nodded. "If we get involved with kidnapping, and we hold that little girl for ransom, there's no way we can stay here. Betty and I like Branscombe, and we like New Hampshire. We like the snow, and Betty has turned into a good little baker, as you may have noticed."

"Listen to them," Woodrow said to Edmund. "You'd think they were Ma and Pa Kettle." He turned to Jed. "What about the fact that you're cheating people with your Internet schemes and stealing from your guests' homes months after their wonderful stay at The Hideaway?"

"That's just to keep me busy! It might not be right, but it's small potatoes compared to kidnapping charges. And even if you did get your lottery ticket back in exchange for that girl, there's no guarantee you'll end up with any money. The day someone tries to collect on that ticket, the lottery office will be swarming with Feds. And Lord knows we can't trust you two to pay me and Betty our share if you somehow *did* collect. Why, you didn't even call us to give us the good news that you'd won, now did you?"

"We were going to . . ." Woodrow said.

"Honestly, we were," Edmund said. "We were just so excited . . ."

"Oh, sure. Let me tell you something. If we let that girl go, ten minutes later every cop in New Hampshire will be hunting us down."

"What are you suggesting?"

"I'm suggesting that if you want to get your ticket back from Duncan, don't say one word to him about the girl. Threaten him about his own safety if you have to. He's getting that other lottery money. Maybe he'll give you back your ticket. But I'm warning you, don't make any deals to exchange Flower for the ticket." Jed glared coldly at the cousins.

"Then what do we do with her?" Edmund asked. "We can't just leave her back there."

"Of course we can't! You think *we* want her around?" Jed exclaimed. "There's only one solution." He lowered his voice. "When it gets dark, we'll put her in the trunk of your car and drive up to the lake at Devil's Pass. We'll weight her down with a block of cement. That lake is big and cold and deep. She'll never be seen again."

Edmund and Woodrow stared at him in shock. "Kidnapping offends you, but murder doesn't?" Edmund asked, his voice barely audible.

Jed shrugged.

"I see," Edmund mumbled weakly.

"Going to prison again is what offends me," Jed said vehemently. "There's a lot better chance we'll get caught if we hold her for ransom. This way she'll disappear without a trace."

"Let me try and trade Flower for the lottery ticket," Woodrow begged. "We promise we'll pay you as soon as we get the money. Just think of all the nice places in the world you can visit . . ."

"We've made our choice," Betty said with finality. "No more running."

Jed looked out the window. "At 5:00 it'll be dark and the whole town will be gathering at that candlelight ceremony. We'll make our move then and get it over with. After that,

Betty and I would appreciate it if you two made yourself scarce. We don't want any more trouble."

"Make ourselves scarce?" Edmund gasped. "We have no place to go and we can't leave Branscombe without that ticket. Your basement actually sounds very nice. Can't we stay there just for tonight?"

23

The celebratory luncheon at the Branscombe Inn was winding up.

Tommy's parents were sitting on either side of him, their attitude fiercely protective, as if a wanton woman might appear at any moment out of nowhere and ensnare their newly wealthy son. "I know Tommy would like to meet the right girl, but now it's going to be even harder," his mother, Ruth, said. "She's going to have to pass the test with us, and believe me, we'll put her through the ringer, right, Burt?" she asked her husband.

As usual, when his wife wanted him to agree, Burt's head nodded affirmatively. "Tommy's a good boy," he declared. "He's always deserved the best, even when he didn't have a dime in his pocket. When you see how someone as smart as Sam Conklin can get swept off his feet and rush into a disaster, it scares you. To think Sam was married all those years to Maybelle, one of the sweetest, nicest ladies who ever walked the face of the earth, and then he marries a woman nobody knows." Burt looked around the table. "What do you all call her, the Raccoon?"

"The Skunk, Dad," Tommy corrected him, increasingly embarrassed by the drift of the conversation. "Don't worry about me, I'll be fine. Believe me."

"That skunk!" Ralph's wife, Judy, cried. "Boy was she guilty of bad timing. I hear things are a mess over at Conklin's right now, and I couldn't be happier!"

"You have?" Muffy asked anxiously. "I hope there won't be any problem with the food for the Festival."

"Don't worry, Muffy," Ralph said with a wave of his hand. "We did so much advance preparation that they should be able to handle it without us."

"I hope so. This is Branscombe's first Festival of Joy, and we want to make a good impression on all our visitors plus everyone who tunes in to the special."

Marion pushed back her chair. "Festival or no Festival, we've got to get to the bank. I won't rest easy until we put that lottery ticket in a safe deposit box and see them lock the vault." She turned to Nora. "I've just loved chatting with you. Hope to see you later."

"We'll all see each other later," Muffy said enthusiastically. "Everyone in town is going to be at the opening of the Festival. I hope Duncan can be there. It's wonderful that he made it back safely from wherever he was. It would have been such a downer if he were still missing."

That's one way of putting it, Luke thought. Since Willy

came into the room without Alvirah, he knew that Nora was chomping at the bit to find out the real reason Alvirah had gone with Regan and Jack. She obviously didn't buy the story that Alvirah was dying to get a look at Branscombe. Luke didn't either.

"Oh Duncan's back, all right," Tommy's mother said to Muffy, a hint of derision in her voice. "And I notice he didn't turn down the chance to be included in the winning group."

"Mom," Tommy said hurriedly. "Remember the number 32. That was Duncan's Powerball number. We wouldn't be sitting here now if he hadn't chosen it."

"I suppose," she acquiesced. "We'll go to the bank with you, son."

Muffy turned to Nora. "I would just love to drive you around our pretty little town this afternoon. We can stop by the church bazaar where we'll get a sneak preview of all the wonderful things that will be on sale starting tonight. They'll be putting the final touches on everything, and I can show you where you'll be doing the story hour tomorrow. Does that sound good?" As was her custom, she answered herself. "I think it sounds great! I just wish Regan were here. Maybe she can catch up with us later. Willy, Luke—does a tour of our village sound agreeable to you?"

"Yes," they both answered quickly, if only to stop the flow of talk.

"Muffy," Nora said, "Luke and Willy and I haven't even

been to our rooms yet. Why don't we meet you in the lobby in twenty minutes?"

"Super!"

The Reillys and Meehans had rooms across the hall from each other on the second floor. As they were getting off the elevator, Nora said, "Willy, could you come into our room for a minute?" It wasn't a question.

Here we go, Luke thought. "Get ready for the interrogation, Willy," he warned.

Willy rolled his eyes. "Regan swore me to secrecy."

"She didn't mean us," Nora assured him.

"Yes, she did," Luke said positively.

"Oh, Luke, stop it," Nora said, laughing, "hurry up and open the door." They were barely inside the room when she spun around. "Willy, what's going on? What made Alvirah take off with them?"

Even Luke's usually unflappable demeanor registered shock and disbelief as Willy filled them in. "You mean to tell me they're riding around with a lottery ticket worth 180 million dollars that belongs to two criminals?" he asked.

"That about sums it up," Willy answered, as he reached for the door handle. "I'd better go powder my nose. I'll see you downstairs in fifteen minutes."

24

The sixtyish receptionist in the emergency room of Branscombe General Hospital looked up when the group appeared at her desk. Spotting Glenda, she smiled. "I saw you on TV. You're one of the lottery winners!"

"Yes, I am," Glenda replied. "Trust me. I still can't believe it. We're here to see my fellow winner, Duncan Graham."

"I just tried to call his girlfriend for him, but her message box was full. What a lucky girl she is! As my grandmother would say, she certainly landed in a tub of butter."

"My mother used that expression, too," Alvirah said, thinking that her mother's version was a little more colorful.

"Granny had a saying for everything," the receptionist said with a laugh. She pointed to a door. "He's right through there. The third cubicle on the right. I shouldn't let you all in at once, but we don't have any serious cases at the moment. Just a bunch of broken bones."

"Is that all?" Jack muttered as they went through the door.

They reached the third curtained cubicle. "Duncan?" Glenda called.

"I'm here," Duncan replied, his voice faint.

Glenda pulled back the curtain.

Alvirah took in the sight of the unshaven, pale, anxious-looking figure on the bed. He doesn't look like he could use any more bad news, she thought.

"Glenda!" Duncan said, trying to sit up. "Do you have my cell phone?"

"Right here." Quickly she handed it to him. "I think you've met Jack Reilly." She began to introduce him to Regan and Alvirah, but Duncan interrupted.

"I'm sorry to be rude but I'm worried about my girl-friend. Maybe she was in an accident . . ." He checked his messages. "She still hasn't called me!"

A nurse approached. "Mr. Graham, it's time to take you in for your cast. And you must turn off that phone. They're not permitted in here." She turned to the others. "This won't take long. You can wait outside."

"Glenda," Duncan said quickly. "Would you please try to reach Flower? Her number must still be on your phone. If you can't reach her, please call her work number. That must be on your phone, too—I called earlier. Ask if they know where she is." His eyes were sick with worry.

"Of course, Duncan. I'll make the calls, and we'll be waiting for you outside." She turned to the nurse. "Will he be able to leave as soon as his cast is on?"

"Absolutely. We'll fit him with crutches, and off he goes."

The four of them retreated to the waiting room. Glenda tried Flower's phone, but her mailbox was still full. She then tried Flower's work number. A woman with a soothing voice answered. "Precious Darlings Day Care."

Not all of them, I'm sure, Glenda thought. "Hello, may I speak to the manager?"

"We're fully enrolled for the next four years," the woman said proudly.

"No, I'm not calling about that," Glenda said. "It's very important I speak to someone about one of the employees. Flower . . ." Glenda realized she didn't know Flower's last name. But how many Flowers could be working there?

"Oh, yes, Flower," the woman said.

"I'm calling for her boyfriend who just broke his leg, and he really wants to reach her."

"Duncan broke his leg?"

"Yes. Do you know him?"

"No. But Flower talks about him all the time. He called earlier."

"Yes, he did. He's concerned that he hasn't been able to reach her and didn't know that she was taking today off."

"Wait a minute. It's mid-afternoon there, right?"

"Yes."

"Oh, dear."

Glenda's heart sank. "What do you mean?"

"Flower was flying in to surprise him today. She took the

red-eye to Boston last night, then was planning to take an early morning bus to where Duncan lives. She should have been there *hours* ago. And it's odd she isn't answering her phone."

"Do you by any chance know what flight she took?"

"I'm sorry, I don't."

"Okay," Glenda said. "If you hear from her, could you please call me or Duncan?" She recited their numbers.

"And if you hear anything, please call us," the woman said. "We love Flower. We were already feeling terrible that we might lose her soon."

25

The *Skunk!*" Rhoda thought as she turned the key in the lock of the three-bedroom home Sam had lived in since his marriage to Maybelle fifty years ago. She slammed the door so hard that several of Maybelle's figurines jiggled on the shelf over the foyer table. Too bad they didn't fall off, Rhoda thought. Sam had reluctantly agreed to allow her to redecorate but had insisted on keeping Maybelle's trinkets in place, which annoyed Rhoda no end. The living room of the colonial house had been done over with black leather couches and chairs, a white shag rug, and modern art that Sam complained he couldn't make head nor tail of. Paintings of mountains and lakes and flowers and animals had been relegated to the attic.

Maybelle's maple dining room furniture, with its corner cupboards and cushioned chairs, had been replaced by a glass table with massive steel legs and chairs shaped like triangles. Upstairs, Richard's boyhood room was now serving as Rhoda's office, and the former guest bedroom was filled with her exercise equipment.

Go back to my lah-dee-dah apartment, she thought, as she yanked off her coat and threw it over the bannister. I can't *wait* to pack up and get out of here! I'll fix his wagon! All I've tried to do for him, and he just takes me for granted. Through the window, she could see that the snow, which had been light and intermittent, was suddenly coming down harder. Oh no, she thought, I can't drive in this. By the time I get my things together, the roads will be slick, and I'll end up getting stuck in all that traffic going into Boston on a Friday night at holiday time. Good riddance to this burg—but not till tomorrow.

I took a shot at the country life, but it's not for me. Rhoda thought of her previous husbands, two of whom she had not mentioned to Samuel. It's not bad to be divorced twice, but *four* times suggests I can't get along with anyone and scares off potential suitors.

Samuel had seemed so easygoing, but she soon found out that he was stubborn as a mule. Getting him to agree to put his employees' bonus money in our retirement fund had been a struggle. I was only looking out for our future, she thought. Oh well, the prenup gives me $200,000 if we get divorced. I'll start off the New Year with that happy thought in mind. If I had known how much that geezer had in his savings account, I'd have insisted on more.

In the six months she'd lived in town, Rhoda had made

exactly one friend, Tishie Thornton, who never had anything nice to say about anyone and was the only human
being in town Rhoda found who couldn't stand Maybelle.
"From the time we were six years old, she was so annoyingly
sweet," Tishie confided to a delighted Rhoda. "I have a beautiful singing voice, but *she* was the one always chosen for the
solos in the school and then in the church choir. I couldn't
bear the sight of her looking so innocent, holding her song
book, singing with her eyes looking up to heaven like she
was an angel. I finally quit the choir and never went back
even after Maybelle died. I didn't want to hear all the talk
about what a saint she was."

Rhoda stood for a moment in the quiet house. I don't
want to hang around here all day, she thought. She hurried
into the kitchen and picked up the phone. Tishie answered
on the first ring.

"Rhoda, I hear you've had a rough day," Tishie said, trying not to sound pleased.

"You wouldn't believe it."

"No bonuses, huh?"

"They got paid well enough all year."

"I bet they did. And now look at them! They don't need
your bonuses. Did you hear about the ring Duncan bought
for his girlfriend?"

"I haven't heard anything. I was too busy picking apples
off the floor."

"Duncan put a deposit on some kind of flowered ring at

Pettie's, and now he's bent out of shape. Turns out Pettie put the ring in the display window next to those Festival charms Luella's told me about at least a hundred times."

"A *flower* ring?" Rhoda repeated.

"Yes. A little diamond surrounded by colored stones shaped like petals."

"Who's his girlfriend?"

"Nobody knows. Who cares?"

"Who cares is right," Rhoda said, her mind flashing to the face of the young girl who was asking for Duncan this morning. "*I* certainly don't."

"So, what's up? I know you can't be calling just to chat what with everything going on at the store."

"Sam and I broke up. We're totally *kaput*. Finished. Bye-bye."

"So soon? I knew you'd be bored to tears by him. But you should have waited to get a Christmas present."

"He already bought it for me. A gorgeous bracelet we got in Boston when we went to see that son of his in a play. Sam almost had a heart attack when he signed the credit slip. The bracelet's in the safe, nicely gift wrapped. Don't worry, it's going with me."

"I'm proud of you, Rhoda. After all, you gave him the best six months of your life."

Rhoda laughed. "It *feels* like the best six years! Tishie, the weather's not great, so I'll have to put up with another night here. I was thinking, why don't we go to The Hideaway for tea this afternoon? That woman Betty is a little annoying with her saccharine sweetness . . ."

"Just like Maybelle was," Tishie interrupted.

"Don't remind me! I don't know if Betty can sing, but she sure knows how to bake. We can sit and gossip, away from all this hullabaloo about the Festival. I'm sick of it."

"Me, too. I can be there in half an hour, okay?"

"Tishie, I'm a city girl. I can't drive so well in the snow. Would you mind picking me up?"

"Not at all."

"Thanks, Tishie. If I hadn't met you, I probably would have been out of here months ago."

"Sorry about that. See you soon."

Rhoda hung up. Even though she could care less about Samuel, she felt a little let down. A sudden thought cheered her. There's got be a holiday singles dance for seniors somewhere in Boston tomorrow night. She'd gone to six of them in the month of December last year. She hadn't met anyone special, but who knows? There might be a new crop of widowers or divorcés that sprung up in the six months she'd been buried here. Maybe my next great romance will begin while Samuel is slaving over chicken potpie at the church supper. She began to hum as she ran upstairs to check her computer.

26

By the time Duncan was wheeled into the waiting room, his right leg in a cast from his knee to his ankle, Jack had learned from his office that Flower had been on a red-eye flight of Pacific Airlines that landed in Boston, where she had bought a bus ticket to Branscombe.

"But there hasn't been any further activity on the credit card she used to buy those tickets," Detective Joe Azzolino reported to his boss. "And that stock certificate is as phony as a three dollar bill."

As they had expected, Duncan's first question when he saw them was, "Have you reached Flower?"

"Not yet," Jack said. "Let's get you out to the car."

Alvirah's heart ached for Duncan as the attendant at the emergency room exit helped him up and handed him his crutches. At least I was able to walk out of the emergency room in New York on two feet, she thought, unconsciously patting the bandage over her eye.

Outside it had begun to snow hard. They were barely in

the car when Duncan asked anxiously, "Glenda, did you call the day care center?"

"Duncan, I'm sure everything's going to be all right . . ."

"What do you mean?" he demanded, his eyes suddenly frantic with worry.

"Flower took the day off. She flew to Boston on the red-eye last night and was planning to surprise you. We know she bought a bus ticket to Branscombe that would have gotten her here at about ten o'clock this morning."

"So where is she then? Why isn't she answering her phone?"

"We don't know, Duncan," Regan said quietly. "We thought we'd go down to the bus depot and make some inquiries to see if anyone remembers seeing her there. Glenda threw a few things in a bag for you because we think you should stay at the Inn tonight. We put a picture of a young woman you had on the mantel in it. We assumed it was Flower."

"Of course it's Flower! Who else would it be? Can I have it?" Duncan asked, his voice cracking.

Glenda retrieved the picture from the bag and gave it to him.

Duncan held it in his hands, his eyes suddenly moist. "Something's happened to her," he said, his voice trembling as he stared at the picture. "I'm sure of it. Even if she wanted to wait until tonight to surprise me, she'd be answering her phone. Those Winthrop thieves were on their way to Boston.

I told them about Flower when I talked to them about my goals in life. Could they have somehow run into her?"

"Did they ever see her picture?" Jack asked.

"No."

"Then it would seem unlikely, Duncan. But we did find out that the stock certificate is fraudulent. We'll have to go to the DA's office where you can swear out a complaint. They'll get an arrest warrant for those crooks."

"I don't care about that now! If they have Flower, it's a far worse crime than selling a phony oil well. Right now I don't care about an arrest warrant. We have to find Flower!"

"Absolutely," Jack agreed.

"I say we go to Conklin's first," Alvirah suggested. "If Flower arrived this morning and didn't know you were in on the lottery, she probably would have gone to see you at work. She doesn't have a key to your house, does she?"

"She's never been there," Duncan said sadly.

"She will be soon," Glenda encouraged. "Alvirah, I think that's a good idea to go directly to Conklin's, although I'm sure Mr. Conklin won't be too happy to see me after we dumped those miserable wedding pictures on his doorstep this morning. But I don't care what he thinks." She turned back to Duncan. "You'd better stay in the car. It's slippery, and all you need is another fall. I'll talk to everyone who's working today."

They reached the end of the hospital parking lot. "Which way, Glenda?" Jack asked.

"Turn right here and keep going."

When they pulled up in front of Conklin's, Regan turned to Glenda. "I'll come in with you. Duncan, how tall is Flower and how old is she?"

"She's twenty-four years old, but she looks younger. She's petite—about 5'3"."

"Can we have the picture, please?"

Reluctantly, Duncan handed it over.

Inside the store, Glenda heard a familiar voice. "Well, look who's here," Paige, a teenaged cashier called. "Don't tell me your ticket's a fake, and you want your job back?"

Glenda and Regan hurried over to Paige's register, where a woman pushing a cart filled with overflowing grocery bags had just been checked out. "Paige, I have to talk to you for a minute."

"Sure." Paige turned off the light at her station. "What's up, Moneybags?"

Glenda introduced her to Regan, held up Flower's picture, and explained the situation. ". . . she was on her way to visit Duncan and seems to be missing."

"Sounds like they make a good pair," Paige cracked as she snapped her gum. "Wasn't he missing overnight? I can't believe you guys cut him in on the lottery. You should have asked me. I would have thrown in a buck."

"Paige, I'm not kidding. This is serious."

"Oh, sorry."

"By any chance did you see this girl in the store today?"

Paige studied the picture. "No, I didn't see her. If she was here and bought anything, she didn't come through my register."

"Okay. We'll go around and speak to the others."

Paige lowered her voice. "Glenda, you missed the fireworks this morning. The Skunk had a shouting match with Mr. Conklin, and she stormed out. He told her to take her apartment in Boston off the market. Everyone here is so psyched! For us, the Festival of Joy is off and running."

"You're *kidding*!" Glenda exclaimed.

"Trust me, I'm not."

"It almost makes me want my job back."

"Oh, sure."

"Is Mr. Conklin in his office?"

"He's back in the kitchen with his sleeves rolled up. He even put on an apron. They have to get the trays of food ready and over to the Festival."

"That makes me feel guilty," Glenda murmured.

"It wouldn't make *me* feel guilty," Paige said, turning her light back on as a shopper approached. "It's his name over the door. Besides, I've never see him in a better mood."

Glenda and Regan showed Flower's picture to the other employees. They had all been there since early morning, and no one could remember seeing her.

"Regan, let's go talk to Mr. Conklin."

Regan followed her into the large kitchen where a half

dozen workers were rushing around, assembling platters of cold cuts and salads.

"Good work everyone!" Sam was saying. "We're getting that old teamwork spirit back in this store!" He turned and spotted Glenda. For a moment they looked at each other uncertainly, then Sam smiled broadly. He opened his arms and hurried toward her. "Glenda, congratulations, I'm so happy for you," he exclaimed as he hugged her.

"I'm sorry we left those pictures outside," Glenda said contritely. "That was mean."

"Don't you worry. I'm having my own private bonfire to get rid of them. I don't know whether you've heard . . ."

"I have," Glenda said.

"I'm so ashamed of myself. I let her nag me into not giving you bonuses. Come to my office, right now. I know you don't need it, but I wrote out the checks I should have given you last night. Glenda, you've been such a wonderful employee the last eighteen years. It's almost like you're my daughter." He hugged her again. "I won't be able to look myself in the mirror until those bonus checks are cashed."

"Mr. Conklin, that's very kind of you, but we can't take the time for that now." Glenda introduced Regan, then showed him Flower's picture. "Duncan's sure that she ran into trouble. You didn't see her in here today, did you?"

Sam studied the picture. "No, I didn't. Did you ask the others?" He nodded toward the front of the store.

"Yes, no one saw her, and no one remembers anyone asking for Duncan."

Quickly Sam showed the photo to everyone in the kitchen. The response was negative. "Do you have any idea what time she might have come in?" he asked as he handed Glenda back the picture.

"Our guess is some time after ten o'clock. That's the time her bus arrived at the station."

"The Skunk was still here then," Sam said. "I wonder if she saw her."

"The Skunk?" Glenda asked.

"Don't act dumb."

"Okay, I won't."

"I could call her if you want to see if she might have talked to Duncan's girlfriend. I'd only make a call to her for something like this."

"If you don't mind. This is important."

Not surprisingly, Rhoda didn't pick up the phone. "She's probably staring at my name on her cell phone right now cussing me out," Sam said. "Why don't you take her number and try her yourself? Maybe you'll have better luck."

But Rhoda Conklin didn't pick up when Regan tried her either. Regan left a message identifying herself and explaining the reason for her call. "Please get back to me as soon as possible."

Sam tapped his finger on the counter. "One of our new kids was working in produce this morning, and Rhoda tried to fire him. He's out loading the truck now." The back door opened. "Oh, here he comes. Hey, Zach," Sam called to the rosy-cheeked young man. "Come here for a minute, would you?"

"Sure, Mr. Conklin." Zach hurried over.

"No," he said, shaking his head when he looked at Flower's picture. "I haven't seen her. But I've got to tell you, she could have been standing in front of me, and I wouldn't have noticed with the way The Skunk kept yelling at me this morning. Mr. Conklin, I'm so glad you got rid of her," he said enthusiastically. "Give me a high five."

"Okay, Zach," Sam said, as he awkwardly raised his hand. "Keep loading the truck. The mayor's wife is getting nervous. We've got a town to feed."

"Yo." Zach picked up another completed tray and headed for the back door.

Glenda sighed. "Thanks, Mr. Conklin. We'd better get going. Duncan's pretty worried right now."

"Isn't it a shame that the day he learns his coworkers are handing him twelve million dollars, he ends up heartsick about his girlfriend? I hope it all works out. Duncan's a nice fellow."

"Maybe Flower's nearby and is going to surprise us all," Glenda suggested. "Hope to see you over the weekend, Mr. Conklin."

Out in the car, they had to tell an increasingly agitated Duncan that no one had seen Flower. "But it's been pretty busy in there today," Regan said, trying to sound positive. "Let's go to the bus depot."

"Everything's going wrong!" Duncan cried. "Alvirah just told me about the ring!" He looked out the window at the heavy clouds and the falling snow. "What if Flower suddenly had amnesia and is walking around in this weather?"

At the depot, Duncan insisted on coming inside. A cleaning woman was mopping the floor near the entrance. Regan showed her Flower's picture and explained why they were looking for her. The woman had only to glance at the picture before saying, "Yes, I saw her this morning. She was in the ladies' room gussying herself up when I went in there to empty the wastebaskets. A pretty little thing."

"You're sure it was her?" Duncan asked.

The woman frowned. "Either that or she was a dead ringer."

Poor choice of words, Regan thought. "Do you remember what she was wearing?"

"Nothing unusual. Blue jeans, I think. A ski jacket. Might have been gray. She had a red knapsack that had a slogan I hadn't seen in years. It said FLOWER POWER."

"That's definitely her," Duncan moaned.

"What time did you see her?" Regan asked the woman.

"I'd say it was around 10:30—right before my break."

The lone agent at the ticket counter had also noticed Flower. "I saw her get off the bus, and then I saw her leave the depot. She definitely hasn't been back," he informed them.

Duncan looked at Glenda and Regan. "She's got to be here somewhere. If I have to ring every doorbell in this town, I will." He turned, leaned on his crutches, and moving as quickly as the bulky cast would allow, made his way back to the car.

27

The one window in Jed's office, high on the wall at the back of the shed, had a shade that was pulled most of the way down. Looking up, Flower could tell the snow was falling rapidly. When they left her, Betty had turned out all the lights, and Jed had shut off his three computers. The room was cold even though they had left one space heater on. Otherwise I'd freeze to death, Flower thought, shivering.

In the semidarkness she had already familiarized herself with her surroundings. This place is unbelievable, she thought fearfully. No one would ever guess it existed. And no one would guess, looking at folksy Jed, that he had an operation like this going on either. Keys were hanging over the workbench. A row of files was padlocked. From where she was sitting, Flower could see a screen that showed the activity recorded by eight different security cameras around the bed and breakfast.

They said they had no TV, radio, or internet access, Flower remembered bitterly as she tried to pick at the knots that bound her wrists together behind her back. But she couldn't reach the knots with her fingers. And this gag is choking me, she thought. She tried to move her jaw, but that only made it harder to breathe. Calm down, she warned herself. But how can I? Even if Duncan gives them the ticket, they'll never let me go. I can identify all of them. My only chance is that if they get the ticket and are able to cash it and escape the country, they just might leave word where I could be found. That's never going to happen.

All of this is my fault, she thought. When I didn't hear from Duncan, I didn't worry for one single minute that something might have happened to him. Is he feeling that way about me right now? Probably not, Flower decided, as tears stung her eyes. He's so good. Even if I do get out of here, I wouldn't blame him if he never wanted to see me again.

On the screen she saw a car pull into the driveway to the left of the Inn and take the first parking space. Three women got out and scurried toward the front door. People will be coming for tea, Flower thought. Some of them may have to park back here near the shed. If I can move this lawn chair and start slamming it against the wall when a car pulls into one of the spots near the shed, I might attract someone's attention.

Slowly, tentatively, she began to lift herself and the chair upward from the floor, inching toward the wall. If this thing lands on its side, I'll never be able to get up, she told herself.

And they'll know I was trying to escape. So what? Heaving her body, she was able to move slowly, painfully across the cement floor. More cars were pulling into the driveway. She reached the wall just as a car pulled up outside the shed. It sounded so close. She heard the doors open and close.

"I tell you, Tishie," a woman said, her tone strident. "Sam Conklin misses me already. I knew he would. But I'm not picking up the phone for anyone. This is time for Rhoda."

"You're darn right," Tishie said.

Instinctively, Flower tried to scream but only a whimper-like sound came from her mouth. That must be Conklin's wife, she thought frantically. I'd recognize that voice any-where. But maybe she can save me. With all her strength Flower hurled her body, tied to the lawn chair, against the wall.

"Rhoda, what was that noise?"

"I didn't hear anything. Come on, Tishie, I'm getting wet."

On the cement floor, Flower was struggling to right the chair and try again when she heard the door to Jed's office slide open.

28

These are the Festival of Joy oven mitts and potholders we'll be selling, starting this evening," Muffy explained to Nora, Luke, and Willy, as they walked through the heavily stocked sales area of the church basement. "Then we have water colors of Branscombe scenes, painted by our Red Barn artists. Red Barn is a haven for seniors who love to paint, and we have two professional artists who volunteer their time to teach a couple of times a week."

Nora examined the paintings carefully. "They're lovely," she said. "Several of them are really fine."

Luke, whose taste in art was more Georgia O'Keefe's style of painting, pretended to study the cozy scenes. Willy remembered that in the sixth grade, Sister Jane had labeled his "Keep Them Flying" poster of an airplane soaring past a flag as resembling "a flying fish wrapped in a rag." She was one tough old bird, he thought. She'd have found fault with the *Mona Lisa*. I'll buy the water color of the Branscombe Inn for Alvirah, he decided. She always likes a memento of places we've stayed.

Alvirah. Where the heck was she? And did she ever get any lunch? She'd been hungry enough on the plane to eat stale pretzels, then had dived into those chocolates he'd bought her at the convenience store. Last night, being hungry had landed her in the emergency room. Who knows what might happen if she got hungry today? He was tempted to call her cell phone, but he knew she'd get back to him when she was ready.

Luke had once suggested that Milton's line, "They also serve who only stand and wait," should be an inspiration to the two of them. Willy remembered he had asked, "Milton who?"

"Didn't the ladies do a beautiful job transforming the basement into a winter wonderland?" Muffy was asking.

"It is so pretty," Nora agreed. "I was raised in a small town in New Jersey, and it had the same feeling I'm experiencing here. Everyone enjoyed pitching in. In fact in our town, when a new parish was started, the men got together and renovated an old barn into a beautiful chapel."

"And a-one, and a-two, and a-three," a voice boomed from a side room.

Like a clap of thunder, a piano began to play, and a chorus of voices rang out, "Deck the halls with boughs of holly . . ."

"The choir's tuning up for this evening," Muffy explained. "Oh, here comes Steve."

They all turned to look as the Mayor of Branscombe

came down the stairs. Something's up, Luke thought as he observed the forced smile on Steve's face and his quick greetings to the Festival volunteers as he hurried across the room. "I just talked to Jack. Looks as if we have to get another search party organized," he said tersely. "Duncan Graham's girlfriend, Flower Bradley, came into town from California to surprise him this morning and is missing. We're having copies of her picture made to post around town. Then, besides searching the woods, we'll start ringing doorbells and making inquiries. She has to have been seen by *someone*."

Nora studied the expression of profound worry on Steve's face. "You haven't told us everything, Steve."

He looked around. There was no one standing within earshot. "Duncan phoned Flower's mother and found out something he never knew about her. When Flower turns twenty-five—which is next month—she comes into a trust fund that's worth a fortune. Her great-grandfather was the founder of Corn Bitsy Cereals. Now her mother is afraid that someone may have followed Flower here and may be holding her for ransom, but she doesn't want that to get out if at all possible."

"How much is the trust fund worth?" Luke asked.

"One hundred million plus."

"Jingle Bells, Jingle Bells," the choir was singing. "Jingle all the way."

29

Glenda's ex-husband, Harvey, met up with a reporter and a camera crew from BUZ outside the house he had shared with Glenda for twelve years. He had more than willingly agreed to a reenactment of his clothes being left on the driveway in trash bags and then run over by a delivery truck. Glenda had not been invited to participate.

With the promise of a full and better-quality replacement of his clothes by the network, Harvey brought along the new wardrobe that he had acquired after a judge ruled that Glenda's action had been malicious. As instructed, Harvey had stuffed the garments into two garbage bags.

"You think this weather is bad?" he asked as he got out of his van, dragging the bags. "This snow can't compare with the way it rained that day. It was terrible. Strong gusty winds. Glenda claimed it wasn't raining when she put the bags on the driveway, but give me a break. It didn't take a rocket scientist to realize the heavens were about to open up."

What a dope, Ben Moscarello, the reporter from BUZ

was thinking as he shook Harvey's hand. "Hello, Harvey. That must have been quite a day. Why don't you leave the bags here on the driveway? We'll get a shot of them with your clothes sticking out."

"It was very insulting. Glenda had no right to treat my stuff that way," Harvey said as he set the bags down, untwisted the ties, and started rummaging through the contents. With great care, he draped the sleeves of some of his favorite sweatshirts over the sides.

"That's the idea, Harvey," Ben said approvingly.

"I gave Glenda a suitcase for her birthday about four years ago. It wouldn't have killed her to pack my clothes nice and neat in it. I would have returned it."

Of *course* you would have, Ben thought sarcastically. "Now Harvey we want you to stand on the front porch and talk about the horror and embarrassment of driving down the block and suddenly seeing the wardrobe you took such pride in blown all over the road, wet, dirty, then covered with tire tracks."

"I'll never forget it as long as I live!" Harvey said. "*Never! It still gives me nightmares.*"

"Save that for when the camera's running," Ben told him as they walked up the path to the house. "Harvey, we don't want to mention that you were late to pick up your gear. That wouldn't be sympathetic."

"I was only five minutes late!" Harvey protested as he positioned himself on the top step of the porch.

"I know, but don't mention it. None of this was your fault. The point is, the viewing public likes victims. They not only like them, they root for them. And there aren't too many victims the public will feel sorrier for than someone whose former spouse hits it big in the lottery."

Harvey's face fell. "I'll never get over it."

"Let's roll the camera," Ben said quickly. "Harvey, you say you're never going to get over this?"

"Never!"

"Would you say the humiliation of seeing your clothes strewn on the street made you depressed?"

"I was furious and depressed, and too broke to replace anything. Thank God the judge made Glenda pay up. I hadn't had gainful employment for about a year before we split. I'd been looking for work, then one day I went into a Go Go Bar and met Penelope and . . ."

"Harvey!" Ben interrupted. "We don't want to know that you didn't find a job because you were too busy with a girl-friend. That isn't sympathetic either."

"You want to know the worst part?" Harvey asked. "Right after the divorce went through, Penelope dumped me."

The cameraman tapped Ben on the shoulder. "We've got to get this scene moving. Right now we're supposed to be taking background shots of the church bazaar, then get over in time to catch Santa climbing into his sleigh."

"Okay," Ben said impatiently, then turned back to Harvey. "Let's pick up with your telling us that after twelve beautiful years you and Glenda split, and how shocked you were when she showed a side of her personality that was mean and vindictive."

"Vindictive?"

"She wasn't nice to you."

Harvey cleared his throat. "Glenda and I got married when she was twenty and I was twenty-four," he began. "She was no Marilyn Monroe, but I thought she was a very nice person. I was wrong."

"Cut!" an exasperated Ben moaned. "Harvey, get this straight. You start knocking your ex-wife's looks and every woman who watches the show will hate you. Stick to how much you loved her."

"I loved my wife," Harvey began dutifully. "I still love her. Glenda is A–number one in my book."

Keep going, Ben prayed.

"I begged her to work things out with me," Harvey continued, warming to his narrative. "But she coldly refused, and we were divorced. Glenda got the house, which I thought was very unfair, but since we had remortgaged it, there wasn't much equity, if you get my drift."

"Harvey," Ben interrupted. "Tell us about the clothes as you walk toward the driveway."

Harvey nodded. Dramatically he pointed at the front door of the house. "It was very unfriendly of Glenda to change the locks on the doors so fast. I hadn't had the chance to get all my stuff out. We agreed she'd leave my clothes out on the driveway." He walked over and pointed at the bags. "They couldn't have been here for two minutes when the storm blew in," he said, blinking as snow pelted his face.

"Good, Harvey," Ben said. "We're going to spread the clothes around the street now and have our truck run over them."

Five minutes later Harvey was standing on the road, looking down, tears in his eyes. "I couldn't believe that the woman I had shared twelve years of my life with could do this to me," he said, pointing at his soggy shirts and pants and sweaters and socks and underwear. "I was so crushed when I came upon this devastating scene. I was crushed worse than my clothes."

Ben made a signal with his arm. A truck came rumbling down the road and ran over Harvey's new wardrobe.

"Cut!" Ben called. "That's a wrap!"

Another segment of the Festival of Joy special was in the can.

30

Before Duncan called Flower's mother, they canvassed the stores along Main Street, just in case Flower had stopped in one of them. They even went to the movie theater in the hopes that she had gone there to kill time before surprising Duncan.

No one had seen her.

Then they called the Branscombe Inn and the two bed-and-breakfasts in town, the Hideaway and the Knolls. She hadn't registered at any of them. That was when Duncan reluctantly phoned Flower's parents. Her mother, Margo Bradley, whom he had never met, was surprised to hear from him.

"Duncan, hello. I tried to call Flower, but her phone is turned off and her mailbox is full. Is anything wrong?" Margo asked quickly.

With a heavy heart, Duncan told her what had happened.

"I was always afraid of this!" Margo cried.

"Why?"

"Flower is an heiress of the Corn Bitsy Cereal Company. Her great-great grandfather founded it. I've had a fear of her being kidnapped ever since she was born."

"An *heiress?*" Duncan had said in disbelief. "I'd never have guessed that in a million years."

"That's the way she wanted it," Margo explained anxiously. "She wanted to meet someone who would love her for herself."

"I do," Duncan said vigorously. "I'm just surprised because when she talked about her life growing up, it seemed just like mine."

"We didn't have a wealthy lifestyle," Margo explained. "Her father and I were never interested in money. I was allowed access to my trust fund at eighteen, and in the following five years ended up giving most of the money away to causes we supported and anyone who asked to borrow. That's why Flower isn't allowed near her trust until she's twenty-five. Our family has shunned publicity, but people know there's money. I'm so afraid, with her trust coming due, that someone might have targeted her."

"Mrs. Bradley, it might have nothing to do with her family money. I won twelve million dollars in the lottery last night, and there's been a lot of publicity about it. If she was targeted, it could have been because of *me*," he admitted.

"Duncan," Margo said impatiently, "Flower's trust is worth over 100 million dollars. I knew she shouldn't go flying across the country to spend time with a man she knows nothing about."

"I *love* Flower," Duncan protested. "And I won't let anything happen to her. I promise you. I will find her."

"Don't talk about her trust fund publicly. If Flower is okay and out there somewhere, let's not give some crazy the idea to try and find her on his own."

When Duncan hung up, he was distraught. Stumbling over his words, he told them what Flower's mother had just revealed.

"Duncan," Jack said. "We'll let Steve know Flower is missing and that it's urgent the police be on the lookout for her. We'll have to tell him why we suspect a serious problem. Otherwise he'll wonder why they're supposed to look for a twenty-four-year-old woman who has only been out of touch for a few hours."

As Jack called Steve, Alvirah thought about the time Willy was kidnapped and held for ransom. She had managed to get a job as a maid in a sleazy hotel where she believed he was being kept. The criminals who took him had planned to kill him once the ransom money was paid, she remembered. Thank God I was able to save him. Where could Flower be? The engagement ring intended for her was in Alvirah's purse. Alvirah realized she was getting one of her funny feelings. Could this ring lead them to Flower?

I've got to talk to the man who found the ring and brought it to the jewelry shop, she decided.

31

In the basement of The Hideaway, Woodrow and Edmund were sitting on a lumpy, dusty old couch that smelled of mildew. A lone lightbulb dangled overhead. Betty had given them a couple of blankets to throw over their legs. Even so, they were both cold and increasingly fearful of Jed and Betty's plans to get rid of Flower.

Edmund's head was in his hands. "Woodrow, I'm scared!" he said.

"Take it easy, Edmund, I'm nervous enough already. My stomach's a little off. I shouldn't have eaten all that candy."

"Woodrow, I don't care about your bellyache. We *can't* be involved in a murder. Did you see the look on that girl's face when we tied her up and left her back there? She's terrified, and she's just a kid."

"What are we going to do?" Woodrow asked angrily, spitting out the words. "Our only choice is to forget about the lottery ticket and drive out of town just the way we planned to do after our last class next week. We won't get the money, but we won't get arrested for murder either."

"We will be if we let Betty and Jed kill her, and we don't try to stop them. With or without us, they're not going to let that girl live." Edmund swallowed hard and ran his fingers through his thinning hair. "If only we had inherited a little money. We were never greedy with our scams. I really don't think we ever took money from that many people who couldn't afford to lose a few bucks."

"Shut up, Edmund. How about Duncan? We cleaned *him* out."

Overhead they could hear the floorboards creaking as Betty hurried back and forth from the kitchen to the living room. Tea time was obviously busy. "Jed," they heard her snap. "You forgot to put preserves on table four."

"She's *mean*," Edmund said, his voice shaking. "Woodrow, what are we going to do? We can't let that girl die. We're pretty bad, but we're not killers. Those two," he pointed toward the ceiling, "seem to have no problem with it. In prison the talk always was that Jed got away with a lot of really bad stuff. He was just stupid and got caught robbing a bank. With a loaded gun."

"What do you suggest?" Woodrow asked sarcastically.

"We get the girl out of here, then contact Duncan. She'll

be our witness that we saved her life. If he won't give us the ticket, we'll just head for the hills."

Woodrow was silent for a moment. "Edmund, how stupid are you? Betty and Jed will never let us get out of here alive with that girl. They probably have guns hidden away in Betty's baking pans. If they think their whole way of life is threatened, they won't be afraid to use them."

"Well then let's go for it while they're busy with their tea party."

"You think the girl's going to come willingly? No way."

"Believe me, Woodrow, she'll trust us more than Betty. If I had a choice of going with us, or staying here with Betty and Jed, I'd go with us."

"And if we save her life, the least Duncan can do is give us back our ticket," Woodrow agreed. "One good turn deserves another, as Aunt Millie aways told us."

Edmund snapped his fingers. "I know! Let's get Aunt Millie involved."

"How?"

"Have her get the ticket back from Duncan. She'll be outraged if she thinks we missed out on 180 million dollars. We'll explain to her we made a little mistake with the oil well, but that we plan to pay everyone back. She doesn't have to know anything about Flower. We'll just tell her to call Duncan and say that if he doesn't give her the lottery ticket she bought at the convenience store when she was visiting us, she'll be very hurt. And her nephews don't want to see her or anyone else hurt. Duncan would have to be an idiot if he doesn't get the message."

"He *is* an idiot."

"So what? I think it could work. We want Aunt Millie to stay completely innocent about Flower. We'll get away from here with Flower, in Jed's van, and head to Canada. I saw Jed's keys on a hook in the shed. No one will be on the lookout for his van—he wouldn't dare report it missing. We'll tell Millie to hire a limo and head to Branscombe. She could be in town by ten o'clock. As soon as we get word she has the ticket in her hot little hands, we'll release Flower."

"And I guess if we get caught, we can comfort ourselves with the thought that there will be some family money when we finally get out of prison," Woodrow said glumly.

"If she doesn't spend it all first."

Woodrow shrugged, as if defeated. "At least we'll know we did the right thing, saving Flower's life."

"Let's call Aunt Millie real fast," Edmund said. "I want to get that girl out of here."

Aunt Millie was on Woodrow's speed dial. Not surprisingly, she answered on the first ring.

"Woodrow, to what do I owe this honor?" she asked crisply. "It's always good to hear from you, but it usually means something's up."

"Edmund and I wanted to see how you were," Woodrow said innocently.

"Bored to tears. I can't go back to the casino until I get

my social security check. Life is a drag when you don't have money. So what do you want?"

"Actually, we have sad news and glad news."

"Fire away."

"We bought a lottery ticket and won 180 million dollars."

"What! I don't believe it! What could possibly be the sad news?"

"We were in the middle of running a scam and . . ."

"You two never learn do you?"

"Listen, we were smart enough to win the lottery."

"That's true."

"But someone stole the ticket from our freezer, and we want you to get it back. We're sure we know who it is. His name is Duncan Graham and wouldn't you know, we sold him stock in a phony oil well."

"You make my head spin. Why on earth would he give it back to me?"

Woodrow hesitated. "He's already in on the other winning ticket that was sold in this lottery so he's getting twelve million dollars anyway. But he stole our ticket and he knows it. We just want to convince him the ticket is yours. And we want him to be afraid that if he doesn't give it to you, the rightful owner, who bought the ticket when you visited your two loving nephews the other day, he'll be sorry. Got it?"

"Oh, what a good idea! Trust me, I know what to do. I get a third, right?"

Woodrow gulped. "Of course, Aunt Millie. We'll even pay for your limo up to Branscombe."

"Give me Duncan's number . . ."

When Woodrow snapped his cell phone closed, he looked at his cousin. "We're lucky to have her," he said to Edmund. "Even if she is a little greedy and wants a third."

"Two-thirds of a loaf is better than none," Edmund replied. "Let's get out of here."

32

"What do you think you're doing?" Betty asked harshly as she pulled Flower's chair upright. "Trying to get help? That's not a good idea. You might be interested to know I got a call to see if you registered here. Maybe your boyfriend didn't intend to dump you after all."

Betty yanked open the drawer of the computer desk and pulled out a thick roll of black duct tape. She dragged the chair to the desk and with quick strokes bound the chair and desk together. Looking down into Flower's terrified eyes, she said, "If you know what's good for you, you won't try anything like that again." She then took a dish towel out of the deep pocket of her apron and blindfolded Flower. "See no evil," she muttered irritably. "I've got to get back to the tea."

She's going to kill me, Flower thought, as the door slid closed. This is the end. Desperately she strained to free herself.

A few minutes later the door slid open again. Oh my God, Flower thought. She's going to kill me now.

Then one of the financial advisers who had helped tie her up said quietly, "Don't be scared, Flower. We're getting you out of here. All we want is our lottery ticket back from your boyfriend. Those two intend to kill you, and we're not going to let it happen."

"Oh, you're not, are you?" Betty cried.

"Huh?" the man said in a panic.

A few seconds later Flower heard his body land with a thud on the cement floor.

33

"Steve wants us to bring Flower's picture over to the church bazaar," Jack said. "We can make copies of it there. He says there are a lot of people around. We can show the photo to all of them. It's a good place to start."

These roads are getting slippery, Duncan worried, and with each passing minute it's getting darker. How can this have happened? he asked himself. How? If only I had just stayed home last night.

It's the calm before the storm with the way some of the streets are deserted, Alvirah thought. Everyone's probably getting ready for the candlelight ceremony and Santa's ride through the snow. But then she saw that the church parking lot was almost full. Jack stopped at the front door. Glenda and Regan jumped out to assist Duncan, who was unsteady on his crutches.

"Jack, I'll keep you company while you park," Alvirah offered.

"Alvirah, that's crazy."

"Please, just park the car. I've got to make a phone call."

When Regan closed the door, Alvirah said, "Jack, I didn't want to say this in front of Duncan. I want to follow up on that man who found the flower ring. It's possible that companion who very likely killed Mrs. O'Keefe's friend Kitty is around here somewhere. And there's always the wild chance that somehow Flower met up with her. If that companion is here, I'm sure she's following the lottery story."

"It's certainly worth checking out," Jack agreed. "That ring didn't walk to Branscombe."

But there was still no answer at Rufus Blackstone's home. "Why doesn't he have an answering machine?" Alvirah grumbled. "In this day and age . . . Let me try Mrs. O'Keefe. I just want to see what she remembers about the companion. She's probably mad at me because I haven't talked to her in so long."

"No one could stay mad at you, Alvirah," Jack said amiably as he pulled into a parking space.

Alvirah began to dial. "I never forget a phone number," she bragged. "Particularly Bridget O'Keefe's. She was always calling me and leaving messages asking if I had seen her glasses or her keys or her address book. . . . Hello, Bridget? This is Alvirah Meehan . . ." She laughed. "No, I'm not too big for my britches. I *do* want to see you for lunch one of these days . . . But the strangest thing happened today. I'm in a little town in New Hampshire, and I spotted Kitty's flower ring in a jewelry shop window. I'm absolutely *sure* it was hers."

On the other end of the phone, Alvirah's former employer, who had been watching her afternoon soap operas, gasped. "That ring has been on my mind lately. How did the jeweler get it?"

"A local man found it. I'm trying to get in touch with him. I wanted to see what you remembered about Kitty's companion. I only saw her once from a distance."

Mrs. O'Keefe lowered the volume on the television. "I still feel so terrible about Kitty. That companion, who we later found out used a fake name, was syrupy sweet in the beginning, then she started to boss Kitty around."

"I remember you were worried about that. But what did she *look* like?"

"She had one of those round faces that always had a phony smile plastered on it. Brown hair. Medium sized, but kind of a big frame. She pretended to act concerned about Kitty and was always saying she wanted to fatten Kitty up. It bugged Kitty, who said the companion's head was always in and out of the oven, baking cakes and cookies, most of which she ate herself. To think she got away with robbing poor Kitty blind, then pushing her down the stairs. We both know she did that. Alvirah, if you find her, I'd love to get the chance to spit in her face."

"Bridget, I would love to find her. Kitty was such a sweet

lady. I'll call you when I get back to New York. I have the ring. As long as Kitty's nephew says it's okay, it's yours. I heard Kitty say so many times that she wanted you to have it."

"Oh, Alvirah, I can't believe how good you are. The ring won't bring Kitty back, but it will make me feel close to her again."

Alvirah said her good-byes and closed her cell phone. "That wasn't much help," she admitted. "The murdering companion likes to bake. Which reminds me, I'm hungry." She reached in her purse for a chocolate caramel. "Jack would you like one?"

"Sure," he said. As he unwrapped the red and green foil he asked, "Alvirah, how's your head feeling?"

Alvirah opened the car door. "I'll think about it when we get Flower back."

Jack put his hand under her arm as they walked carefully through the parking lot. Inside the church, they went down the steps to the basement, which was cheerfully decorated and abuzz with smiling volunteers. They could hear the choir rehearsing nearby. "Nine ladies dancing, eight maids a-milking, seven swans a-swimming, six geese a-laying . . ."

Alvirah turned to Jack. "Five gooolden rings," she sang off-key.

"Jack!"

They both turned. Regan was hurrying toward them. "Duncan just got a phone call from the Winthrops' elderly aunt. They know Duncan has the lottery ticket. She said he'd better not cash it because it belongs to her, and she wants it back or she'll be very hurt."

"Hurt?" Jack repeated.

"That's what she said. Duncan is sure it's a threat and that those guys have Flower, but the aunt hung up before he could question her."

"How is he supposed to get the ticket to her?" Alvirah asked.

"She said she'd call back later. Duncan knows she didn't buy the ticket, but he doesn't care. He's going to give it to her anyway."

Alvirah's heart sank. She'd been hoping against hope that Flower had maybe gone skiing for the day and was going to surprise Duncan tonight. These kidnapping situations usually don't end well, she thought. There's always the fear the kidnappers will panic, and then . . .

She knew that Regan and Jack were thinking the same thing.

34

You two-timing jerk!" Betty cried as she stood over a stunned Edmund, whom she'd karate chopped in the back of the head. Dazed, he began to struggle clumsily to his feet.

"Don't bother," Jed said quietly from the doorway, pointing a pistol at Edmund. "Betty, let's get him tied up."

"What do you think I'm doing?" she asked impatiently, grabbing the duct tape. "I've got to get back inside. People are wolfing down my scones." With swift movements she secured Edmund's hands behind his back and twisted tape around his legs.

They heard the outer door of the shed open and close. "Here comes 911," Jed scoffed in a low voice.

As Betty was about to stuff Edmund's mouth, he cried out, "Woodrow, run!"

But it was too late.

A moment later Jed was escorting Woodrow back to his

office, his gun pointed at Woodrow's ear. "Betty, it looks like you're going to have to help me up at Devil's Pass. We now have three people going for a dip tonight."

"Jed, what are you talking about?" Woodrow asked, his voice trembling.

"Your cousin here said you wanted to let this little girl go. That wouldn't have been so good for me and Betty, now would it?"

"We weren't going to let her go."

"Then what were you planning to do?" Betty asked harshly as she pulled his arms behind him and started to bind them with the tape.

"Let's work this out," Woodrow pleaded. "When we cash in the lottery ticket, we'll only take ten percent. The rest is yours."

"Only if you throw in a couple oil wells," Betty snapped. "I'm tired of listening to your lies." She stuffed his mouth with a gag.

Within five minutes, their three captives securely bound and gagged, Betty was back in the parlor.

Rhoda Conklin and Tishie Thornton were talking animatedly to two women at a neighboring table.

"They actually put Duncan's girlfriend's ring on display at Pettie's jewelry store," Tishie was telling her enthralled listeners. "He was furious."

"Some girl came into the store looking for him this

morning," Rhoda said. "I don't see how that could be his girlfriend though. She seemed stunned when I told her he'd quit because he won the lottery."

One of the women waved her hand dismissively. "Maybe it was someone who did know he had won and was hoping to meet him."

"But who would go to work when they just came into twelve million dollars?" the other woman asked. She laughed. "Right, Rhoda?"

"It's not my problem anymore who does or doesn't come to work," Rhoda snarled. "Or who Duncan's girlfriend is."

They don't know she's missing yet, Betty thought gratefully as she started to clear a vacated table. We have to get Flower and the others out of here the minute it gets dark. Rhoda spotted her and beckoned. "Could we have our check now? I was wondering where you were. We would have liked another cup of tea, but it's too late now. I even went looking for you in the kitchen."

Did she look into the laundry room? Betty wondered uneasily. She had stuffed Flower's coat in the hamper and tossed her knapsack behind it. Could Rhoda have seen it? "Sorry," Betty said with a smile. "Things have been so busy with the Festival. I've had my hands full."

"We don't care about the Festival," Tishie said. "Bah, humbug."

"Bah, humbug is right," Rhoda agreed as she reached for her purse. "This is my treat, Tishie. Thanks for picking me up. I knew I couldn't drive in this mess. Thank God I'm moving back to Boston tomorrow."

Thank God is right, Betty thought.

35

After the lottery ticket was securely locked away in the vault of Branscombe's only bank, Ralph, Tommy, and Marion agreed to meet at the start of the candlelight ceremony. Ralph and Judy, hand in hand, had headed toward their car; Tommy, closely guarded by his parents, had gotten behind the wheel of their ten-year-old sedan; Marion had driven home through the snow by herself.

Inside her house, Marion put the keys on the kitchen counter and went into her bedroom. I'll get out of my dress-up clothes and put a robe on, she thought. I'll make myself a cup of tea and relax for a few hours. I hardly closed an eye last night, but I know I'll never sleep now.

Out of the blue, she burst into tears. Grabbing a hanky from her drawer, she dabbed her eyes. I feel so alone, she thought. This money is wonderful, but I'm going to miss seeing my friends every day—the people I worked with, excluding The Skunk, and our regular customers. What am I going to *do* with myself when I wake up in the morning?

She put on her robe, tied the sash, and told herself how silly she was being. So many people would give their eye-teeth to be in my shoes right now, she thought. But if only Gus were still alive. We'd have so much fun planning trips. She remembered the dozens of pictures of penguins a Conklin's customer had shown her, taken on a cruise to Antarctica. I think Gus and I would have skipped the penguins and gone to someplace warm, Marion decided wistfully.

In the kitchen, she turned on the kettle, opened the cabinet, got out a cup and a tea bag. I should call Glenda. Reaching for the phone, she looked at the list of numbers taped to the side of the refrigerator and dialed. When Glenda answered, Marion could hear the buzz of activity in the background. "Glenda, the ticket is locked up," she began brightly. "How's Duncan?"

"Not good," Glenda said quickly. "His girlfriend is missing."

"What?"

Glenda filled her in. "I'm at the church bazaar. We're showing her picture to everyone. On top of that, we picked up the flower ring from the jewelry store, and it turns out it was stolen eight years ago."

"Flower's ring was stolen?"

"Actually, what I mean is that the ring Duncan bought for her is in the shape of a flower, and . . . I'm sorry, Marion, I can't talk now."

"I want to help!" Marion cried.

"We can't have you walking around in the snow ringing doorbells."

"Glenda, don't put me out to pasture! Don't forget, until this morning I stood on my feet all day at the bakery."

"I know what you can do. I'll have someone here e-mail you Flower's picture. Go down to Conklin's, stand inside the entrance, and show it to everyone who comes in. Maybe someone saw her."

"Conklin's?" Marion asked tentatively.

"Oh, I didn't tell you. The Skunk is gone for good. She and Sam broke up this morning. He's thrilled."

"Send me that e-mail ASAP. I'm on my way!" Marion hung up. A flower-shaped ring, she thought as she rushed back into the bedroom. I know I've seen somebody wearing one.

But who?

And where?

36

Betty carried the last tray of tea cups and dessert plates into the kitchen. She dropped the tray next to the sink and with heavy steps strode to the door of the laundry room.

"What are you doing?" Jed asked.

"Checking to see if that knapsack is visible. Rhoda Conklin was in the kitchen when we were in the shed. She saw Flower this morning at the market, and she may have noticed she was carrying a red knapsack." Betty stared at the red fabric sticking up from behind the hamper. "You can see a little bit of it, but not so much that you'd pay attention. If that 'Flower Power' logo had been visible, we could have been sunk." She grabbed the knapsack and Flower's coat and threw them at Jed. "Pull the van up next to the shed and hide these in it. We've got to move the three of them into the van and off this property fast."

"Betty, it's not dark yet."

"Jed, stop being so stupid. Rhoda Conklin, that gossip Tishie Thornton, and some other women were all talking about Flower. They don't know that she's missing yet, but I'm sure word has gotten out. Someone's already called here to see if she checked in. We can't take a chance that the police may stop by and start snooping around. They don't need a search warrant to walk around the back and see the Winthrops' car behind the shed. Let me remind you—they told us the cops were probably looking for them."

"Keep your voice down," Jed snapped. "Someone may be upstairs."

"No one is upstairs. Why would the television people be here when they have the Festival to cover?" she snapped back.

"Betty, we have to wait until it gets dark," he said firmly. "It'll only be another half hour."

"Then just pull the van around and stay with them in the shed until we leave. That girl is smart. She already figured out a way to attract attention. Someone could have heard her kicking the wall if I hadn't stopped her."

"So, you stopped her. But remember, this is *your* fault. You should have handled it better when the Winthrops showed up."

"And you should never have become friends with them in prison!" Nervously, Betty began to rinse the cups. "Jed, after we get rid of them we'd better think about moving on from here, and soon. There are going to be a lot of questions asked when Flower doesn't show up, never mind the other two. If anyone starts digging deep, it won't take them long to find out that the real Betty and Jed Elkins died when their touring bus crashed in Germany six years ago."

37

"Duncan, if you perceive that woman's call as being a threat, then you might be right that those guys have Flower," Jack said bluntly.

"We'd better talk in the office," Steve suggested. "It's through that door in the corner."

Steve and Muffy, the Reillys, Alvirah and Willy, and Glenda and Duncan followed Steve into the office, and Jack closed the door behind them.

"They must have Flower," Duncan blurted. "That's why I'm going to give that ticket to their aunt. Why did she hang up? I didn't say I wouldn't give her the ticket."

"She's playing with you, Duncan," Regan said. "She knows exactly what she's doing."

Duncan pointed to the window. "It's going to be dark soon. I can't just sit around and wait for that woman to call back. We've got to look for Flower. It may sound stupid to you, but I feel as if she's pleading with me to find her before it's too late."

"We will, Duncan," Jack said quickly. "But we can't officially treat this as a kidnapping yet. You did take the ticket
they bought, and they want it back. It could be just a coinci-
dence that Flower is missing. And her disappearance could
involve someone else, now that we know she's an heiress.
The thing you have to take heart about is that she's an adult,
and hasn't been out of touch for all that long. She tried to
reach you a few times this morning. She could walk in the
door of this bazaar any minute."

"That's not going to happen," Duncan said flatly. "I know
she's out there, and I know she needs my help."

"Well then let's get started," Regan said briskly. "Steve,
can we use one of these machines to duplicate Flower's
picture?"

"Yes."

"This is where we've been doing the mailings for the Festival," Muffy informed them. "I'll scan the picture into the
computer and print out copies. Then we can do an e-mail
blast. We must have the e-mail address of almost everyone in
town. I'll send out an emergency alert, with Flower's picture
and description."

"That'd be great," Regan said.

"I promised Marion I'd send her Flower's picture,"
Glenda said. "She's going to go over to Conklin's and show it
to everyone who comes through the door."

"I'll call our chief of police," Steve said. "We reserve a few
numbers that we use for emergencies. He'll give me one of

them to put on the e-mail, so people can call in if they've seen her."

Duncan hadn't let go of Flower's picture since Glenda gave it back to him after they had canvassed Main Street. Now he carefully took the picture out of the frame and handed it to Muffy. She sat down at the computer and got to work.

The activity obviously sparked a flicker of hope in Duncan.

"Duncan, we'll show her picture to all the volunteers here now," Alvirah said comfortingly. "Then we'll take to the streets. There's no reason we can't reach everyone in Branscombe in the next hour."

"Steve and I are heading over to the park in a few minutes," Muffy said as the printer was spitting out copies of Flower's picture. "We're supposed to be at the reviewing stand when Santa arrives. We'll get some of the Festival workers over there to distribute Flower's picture."

"Aren't there going to be people lining Santa's route?" Nora asked.

"Yes," Steve answered. "They're gathering already. Some people don't mind waiting in the cold and snow to get a good view."

"Luke and I would be happy to go out along the route with Flower's picture and show it to the people who are already out there."

"Absolutely," Luke confirmed. He put his hand on

Duncan's shoulder but didn't know what to say. He remembered how terrified he had been when he and his driver were kidnapped and left to die in a leaky boat. "Let's move fast, everyone," he urged.

"I'll go with you and Nora," Willy offered. "I might not look it, but I'm quick on my feet. I know Alvirah will want to stay close to Regan and Jack and Duncan. It's best if we fan out and cover as much ground as possible."

"Muffy, before we all split up," Alvirah said, "do you know Rufus Blackstone?"

"Rufus Blackstone? Of course I do. He's playing Scrooge in 'A Christmas Carol.' They were rehearsing across the street at town hall, but they should be about wrapped up by now. Why?"

"I've been trying to reach him for the last couple of hours. He found the ring that Duncan bought for Flower. I wanted to ask him about it. It turns out it was stolen years ago. Leave no stone unturned," she said.

Regan looked at Alvirah. "I'll go over there with you right now," she said. She turned to Jack. "We'll be back in a few minutes. Why don't you and Glenda and Duncan show the pictures to the volunteers here?"

"Good idea."

They all left the office together, armed with stacks of Flower's picture. Steve beckoned to a male volunteer. "I need you to drop these people," he pointed to Luke and Nora, "along Santa's route."

"Sure, Mr. Mayor."

"And if you could drop this other gentleman at the halfway point to the park."

Regan and Alvirah hurried out of the church and across the street. The rehearsal had ended. Quickly they showed Flower's picture to the last actors who were on their way out the door.

"Sorry," they all said.

"I'd like to talk to Rufus Blackstone," Alvirah told them. "Is he still here?"

"He's the tall guy with the white hair and beard helping his wife on with her coat over there. They're talking to the director. Rufus always has a few suggestions at the end of every rehearsal."

"Mr. Blackstone!" Alvirah bellowed. "I need to speak to you."

Seeing the displeased look on his face, Alvirah and Regan hurried over to him and introduced themselves. "We're friends of the young man who bought the flower ring you found."

"You mean Duncan? Everyone's talking about him. He was missing all night and then won the lottery, right?"

"Yes, he did," Alvirah said quickly. "Mr. Pettie said you found the ring on the street."

"That's right."

"Where did you find it?"

He squinted. "Why do you want to know that?"

414 Mary Higgins Clark & Carol Higgins Clark

"Because it may have been dropped by the person who stole it eight years ago."

"My word!" Rufus's wife, Agatha, said. "It was stolen?"

"Yes," Alvirah answered. "And by someone who may be responsible for the death of the woman who owned it."

"Well, no wonder no one answered my lost-and-found ad in the paper," Rufus said. "I had it in there for weeks. I figured some tourist must have lost it."

"Lost it where?" Regan asked.

"In front of Conklin's market."

"Conklin's Market?" Alvirah repeated. "That place has seen a lot of action lately."

"The band on the ring was old and had broken. It may have split and fallen off someone's finger."

"Someone who shouldn't have been wearing it," Alvirah said, thinking of Kitty's companion.

Agatha's mouth was now agape. "I had joked with Rufus that Scrooge was a perfect role for him. He didn't want to let me have the ring. He wanted to sell it for whatever he could get. I'm kinda glad now, huh? Who wants to wear a ring that was on the finger of a murderer? Not me. Right, Rufus?"

"I suppose. Let's get going. We want to make the opening ceremony. Although what we should be doing is having another rehearsal. This play isn't ready for public viewing."

"I know you want to get going," Regan said quickly. "But if you could just take a look at this picture for a minute. It's

Duncan's girlfriend. She's been missing since this morning. You didn't happen to see her anywhere today, did you?"

"Nope," Rufus said brusquely after glancing at the photo.

Agatha scrunched up her eyes and studied the picture. Her jaw dropped even further. "Ohhh. Ohhhh. Wait just a minute. Ohhh. Yes, I did see her."

"Where?" Regan and Alvirah cried together.

"The poor little thing was crying. I passed her on Main Street. She was going one way, and I was going the other. I'd just come out of the beauty parlor."

"Did you see where she went?" Alvirah asked.

"I turned around because I wanted to see if I could help her. She seemed so upset. But she ducked down the alley. I couldn't have kept up with her if I tried. Besides, Rufus is always telling me to mind my own business!"

"Where exactly is the alley?" Regan asked.

"It's between Conklin's and the beauty parlor. You can't miss it. It's the only one there."

"We can't thank you enough," Regan said.

Alvirah was already racing out the door.

38

Warmly dressed in a sweater, slacks, snow boots, and a parka, Marion opened the door of Conklin's and looked around to see if she could spot Sam. The market was crowded with last minute shoppers. She was greeted with smiles and congratulations from all sides.

"If you're looking for Mr. Conklin, he's in the kitchen," Paige the cashier called to her. "Glenda stopped in before. Did you hear about Duncan's girlfriend?"

"That's why I'm here. I want to show her picture to the customers as they come in, but first I have to let Mr. Conklin know what I'm doing."

Marion walked back past the bakery and was startled to see that the shelves in the glass case were nearly empty. Lisa, the kid who assisted her at the counter, looked exhausted. She was ringing up a sale of the last two corn muffins and an apple tart.

The customer who reached out to take the package, a young woman in her twenties, was wearing a wide gold wedding ring. Marion stared at it. This is where I noticed the flower ring, she remembered excitedly. It was when I was handing someone her purchase. But who was it? Maybe it will come back to me.

In the kitchen, Marion was surprised to see Sam's son, Richard, slicing a ham. She'd known him since he was a little boy. "Marion," he said happily. "You spent all your money already?" He hurried over.

"Richard," she said, hugging him. "You look wonderful. I really meant to come see you in your play."

"That's okay. You can come to see the next one with Dad. I guess you heard he's flying solo."

"Yes," Marion said, blushing as Sam turned and spotted them. He looked tired but happy as he took her hands in his. "Marion this place isn't the same without you," he said heartily. "I told Glenda I have your bonus checks."

"Sam, please don't worry about that now," Marion said. "I was wondering if you'd mind if I stand at the front door and hand out Duncan's girlfriend's picture. She hasn't shown up yet, and he's terribly upset."

"Please," Sam said, still holding her hands in his. "Stay as long as you want."

Marion quickly posted herself just inside the entrance of the store. As she handed out Flower's picture, she kept thinking about the flower ring and how she had seen it on a customer's hand at her bakery counter. Think, Marion, she urged herself. It could be very important. She remembered how shy she was when she was a young girl. In the seventh grade when she was called on, she'd get flustered and everything would go out of her mind. Mrs. Griner, her English teacher, had been so understanding. She'd say, "Marion, you know the answer. Give yourself a minute to think. It will come to you."

It always did. But it's not coming to me now. I guess it's my age. I've done so many crossword puzzles to keep my brain sharp, she thought with frustration.

I've *got* to remember who was wearing that ring!

39

We'll retrace her steps," Jack said quickly. "I'll pull the car around."

"Flower was crying. Oh God!" Duncan moaned as he labored, on crutches, up the steps from the church basement to the outside.

"Main Street will be closed off by now," Glenda said when they got in the car. "That alley leads out to a tiny little street. That bed and breakfast I phoned, The Hideaway, is there. But the woman who owns it said Flower wasn't registered."

Regan and Alvirah looked at each other. "Let's go directly there," Regan said. "Maybe she registered under a different name."

"You think that's a possibility?" Duncan asked hopefully. "The owners of that place, Betty and Jed Elkins, are regular customers of Conklin's."

"It's worth a try," Regan said. "We'll start there."

Jack drove carefully through the snowy streets as Glenda directed him.

"People like to go to The Hideaway for tea," she said. "We're almost there. Take the next right."

They turned down a narrow road. On the left was a row of high hedges. "Those hedges hide the parking lot behind the stores. Up here to the left is the alley," Glenda explained. "It's almost directly opposite The Hideaway."

Jack parked the car in front of the Inn. "Glenda, this is your territory. Why don't you and I check the alley?"

"Alvirah and I will run inside and see what we can find out," Regan said.

"I'm coming with you," Duncan insisted.

"Duncan, we'll move faster if you wait here. Look at all those steps to the porch. Sit in the car with your cell phone on, and see if the Winthrops' aunt calls back," Regan suggested.

"All right, Regan," Duncan agreed, as he leaned back wearily against the seat.

40

Flower was wedged between Edmund and Woodrow in the back of Jed's van. Together Jed and Betty had carried each of them out of the shed and covered them with blankets. Flower's gag was so tight that she couldn't utter a sound, but both men were trying desperately to call for help through their taped mouths. The only sounds they managed to make were muted whimpers that no one outside the van could possibly hear.

I'm never going to see Duncan again, Flower thought.

"Come on, Betty," Jed said impatiently.

"I have to put a sign at the front desk that we're out at the candlelight ceremony and will be back later."

"You didn't do that yet?"

"No, Jed, I was too busy having my nails done," Betty retorted. "Get in the car. I'll be right back." She went in the kitchen door in time to hear the bell ring and the sound of the front door opening.

Oh no, she thought. But at least I didn't put the note out yet. I don't want anyone to see us driving away.

"This place feels deserted," Regan said as they waited at the registration desk. Then they heard heavy footsteps coming down the hall. A large woman was coming toward them with a welcoming smile.

"Hello, there. What I can I do for you nice ladies?"

"Are you Betty Elkins?" Regan asked.

"Yes, I am."

Regan handed her the flyer with Flower's picture. "We called before," she said. "This young woman, Flower Bradley, is still missing. We wondered if by any chance she registered here under a different name."

Betty pretended to study Flower's picture. "I'm so terribly sorry I can't help you, but I haven't seen her at all. And as I explained to Glenda, when she called before, we've been fully booked for weeks. No one could have walked in this morning and booked a room." With a sympathetic smile, she handed the flyer back to Regan. "What a shame. She looks like a lovely girl. I hope everything turns out all right."

Regan noticed that Betty Elkins was perspiring and seemed out of breath. "Would you mind keeping the picture and showing it to your other guests?"

"I wouldn't mind at all."

Neither Regan or Alvirah wanted to leave. They both

sensed the acute anxiety that Betty Elkins was trying to hide. I've never seen a phonier smile in my life, Alvirah thought.

"I hear that you serve wonderful teas every day," Regan said, stalling for time.

"You must come to one. I'm proud to say my scones are delicious, and I'm told I make a mean chocolate cake. Now if you'll excuse me, I have something on the stove."

Alvirah could almost hear Bridget O'Keefe's voice. ". . . she had a round face with a phony smile plastered on it. Her head was always in and out of the oven, baking cookies and cakes. . . . She ate most of them herself . . ." Alvirah looked from Betty's round face to the mechanical Santa on the reception desk, waving and bowing. Bridget O'Keefe was always telling me I must have thrown out her mechanical Santa by mistake. I always told her she'd open a drawer some day and find it. "This Santa is so cute," Alvirah began. "I had a friend, Kitty Whalen, who came to visit the woman I worked for . . ."

Alvirah noticed the twitch in Betty's cheek as Betty interrupted her. "I'm so sorry," Betty said, "but I do have to get back to the kitchen. And I'd like to be at the park when the candlelight ceremony begins."

"Thanks for your time," Regan said. As she and Alvirah reluctantly turned to go, the front door burst open, and Glenda rushed in, her eyes wide with excitement.

"Marion just called! Betty, maybe you can help us. Marion remembers seeing you wearing a flower ring. Of course you wouldn't have realized it was stolen. I mean, if it's the same one that Duncan bought . . ."

Alvirah's head swiveled around to Betty. Their eyes met. The smiling mask had been replaced by a look of malevolent fury. In one quick move, Betty overturned the desk and pushed it at them. As they jumped back, Betty ran down the hall with astonishing speed.

"You killed Kitty Whalen!" Alvirah shouted after her.

Regan climbed over the desk and ran down the hall, Alvirah a few steps behind her. When they reached the kitchen, it was empty, but the back door was open. They could hear the sound of a car tearing out of the driveway.

Alvirah's eyes caught sight of crumpled red and green foil candy wrappers on the counter. It was the same as the wrapper on the candy Willy had bought for her at the convenience store—the convenience store where the other lottery ticket had been bought by the financial crooks. The guy at the store had told her he had hardly sold any of them. "Regan!" she cried as she scooped up the scraps of foil. "Those financial advisers who we think have Flower might have been here. Maybe they're in cahoots with Betty!"

They raced back down the hall and out the front door. Glenda had run across the street to the alley to get Jack.

"In the car!" he shouted. "We can't lose them!"

41

"What happened, Betty?" Jed screamed as he floored the accelerator and raced out of the driveway past Jack's car. "While I was waiting for you I heard some guy yelling Flower's name."

"O'Keefe's cleaning lady recognized me."

"What?" Driving at a reckless speed, he turned left at the end of their block.

"Which way are we going?" Betty asked, her voice panicky as the wheels of the van began to slide. "They're following us."

"Be quiet! I found out which streets they're closing off and figured out the fastest way up to Devil's Pass."

Half choked under the stuffy blankets, Flower felt for the first time that there might be hope. She had heard Duncan calling her name. He had to be in the car that was following them. Keep up with us, she prayed.

Edmund wished he could comfort Flower. Who could believe this started with me and Woodrow winning the lottery? he asked himself.

Jed made a sharp left. The rear tires skidded, but he

managed to keep control. "We'll take this road straight out," he told Betty as he looked in the rear view mirror. "I think we lost them."

"Jed, be careful!" Betty screamed as the road curved to the right. Their headlights shone on an unexpected road block. Santas on horse-drawn sleighs could be seen everywhere. As a special surprise for the Festival of Joy, Santas from all over the state of New Hampshire had gathered in Branscombe and were now ready to participate in the opening ceremony.

Jed slammed on the brakes. The van spun around three times and slid to the side of the road. The troopers at the roadblock hurried over as the Reillys' car pulled up behind the Elkins's van.

"Careful, they may be armed," Jack shouted as he jumped out of the car.

Guns drawn, the troopers surrounded the van. The driver's door opened, and Jed, his hands up, stepped out onto the snowy road. At the same time, Betty opened the passenger door. "The gun is in the glove compartment, and there are folks in the back," she said bitterly.

Jack pulled open the back door of the van. He and Regan yanked away the blankets. Three people were struggling to free themselves. They had been blindfolded, gagged, and tied up.

"She's here, Duncan," Regan cried as she jumped in, pulled off Flower's blindfold, and untied her gag.

"Flower!" Duncan cried as he hobbled toward them.

Jack lifted Flower out and set her on her feet, holding her upright as a trooper cut the twine that bound her hands and feet.

"Oh, Duncan," Flower said weakly. "I wanted to surprise you."

"You sure did," Duncan cried. He dropped his crutches and threw his arms around her.

"I thought I'd never see you again," Flower whispered as he held her tight. Then she began to giggle as the troopers pulled the Winthrops out of the van. "Hey, Duncan, here are your financial advisers. Do you have any questions for them now that you finally won the lottery?"

Duncan laughed. "No! And I'm never going to reuse a plastic bag again." He brushed Flower's hair back from her forehead. "And I don't need any more of their advice to plan my life. The only thing I want to plan now is our wedding. Will you marry me, Flower?"

"As soon as possible."

Alvirah wiped a tear from her eye. "Isn't that beautiful?" she asked Regan and Glenda. "I hope they invite us to the wedding."

The roadblock was being pushed aside. "Time to get this show on the road," one of the cops called. As horses neighed and shook snow from their manes, the Festival of Joy began.

42

Sunday, December 14th

On Sunday morning, the church basement was filled with the tantalizing aroma of blueberry pancakes.

The weekend had been a rousing success with everyone from Branscombe participating in the Festival—everyone except Betty and Jed, that is. With kidnapping and intent to murder charges pending, they would not be attending any candlelight ceremonies or pancake breakfasts for years to come.

Rufus Blackstone had taken three curtain calls when "A Christmas Carol" ended. Nora's story hour with the children had been standing room only, bringing out not only the kids, but the kids at heart. The lottery winners had all pitched in at Conklin's to help cater the Festival, Sam and Marion working side by side all weekend.

At the table where Alvirah and Willy, Regan and Jack, Nora and Luke, Muffy and Steve, Duncan and Flower, and

Duncan's fellow lottery winners were seated, they were all exultant.

"I hope they don't throw the book at the Winthrops," Flower said. "They *did* try to save me and almost lost their lives because of it."

"The one I feel sorry for is their Aunt Millie," Duncan said. "When she showed up here the other night to get the ticket from me, she almost fainted when she saw the cops and they told her that her nephews were in jail. Then when she tried to describe the convenience store where she supposedly bought the ticket, it was classic. I wish I'd had a camera with me." He laughed. "She said it was on a busy street and she couldn't remember whether there was a gas pump out front or not. When I handed that ticket over to the police, I think they were stunned. It'll be interesting to see what happens with it."

"A judge will rule on that," Jack explained. "Those two crooks were on parole and shouldn't have been gambling. Who knows what the judge will decide?"

"I just can't believe that I never suspected Betty Elkins of being so evil," Glenda said, shaking her head. "Boy was I dumb."

"Glenda if you hadn't come running into The Hideaway like that," Regan said, "Betty and Jed would have been on their way to that lake with Flower, and it might have been too late to stop them."

Duncan squeezed Flower's hand, then looked around

the table. "I can't tell you how grateful Flower and I are to all of you." He started to get choked up.

Flower smiled at him then looked at Alvirah. "It was so sweet of your friend Mrs. O'Keefe to offer to let us have the ring Duncan chose for me."

"She meant it but was thrilled when you turned her down," Alvirah laughed.

"Mr. Pettie is going to make a special flower ring for us," Duncan said. "I admit that I was really angry that he put the ring in the window, but if he hadn't—"

He didn't finish the sentence.

"We're going to get married on St. John's Island at the end of January," Flower said. "We want you and your families to be our guests for a long weekend at the resort there."

"We can make it," Willy said emphatically.

"We all can!" Tommy agreed.

43

Friday, January 30th

Six weeks later, Duncan fresh out of his cast, the whole group was sunning themselves on the beach the day before the wedding. Glenda's cell phone rang. She looked at the caller ID. "It's Harvey!" she said, exasperated. "Why won't he just leave me alone?" She answered. "What now, Harvey?"

"Glenda," he cried. "I just heard the judge's ruling on that other lottery ticket. He said it was null and void since those crooks had no right to buy it in the first place."

"I'm glad about that," Glenda said. "I've got to go."

"Wait! He also ruled that there was only one winning ticket. You people are going to get the whole pot!"

"The whole pot?" Glenda gasped.

"Twenty-four million each!" Harvey's voice cracked. "Glenda, we had a good thing going . . . We just hit a bump in the road . . ."

"Harvey, you've *got* to be kidding! I'll tell you what. I'll make a donation in your name to the BUZ network's favorite cause." She hung up. The others were looking at her expectantly. "The judge has ruled that our ticket takes the whole pot!" she screamed. "The whole 360 million!"

Whoops and hollers could be heard the length of the beach. Tommy's mother jumped out of her chair. Ralph and Judy's daughters went running into the surf and began splashing each other. Marion and Sam looked stunned. "That's a lot of jelly donuts," Sam said. Duncan and Flower just smiled. At this point, another twelve million more or less didn't mean that much to them.

Regan, Jack, Nora, Luke, Muffy, and Steve just looked at each other.

"And I thought I was 'doing nice,' " Nora laughed.

Alvirah leaned forward. "This is all wonderful. But you must remember that much is expected of those to whom much has been given."

"Alvirah, don't worry. We're all planning to give to charity," Ralph assured her.

"That's good. And now, more than ever, I must insist you become members of my Lottery Winners Support Group. . . ."

Jack turned to Regan, his right eyebrow raised. "That's one group I wouldn't mind being asked to join."

Silent Night

by Mary Higgins Clark

1

It was Christmas Eve in New York City. The cab slowly made its way down Fifth Avenue. It was nearly five o'clock. The traffic was heavy and the sidewalks were jammed with last-minute Christmas shoppers, homebound office workers, and tourists anxious to glimpse the elaborately trimmed store windows and the fabled Rockefeller Center Christmas tree.

It was already dark, and the sky was becoming heavy with clouds, an apparent confirmation of the forecast for a white Christmas. But the blinking lights, the sounds of carols, the ringing bells of sidewalk Santas, and the generally jolly mood of the crowd gave an appropriately festive Christmas Eve atmosphere to the famous thoroughfare.

Catherine Dornan sat bolt upright in the back of the cab, her arms around the shoulders of her two small sons. By the rigidity she felt in their bodies, she knew her mother had been right. Ten-year-old Michael's surliness and seven-year-old Brian's silence were sure signs that both boys were intensely worried about their dad.

Earlier that afternoon when she had called her mother from the hospital, still sobbing despite the fact that Spence Crowley, her husband's old friend and doctor, assured her that Tom had come through the operation better than expected, and even suggested that the boys visit him at seven o'clock that night, her mother had spoken to her firmly: "Catherine, you've got to pull yourself together," she had said. "The boys are so upset, and you're not helping. I think it would be a good idea if you tried to divert them for a little while. Take them down to Rockefeller Center to see the tree, then out to dinner. Seeing you so worried has practically convinced them that Tom will die."

This isn't supposed to be happening, Catherine thought With every fiber of her being she wanted to undo the last ten days, starting with that terrible moment when the phone rang and the call came from St. Mary's Hospital. "Catherine, can you come right over? Tom collapsed while he was making his rounds."

Her immediate impression had been that there had to be a mistake. Lean, athletic, thirty-eight-year-old men don't collapse. And Tom always joked that pediatricians had birthright immunization to all the viruses and germs that arrived with their patients.

But Tom didn't have immunization from the leukemia that necessitated immediate removal of his grossly enlarged spleen. At the hospital they told her that he must have been ignoring warning signs for months. And I was too stupid to notice, Catherine thought as she tried to keep her lip from quivering.

She glanced out the window and saw that they were passing the Plaza Hotel. Eleven years ago, on her twenty-third birthday, they'd had their wedding reception at the Plaza. Brides are supposed to be nervous, she thought. I wasn't. I practically ran up the aisle.

Ten days later they'd celebrated little Christmas in Omaha, where Tom had accepted an appointment in the prestigious pediatrics unit of the hospital. We bought that crazy artificial tree in the clearance sale, she thought, remembering how Tom had held it up and said, "Attention Kmart shoppers . . ."

This year, the tree they'd selected so carefully was still in the garage, its branches roped together. They'd decided to come to New York for the surgery. Tom's best friend, Spence Crowley, was now a prominent surgeon at Sloan-Kettering.

Catherine winced at the thought of how upset she'd been when she was finally allowed to see Tom.

The cab pulled over to the curb. "Okay, here, lady?"

"Yes, fine," Catherine said, forcing herself to sound cheerful as she pulled out her wallet. "Dad and I brought you guys down here on Christmas Eve five years ago. Brian, I know you were too small, but Michael, do you remember?"

"Yes," Michael said shortly as he tugged at the handle on the door. He watched as Catherine peeled a five from the wad of bills in her wallet. "How come you have so much money, Mom?"

"When Dad was admitted to the hospital yesterday, they made me take everything he had in his billfold except a few dollars. I should have sorted it out when I got back to Gran's."

She followed Michael out onto the sidewalk and held the door open for Brian. They were in front of Saks, near the corner of Forty-ninth Street and Fifth Avenue. Orderly lines of spectators were patiently waiting to get a close-up look at the Christmas window display. Catherine steered her sons to the back of the line. "Let's see the windows, then we'll go across the street and get a better look at the tree."

Brian sighed heavily. This was some Christmas! He hated standing in line—for anything. He decided to play the game he always played when he wanted time to pass quickly. He would pretend he was already where he wanted to be, and tonight that was in his dad's room in the hospital. He could hardly wait to see his dad, to give him the present his grandmother had said would make him get well.

Brian was so intent on getting on with the evening that when it was finally their turn to get up close to the windows, he moved quickly, barely noticing the scenes of whirling snowflakes and dolls and elves and animals dancing and singing. He was glad when they finally were off the line.

Then, as they started to make their way to the corner to cross the avenue, he saw that a guy with a violin was about to start playing and people were gathering around him. The air suddenly was filled with the sound of "Silent Night," and people began singing.

Catherine turned back from the curb. "Wait, let's listen for a few minutes," she said to the boys.

Brian could hear the catch in her throat and knew that she was trying not to cry. He'd hardly ever seen Mom cry until that morning last week when someone phoned from the hospital and said Dad was real sick.

Cally walked slowly down Fifth Avenue. It was a little after five, and she was surrounded by crowds of last-minute shoppers, their arms filled with packages. There was a time when she might have shared their excitement, but today all she felt was achingly tired. Work had been so difficult. During the Christmas holidays people wanted to be home, so most of the patients in the hospital had been either depressed or difficult. Their bleak expressions reminded her vividly of her own depression over the last two Christmases, both of them spent in the Bedford correctional facility for women.

She passed St. Patrick's Cathedral, hesitating only a moment as a memory came back to her of her grandmother taking her and her brother Jimmy there to see the crèche. But that was twenty years ago; she had been ten, and he was six. She wished fleetingly she could go back to that time, change things, keep the bad things from happening, keep Jimmy from becoming what he was now.

Even to *think* his name was enough to send waves of fear coursing through her body. Dear God, make him leave me alone, she prayed. Early this morning, with Gigi clinging to her, she had answered the angry pounding on her door to find

Detective Shore and another officer who said he was Detective Levy standing in the dingy hallway of her apartment building on East Tenth Street and Avenue B.

"Cally, you putting up your brother again?" Shore's eyes had searched the room behind her for signs of his presence.

The question was Cally's first indication that Jimmy had managed to escape from Riker's Island prison.

"The charge is attempted murder of a prison guard," the detective told her, bitterness filling his voice. "The guard is in critical condition. Your brother shot him and took his uniform. This time you'll spend a lot more than fifteen months in prison if you help Jimmy to escape. Accessory after the fact the second time around, when you're talking attempted murder—or murder—of a law officer. Cally, they'll throw the book at you."

"I've never forgiven myself for giving Jimmy money last time," Cally had said quietly.

"Sure. And the keys to your car," he reminded her. "Cally, I warn you. Don't help him *this* tune."

"I won't. You can be sure of that. And I did not know what he had done before." She'd watched as their eyes again shifted past her. "Go ahead," she had cried. "Look around. He isn't here. And if you want to put a tap on my phone, do that, too. I want you to hear me tell Jimmy to turn himself in. Because that's all I'd have to say to him."

But surely Jimmy *won't* find me, she prayed as she threaded her way through the crowd of shoppers and sightseers. Not this time. After she had served her prison sentence, she took Gigi from the foster home. The social worker had located the tiny apartment on East Tenth Street and gotten her the job as a nurse's aide at St. Luke's-Roosevelt Hospital.

This would be her first Christmas with Gigi in two years! If only she had been able to afford a few decent presents for her, she thought. A four-year-old kid should have her own new doll's carriage, not the battered hand-me-down Cally'd been forced to get for her. The coverlet and pillow she had bought wouldn't hide the shabbiness of the carriage. But maybe she could find the guy who was selling dolls on the street around here last week. They were only eight dollars, and she remembered that there was even one that looked like Gigi.

She hadn't had enough money with her that day, but the guy said he'd be on Fifth Avenue between Fifty-seventh and Forty-seventh Streets on Christmas Eve, so she had to find him. O God, she prayed, let them arrest Jimmy before he hurts anyone else. There's something wrong with him. There always has been.

Ahead of her, people were singing "Silent Night." As she got closer, though, she realized that they weren't actually carolers, just a crowd around a street violinist who was playing Christmas tunes.

"*. . . Holy infant, so tender and mild . . .*"

Brian did not join in the singing, even though "Silent Night" was his favorite and at home in Omaha he was a member of his church's children's choir. He wished he was there now, not in New York, and that they were getting ready to trim the Christmas tree in their own living room, and everything was the way it had been.

He liked New York and always looked forward to the summer visits with his grandmother. He had fun then. But he didn't like this kind of visit. Not on Christmas Eve, with Dad in the hospital and Mom so sad and his brother bossing him around, even though Michael was only three years older.

Brian stuck his hands in the pockets of his jacket. They felt cold even though he had on his mittens. He looked impatiently at the giant Christmas tree across the street, on the other side of the skating rink. He knew that in a minute his mother was going to say, "All right. Now let's get a good look at the tree."

It was so tall, and the lights on it were so bright, and there was a big star on top of it. But Brian didn't care about that now, or about the windows they had just seen. He didn't want to listen to the guy playing the violin, either, and he didn't feel like standing here.

They were wasting time. He wanted to get to the hospital and watch Mom give Dad the big St. Christopher medal that had saved Grandpa's life when he was a soldier in World War II. Grandpa had worn it all through the war, and it even had a dent in it where a bullet had hit it.

Gran had asked Mom to give it to Dad, and even though she had almost laughed, Mom had promised but said, "Oh, Mother, Christopher was only a myth. He's not considered a saint anymore, and the only people he helped were the ones who sold the medals everybody used to stick on dashboards."

Gran had said, "Catherine, your father believed it helped him get through some terrible battles, and that is all that matters. He believed and so do I. Please give it to Tom and have faith."

Brian felt impatient with his mother. If Gran believed that Dad was going to get better if he got the medal, then his mom had to give it to him. He was positive Gran was right.

"... *sleep in heavenly peace.*" The violin stopped playing, and a woman who had been leading the singing held out a basket. Brian watched as people began to drop coins and dollar bills into it.

His mother pulled her wallet out of her shoulder bag and took out two one-dollar bills. "Michael, Brian, here. Put these in the basket."

Michael grabbed his dollar and tried to push his way through the crowd. Brian started to follow him, then noticed that his mother's wallet hadn't gone all the way down into her shoulder bag when she had put it back. As he watched, he saw the wallet fall to the ground.

He turned back to retrieve it, but before he could pick it up, a hand reached down and grabbed it. Brian saw that the hand belonged to a thin woman with a dark raincoat and a long ponytail.

"*Mom!*" he said urgently, but everyone was singing again, and she didn't turn her head. The woman who had taken the wallet began to slip through the crowd. Instinctively, Brian began to follow her, afraid to lose sight of her. He turned back to call out to his mother again, but she was singing along now, too, "*God rest you merry, gentlemen ...*" Everyone was singing so loud he knew she couldn't hear him.

For an instant, Brian hesitated as he glanced over his shoulder at his mother. Should he run back and get her? But he thought again about the medal that would make his father better; it was in the wallet, and he couldn't let it get stolen.

The woman was already turning the corner. He raced to catch up with her.

Why did I pick it up? Cally thought frantically as she rushed east on Forty-eighth Street toward Madison Avenue. She had abandoned her plan of walking down Fifth Avenue to find the peddler with the dolls. Instead, she headed toward the Lexington Avenue subway. She knew it would be quicker to go up to Fifty-first Street for the train, but the wallet felt like a hot brick in her pocket, and it seemed to her that everywhere she turned everyone was looking at her accusingly. Grand Central Station would be mobbed. She would get the train there. It was a safer place to go.

A squad car passed her as she turned right and crossed the street. Despite the cold, she had begun to perspire.

It probably belonged to that woman with the little boys. It was on the ground next to her. In her mind, Cally replayed the moment when she had taken in the slim young woman in the rose-colored all-weather coat that she could see was fur-lined from the turned-back sleeves. The coat obviously was expensive, as were the woman's shoulder bag and boots; the dark hair that came to the collar of her coat was shiny. She didn't look like she could have a care in the world.

Cally had thought, I wish I looked like that. She's about my age and my size and we have almost the same color hair. Well, maybe by next year I can afford pretty domes tor Gigi and me.

Then she'd turned her head to catch a glimpse of the Saks windows. So I didn't see her drop the wallet, she thought. But as she passed the woman, she'd felt her foot kick something and she'd looked down and seen it lying there.

Why didn't I just ask if it was hers? Cally agonized. But in that instant, she'd remembered how years ago, Grandma had come home one day, embarrassed and upset. She'd found a wallet on the street and opened it and saw the name and address of the owner. She'd walked three blocks to return it even though by then her arthritis was so bad that every step hurt.

The woman who owned it had looked through it and said that a twenty-dollar bill was missing.

Grandma had been so upset. "She practically accused me of being a thief."

That memory had flooded Cally the minute she touched the wallet. Suppose it did belong to the lady in the rose coat and she thought Cally had picked her pocket or taken money out of it? Suppose a policeman was called? They'd find out she was on probation. They wouldn't believe her any more than they'd believed her when she lent Jimmy money and her car because he'd told her if he didn't get out of town right away, a guy in another street gang was going to kill him.

Oh God, why didn't I just leave the wallet there? she thought. She considered tossing it in the nearest mailbox. She couldn't risk that. There were too many undercover cops around midtown during the holidays. Suppose one of them saw her and asked what she was doing? No, she'd get home right away. Aika, who minded Gigi along with her own grandchildren after the day-care center closed, would be bringing her home. It was getting late.

I'll put the wallet in an envelope addressed to whoever's name is in it and drop in in the mailbox later, Cally decided. That's all I can do.

Cally reached Grand Central Station. As she had hoped, it was mobbed with people rushing in all directions to trains and subways, hurrying home for Christmas. She shouldered her way across the main terminal, finally making it down the steps to the entrance to the Lexington Avenue subway.

As she dropped a token in the slot and hurried for the express train to Fourteenth Street, she was unaware of the small boy who had slipped under a turnstile and was dogging her footsteps.

2

"*God rest you merry, gentlemen, let nothing you dismay ...*" The familiar words seemed to taunt Catherine, reminding her of the forces that threatened the happily complacent life she had assumed would be hers forever. Her husband was in the hospital with leukemia. His enlarged spleen had been removed this morning as a precaution against it rupturing, and while it was too early to tell for sure, he seemed to be doing well. Still, she could not escape the fear that he was not going to live, and the thought of life without him was almost paralyzing.

Why didn't I realize Tom was getting sick? she agonized. She remembered how only two weeks ago, when she'd asked him to take groceries from the car, he'd reached into the trunk for the heaviest bag, hesitated, then winced as he picked it up.

She'd laughed at him. "Play golf yesterday. Act like an old man today. Some athlete."

"Where's Brian?" Michael asked as he returned from dropping the dollar in the singer's basket.

Startled from her thoughts, Catherine looked down at her son. "Brian?" she said blankly. "He's right here." She glanced down at her side, and then her eyes scanned the area. "He had a dollar. Didn't he, go with you to give it to the singer?"

"No," Michael said gruffly. "He probably kept it instead. He's a dork."

"Stop it," Catherine said. She looked around, suddenly alarmed. "Brian," she called "Brian." The carol was over, the crowd dispersing. Where was Brian? He wouldn't just walk away, surely. *"Brian,"* she called out again, this time loudly, alarm clear in her voice.

A few people turned and looked at her curiously. "A little boy," she said, becoming frightened, "He's wearing a dark blue ski jacket and a red cap. Did anyone see where he went?"

She watched as heads shook, as eyes looked around, wanting to help. A woman pointed behind them to the lines of people waiting to see the Saks windows. "Maybe he went there?" she said in a heavy accent

"How about the tree? Would he have crossed the street to get up close to it?" another woman suggested.

"Maybe the cathedral," someone volunteered.

"No. No, Brian wouldn't do that. We're going to visit his father. Brian can't wait to see him." As she said the words, Catherine knew that something was terribly wrong. She felt the tears that now came so easily rising behind her eyes. She fumbled in her bag for a handkerchief and realized something was missing: the familiar bulk of her wallet.

"Oh my God," she said. "My wallet's gone."

"Mom!" And now Michael lost the surly look that had become his way of disguising the worry about his father. He was suddenly a scared ten-year-old. "Mom. Do you think Brian was kidnapped?"

"How could he be? Nobody could just drag him off. That's impossible." Catherine felt her legs were turning to rubber. "Call the police," she cried. "My little boy is missing.

The station was crowded. Hundreds of people were rushing in every direction. There were Christmas decorations all over the place. It was noisy, too. Sound of all kinds echoed through the big space, bouncing off the ceiling high above him. A man with his arm full of packages bumped a sharp elbow into Brian's ear. "Sorry, kid."

He was having trouble keeping up with the woman who had his mom's wallet. He kept losing sight of her. He struggled to get around a family with a couple of kids who were blocking his way. He got past them, but bumped into a lady who glared down at him. "Be careful," she snapped.

"I'm sorry," Brian said politely, looking up at her. In that second he almost lost the woman he was following, catching up to her again as she went down a staircase and hurried through a long corridor that led to a subway station. When she went through a turnstile, he slipped under the next one and followed her onto a train.

The car was so crowded he could hardly get in. The woman was standing, hanging onto a bar that ran over the seats along the side. Brian stood near her, his hand gripping a pole. They went only one long stop, then she pushed her way to the opening doors. So many people were in Brian's way that he almost didn't get out of the subway car in time, and then he had to hurry to catch up with her. He chased after her as she went up the stairs to another train.

This time the car wasn't as crowded, and Brian stood near an old lady who reminded him of his grandmother. The woman in the dark raincoat got off at the second stop and he followed her, his eyes fixed on her ponytail as she practically ran up the stairs to the street.

They emerged on a busy corner. Buses raced past in both directions, rushing to get across the wide street before the light turned red. Brian glanced behind him. As far as he could see down the block there were nothing but apartment houses. Light streamed from hundreds of windows.

The lady with the wallet stood waiting for the light to turn. The WALK sign flashed on, and he followed his quarry across the street. When she reached the other side she turned left and walked quickly down the now sloping sidewalk. As he followed her, Brian took a quick look at the street sign. When they visited last summer, his mother had made a game of teaching him about street signs in New York. "Gran lives on Eighty-seventh Street," she had said. "We're on Fiftieth. How many blocks away is her apartment?" This sign said Fourteenth Street. He had to remember that, he told himself, as he fell in step behind the woman with his mom's wallet.

He felt snowflakes on his face. It was getting windy, and the cold stung his cheeks. He wished a cop would come along so he could ask for help, but he didn't see one anywhere. He knew what he was going to do anyway—he would follow the lady to where she lived. He still had the dollar his mother had given him for the man who was playing the violin. He would get change and call his grandmother, and she'd send a cop who would get his mom's wallet back.

It's a good plan, he thought to himself. In fact, he was *sure* of it. He had to get the wallet, and the medal that was inside. He thought of how after Mom had said that the medal wouldn't do any good, Gran had put it in her hand and said, *Please give it to Tom and have faith.*

The look on his grandmother's face had been so calm and so sure that Brian knew she was right. Once he got the medal back and they gave it to his dad, he would get well. Brian *knew* it.

The woman with the ponytail started to walk faster. He chased after her as she crossed one street and went to the end of another block. Then she turned right.

The street they were on now wasn't bright with decorated store windows like the one they had just left. Some places were boarded up and there was a lot of writing on the buildings and some of the streetlights were broken. A guy with a beard was sitting on the curb, clutching a bottle. He stretched out his hand to Brian as he passed him.

For the first time, Brian felt scared, but he kept his eyes on the woman. The snow was falling faster now, and the sidewalk was getting slippery. He stumbled once, but managed not to fall. He was out of breath trying to keep up with the lady. How far was she going? he wondered. Four blocks later he had his answer. She stepped into the entranceway to an old building, stuck her key in the lock, and went inside. Brian raced to catch the door before it closed behind her, but he was too late. The door was locked.

Brian didn't know what to do next, but then through the glass he saw a man coming toward him. As the man opened the door and hurried past him, Brian managed to grab it and to duck inside before it closed again.

The hall was dark and dirty, and the smell of stale food hung in the air. Ahead of him he could hear footsteps going up the stairs. Gulping to swallow his fear, and trying to not make noise, Brian slowly began to climb to the first landing. He would see where the lady went; then he would get out of there and find a telephone. Maybe instead of calling Gran, he would dial 911, he thought.

His mom had taught him that that was what he should do when he *really* needed help.

Which so far he didn't.

*

"All right, Mrs. Dornan. Describe your son to me," the police officer said soothingly.

"He's seven and small for his age," Catherine said. She could hear the shrillness in her voice. They were sitting in a squad car, parked in front of Saks, near the spot where the violinist had been playing.

She felt Michael's hand clutch hers reassuringly.

"What color hair?" the officer asked.

Michael answered, "Like mine. Kind of reddish. His eyes are blue. He's got freckles and one of his front teeth is missing. He has the same kind of pants I'm wearing, and his jacket is like mine 'cept it's blue and mine is green. He's skinny."

The policeman looked approvingly at Michael "You're a real help, son. Now, ma'am, you say your wallet is missing? Do you think you might have dropped it, or did anyone brush against you? I mean, could it have been a pickpocket?"

"I don't know," Catherine said. "I don't care about the wallet. But when I gave the boys money for the violinist, I probably didn't push it down far enough in my purse. It was quite bulky and might have just fallen out."

"Your son wouldn't have picked it up and decided to go shopping?"

"No, no, no," Catherine said with a flash of anger, shaking her head emphatically. "Please don't waste time even considering that."

"Where do you live, ma'am? What I mean is, do you want to

call anyone?" The policeman looked at the rings on Catherine's left hand. "Your husband?"

"My husband is in Sloan-Kettering hospital. He's very ill. He'll be wondering where we are. In fact, we should be with him soon. He's expecting us." Catherine put her hand on the door of the squad car. "I can't just sit here. I've got to look for Brian."

"Mrs. Dornan, I'm going to get Brian's description out right now. In three minutes every cop in Manhattan is going to be on the lookout for him. You know, he may have just wandered away and gotten confused. It happens. Do you come downtown often?"

"We used to live in New York, but we live in Nebraska now," Michael told him. "We visit my grandmother every summer. She lives on Eighty-seventh Street. We came back last week because my dad has leukemia and he needed an operation. He went to medical school with the doctor who operated on him."

Manuel Ortiz had been a policeman only a year, but already he had come in contact with grief and despair many times. He saw both in the eyes of this young woman. She had a husband who was very sick, now a missing kid. It was obvious to him that she could easily go into shock.

"Dad's gonna know something's wrong," Michael said, worried. "Mom, shouldn't you go see him?"

"Mrs. Dornan, how about leaving Michael with us? We'll stay here in case Brian tries to make his way back. We'll have all our guys looking for him. We'll fan out and use bullhorns to get him to contact us in case he's wandering around in the neighborhood somewhere. I'll get another car to take you up to the hospital and wait for you."

"You'll stay right here in case he comes back?"

"Absolutely."

"Michael, will you keep your eyes peeled for Brian?"

"Sure, Mom. I'll watch out for the Dork."

"Don't call him. ..." Then Catherine saw the look on her son's face. He's trying to get a rise out of me, she thought. He's trying to convince me that Brian is fine. That he'll be fine.

She put her arms around Michael and felt his small, gruff embrace in return.

"Hang in there, Mom," he said.

3

Jimmy Siddons cursed silently as he walked through the oval near Avenue B in the Stuyvesant Town apartment complex. The uniform he had stripped from the prison guard gave him a respectable look but was much too dangerous to wear on the street. He'd managed to lift a filthy overcoat and knit cap from a homeless guy's shopping cart. They helped some, but he had to find something else to wear, something decent.

He also needed a car. He needed one that wouldn't be missed until morning, something parked for the night, the kind of car that one of these middle-class Stuyvesant Town residents would own: medium-sized, brown or black, looking like every other Honda or Toyota or Ford on the road. Nothing fancy.

So far he hadn't seen the right one. He had watched as some old geezer got out of a Honda and said to his passenger, "Sure's good to get home," but he was driving one of those shiny red jobs that screamed for attention.

A kid pulled up in an old heap and parked, but from the

sound of the engine, Jimmy wanted no part of it. Just what he'd need, he thought; get on the Thruway and have it break down.

He was cold and getting hungry. Ten hours in the car, he told himself. Then I'll be in Canada and Paige will meet me there and we'll disappear again. She was the first real girlfriend he'd ever had, and she'd been a big help to him in Detroit. He knew he never would have been caught last summer if he had cased that gas station in Michigan better. He should have known enough to check the John outside the office instead of letting himself be surprised by an off-duty cop who stepped out of it while he was holding a gun on the attendant.

The next day he was on his way back to New York. To face trial for killing a cop.

An older couple passed him and threw a smile in his direction. "Merry Christmas."

Jimmy responded with a courteous nod of the head. Then he paid close attention as he heard the woman say, "Ed, I can't believe you didn't put the presents for the children in the trunk. Who leaves anything in sight in a car overnight in this day and age?"

Jimmy went around the corner and then stepped into the deep shadows on the grass as he returned to watch the couple stop in front of a dark-colored Toyota. The man opened the door. From the backseat he took a small rocking horse and handed it to the woman, then scooped up a half-dozen brightly wrapped packages. With her help he transferred everything to the trunk, relocked the car, and got back on the sidewalk.

Jimmy listened as the woman said, "I guess the phone's all right in the glove compartment," and her husband answered, "Sure it is. Waste of money, as far as I'm concerned. Can't wait to see Bobby's face tomorrow when he opens everything."

He watched as they turned the corner and disappeared. Which meant from their apartment they wouldn't be able to glance out and notice an empty parking space.

Jimmy waited ten minutes before he walked to the car. A few snowflakes swirled around him. Two minutes later he was driving out of the complex. It was quarter after five. He was headed to Cally's apartment on Tenth and B. He knew she'd be surprised to see him. And none too happy. She probably thought he couldn't find her. Why did she suppose that he didn't have a way to keep track of her even from Riker's Island? he wondered.

Big sister, he thought, as he drove onto Fourteenth Street, you promised Grandma you'd take care of me! "Jimmy needs guidance," Grandma had said. "He's in with a bad crowd. He's too easily led." Well, Cally hadn't come to see him *once* in Riker's. Not once. He hadn't even heard from her.

He'd have to be careful. He was sure the cops would be watching for him around Cally's building. But he had that figured out, too. He used to hang around this neighborhood and knew how to get across the roofs from the other end of the block and into the building. A couple of times he'd even pulled a job there when he was a kid.

Knowing Cally, he was sure she still kept some of Frank's

clothes in the closet. She'd been crazy about him, probably still had pictures of him all over the place. You'd never think he'd died even before Gigi was born.

And knowing Cally, she'd have at least a few bucks to get her little brother through the tolls, he figured. He'd find a way to convince her to keep her mouth shut until he was safely in Canada with Paige.

Paige. An image of her floated through his mind. Luscious. Blond. Only twenty-two. Crazy about him. She'd arranged everything, gotten the gun smuggled in to him. She'd never let him down or turn her back on him.

Jimmy's smile was unpleasant. You never tried to help me while I was rotting in Riker's Island, he thought—but once again, sister dear, you're going to help me get away, like it or not.

He parked the car a block from the rear of Cally's building and pretended to be checking a tire as he looked around. No cops in sight. Even if they were watching Cally's place, they probably didn't know you could get to it through the boarded-up dump. As he straightened up he cursed. Damn bumper sticker. Too noticeable, WE'RE SPENDING OUR GRANDCHILDREN'S INHERITANCE. He managed to pull most of it off.

Fifteen minutes later, Jimmy had picked the flimsy lock of Cally's apartment and was inside. Some dump, he thought, as he took in the cracks in the ceiling and the worn linoleum in the tiny entranceway. But neat. Cally was always neat. A

Christmas tree in the corner of what passed for a living room
had a couple of small, brightly wrapped packages under it.

Jimmy shrugged and went into the bedroom, where he ran-
sacked the closet to find the clothes he knew would be there. After
changing, he went through the place looking for money but found
none. He yanked open the doors that separated the stove, refrigerator, and sink from the living room, searched unsuccessfully for a
beer, settled for a Pepsi, and made himself a sandwich.

From what his sources had told him, Cally should be home
by now from her job in the hospital. He knew that on the way
she picked up Gigi from the baby-sitter. He sat on the couch, his
eyes riveted on the front door, his nerves jangling. He'd spent
most of the few dollars he found in the guard's pockets on food
from street vendors. He had to have money for the tolls on the
Thruway, as well as enough for another tank of gas. Come on,
Cally, he thought, where the hell are you?

At ten to six, he heard the key inserted in the lock. He
jumped up and in three long strides was in the entryway, flat-
tened against the wail. He waited until Cally stepped in and
closed the door behind her, then put his hand over her mouth.

"*Don't scream!*" he whispered, as he muffled her terrified
moan with his palm. "Understand?"

She nodded, eyes wide open in fear.

"Where's Gigi? Why isn't she with you?"

He released his grip long enough to let her gasp in an almost
inaudible voice, "She's at the baby-sitter's. She's keeping her

longer today, so I can shop. Jimmy, what are you *doing* here?"

"How much money have you got?"

"Here, take my pocketbook." Cally held it out to him, praying that he would not think to look through her coat pockets. Oh God, she thought, make him go away.

He took the purse and in a low and menacing tone warned, "Cally, I'm going to let go of you. Don't try anything or Gigi won't have a mommy waiting for her. Understand that?"

"Yes. Yes."

Cally waited until he released his grip on her, then slowly turned to face him. She hadn't seen her brother since that terrible night nearly three years ago when, with Gigi in her arms, she had come home from her job at the day-care center to find him waiting in her apartment in the West Village.

He looks about the same, she thought, except that his hair is shorter and his face is thinner. In his eyes there wasn't even a trace of the occasional warmth that at one time made her hope there was a possibility he might someday straighten out. No more. There was nothing left of the frightened six-year-old who had clung to her when their mother dumped them with Grandma and disappeared from their lives.

He opened her purse, rummaged through it, and pulled out her bright green combination change purse and billfold. "Eighteen dollars," he said angrily after a quick count of her money. "Is that all?"

"Jimmy, I get paid the day after tomorrow," Cally pleaded.

"Please just take it and get out of here. Please leave me alone."

There's half a tank of gas in the car, Jimmy thought. There's money here for another half tank and the tolls. I might just be able to make Canada. He'd have to shut Cally up, of course, which should be easy enough. He would just warn her that if she put the cops onto him and he got caught, he'd swear that she got someone to smuggle the gun in to him that he'd used on the guard.

Suddenly a sound from outside made him whirl around. He put his eye to the peephole in the door but could see no one there. With a menacing gesture to Cally, indicating that she had better keep quiet, he noiselessly turned the knob and opened the door a fraction, just in time to see a small boy straighten up, turn, and start to tiptoe to the staircase.

In one quick movement, Jimmy flung open the door and scooped up the child, one arm around his waist, the other covering his mouth, and pulled him inside, then roughly set him down.

"Eavesdropping, kid? Who is this, Cally?"

"Jimmy, leave him alone. I don't know who he is," she cried. "I've never seen him before."

Brian was so scared he could hardly talk. But he could tell the man and woman were mad at each other. Maybe the man would help him get his mother's wallet back, he thought. He pointed to Cally. "She has my mom's wallet."

Jimmy released Brian. "Well, now *that's* good news," he said with a grin, turning to his sister. "Isn't it?"

4

A plainclothesman in an unmarked car drove Catherine to the hospital. "I'll wait right here, Mrs. Dornan," he said. "I have the radio on so we'll know the minute they find Brian."

Catherine nodded. *If they find Brian* raced through her mind. She felt her throat close against the terror that thought evoked.

The lobby of the hospital was decorated for the holiday season. A Christmas tree was in the center, garlands of evergreens were hung, and poinsettias were banked against the reception desk.

She got a visitor's pass and learned that Tom was now in room 530. She walked to the bank of elevators and entered a car already half full, mostly with hospital personnel—doctors in white jackets with the telltale pen and notebook in their breast pockets, attendants in green scrub suits, a couple of nurses.

Two weeks ago, Catherine thought, Tom was making his rounds at St. Mary's in Omaha, and I was Christmas shopping. That evening we took the kids out for hamburgers. Life was normal and good and fun, and we were joking about how last year Tom had had so much trouble getting the Christmas tree in the stand, and I promised him I'd buy a new stand before this Christmas Eve. And once again I thought Tom looked so tired, and I did nothing about it.

Three days later he collapsed.

"Didn't you push the fifth floor?" someone asked.

Catherine blinked. "Oh, yes, thank you." She got off the elevator and for a moment stood still, getting her bearings. She found what she was looking for, an arrow on the wall pointing toward rooms 515 to 530.

As she approached the nurses' station, she saw Spence Crowley. Her mouth went dry. Immediately following the operation this morning, he had assured her that it had gone smoothly, and that his assistant would be making the rounds this afternoon. Then why was Spence here now? she worried. Could something be wrong?

He spotted her and smiled. Oh God, he wouldn't smile if Tom were ... It was another thought she could not finish.

He walked quickly around the desk and came to her. "Catherine, if you could *see* the look on your face! Tom's doing fine. He's pretty groggy, of course, but the vital signs are good."

Catherine looked up at him, wanting to believe the words she heard, wanting to trust the sincerity she saw in the brown eyes behind rimless glasses.

Firmly he took her arm and ushered her into the cubicle

behind the nurses' station. "Catherine, I don't want to bully you, but you have to understand that Tom has a good chance of beating this thing. A very good chance. I have patients who've led useful, full lives with leukemia. There are different types of medicine to control it. The one I plan to use with Tom is Interferon. It's worked miracles with some of my patients. It will mean daily injections at first, but after we get the dosage adjusted, he'll be able to give them to himself. When he recuperates fully from the operation, he can go back to work, and I swear to you that's going to happen." Then he added quietly, "But there is a problem."

Now he looked stern. "This afternoon when you saw Tom in ICU, I understand you were pretty upset."

"Yes." She had tried not to cry but couldn't stop. She'd been so worried, and knowing that he had made it through the operation was such a relief that she couldn't help herself.

"Catherine, Tom just asked me to level with him. He thinks I told you it was hopeless. He's starting to not trust me. He's beginning to wonder if maybe I'm hiding something, that maybe things are worse than I'm telling him. Well, Catherine, that is simply not so, and your job is to convince him that you have every expectation that you two will have a long life together. He mustn't get it in his head that he has a very limited time, not only because that would be harmful to him, but equally important because I don't believe that's *true*. In order to get well, Tom needs faith in his chances to get better, and a great deal of that has to come from you."

"Spence, I should have *seen* he was getting sick." Spence put his arms around her shoulders in a brief hug. "Listen," he said, "there's an old adage, 'Physician, heal thyself.' When Tom is feeling better, I'm going to rake him over the coals for ignoring some of the warnings his body was giving him. But now, go in there with a light step and a happy face. You can do it."

Catherine forced a smile. "Like this?"

"Much better," he nodded. "Just keep smiling. Remember, it's Christmas. Thought you were bringing the kids tonight?"

She could not talk about Brian being missing. Not now. Instead, she practiced what she would tell Tom. "Brian was sneezing, and I want to make sure he's not starting with a cold."

"That was wise. Okay. See you tomorrow, kiddo. Now remember, keep that smile going. You're gorgeous when you smile."

Catherine nodded and started down the hall to room 530. She opened the door quietly. Tom was asleep. An IV unit was dripping fluid into his arm. Oxygen tubes were in his nostrils. His skin was as white as the pillowcase. His lips were ashen.

The private duty nurse stood up. "He's been asking for you, Mrs. Dornan. I'll wait outside."

Catherine pulled up a chair next to the bed. She sat down and placed her hand over the one lying on the coverlet. She studied her husband's face, scrutinizing every detail: the high forehead framed by the reddish brown hair that was exactly the color of Brian's; the thick eyebrows that always looked a bit unruly; the well-shaped nose and the lips that were usually parted in a smile.

She thought of his eyes, more blue than gray, and the warmth and understanding they conveyed. He gives confidence to his patients, she thought. Oh, Tom, I want to tell you that our little boy is missing. I want you to be well and with me, looking for him.

Tom Dornan opened his eyes. "Hi, Love," he said weakly.

"Hi, yourself." She bent over and kissed him. "I'm sorry I was such a wimp this afternoon. Call it PMS or just old-fashioned relief. You know what a sentimental slob I am. I even cry at happy endings."

She straightened up and looked directly into his eyes. "You're doing great. You really are, you know."

She could see he did not believe her. *Not yet*, she thought determinedly.

"I thought you were bringing the kids tonight?" His voice was low and halting.

She realized that with Tom it was not possible to utter Brian's name without breaking down. Instead she said quickly, "I was afraid they'd be hanging all over you. I thought it was a good idea to let them wait until tomorrow morning."

"Your mother phoned," Tom said drowsily. "The nurse spoke to her. She said she sent a special present for you to give me. What is it?"

"Not without the boys. They want to be the ones to give it to you."

"Okay. But be sure to bring them in the morning. I want to see them."

"For sure. But since it's just the two of us now, maybe I should climb in the sack with you."

Tom opened his eyes again. "Now you're talking." A smile flickered on his lips. And then he was asleep again.

For a long moment, she laid her head on the bed, then got up as the nurse tiptoed back in. "Doesn't he look fantastic?" Catherine asked brightly as the nurse put her fingers on Tom's pulse.

She knew that even slipping into sleep, Tom might hear her. Then with a last glance at her husband, she hurried from the room, down the corridor and to the elevator, then through the lobby, and into the waiting police car.

The plainclothesman answered her unasked question: "No word so far, Mrs. Doman."

5

"I said, give it to me," Jimmy Siddons said ominously.

Cally tried to brave it out. "I don't know what this boy is talking about, Jimmy."

"Yes, you do," Brian said. "I saw you pick up my mom's wallet. And I followed you because I have to get it back."

"Aren't you a smart kid?" Siddons sneered. "Always go where the buck is." His expression turned ugly as he faced his sister. "Don't make me take it from you, Cally."

There was no use trying to pretend she didn't have it. Jimmy knew the boy was telling the truth. Cally still had her coat on. She reached into the pocket and took out the handsome Moroccan leather wallet. Silently she handed it to her brother.

"That belongs to my mother," Brian said defiantly. Then the glance the man gave him made him shiver. He had been about to try to grab the wallet; instead, now suddenly fearful, he dug his hands deep in his pockets.

Jimmy Siddons opened the billfold. "My, my," he said, his

tone now admiring. "Cally, you surprise me. You run rings around some of the pickpockets I know."

"I didn't steal it," Cally protested. "Someone dropped it, I found it. I was going to mail it back."

"Well, you can forget that," Jimmy said. "It's mine now, and I need it."

He pulled out a thick wad of bills and began counting. "Three hundred-dollar bills, four fifties, six twenties, four tens, five fives, three ones. Six hundred and eighty-eight dollars. Not bad, in fact, it'll do just fine."

He stuffed the money in the pocket of the suede jacket he had taken from the bedroom closet and began to dig through the compartments in the wallet. "Credit cards. Well, why not? Driver's license—no, two of them: Catherine Dornan and Dr. Thomas Dornan. Who's Dr. Thomas Dornan, kid?"

"My dad. He's in the hospital." Brian watched as the deep compartment in the wallet revealed the medal.

Jimmy Siddons lifted it out, held it up by the chain, then laughed incredulously. "St. Christopher! I haven't been inside a church in years, but even I know they kicked him out long ago. And when I think of all the stories Grandma used to tell us about how he carried the Christ child on his shoulders across the stream or the river or whatever it was! Remember, Cally?" Disdainfully he let the medal clatter to the floor.

Brian swooped to retrieve it. He clutched it in his hand, then slipped it around his neck. "My grandpa carried it all through the war and came home safe. It's going to make my dad get better. I don't care about the wallet. You can have it. This is what I really wanted. I'm going home now." He turned and ran for the door. He had twisted the knob and pulled the door open before Siddons reached him, clapped a hand over his mouth, and yanked him back inside.

"You and St. Christopher are staying right here with me, buddy," he said as he shoved him roughly to the floor.

Brian gasped as his forehead slammed onto the cracked linoleum. He sat up slowly, rubbing his head. He felt like the room was spinning, but he could hear the woman he had followed pleading with the man. "Jimmy, don't hurt him. Please. Leave us alone. Take the money and go. But get out of here."

Brian wrapped his arms around his legs, trying not to cry. He shouldn't have followed the lady. He knew that now. He should have yelled instead of following her so that maybe somebody would stop her. This man was bad. This man wasn't going to let him go home. And nobody knew where he was. Nobody knew where to look for him.

He felt the medal dangling against his chest and closed his fist around it. Please get me back to Mom, he prayed silently, so I can bring you to Dad.

He did not look up to see Jimmy Siddons studying him. He did not know that Jimmy's mind was racing, assessing the situation. This kid followed Cally when she took the wallet, Siddons thought. Did anyone follow him? No. If they had, they'd be here by now. "Where did you get the wallet?" he asked his sister.

"On Fifth Avenue. Across from Rockefeller Center." Cally was terrified now. Jimmy would stop at nothing to get away. Not at killing her. Not at killing this child. "His mother must have dropped it. I picked it up off the sidewalk. I guess he saw me."

"I guess he did." Jimmy looked at the phone on the table next to the couch. Then, grinning, he reached for the cellular phone he had taken from the glove compartment of the stolen car. He also took out a gun and pointed it at Cally. "The cops may have your phone tapped." He pointed at the table next to the couch. "Go over there. "I'm going to dial your number and tell you I'm turning myself in and I want you to call that public defender who is representing me. All you have to do is act nice and nervous, just like you are now. Make a mistake and you and this kid are dead."

He looked down at Brian. "One peep out of you and ..." He left the threat unspoken.

Brian nodded to show he understood. He was too scared to even promise that he'd be quiet.

"Cally, you got all that straight?"

Cally nodded. How stupid I've been, she thought. I was fool enough to believe I'd gotten away from him. No chance. He even knows this phone number.

He finished dialing and the phone beside her rang. "Hello." Her voice was low and muffled.

"Cally, it's Jimmy. listen, I'm in trouble. You probably know by now. I'm sorry I tried to get away. I hope that guard will be all right I'm broke and I'm scared." Jimmy's voice was a whine. "Call Gil Weinstein. He's the public defender assigned to me. Tell him I'll meet him at St. Patrick's Cathedral when midnight Mass is over. Tell him I want to turn myself in and I want him to be with me. His home number is 555-0267. Cally, I'm sorry I messed up everything so badly."

Jimmy pressed the disconnect on the cellular phone and watched as Cally hung up as well. "They can't trace a cellular phone call, you know that, don't you? Okay, now phone Weinstein and give him the same story. If the cops are listening, they must be jumping up and down right now."

"Jimmy, they'll think I . . ."

In two steps Jimmy was beside her, the gun to her head. "Make the call."

"Your lawyer may not be home. He may refuse to meet you."

"Naw. I know him. He's a jerk. Hell want the publicity. Get him."

Cally did not need to be told to make it quick. The moment Gil Weinstein was on the line, she rushed to say, "You don't know me. I'm Cally Hunter. My brother, Jimmy Siddons, just called. He wants me to tell you . . ." In a quavering voice she delivered the message.

"I'll meet him," the lawyer said. "I'm glad he's doing this, but if that prison guard dies, Jimmy is facing a death-penalty trial. He could get life without parole for the first killing, but now . . ." His voice trailed off.

"I think he knows that." Cally saw Jimmy's gesture. "I have to go now. Good-bye, Mr. Weinstein."

"You make a great accomplice, big sister," Jimmy told her. He looked down at Brian. "What's your name, kid?"

"Brian," he whispered.

"Come on, Brian. We're getting out of here."

"Jimmy, leave him alone. Please. Leave him here with me."

"No way. There's always the chance you'd go running to the cops even though the minute they talk to that kid, you're in big trouble yourself. After all, you *did* steal his mama's wallet. No, the kid comes with me. No one is looking for a guy with his little boy, are they? I'll let him go tomorrow morning when I get to where I'm headed. After that you can tell them anything you like about me. The kid'll even back you up, won't you, sonny?"

Brian shrank against Cally. He was so afraid of the man that he was trembling. Was the man going to make him go away with him?

"Jimmy, leave him here. Please." Cally thrust Brian behind her.

Jimmy Siddons's mouth twisted in anger. He grabbed Cally's arm and yanked her toward him, roughly twisting her arm behind her.

She screamed as she lost her grip on Brian and slipped to the floor.

With eyes that denied any history of affection between them, Jimmy stood over his sister, again holding the gun to her head.

"If you don't do what I tell you, you'll get more of that ... and worse. They won't take me alive. Not you, not nobody else is gonna send me to the death chamber. Besides, I got a girlfriend waiting for me. So just keep your mouth shut. I'll even make a deal. You don't say nothing, and I'll let the kid live. But if the cops try to close in on me, he gets a bullet in the head. It's as simple as that. Got it straight?"

He stuck the gun back inside his jacket, then reached down and roughly pulled Brian to his feet. "You and I are gonna get to be real pals, sonny," he said. "Real pals." He grinned. "Merry Christmas, Cally."

6

The unmarked van parked across the street from Cally's apartment building was the lookout post for the detectives watching Cally's building for any sign of Jimmy Siddons. They had observed Cally come home at just a little after her usual time.

Jack Shore, the detective who had visited Cally in the morning, pulled off his earphones, swore silently, and turned to his partner. "What do you think, Mort? No, wait a minute. I'll tell you what I think. It's a trick. He's trying to buy time to get as far away from New York as possible while we take up the collection at St. Pat's looking for him."

Mort Levy, twenty years younger than Shore and less cynical, rubbed his chin, always a sign that he was deep in thought. "If it is a trick, I don't think the sister is a willing accomplice. You don't need a meter to hear the stress level in her voice."

"Listen, Mort, you were at Bill Grasso's funeral. Thirty years old, with four little kids, and shot between the eyes by that bum

Siddons. If Cally Hunter had come clean with us and told us that she'd given that rat brother of hers money and the keys to her car, Grasso would have known what he was up against when he stopped him for running a light."

"I still believe that Cally had bought Jimmy's story about trying to get away because he'd been in a gang fight and the other gang was after him. I don't think she knew that he'd wounded a clerk in a liquor store. Up till then he hadn't been in really serious trouble."

"You mean he'd gotten away with it till then," Shore snapped. "Too bad that judge couldn't put Cally away as an accessory to murder instead of just for aiding a fugitive. She got off after serving fifteen months. Bill Grasso's widow is trimming the tree without him tonight."

His face reddened with anger. "I'll call in. Just in case that louse meant what he said, we've got to cover the cathedral. You know how many people go to midnight Mass there tonight? Take a guess."

Cally sat on the worn velour sofa, her hands clasped around her knees, her head bent, her eyes closed. Her entire body was trembling. She was beyond tears, beyond fatigue. Dear God, dear God, *why* did all this happen?

What should she do?

If anything happened to Brian, she would be responsible. She had picked up his mother's wallet, and that's why he'd followed her. If the child was right, his dad was very ill. She thought of the attractive young woman in the rose-colored coat and how she had been sure everything in her life was perfect.

Would Jimmy let the boy go when he got to wherever was his destination? How could he? she reasoned. Wherever that was, they'd start searching for Jimmy in that area. *And if he does let him go, Brian will tell how he followed me because I took the wallet,* she reminded herself.

But Jimmy had said he would shoot the child if the cops closed in on him. And he meant it, she was certain of that. So if I tell the cops, Brian doesn't have a chance, she thought.

If I don't say anything now and Jimmy does let him go, then I can honestly say that I didn't tell because he threatened to kill the kid if the cops got near him, and I knew he meant it. And I know he does mean it, Cally thought. That's the worst part.

Brian's face loomed in Cally's mind. The reddish brown hair that fell forward on his forehead, the large, intelligent blue eyes, the spatter of freckles on his cheeks and nose. When Jimmy dragged him in, her first impression was that he wasn't more than five; from the way he spoke, though, she was sure he was older. He was so scared when Jimmy made him go with him out the window and onto the fire escape. He had looked back at her, his eyes pleading.

The phone rang. It was Aika, the wonderful black woman who minded Gigi along with her own grandchildren each afternoon after the day-care center closed.

"Just checking to see if you're home, Cally," Aika said, her voice rich and comforting. "Did you find the doll man?"

"I'm afraid not."

"Too bad. You need more time to shop?"

"No, I'll come right over now and get Gigi."

"No, that's okay. She already ate dinner with my gang. I need milk for breakfast, so I've got to go out anyway. I'll drop her off in half an hour or so."

"Thanks, Aika." Cally put down the receiver, aware that she still had her coat on and that the apartment was dark except for the entryway light. She took off the coat, went into the bedroom, and opened the closet door. She gasped when she saw that when he took Frank's suede jacket and brown slacks, Jimmy had left other clothes crumpled on the floor, a jacket and pants, and a filthy overcoat.

She bent down and picked up the jacket. Detective Shore had told her that Jimmy had shot a guard and stripped him of his uniform. Obviously, this was the uniform—and there were bullet holes in the jacket.

Frantically, Cally wrapped the jacket and pants inside the overcoat. Suppose the cops came in with a search warrant! They'd never believe her, that Jimmy broke into her place. They'd be sure she gave him clothes. She'd go back to prison. And she'd lose Gigi for good! What should she do?

She looked around the closet, wildly searching for a solution. The storage box on the overhead shelf. In it she kept whatever summer clothes she and Gigi had. She yanked the box down, opened it, pulled out the contents, and threw them on the shelf. She folded the uniform and coat into the box, closed it, ran to the bed, and fished under it for the Christmas wrappings she had stored there.

With frantic fingers she wrapped candy-cane paper around the box and tied it with a ribbon. Then she carried it into the living room and put it under the tree. She had just completed the task when she heard the downstairs buzzer. Smoothing back her hair, and forcing a welcoming smile for Gigi, she went to answer it.

It was Detective Shore and the other detective who had been with him this morning who came up the stairs. "Playing games again, Cally?" Shore asked. "I hope not."

7

Brian huddled in the passenger seat as Jimmy Siddons drove up the East River Drive. He had never felt so afraid before. He'd been scared when the man made him climb up that fire escape to the roof. Then he'd practically been dragged from one roof to another as they went the length of the block, finally going down through an empty building and onto the street where this car was parked.

The man had pushed Brian into the car and snapped on the seat belt. "Just remember to call me Daddy if anyone stops us," he had warned him.

Brian knew the man's name was Jimmy. That was what the woman had called him. She had looked so worried about Brian. When Jimmy pulled him through the window, she had been crying, and Brian could tell how scared she was for him. She knew his parents' names. Maybe she would call the cops. If she did, would they come looking for him? But Jimmy said he'd kill him if the cops came. Would he?

Brian huddled deeper in the seat. He was scared and hungry. And he had to go to the bathroom, but he was afraid to ask. His only comfort was the medal that now lay against his chest on the outside of his jacket. It had brought Grandpa home from the war. It was going to make Daddy well. And it was going to get him home safe, too. He was sure of it.

Jimmy Siddons glanced briefly at his small hostage. For the first time since he had broken out of the prison, he was beginning to relax. It was still snowing, but if it didn't get any worse than this, it was nothing to worry about. Cally wouldn't call the cops. He was positive of that. She knew him well enough to believe him when he said he would kill the kid if he was stopped.

I'm not going to rot in prison for the rest of my life, he thought, and I'm not giving them the chance to pump me full of poison. Either I make it, or I don't.

But I *will*. He smiled grimly. He knew there had to be an APB out on him and they'd be watching all the bridges and tunnels out of New York. But they had no idea where he was heading, and they certainly weren't looking for a father and son traveling in a car that wasn't reported stolen yet.

He'd pulled out all the presents he had seen the couple stash in the trunk. Now they were piled on the backseat, bundles of Christmas cheer. Those presents, coupled with the kid in the front, meant even if toll takers had been alerted to be on the lookout, they'd never glance twice at him now.

And in eight or nine hours he would be across the border and into Canada, where Paige would be waiting. And then he would find a nice deep lake that would be the final destination of this car and all the nice presents in the backseat.

And this kid with his St. Christopher medal.

The awesome power of the New York City Police Department ground methodically into gear as plans were laid to assure that Jimmy Siddons did not slip between their fingers, just in case, at the last minute, he panicked and decided not to surrender after midnight Mass.

As soon as their wiretap recorded Cally's phone calls from Jimmy, and to his lawyer, Jack Shore had called in the information. He had let the higher-ups know exactly what he thought of Siddons's "decision" to surrender. "It's an out-and-out crock," he had barked. "We tie up a couple of hundred cops till one-thirty or two in the morning, and he's halfway to Canada or Mexico before we find out that he's made us look like a bunch of fools."

Finally the deputy police commissioner in charge of the manhunt had snapped, "All right, Jack. We *know* what you think. Now let's get on with it. There's been no sign of him around his sister's place?"

"No, sir," Jack Shore had said and hung up, and then he and his partner, Mort, had gone to visit Cally. When they got back to the van, Shore again reported in to headquarters. "We just were back to Hunter's apartment, sir. She's fully aware of the consequences if she helps her brother in any way. The baby-sitter dropped off her kid as we were leaving, and my guess is Cally's in for the night."

Mort Levy frowned as he listened to his partner's conversation with the deputy police commissioner. There was something about that apartment that was *different* from the way it had looked this morning, but he couldn't figure out what it was. Mentally he reviewed the layout: the small entryway, the bathroom directly off it, the narrow combination living room-kitchen, the cell-like bedroom, barely large enough to hold a single bed, a cot for the little girl, and a three-drawer dresser.

Jack had asked Cally if she would mind if they looked around again, and she had nodded assent. Certainly no one was hiding in that place. They had opened the door to the bathroom, looked under the beds, poked in the closet. Levy had felt unwilling pity for Cally Hunter's attempts to brighten the dismal flat. All the walls were painted a bright yellow. Floral pillows were randomly piled on the old couch. The Christmas tree was bravely decorated with tons of tinsel and strings of red and green lights. A few brightly wrapped presents were placed under it.

Presents? Mort did not know why this word triggered something in his subconscious. He thought for a moment, then shook his head. Forget it, he told himself.

He wished Jack hadn't bullied Cally Hunter. It was easy to

see that she was terrified of him. Mort hadn't been in on her case, which had been tried over two years ago, but from what he'd heard, he believed that Cally honestly thought that her troublesome kid brother had been in a gang fight and that the members of the other gang were hunting him.

What am I trying to remember about her apartment? Mort asked himself. *What was different?*

They were normally scheduled to go off duty at eight o'clock, but tonight both he and Jack were going back to headquarters instead. Like dozens of others, they would be working overtime at least until after midnight Mass at the cathedral. Maybe, just maybe, Siddons would show up as he had promised. Levy knew that Shore was aching to make the arrest personally. "I could spot that guy if he was wearing a nun's habit," he kept saying, over and over again.

There was a tap at the back door of the van, signifying that their replacements had arrived. As Mort stood up, stretched, and stepped down onto the street, he was glad that just before he left Cally Hunter's apartment, he had slipped her his card and whispered, "If you want to talk to anyone, Mrs. Hunter, here's a number where you can reach me."

8

The crowds on Fifth Avenue had thinned out, although there were still some onlookers around the tree in Rockefeller Center. Others were still lined up waiting to see Saks's window display, and there was a steady stream of visitors slipping in and out of St. Patrick's Cathedral.

But as the car she was in pulled up behind the squad car where Officer Ortiz and Michael were waiting, Catherine could see that most of the last-minute shoppers were gone.

They're on their way home, she thought, to do the final gift wrapping and to tell each other that next year, for sure, they won't be rushing around to stores on Christmas Eve.

Everything at the last minute. That had been her own pattern until twelve years ago, when a third-year resident, Dr. Thomas Doman, came into the administration office of St. Vincent's Hospital, walked over to her desk, and said, "You're new here, aren't you?"

Tom, so easygoing, but so organized. If she were the one who was sick, Tom wouldn't have stuffed all her money and identification into his own bulging wallet. He wouldn't have dropped it into his pocket so carelessly that someone either reached in and grabbed it or picked it up off the ground.

That was the thought that was torturing Catherine as she opened the car door and, through the swirling snow, ran the few steps to the squad car. Brian would never have wandered away on his own, she was sure of that. He was so anxious to get to Tom, he hadn't even wanted to take the time to look at the Rockefeller Center tree. He must have set off on some mission. That was it. If somebody hadn't actually kidnapped him—and that seemed unlikely—he must have seen whoever took or picked up the wallet and followed that person.

Michael was sitting in the front seat with Officer Ortiz, sipping a soda. A brown paper bag with remnants of a packet of ketchup was standing on the floor in front of him. Catherine squeezed in beside him on the front seat and smoothed his hair.

"How's Dad?" he asked anxiously. "You didn't tell him about Brian, did you?"

"No, of course not. I'm sure we'll find Brian soon, and there was no need to worry him. And he's doing just great. I saw Dr. Crowley. He's a happy camper about Dad." She looked over Michael's head at Officer Ortiz. "It's been almost two hours," she said quietly.

He nodded. "Brian's description will keep going out every hour to every cop and car in the area. Mrs. Dornan, Michael ahd I have been talking. He's sure Brian wouldn't deliberately wander away."

"No, he's right He wouldn't."

"You talked to the people around you when you realized he was missing?"

"Yes."

"And no one noticed a kid being pulled or carried away?"

"No. People remember seeing him, then they didn't see him."

"I'll level with you. I don't know any molester who would even attempt to kidnap a child from his mother's side and work his way through a crowd of people. But Michael thinks that maybe Brian would have taken off after someone he saw take your wallet."

Catherine nodded. "I've been thinking the same thing. It's the only answer that makes sense."

"Michael tells me that last year Brian stood up to a fourth-grade kid who shoved one of his classmates."

"He's a gutsy kid," Catherine said. Then the import of what the policeman had said hit her. *He thinks that if Brian followed whoever took my wallet, he may have confronted that person.* Oh God, no!

"Mrs. Dornan, if it's all right with you, I thyink it would be a good idea if we tried to get cooperation from the media. We might be able to get some of the local TV stations to show Brian's picture if you have one."

"The one I carried is in my wallet," Catherine said, her voice a monotone. Images of Brian standing up to a thief flashed in her mind. My little boy, she thought, would someone hurt my little boy?

What was Michael saying? He was talking to the cop Ortiz.

"My grandmother has a bunch of pictures of us," Michael was telling him. Then he looked up at his mother. "Anyhow, Mom, you gotta call Gran. She's going to start worrying if we're not home soon."

Like father, like son, Catherine thought. Brian looks like Tom. Michael thinks like him. She closed her eyes against the waves of near panic that washed through her. Tom. Brian. Why?

She felt Michael fishing in her shoulder bag. He pulled out the cellular phone. "I'll dial Gran," he told her.

9

In her apartment on Eighty-seventh Street, Barbara Cavanaugh clutched the phone, not wanting to believe what her daughter was telling her. But there was no disputing the dreadful news that Catherine's quiet, almost emotionless voice had conveyed. Brian was missing, and had been missing for over two hours now.

Barbara managed to keep her voice calm. "Where are you, dear?"

"Michael and I are in a police car at Forty-ninth and Fifth. That's where we were standing when Brian ... just suddenly wasn't next to me."

"I'll be right there."

"Mom, be sure to bring the most recent pictures you have of Brian. The police want to give them out to all the news media. And the news radio station is going to have me on in a few minutes to make an appeal. And Mom, call the nurses' station on the fifth floor of the hospital. Tell them to make absolutely sure that Tom isn't allowed to turn on the TV in his room. He doesn't have a radio. If he ever found out that Brian was missing . . ." Her voice trailed off.

"I'll call right away but, Catherine, I don't have any recent pictures here," Barbara cried. "All the ones we took last summer are in the Nantucket house." Then she wanted to bite her tip. She'd been asking for new pictures of the boys and hadn't received any. Only yesterday Catherine had told her that her Christmas present, framed portraits of them, had been forgotten in the rush to get Tom to New York for the operation.

"I'll bring what I can find," she said hurriedly. "I'm on my way."

For an instant after she finished delivering the message to the hospital, Barbara Cavanaugh sank into a chair and rested her forehead in her palm. Too much, she thought, too much.

Had there always been a feeling haunting her that everything was too good to be true? Catherine's father had died when she was ten, and there had always been a lingering touch of sadness in her eyes, until at twenty-two she met Tom. They were so happy together, so perfect together. The way Gene and I were from day one, Barbara thought.

For an instant her mind rushed back to that moment in 1943, when at age nineteen and a sophomore in college, she'd been introduced to a handsome young Army officer, Lieutenant Eugene Cavanaugh. In that first moment they'd both known that they were perfect for each other. They were married two months later, but it was eighteen years before their only child was born.

With Tom, my daughter has found the same kind of relationship with which I was blessed, Barbara thought, but now . . . She jumped up. She *had* to get to Catherine, Brian *must* have just wandered away. They just got separated, she told herself. Catherine was strong, but she must be close to the breaking point by now. Oh, dear God, let someone find him, she prayed.

She rushed through the apartment, yanking framed photographs from mantels and tabletops. She'd moved here from Beekman Place ten years ago. It was still more space than she needed, with a formal dining room, library, and guest suite. But now it meant that when Tom and Catherine and the boys came to visit from their home in Omaha, there was plenty of room for them.

Barbara tossed the pictures into the handsome leather carry-all Tom and Catherine had given her for her birthday, grabbed a coat from the foyer closet, and, without bothering to double lock the door, rushed outside in time to press the button for the elevator as it began to descend from the penthouse.

Sam, the elevator operator, was a longtime employee. When he opened the door for her, his smile was replaced by a look of concern. "Good evening, Mrs. Cavanaugh. Merry Christmas. Any further word on Dr. Dornan?"

Afraid to speak, Barbara shook her head.

"Those grandkids of yours are real cute. The little one,

Brian, told me you gave his mom something that would make his dad get well. I sure hope that's true."

Barbara tried to say, "So do I," but found that her lips could not form the words.

"Mommy, why are you sad?" Gigi asked as she settled onto Cally's lap.

"I'm not sad, Gigi," Cally said. "I'm always happy when I'm with you."

Gigi shook her head She was wearing a red-and-white Christmas nightgown with figures of angels carrying candles. Her wide brown eyes and wavy golden-brown hair were legacies from Frank. The older she gets, the more she looks like him, Cally thought, instinctively holding the child tighter.

They were curled up together on the couch across from the Christmas tree. "I'm glad you're home with me, Mommy," Gigi said, and her voice became fearful. "You won't leave me again, will you?"

"No. I didn't want to leave you last time, sweetheart."

"I didn't like visiting you at that place."

That place. The Bedford correctional facility for women.

"I didn't like being there." Cally tried to sound matter-of-fact.

"Kids should stay with their mothers."

"Yes. I think so too."

"Mommy, is that big present for me?" Gigi pointed to the box that held the uniform and coat Jimmy had discarded.

Cally's lips went dry. "No, sweetheart, that's a present for Santa Claus. He likes to get something for Christmas, too. Now come on, it's past your bedtime."

Gigi automatically began to say, "I don't want to ... ," then she stopped. "Will Christmas come faster if I go to bed now?"

"Uh-huh. Come on, I'll carry you in."

When she had tucked the blankets around Gigi and given her her "bee," the tattered blanket that was her daughter's indispensable sleeping companion, Cally went back to the living room and once again sank down onto the couch.

Kids should stay with their mothers ... Gigi's words haunted her. Dear God, where had Jimmy taken that little boy? What would he do to him? What should she do?

Cally stared at the box with the candy-cane paper. *That's for Santa Claus.* A vivid memory of its contents flashed through her mind. The uniform of the guard Jimmy had shot, the side and sleeve still sticky with blood. The filthy overcoat—God knew where he'd found or stolen *that.*

Jimmy was *evil.* He had no conscience, no pity. Face it, Cally told herself fiercely—he won't hesitate to kill that little boy if it helps his chances to escape.

She turned on the radio to the local news. It was seven-thirty. The breaking news was that the condition of the prison guard who had been shot at Riker's Island was still critical, but was now stable. The doctors were cautiously optimistic that he would live.

If he lives, Jimmy isn't facing the death penalty, Cally told herself. They can't execute him now for the cop's death three years ago. He's smart. He won't take a chance on murdering the little boy once he knows that the guard isn't going to die. He'll let him go.

The announcer was saying, "In other news, early this evening, seven-year-old Brian Dornan became separated from his mother on Fifth Avenue. The family is in New York because Brian's father . . ."

Frozen in front of the radio, Cally listened as the announcer gave a description of the boy, then said, "Here is a plea from his mother, asking for your help."

As Cally listened to the low, urgent voice of Brian's mother, she visualized the young woman who had dropped the wallet. Early thirties at the most. Shiny, dark hair that just reached the collar of her coat. She'd only caught a glimpse of her face, but Cally was sure that she was very pretty. Pretty and well dressed and secure.

Now, listening to her begging for help, Cally put her hands over her ears, then ran to the radio and snapped it off. She tiptoed into the bedroom. Gigi was already asleep, her breathing soft and even, her cheek pillowed in her hand, the other hand holding the ragged baby blanket up to her face.

Cally knelt beside her. I can reach out and touch her, she thought. That woman can't reach out to her child. What should I do? But if I call the police and Jimmy does harm that little boy, they'll say it's my fault, just the way they said that the cop's death was my fault.

Maybe Jimmy will just leave him somewhere. He *promised* he would ... Even Jimmy wouldn't hurt a little boy, surely? I'll just wait and pray, she told herself.

But the prayer she tried to whisper—"Please God, keep little Brian safe"—sounded like a mockery and she did not complete it.

Jimmy had decided that his best bet was to go over the George Washington Bridge to Route 4, then take Route 17 to the New York Thruway. It might be a little farther that way than going up through the Bronx to the Tappan Zee, but every instinct warned him to get out of New York City fast. It was good that the GW had no toll gate at the outgoing side where they might stop him.

Brian looked out the window as they crossed the bridge. He knew they were going over the Hudson River. His mother had cousins who lived in New Jersey, near the bridge. Last summer, when he and Michael spent an extra week with Gran after they came back from Nantucket, they had visited them there.

They were nice. They had kids just about his age, too. Just thinking about them made Brian want to cry. He wished he could open the window and shout, "*I'm here. Come get me, please!*"

He was so hungry, and he really had to go to the bathroom. He looked up timidly. "I ... could I please ... I mean, I have to go to the bathroom." Now that he'd said it, he was so afraid the man would refuse that his lip began to quiver. Quickly he bit down on it. He could just hear Michael calling him a crybaby. But even that thought made him feel sad. He wouldn't even mind seeing Michael right now.

"You gotta pee?"

The man didn't seem too mad at him. Maybe he wouldn't hurt him after all. "Uh-huh."

"Okay. You hungry?"

"Yes, sir."

Jimmy was starting to feel somewhat secure. They were on Route 4. The traffic was heavy but moving. Nobody was looking for this car. By now, the guy who parked it was probably in his pj's watching *It's a Wonderful Life* for the fortieth time. By tomorrow morning, when he and his wife started to holler about their stolen Toyota, Jimmy would be in Canada with Paige. God he was crazy about her. In his life, she was the closest he had ever come to a sure thing.

Jimmy didn't want to stop to eat yet. On the other hand, to be on the safe side, he probably should fill up the tank now. There was no telling what hours places would keep on Christmas Eve.

"All right," he said, "in a couple minutes we'll get some gas, go to the John, and I'll buy sodas and potato chips. Later on, we'll stop at a McDonald's and get a hamburger. But just remember when we stop for gas, you try to attract attention and . . ." He pulled the pistol from his jacket, pointed it at Brian, and made a clicking noise. "*Bang*," he said.

Brian looked away. They were in the middle lane of the three-lane highway. A sign pointed to the exit marked Forest Avenue. A police car pulled abreast of them, then turned off into the parking lot of a diner. "I won't talk to anyone. I promise," he managed to say.

"I promise, *Daddy*," Jimmy snapped.

Daddy. Involuntarily, Brian's hand curled around the St. Christopher medal. He was going to bring this medal to Daddy and then Daddy was going to get better. Then his dad would find this guy, Jimmy, and beat him up for being so mean to his kid. Brian was sure of it. As his fingers traced the raised image of the towering figure carrying the Christ child, he said in a clear voice, "I promise, *Daddy*."

10

At lower Manhattan's One Police Plaza, the command post for the Jimmy Siddons manhunt, the escalating tension was visibly evident. Everyone was keenly aware that to make good his escape, Siddons would not hesitate to kill again. They also knew he had the weapon smuggled in to him.

"*Armed and Dangerous*" was the caption under his picture on the flyers that were being distributed all over the city.

"Last time, we got two thousand useless tips, followed up every useless one of them, and the only reason we ever got him behind bars last summer was because he was dumb enough to hold up a gas station in Michigan while a cop was on the premises," Jack Shore growled to Mort Levy, as in disgust he watched a team of officers answer the flood of calls on the hot line.

Levy nodded absently. "Anything more about Siddons's girlfriend?" he asked Shore.

An hour ago one of the prisoners in Siddons's cellblock had told a guard that last month Siddons had bragged about a girlfriend named Paige, who he said was a world-class stripper.

They were crying to trace her in New York, but on the hunch that she might have been involved with Siddons in Michigan, Shore had contacted the authorities there.

"No, nothing so far. Probably another dead end."

"Call for you from Detroit, Jack," a voice bellowed above the din in the room. Both men turned quickly. In two strides Shore was at his desk and had grabbed the phone.

His caller did not waste time. "Stan Logan, Jack. We met when you came out to pick up Siddons last year. I may have something interesting for you."

"Let's have it."

"We never could find out where Siddons was hiding before he tried to pull the holdup here. The tip about Paige may be the answer. We've got a rap sheet on a Paige Laronde who calls herself an exotic dancer. She left town two days ago. Told a friend she didn't know if she'd be back, that she expected to join her boyfriend."

"Did she say where she was going?" Shore snapped.

"She said California, then Mexico."

"California and Mexico! Hell, if he makes it to Mexico we may never find him."

"Our guys are checking the train and bus stations as well as the airports, to see if we can pick up her trail. We'll keep you posted," Logan promised, then added, "We're about to fax her rap sheet and publicity pictures. Don't show them to your kids."

Shore slammed down the phone. "If Siddons managed to get out of New York this morning, he could be in California right now, maybe even Mexico."

"It would be pretty rough to get a plane reservation at the last minute on Christmas Eve," Levy reminded him cautiously.

"Listen, somebody got a gun in to him. That same somebody may have had clothes and cash and an airline ticket waiting for him. Probably managed to get him to an airport in Philadelphia or Boston, where no one's looking for him. My guess is that he's met up with his girlfriend by now and the two of them are heading south of the border, if they're not already eating enchiladas. And I still say one way or the other the go-between had to be Siddons's sister."

Frowning, Mort Levy watched Jack Shore go to the communications room to await the faxes from Detroit. The next step would be to forward pictures of both Siddons and his girlfriend to the border patrol in Tijuana, with the warning to be on the lookout for them.

But we still have to cover the cathedral tonight on the one-in-a-million chance that Jimmy's offer to surrender was on the level, Mort thought. Somehow neither possibility rang true to him—not Mexico, not the surrender. Would this Paige be smart enough to lie to her friend on the chance that the cops might come looking for her?

The coffee and sandwiches they had ordered were just being delivered. Mort went over to get his ham on rye. Two of the women officers were talking together.

He heard one of them, Lori Martini, say, "Still no sign of that missing kid. For sure some nut must have picked him up."

"What missing kid?" Levy asked.

Soberly he listened to the details. It was the one kind of case no one in the department could work on without becoming emotionally involved. Mort had a seven-year-old son. He knew what must be going through that mother's mind. And the father so sick he hadn't even been told his son was missing. And all this at Christmastime. God, some people really get it in spades, hye thought.

"Call for you, Mort," a voice shouted from across the room.

Carrying the coffee and sandwich, Mort returned to his desk. "Who is it?" he asked as he took the receiver.

"A woman. She didn't give her name."

As Mort pressed the phone to his ear, he said, "Detective Levy."

He heard the sound of frightened breathing. And then a faint click as the line went dead.

WCBS reporter Alan Graham approached the squad car where he'd interviewed Catherine Doman an hour earlier when he had done an update on the story.

It-was eight-thirty, and the intermittent gusts of snow had become a steady flow of large white flakes again.

Through his earphone, Graham heard the anchorman give the latest information about the escaped prisoner. "The condition of Mario Bonardi, the injured prison guard, is still extremely critical Mayor Giuliani and Police Commissioner Bratton have paid a second visit to the hospital where he is in intensive care after delicate surgery. According to the latest report, the police are following up on a tip that his assailant, alleged murderer Jimmy Siddons, may be meeting a girlfriend in California with the final destination, Mexico. The border patrol at Tijuana has been alerted."

One of the newsmen had been tipped off that Jimmy's lawyer claimed Siddons was turning himself in after midnight Mass at St. Patrick's. Alan Graham was glad that the decision had been made not to air that story. None of the police brass really believed it, and they didn't want the worshipers distracted by the rumor.

There were few pedestrians now on Fifth Avenue. It occurred to Graham that there was something almost obscene about the breaking stories they were covering this Christmas Eve: an escaped cop killer; a prison guard clinging to life; a seven-year-old missing boy, who was now the suspected victim of foul play.

He tapped on the window of the squad car. Catherine glanced up, then opened it halfway. Looking at her, he wondered how long she would be able to maintain her remarkable composure. She was sitting in the passenger seat of the car next to Officer Ortiz. Her son Michael was in the back with a handsome older woman whose arm was around him.

Catherine answered his unasked question. "I'm still waiting," she said quietly. "Officer Ortiz has been good enough to stay with me. I don't know why, but I feel as though somehow I'll find Brian right here." She turned slightly. "Mom, this is Alan Graham from WCBS. He interviewed me right after I spoke with you."

Barbara Cavanaugh saw the compassion on the face of the young reporter. Knowing that if there were anything to tell, they would have heard it by now, she still could not stop herself from asking, "Any word?"

"No, ma'am. We've had plenty of calls to the station, but they were all to express concern."

"He's vanished," Catherine said, her voice lifeless. "While Tom and I have raised the boys to basically trust people, they also know how to deal with emergencies. Brian knew enough to go to a policeman if he was lost. He knew to dial 911. Somebody has taken him. Who would take and hold a seven-year-old child unless . . . ?"

"Catherine, dear, don't torture yourself," her mother urged. "Everyone who heard you on the radio is praying for Brian. You must have faith."

Catherine felt frustration and anger rising inside her. Yes, she supposed she should have "faith." Certainly Brian had faith—he believed in that St. Christopher medal, probably enough to have followed whoever picked up my wallet. He knew it was inside, she reasoned, and felt he had to get it back. She looked back at her mother, and at Michael beside her. She felt her anger ebb. It wasn't her mother's fault that any of this had happened. No, faith—even in something as unlikely as a St. Christopher medal—was a good thing.

"You're right, Mom," she said.

From the receiver in his ear, Graham heard the anchorman say, "Over to you, Alan."

Stepping back from the car, he began, "Brian Dornan's mother is still keeping watch at the spot where her son disappeared shortly after 5:00 P.M. Authorities believe Catherine Dornan's theory that Brian may have seen someone steal her wallet and followed that person. The wallet contained a St. Christopher medal, which Brian was desperately anxious to bring to his father's hospital bed."

Graham handed the microphone to Catherine. "Brian believes the St. Christopher medal will help his father get well. If I had had Brian's faith, I would have guarded my wallet more carefully because the St Christopher medal was in it. I want my husband to get better. I want my child," she said, her voice steady despite her emotion. "In the name of God, if anyone knows what happened to Brian, who has him, or where he is, please, *please* call us."

Graham stepped back from the squad car. "If anyone who knows anything about Brian's whereabouts is listening to that young mother's pain, we beg you to call this number, 212-555-0748."

11

Her eyes filled with tears, her lip quivering, Cally turned off the radio. *If anyone knows what happened to Brian . . .*

I *tried*, she told herself fiercely. I tried. She had dialed Detective Levy's number, but when she heard his voice, the enormity of what she was about to do overwhelmed her. They would arrest her. They would take Gigi away from her again and would put her with a new foster family. *If anyone knows anything about Brian's whereabouts . . .*

She reached for the phone.

From inside die bedroom she heard a wail and spun around. Gigi was having another nightmare. She rushed inside, sat down on the bed, garnered her child in her arms, and began rocking her. "Sshh, it's okay, everything's fine."

Gigi clung to her. "Mommy, Mommy. I dreamed that you were gone again. Please don't go, Mommy. Please don't leave me. I don't want to live with other people ever, ever."

"That won't happen, sweetheart, I promise."

She could feel Gigi relax. Gently she laid her back on the pillow and smoothed her hair. "Now go bacik to sleep, angel."

Gigi closed her eyes, then opened them, again. "Can I watch Santa Claus open his present?" she murmured.

Jimmy Siddons lowered the volume on the radio. "Your mom sure is flipping out about you, kid."

Brian had to keep himself from reaching out to the dashboard and touching the radio. Mom sounded so worried. He had to get back to her. Now she believed in the St. Christopher medal too. He was sure of it.

There were a lot of cars on the highway, and even though it was really snowing now, they were all going pretty fast. But Jimmy was in the far right lane, so no cars were coming up on that side. Brian began to plan.

If he could open the door real fast and roll out onto the road, he could keep rolling to the side. That way nobody would run over him. He pressed the medal for an instant, and then his hand crept to the handle on the door. When he put faint pressure on it, it moved slightly. He was right. Jimmy hadn't put the lock on after they stopped for gas.

Brian was about to throw open the door when he remembered his seat belt. He'd have to unfasten that just as the door swung open. Careful not to attract Jimmy's attention, he laid the index finger of his left hand on the seat belt's release button.

Just as Brian was about to pull on the handle and push the release, Jimmy swore. A car, weaving erratically, was coming up behind them on the left. An instant later it was so close it was almost touching the Toyota. Then it cut in front of them. Jimmy slammed on the brakes. The car skidded and fish-tailed, as around them came the sound of metal impacting metal. Brian held his breath. Crash, he begged, *crash!* Then someone would help him.

But Jimmy righted the car and drove around the others. Just ahead, Brian could hear the wail of sirens and see the brilliance of flashing lights gathered around another accident, which they quickly drove past as well.

Jimmy grinned in savage satisfaction. "We're pretty lucky, aren't we, kiddo?" he asked Brian, as he glanced down at him.

Brian was still clutching the handle.

"Now you weren't thinking of jumping out if we'd gotten stuck back there, were you?" Jimmy asked. He clicked the control that locked the doors. "Keep your hand away from there. I see you touch that handle again and I'll break your fingers," he said quietly.

Brian didn't have the slightest doubt he would do just that.

12

It was five after ten. Mort Levy sat at his desk, deep in thought. He had only one explanation for the disconnected call: Cally Hunter. The tap from the police surveillance van outside Cally's building confirmed that she had dialed him. The men on duty there offered to go up and talk to her if Mort wanted them to. "No. Leave her alone," he ordered. He knew it would be pointless. She'd only repeat exactly what she'd told them before. But she knows something and she is afraid to tell, he thought. He had tried to phone her twice, but she had not answered. He knew she was there, though. The lookouts in the van would have notified them if she'd left the apartment. So why wasn't she answering? Should he go over to see Her himself? Would it do any good?

"What's with you?" Jack Shore asked impatiently. "You forgot how to hear?"

Mort looked up. The rotund senior detective stood glowering down at him. No wonder Cally's afraid of you, Mort thought, remembering the fear in her eyes at Jack's anger and open hostility.

"I'm thinking," Mort said curtly, resisting the impulse to suggest that Shore try it sometime.

"Well, think with the rest of us. We've gotta go over the plans to cover the cathedral." Then Shore's scowl softened. "Mort, why don't you take a break?"

He isn't as bad as he tries to seem, Mort thought. "I don't see you taking a break, Jack," he replied.

"It's just that I hate Siddons worse than you do."

Mort got up slowly. His mind was still focused on the elusive memory of some important clue that had been overlooked, something he knew was there, right in front of him, but that he just couldn't make himself see. They'd seen Cally Hunter at seven-fifteen this morning. She'd already been dressed for work. They had seen her again nearly twelve hours later. She looked exhausted and desperately worried. She was probably in bed asleep now. But every nerve in his body was telling him that he should talk to her. Despite her denial, he believed she held the key.

As he turned away from his desk, the phone rang. When he picked it up, he again heard the terrified breathing. This time he took the initiative. "Cally," Mort said urgently. "Cally, *talk* to me. Don't be afraid. Whatever it is, I'll try to help you."

Cally could not even mink of going to bed. She had listened to the all-news station, hoping but at the same time tearing that the cops had found Jimmy, praying that little Brian was safe.

At ten o'clock she had turned on the television to watch the Fox local news, then her heart sank. Brian's mother was seated next to the anchorman, Tony Potts. Her hair seemed looser now, as though she'd been standing outside in the wind and snow. Her face was very pale, and her eyes were filled with pain. There was a boy sitting next to her who seemed to be about ten or eleven years old.

The anchorman was saying, "You may have heard Catherine Dornan's appeals for help in finding her son Brian. We've asked her and Brian's brother, Michael, to be with us now. There were crowds of people on Fifth Avenue and Forty-ninth Street shortly after five o'clock this evening. Maybe you were one of mem. Maybe you noticed Catherine with her two sons, Michael and Brian. They were in a group listening to a violinist playing Christmas carols, and singing along. Seven-year-old Brian disappeared from his mother's side. His mother and brother need your help in finding him."

The anchorman turned to Catherine. "You're holding a picture of Brian."

Cally watched as the picture was held up, listened as Brian's mother said, "It's not very clear, so let me tell you a little more about him. He's seven but looks younger because he's small. He has dark reddish brown hair and blue eyes and freckles on his nose . . ." Her voice faltered.

Cally shut her eyes. She couldn't bear to look at the stark agony on Catherine Dornan's face.

Michael put his hand over his mother's. "My brother's wearing a dark blue ski jacket just like mine, 'cept mine is green, and a red cap. And one of his front teeth is missing." Then he burst out, "We gotta get him back. We can't tell my Dad that Brian is missing. Dad's too sick to be worried." Michael's voice became even more urgent "I know my dad. He'd try to do something. He'd get out of bed and start looking for Brian, and we can't let him do that. He's sick, real sick."

Cally snapped off the set. She tiptoed into the bedroom where Gigi was at last sleeping peacefully and went over to the window that led to the fire escape. She could still see Brian's eyes as he glanced over his shoulder, begging her to help him, his one hand in Jimmy's grasp, his other holding the St. Christopher medal as though it would somehow save him. She shook her head. That medal, she thought. He hadn't cared about the money. He followed her because he believed that medal would make his father get well.

Cally ran the few steps back into the living room and grabbed Mort Levy's card.

When he answered, her resolve almost crumbled again, but then his voice was so kind when he said, "Cally, *talk* to me. Don't be afraid."

"Mr. Levy," she blurted out, "can you come here, quick? I've got to talk to you about Jimmy—and that little boy who's missing."

13

All that was left of the snack Jimmy had purchased when they stopped for gas were the empty Coca-Cola cans and the crumpled bags that had held potato chips. Jimmy had thrown his on the floor in front of Brian, while Brian had placed his in the plastic waste-basket attached under the dashboard. He couldn't even remember what the chips had tasted like. He was so hungry that, scared as he felt, being hungry was all he could think about.

He knew that Jimmy was really mad at him. And ever since the time they'd nearly crashed and Jimmy realized that he had been planning to try to jump out of the car, he'd seemed real nervous. He kept opening and closing his fingers on the steering wheel, making a scary snapping sound. The first time he did it, Brian had flinched and jumped, and Jimmy had grabbed him by the shoulder, snarling at him to stay away from the door.

The snow was coming down faster now. Ahead of them

someone braked. The car swung around in a circle, then kept going. Brian realized that it hadn't slammed into another car only because all the drivers on the road were trying to keep from getting too close to other cars.

Even so, Jimmy began to swear, a low steady stream of words, most of which Brian had never heard, even from Skeet, the kid in his class who knew all the good swear words.

The spinning car confirmed Jimmy's growing sense that near as he was to escaping the country something could still go wrong any minute. It didn't sound as though that prison guard he shot was going to make it. If the guard died . . . Jimmy had meant it when he told Cally that they wouldn't take him alive.

Then Jimmy tried to reassure himself. He had a car that probably nobody even realized was missing yet. He had decent clothes and money. If they'd been stuck back there when that crazy fool caused the accident, the kid might have managed to jump out of the car. If that jerk who just spun around had hit the Toyota, I might have been hurt, Jimmy thought. On my own, maybe I could've bluffed it, but not with the kid along. On the other hand, nobody knew he had the kid, and in a million years no cop was on the lookout for a guy in a nice car with a bunch of toys in the backseat and a little boy beside him.

They were near Syracuse now. In three or four hours he'd be across the border with Paige.

There was a McDonald's sign on the right. Jimmy was hungry, and this would be a good place to get something to eat.

It would have to last him until he reached Canada. He'd pull up to the drive-in window, order for the two of them, then get back on the road fast.

"What's your favorite food, kid?" he asked, his tone almost genial.

Brian had spotted the McDonald's sign and held his breath, hoping that this meant they were going to get something to eat. "A hamburger and french fries, and a Coke," he said timidly.

"If I stop at McDonald's, can you look like you're sleeping?"

"Yes, I promise."

"Do it men. Lean against me with your eyes closed."

"Okay." Obediently Brian slumped against Jimmy and squeezed his eyes shut. He tried not to show how scared he was.

"Let's see what kind of actor you are," Jimmy said. "And you'd better be good."

The St. Christopher medal had slipped to the side. Brian straightened it so that he could feel it, heavy and comforting against his chest.

It was scary to be so close to this guy, not like being sleepy when he was driving with Dad and curling up against him and feeling Dad's hand patting his shoulder.

Jimmy pulled off the highway. They had to wait on line at the drive-in window. Jimmy froze when he saw a state trooper pull in behind them, but had no choice except to stay put and not draw attention to himself. When it was their turn and he placed the order and paid, the attendant didn't even glance into the

car. But at the pickup spot, the woman looked over the counter
to where the light from behind her shone on Brian.

"I guess he just can't wait to see what Santa Claus is going to
bring him, can he?"

Jimmy nodded and tried to smile in agreement as he reached
for the bag.

She leaned way forward and peered into the car. "My goodness, is he wearing a St. Christopher medal? My dad was named
after him and used to try to make a big deal of it, but my mom
always jokes about St. Christopher being dropped from the
calendar of saints. My dad says it's too bad Mom wasn't named
Philomena. She's another saint the Vatican said didn't exist."
With a hearty laugh the young woman handed over the bag.

As they drove back onto the highway, Brian opened his eyes. He
could smell the hamburgers and the french fries. He sat up slowly.

Jimmy looked at him, his eyes steely, his face rigid. Through
lips that barely parted, he quietly ordered, "Get that goddamn
medal off your neck."

Cally had to talk to him about her brother and the missing child. After
promising to be right over, Mort Levy hung up the phone,
stunned. What possible connection could there be between Jimmy
Siddons and the little boy who disappeared on Fifth Avenue?

He dialed the lookout van. "You recorded that call?"

"Is she crazy, Mort? She can't be talking about the Dornan
kid, can she? Want us to pick her up for questioning?"

"That's just what I *don't* want you to do!" Levy exploded. "She's scared to death as it is. Sit tight until I get there."

He had to inform his superiors, starting with Jack Shore, about Cally Hunter's call. Mort spotted Shore leaving the chief of detectives' private office, was out of his chair and across the room in seconds. He grabbed Shore's arm. "Come back inside."

"I told you to take a break." Shore tried to shake off his hand. "We just heard from Logan in Detroit again. Two days ago a woman whose description matches Siddons's girlfriend got a ride from a private car service over the border to Windsor. Logan's guys think that Laronde told her girlfriend about California and Mexico to throw them off her trail. The girlfriend was questioned again. This time it occurred to her to mention that she offered to buy Laronde's fur coat because it wouldn't be needed in Mexico. Laronde refused."

I never bought that Mexico story, Mort Levy thought. He didn't relinquish his grip on Shore's arm as he shoved open the chiefs door.

Five minutes later, a squad car was racing up the East Side Drive to Avenue B and Tenth Street. A bitterly frustrated Jack Shore had been ordered to wait in the lookout van while Mort and the chief, Bud Folney, went upstairs to talk to Cally.

Mort knew that Shore would not forgive him for insisting that he stay out of it. "Jack, when we were there earlier, I knew there was something she was holding back. You've scared her to death. She thinks you'd do anything to see her back behind bars. For God's sake, can't you look at her as a human being? She's got a four-year-old child, her husband is dead, and she got the book thrown at her when she made the mistake of helping the brother she'd practically raised."

Now Mort turned to Folney. "I don't know how Jimmy Siddons ties into that missing child, but I do know that Cally has been too frightened to talk. If she tells us now whatever she knows, it will be because she feels that the department . . . you . . . aren't out to get her."

Forney nodded. He was a soft-spoken, lean man in his late forties, with a scholarly face. He had in fact spent three years as a high school teacher before realizing his passion was law enforcement. It was widely believed among the ranks that one day he'd be police commissioner. Already he was one of the most powerful men in the department.

Mort Levy knew that if there was anyone who could help Cally, assuming she had in some way been forced to cover for Jimmy again, it was Folney. But the missing child—how could Siddons be involved in this?

It was a question they were all frantic to ask.

When the squad car pulled up behind the surveillance van, Shore made one last appeal. "If I keep my mouth shut . . ."

Folney answered, "I suggest you start right now, Jack. Get in the van."

14

Pete Cruise had been about to call it a day. He'd discovered where Cally Hunter lived when he tried to interview her after she was released from prison, and now he was hoping her brother would show up. But there'd been nothing to watch for hours except the on-again-off-again falling snow. Now at least it seemed to have stopped for good. The van that he knew was a police van was still parked across the street from Cally's apartment, but probably all they were doing was monitoring her calls. The likelihood of Jimmy Siddons suddenly showing up at his sister's house now was about the same as two strangers having matching DNA.

All the hours of hanging around Hunter's building were a waste, Pete decided. From the time he'd seen Cally come home shortly before six, and the two detectives stop in around seven, it had been a big nothing.

He'd kept his powerful portable radio on the whole time he waited, switching between the police band, his station, WYME, and the WCBS news station. No word of Siddons at all. Shame about that missing kid.

When the ten o'clock news came on WYME, Pete thought for the hundredth time that the anchor in that slot sounded like a wimp. But she did have some real emotion when she talked about the missing seven-year-old. Maybe we need a missing kid every day, Pete thought sarcastically, then was immediately ashamed of himself.

There was a lot of activity in Hunter's building, people coming and going. Many of the churches had moved up the midnight services to ten o'clock. No matter what time they schedule them, some people will always be late, Pete thought as he saw an elderly couple hurry from the building and turn up Avenue B. Probably heading for St. Emeric's.

The woman who had brought Hunter's kid home earlier was coming up the block. Was she headed for Hunter's apartment? Cally planning to go out? he wondered.

Pete shrugged. Maybe Hunter had a late date or was going to church herself. Obviously, today wasn't the day to get the story that was going to make his name as a reporter.

It'll happen, Pete promised himself. I won't always be working on this lousy ten-watt station. His buddy who worked at WNBC loved to ride Pete about his job. A favorite put-down was that the only audience for WYME were two cockroaches and three stray cats. 'This is station Why-Me," he'd joke.

Pete started his car. He was just about to pull out when a

squad car raced down the block and stopped in front of Cally's building.

Through narrowed eyes, Pete observed three men emerge. One he recognized as Jack Shore crossed the street and got into the van. Then in the light from the building entrance he could make out Mort Levy. He didn't get a good look at the other one.

Something was breaking. Pete turned off the engine, suddenly interested again.

While she waited for Mort Levy, Cally took Gigi's Christmas presents from their hiding place behind the couch and set them in front of the tree. The secondhand doll's carriage didn't look that bad, she decided, with the pretty blue satin coverlet and pillowcase. She'd put the baby doll she'd picked up for a couple of dollars last month in it, but it wasn't nearly as cute as the one that she'd wanted to buy from the peddler on Fifth Avenue. That one had Gigi's golden-brown hair and was wearing a blue party dress. *If she hadn't been looking for that peddler, she wouldn't have seen the wallet, and the boy wouldn't have followed her, and . . .*

She put that thought aside. She was past feeling now. Carefully, she stacked the presents she'd wrapped with candy-cane paper: an outfit from The Gap—leggings and a polo shirt; crayons and a coloring book; some furniture for Gigi's dollhouse. Everything, even the two pieces of the Gap outfit, was in separate boxes so at least it looked as though Gigi had a stack of gifts to open.

She tried to avoid looking at the largest package under the tree, the package that Gigi thought was their gift for Santa Claus.

Finally she phoned Aika. Aika's grandchildren always went home to sleep, so she was sure she could come over and stay with Gigi in case the cops arrested Cally after she told them about Jimmy and the tittle boy.

Aika answered on the first ring. "Hello." Her voice was filled with her normal warmth. If only they'd let Gigi stay with Aika if they put me in prison again, Cally thought. She swallowed over the lump in her throat, then said, "Aika, I'm in trouble. Can you come over in about half an hour and maybe stay overnight?"

"You bet I can." Aika did not ask questions, simply clicked off.

As Cally replaced the receiver, the buzzer from the downstairs door resounded through the apartment

"The switchboard's on fire, Mrs. Dornan," Leigh Ann Winkle, the producer of Fox 5 Ten O'clock News told Catherine as, carefully avoiding the floor cables, she and Michael left the broadcast area. "It looks as though everyone in our viewing area wants you to know that they're rooting and praying for Brian and your husband."

'Thank you." Catherine tried to smile. She looked down at Michael. He had been trying so hard to keep up his spirits for her sake. It was only when she had listened to his on-camera plea that she had fully realized what this was doing to him.

Michael's hands were in his pockets, his shoulders hunched

under his ears. It was exactly the same posture Tom unconsciously fell into when he was worried about a patient. Catherine squared her own shoulders and put her arm around her older son as the door from the studio dosed behind them.

The producer said, "Our operators are thanking everyone in your name, but is there anything else you'd like us to tell our audience?"

Catherine drew a deep breath, and her arm tightened around Michael. "I wish you'd tell them that we think I dropped my wallet, and that Brian apparently followed whoever picked it up. The reason he was so anxious to get it back is that my mother had just given me a St. Christopher medal that my rather wore through World War II. My father believed the medal kept him safe. It even has a dent where a bullet glanced off it, a bullet that might have killed him. Brian has the same wonderful faith that St. Christopher or what he represents is going to take care of us again ... and so do I. St. Christopher will carry Brian back to us on his shoulders, and he will help my husband get well."

She smiled down at Michael "Right, pal?"

Michael's eyes were shining. "Mom, do you really believe that?"

Catherine drew a deep breath. *I believe, Lord, help my unbelief.* "Yes, I do," she said firmly.

And maybe because it was Christmas Eve, for the first time, she really did.

15

S tate Trooper Chris McNally tuned out as Deidre Lenihan droned on about just seeing a St. Christopher medal, and how her father was named after St. Christopher. She was a well-meaning young woman, but every time he stopped for coffee at this McDonald's, she seemed to be on duty and always wanted to talk.

Tonight Chris was too preoccupied with thoughts of getting home. He wanted to get at least some sleep before his kids got up to open all their Christmas presents. He also had been thinking about the Toyota he had just seen pull out in front of him. He'd been thinking of buying one himself, although he knew his wife wouldn't want a brown one. A new car meant monthly payments to worry about. He noticed the remnant of a bumper sticker on the Toyota, a single word, *inheritance.* He knew the sticker had originally said, "We're spending our grandchildren's inheritance." We could use an inheritance, he thought.

"And my father said . . ."

Chris forced himself to refocus. Deidre's nice, he thought, but she talks too much. He reached for the bag she was dangling in her hand, but it was clear she was not going to relinquish it yet, not until she had told how her dad said it was too bad that her mother hadn't been named Philomena.

Still she wasn't finished. "Years ago my aunt worked in Southampton and belonged to St. Philomena's parish. When they had to rename it, the pastor had a contest to decide which saint they should choose and why. My aunt suggested St. Dymphna because she said she was the saint of the insane and most of the people in the parish were nuts."

"Well, I was named after St. Christopher myself," Chris said, managing to snare the bag. "Merry Christmas, Deidre."

And it will be Christinas before I get a bite out of this Big Mac, he thought as he drove back onto the Thruway. With one hand, he deftly opened the bag, freed the burger, and gratefully took a large bite. The coffee would have to wait until he got back to his post.

He'd be off duty at midnight, and then, he thought, smiling to himself, it would be time to grab a little shut-eye. Eileen would try to keep the kids in bed till six, but lots of luck. It hadn't happened last year and it wouldn't happen this year if he knew his sons.

He was approaching exit 40 and drove the car to the official turnaround, from which he could observe errant drivers. Christmas Eve was nothing like New Year's Eve for nabbing drinkers, but Chris was determined that no one who was speeding or weaving on the road was going to get past him. He'd witnessed a couple of accidents where some drunk turned the holiday into a nightmare for innocent people. Not tonight if he could help it. And the snow had made driving that much more treacherous.

As Chris opened the lid on his coffee, he frowned. A Corvette doing at least eighty was racing up the service lane. He snapped on his dome lights and siren, shifted into gear, and the squad car leaped in pursuit.

Chief of Detectives Bud Folney listened with no expression other than quiet attentiveness as a trembling Cally Hunter told Mort Levy about finding the wallet on Fifth Avenue. She had waived her Miranda warning, saying impatiently, "This can't wait any longer."

Folney knew the basics of her case: older sister of Jimmy Siddons, had served time because a judge had not believed her story that she thought she was helping her brother get away from a rival gang bent on killing him. Levy had told him that Hunter seemed to be one of the hard-luck people of this world—raised by an elderly grandmother, who died, leaving her to try to straighten out her louse of a younger brother when she was only a kid herself; then her husband killed by a hit-and-run driver when she was pregnant.

About thirty, Folney thought, and could be pretty with a little meat on her. She still had the pale, haunted expression he had seen on other women who had been imprisoned and carried with them the horror that someday they might be sent back.

He looked around. The neat apartment, the sunny, yellow paint on the cracked walls, the bravely decorated but skimpy Christmas tree, the new coverlet on the battered doll carriage, they all told him something about Cally Hunter.

Folney knew that, like himself, Mort Levy was desperate to know what connection Hunter could give them between Siddons and the missing Dornan child. He approved of Mort's gentle approach. Cally Hunter had to tell it her way. It's a good thing we didn't bring in the raging bull, Folney thought. Jack Shore was a good detective, but his aggressiveness often got on Folney's nerves.

Hunter was talking about seeing the wallet on the sidewalk. "I picked it up without thinking. I guessed it belonged to that woman, but I wasn't sure. I honestly wasn't sure," she burst out, "and I thought if I tried to give it back to her, she might say something was missing from it. That happened to my grandmother. And then you'd send me back to prison and . . ."

"Cally, take it easy," Mort said. "What happened then?"

"When I got home . . ."

She told them about finding Jimmy in the apartment, wearing her deceased husband's clothes. She pointed to the big package under the tree. "The guard's uniform and coat are in there," she said. "It was the only place I could think to hide them in case you came back."

That's it, Mort thought. When we looked around the apartment the second time, there was something different about the closet. The box on the shelf and the man's jacket were missing.

Cally's voice became ragged and uneven as she told them about Jimmy taking Brian Dornan and threatening to kill him if he spotted a cop chasing him.

Levy asked, "Cally, do you think Jimmy can be trusted to let Brian go?"

"I wanted to think so," she said tonlessly. "That was what I told myself when I didn't call you immediately. But I know he's desperate. Jimmy will do anything to keep from going to prison again."

Folney finally asked a question. "Cally, why did you call us now?"

"I saw Brian's mother on television, and I knew that if Jimmy had taken Gigi, I'd want you to help me get her back." Cally clasped her hands together. Her body swayed slightly forward then back in the ancient posture of grief. 'The look on that little boy's face, the way he put that medal around his neck and was holding on to it like it was a life preserver . . . if anything happens to him, it's my fault."

The buzzer sounded If that's Shore . . . Folney thought as he jumped up to answer it.

It was Aika Banks. When she entered the apartment, she looked at the policemen searchingly, then rushed to Cally and hugged her. "Baby, what is it? What's wrong? Why do you need me to stay with Gigi? What do these people want?"

Cally winced in pain.

Aika peeled up her friend's sleeve. The bruises caused by Jimmy's fingers were now an ugly purple. Any doubts that Bud Folney had about Hunter's possible cooperation with her brother disappeared. He squatted in front of her. "Cally, you're not going to get into trouble. I promise you. I believe you found that wallet. I believe you didn't know what was best for you to do. But now you've got to help us. *Have you any idea where Jimmy might have gone?*"

Ten minutes later, when they left Cally's apartment, Mort Levy was carrying the bulky gift-wrapped package that held the guard's uniform.

Shore joined them in the squad car and impatiently fired questions at Mort. As they were driven downtown, they agreed that the search for Jimmy Siddons would be based on the assumption that he might be trying to reach Canada.

"He's got to be in a car," Folney said flatly. 'There's no way he'll travel on public transportation with that child."

Cally had told them that from the time he was twelve years old, Jimmy could hot-wire and steal any car; she was sure he must have had one waiting near the apartment.

"My guess is that Siddons would want to get out of New York State as soon as possible," Folney said. "Which means he'd drive through New England to the border. But it's only a guess. He could be on the Thruway, headed for 187. That's the fastest route."

And Siddons's girlfriend was probably in Canada. It all fit together.

They also accepted Cally's absolute certainty that Jimmy Siddons would not be taken alive and that his final act of vengeance would be to kill his hostage.

So they were faced with an escaped murderer with a child, possibly driving a car they could not describe, probably headed north in a snowstorm. It would be like looking for a needle in a haystack. Siddons would be too smart to attract attention by speeding. The border was always mobbed with holiday traffic on Christmas Eve. He dictated a message to be sent to state police throughout New England as well as New York. "Has threatened to kill the hostage," he emphasized.

They calculated that if Siddons had left Cally Hunter's apartment shortly after six, depending on driving conditions, he'd be between two and three hundred miles away. The alert that went out to the state police contained Cally's final certainty: *On a chain around his neck, the child may be wearing a bronze St. Christopher medal the size of a silver dollar.*

Pete Cruise watched as the detectives emerged from Cally Hunter's building some twenty minutes after arriving there. He noted that Levy was carrying a bulky package. Shore immediately jumped out of the van and joined them.

This time Pete got a good look at the third man, then whistled silently. It was Bud Folney, chief of detectives and in line to be the next police commissioner. Something was breaking. Something big.

The squad car took off with its dome light flashing. A block away its siren was turned on. Pete sat for a moment, debating what to do. The cops in the van might stop him if he tried to go in to see Cally, but obviously something major was going down here, and he was determined to scoop everyone on this.

As he was wondering about looking for a back entrance to the building, he saw the woman he knew to be Cally's babysitter leave. In a flash he was out of the car and following her. He caught up with her when she turned the corner and they were out of sight of the cops in the van. "I'm Detective Cruise," he said. "I've been instructed to see you safely home. How is Cally doing?"

"Oh, that poor girl," Aika began. "Officer, you people have to believe her. She thought she was doing the right thing when she didn't phone you about her brother kidnapping that little boy ..."

Even though Brian was hungry, the hamburger was hard to swallow. His throat felt like mere was something stuck in it. He knew that Jimmy was the reason for that. He took a giant swallow of Coke and tried to think about how Daddy would beat Jimmy up for being so mean to him.

But now when he thought about Daddy it was hard to remember anything except all the plans they had made for Christmas Eve. Daddy had planned to come home early, and they were all going to trim the tree together. Then they were going to have dinner and go around their neighborhood singing Christmas carols with a bunch of their friends.

That was all he could think about now, because that was all he wanted, to be home and have Daddy and Mommy smiling a lot the way they always did when they were together. When they came to New York because Dad was sick, Mom had told him and Michael that their big presents, the ones they really wanted, would be waiting for them when they got back home. She said that Santa Claus would keep the presents on his sleigh until he knew they were in their own house again.

Michael had said, "Yeah, really," under his breath to Brian. But Brian believed in Santa Claus. Last year Dad had pointed out marks on the roof of the garage where Santa's sleigh had landed and where the reindeer had stood. Michael told him he heard Mom tell Dad it was a good thing Dad hadn't broken his neck sliding around on the icy roof and making tracks all over it, but Brian didn't mind what Michael said, because he didn't believe it. Just like he didn't mind that Michael sometimes called him the Dork; he knew he wasn't a dork.

He knew things were bad when you wished your jerk brother, who could be such a pain in the neck, was there with you, and that was just how he felt now.

As Brian swallowed over that feeling of something in his throat, the plastic container almost jumped out of his hand. He realized Jimmy had switched lanes fast.

Jimmy Siddons swore silently. He had just passed a state trooper's car stopped in back of a sports car. The sight of a trooper made him sweat all over, but he shouldn't have switched lanes like that. He was getting jumpy.

Sensing the animosity that bristled from Jimmy, Brian put the uneaten hamburger and the soda back in the bag and, moving slowly so Jimmy could see what he was doing, leaned down and put the bag on the floor. Then he straightened up, huddled against the back of the seat and hugged his arms against his sides. The fingers of his right hand groped until they closed around the St. Christopher medal, which he had laid on the seat next to him when he opened the package of food.

With a sense of relief he closed his hand over it and mentally pictured the strong saint who carried the little kid across the dangerous river, who had taken care of his grandfather, who would make Dad get better and who ... Brian closed his eyes ... He didn't finish the wish, but in his mind he could see himself on the shoulders of the saint.

16

Barbara Cavanaugh was waiting for Catherine and Michael in the green room at Channel 5. "You both did a great job," she said quietly. Then, seeing the exhaustion on her daughter's face, she said, "Catherine, please come back to the apartment. The police will get in touch with you there as soon as they have any word about Brian. You look ready to drop."

"I can't, Mother," Catherine said. "I know it's foolish to wait on Fifth Avenue. Brian isn't going to get back there on his own, but while I'm out and about I at least feel as though I'm doing something to find him. I don't really know what I'm saying except that when I left your apartment, I had my two little boys with me, and when I go back they're going to be with me, too."

Leigh Ann Winick made a decision. "Mrs. Dornan, why not stay right here at least for the present? This room is comfortable. We'll send out for some hot soup or a sandwich or whatever you want. But you've said yourself, there's no point in just waiting on Fifth Avenue indefinitely."

Catherine considered. "And the police will be able to reach me here?"

Winick pointed to the phone. "Absolutely. Now tell me what I can order for you."

Twenty minutes later, as Catherine, her mother, and Michael were sipping steaming hot minestrone, they watched the green room's television monitor. The news bite was about Mario Bonardi, the wounded prison guard. Although still critical, his condition had stabilized.

The reporter was with Bonardi's wife and teenage children in the waiting room of the intensive care unit. When asked for a comment, a weary Rose Bonardi said, "My husband is going to make it. I want to thank everyone who has been praying for him today. Our family has known many happy Christmases, but this will be the best ever because we know what we so nearly lost."

"That's what we'll be saying, Michael," Catherine said determinedly. "Dad is going to make it and Brian is going to be found."

The reporter with the Bonardi family said, "Back to you at the news desk, Tony."

"Thanks, Ted. Glad to hear that it's going so well. That's the kind of Christmas story we want to be able to tell." The anchor's smile vanished. "There is still no trace of Mario Bonardi's assailant, Jimmy Siddons, who was awaiting trial for the murder of a police officer. Police sources are quoted as saying that he may be planning to meet his girlfriend, Paige Laronde, in

Mexico. Airports, train stations, and bus terminals are under heavy surveillance. It was nearly three years ago, while making his escape after an armed robbery, that Siddons shot and fatally wounded Officer William Grasso, who had stopped him for a traffic violation. Siddons is known to be armed and should be considered extremely dangerous."

As the anchorman spoke, Jimmy Siddons's mug shots were flashed on the screen.

"He looks mean," Michael observed as he studied the cold eyes and sneering lips of the escaped prisoner.

"He certainly does," Barbara Cavanaugh agreed. Then she looked at her grandson's face. "Mike, why don't you close your eyes and rest for a little while?" she suggested.

He shook his head. "I don't want to go to sleep."

It was one minute of eleven. The newscaster was saying, "In an update, we have no further information about the whereabouts of seven-year-old Brian Dornan, who has been missing since shortly after five o'clock today.

"On this very special evening, we ask you to continue to pray that Brian is safely returned to his family, and wish you and all of your loved ones a very Merry Christmas."

In an hour it will be Christmas, Catherine thought. *Brian, you have to come back, you have to be found. You have to be with me in the morning when we go see Dad. Brian, come back. Please come back.*

The door of the green room opened. Winick ushered in a tall man in his late forties, followed by Officer Manuel Ortiz.

"Detective Rhodes wants to talk to you, Mrs. Dornan," Winick said. "I'm outside if you need me."

Catherine saw the grave look on the faces of both Rhodes and Ortiz, and fear paralyzed her. She was unable to move or speak.

They realized what she was thinking. "No, Mrs. Dornan, it isn't that," Ortiz said quickly.

Rhodes took over. "I'm from headquarters, Mrs. Dornan. We have information about Brian, but let me begin by saying that as far as we know he's alive and unharmed."

"Then where is he?" Michael burst out. 'Where's my brother?"

Catherine listened as Detective Rhodes explained about her wallet being picked up by a young woman who was the sister of escaped prisoner Jimmy Siddons. Her mind did not want to accept that Brian had been abducted by the murderer whose face she had just seen on the television screen. No, she thought, no, that can't be.

She pointed to the monitor. "They just reported that that man is probably on his way to Mexico. Brian disappeared six hours ago. He could be in Mexico right now."

"At headquarters we don't buy that story," Rhodes told her. "We think he's heading for Canada, probably in a stolen car. We're concentrating the search in that direction."

Suddenly Catherine could feel no emotion. It was like when she was in the delivery room and was given the shot of Demerol and all die pain miraculously stopped. *And she'd looked up to see Tom wink at her. Tom, always there for her. "Feels better doesn't it, Babe?" he had asked. And her mind, no longer clouded with pain, had become so clear.* It was that way now, as well. "What kind of car are they in?"

Rhodes looked uncomfortable. "We don't know," he said. "We're only guessing that he's in a car, but we feel sure it's the right guess. We have every trooper throughout New York and New England on the alert for a man traveling with a young boy who is wearing a St. Christopher medal."

"Brian is wearing the medal?" Michael exclaimed. "Then he'll be all right. Gran, tell Mom that the medal will take care of Brian like it took care of Grandpa."

"Armed and dangerous," Catherine repeated.

"Mrs. Dornan," Rhodes said urgently. "If Siddons is in a car, he's probably listening to the radio. He's smart. Now that Officer Bonardi is out of danger, Siddons knows he isn't facing a death sentence. Capital punishment had not been reinstated when he killed the police officer three years ago. And he did tell his sister that he'd let Brian go tomorrow morning."

Her mind was so clear. "But you don't believe that, do you?"

She did not need to see the expression on his face to know that Detective Rhodes did not believe that Jimmy Siddons would voluntarily release Brian.

"Mrs. Dornan, if we're right and Siddons is heading for the Canadian border, he's not going to get there for at least another three or four hours. Although the snow has stopped in some areas, the roads are still going to be something of a mess all night. He can't be traveling fast, and he doesn't know that we know he has Brian. That's being kept from the media. In Siddons's mind, Brian will be an asset—at least until he reaches the border. We will find him before then."

The television monitor was still on with the volume low. Catherine's back was to it. She saw Detective Rhodes's face change, heard a voice say, "We interrupt this program for a news bulletin. According to a report that has just been broadcast by station WYME, seven-year-old Brian Dornan, the boy who has been missing since this afternoon, has fallen into the hands of alleged murderer Jimmy Siddons, who told his sister that if the police close in on him, he will put a bullet through the child's head. More later, as news comes in."

17

After Aika left, Cally made a cup of tea, wrapped herself in a blanket, turned the television on, and pressed the MUTE button. This way I'll know if there's any news, she thought. Then she turned on the radio and tuned in a station playing Christmas music, but she kept the volume low.

"*Hark, the herald angels sing . . .*" Remember how Frank and I sang that together when we were trimming the tree? she thought. Five years ago. Their one Christmas together. They'd just learned that she was pregnant. She remembered all the plans they'd made. "Next year we'll have help trimming the tree," Frank had said.

"Sure we will. A three-month-old baby will be a big help," she'd said, laughing.

She remembered Frank lifting her up so that she could place the star on the top of the tree.

Why?

Why had everything gone so wrong? There wasn't a next year.

Just one week later Frank was killed by a hit-and-run driver. He'd been on his way home from a trip to the deli for a carton of milk.

We had so little time, Cally thought, shaking her head. Sometimes she wondered if those months were just a dream. It seemed so long ago now.

"O *come, all ye faithful, joyful and triumphant ...*" "Ad-este Fideles." Was it just yesterday that I was feeling so good about life? Cally wondered. At work the hospital administrator had said, "Cally, I've been hearing wonderful reports on you. They tell me you've got the makings of a born nurse. Have you ever thought of going to nursing school?" Then she'd talked about scholarships and how she was going to look into it.

That little boy, Cally thought. Oh God, don't let Jimmy hurt him. I should have called Detective Levy immediately. I know I should have. Why didn't I? she wondered, then immediately answered her own question: Because I wasn't just afraid for Brian. I was afraid for myself, too, and that may cost Brian his life.

She got up and went in to look at Gigi. As usual, the little girl had managed to work one foot out from under the covers. She did it every night, even when the room was cold.

Cally tucked the covers around her daughter's shoulders, then touched the small foot and tucked that in, too. Gigi stirred. "Mommy," she said drowsily.

"I'm right here."

Cally went back to the living room and glanced over at the television for a moment, then rushed to turn up the volume. No! No! she thought as she heard the reporter explain that police now had information that the missing boy had been kidnapped by escaped cop killer Jimmy Siddons. The police will blame the leak on me, she thought frantically. They'll think I told someone. I know they will.

The phone rang. When she picked it up and heard Mort Levy's voice, the pent-up emotions that had seemed so frozen erupted suddenly. "I didn't do it," she sobbed. "I didn't tell anyone. I swear, I swear I didn't tell."

The steady rise and fall of Brian's chest told Jimmy Siddons that his hostage was asleep. Good, he thought, better for me. The problem was that the kid was smart. Smart enough to know that if he had managed to throw himself out of the car next to the breakdown lane, he wouldn't risk getting run over. If that jerk hadn't spun out and caused the fender-bender, it would be all over for me now, Jimmy thought. The kid would have gotten out and the troopers would have been on my tail right then.

It was past eleven o'clock. The kid should be tired. With luck he'd sleep for a couple of hours anyhow. Even with the snow on the roads, they should be at the border in, at most, three or four hours. It'll still be dark for a long time after that, Jimmy thought with satisfaction. He knew he could count on Paige to be waiting on the Canadian side. They'd worked out a rendezvous point in the woods about three miles from the customs check.

Jimmy debated about where he should leave the Toyota. There was nothing to tie him to it as long as he made sure he wiped it dean of fingerprints. Maybe he'd ditch it in one of the wooded areas.

On the other hand ... He thought of the Niagara River, where he would make the border crossing. It had a strong current, so chances were it wouldn't be frozen. With luck, the car might never surface.

What about the kid? Even as he asked himself the question, Jimmy knew there was no way he'd take a chance on the kid being found near the border and able to talk about him.

Paige had told all her friends she was going to Mexico.

Sorry, kid, Jimmy thought. That's where I want the cops looking for me.

He reflected for a moment, then decided the river would take care of the car *and* the kid.

That decision made, Jimmy felt some of the tension ease from his body. With every mile, he felt more sure that he was going to make it, that Canada and Paige and freedom were within reach. And with each mile he felt more anxious—and more determined—that nothing happen to screw it up.

Like last time. He'd been all set. He'd had Cally's car, a hundred bucks, and was heading for California. Then he ran a lousy caution light on Ninth Avenue and got pulled over.

The cop, a guy about thirty, thought he was a big shot. He had come to the driver's window and said real sarcastically, "Driver's license and registration, *sir.*"

That's all he would have needed to see, Jimmy thought, remembering the moment as though it were yesterday, a license issued to James Siddons. He had had no choice. He would have been arrested on the spot. He'd reached into his breast pocket, pulled out his gun, and fired. Before the cop's body hit the ground, Jimmy was out of the car and on the street, blending into the crowd around the bus terminal. He had looked at the departure schedule board and rushed to buy a ticket on a bus leaving in three minutes, destination: Detroit.

That was a lucky decision, Jimmy thought. He'd met Paige the first night, moved in with her, then got some phony ID and a job with a low-lite security firm. For a while he and Paige had even had a kind of normal life. Their only real arguments were when he got sore at the way she encouraged the guys who made passes at her in the strip joint. But she said it was her job to make them *want* to make passes at her. For the first time, everything was actually working out. Until he was dumb enough to hit the service station without taking enough time to case it.

He focused his attention back on the snow-covered road ahead of him. He could tell from the feel of the tires that it was getting icy. Good thing this car had snow tires, Jimmy thought. He flashed back to the couple who owned the car—what had the guy said to his wife? Something about can't wait to see

Bobby's face? Yeah, that was it, Jimmy thought, grinning as he imagined their faces when they found an empty space where their car had been parked, or more likely another car taking up the space.

He had the radio turned on, but the volume was low. It was tuned to a local station to get an update on the weather, but now the sound was fading and static was breaking up the signal. Impatiently Jimmy twiddled the dial until he found an all-news station, then froze as an announcer's urgent voice reported: "Police have reluctantly confirmed the story broken by station WYME that seven-year-old Brian Dornan, missing since five o'clock this evening, has fallen into the hands of alleged murderer Jimmy Siddons, who is believed to be heading for Canada."

Swearing steadily, Jimmy snapped off the radio. Cally. She must have called the cops. The Thruway's probably already lousy with them, all looking for me—and the kid, he reasoned frantically. He glanced to the left, at the car just passing him. Probably dozens of unmarked cars around here, he thought.

Calm. Keep it calm, he told himself. They didn't know what kind of car he was driving. He wasn't going to be dumb enough to speed or, worse yet, crawl so far below the speed limit that they'd get suspicious.

But the kid was a problem. He had to get rid of him right away. He thought the situation through quickly. He'd get off at the nearest exit, take care of him, dump him fast, and then get back on the road. He looked at the boy sleeping beside him. Too bad, kid, but that's the way it's got to be, he said to himself.

On the right he saw an exit sign. That's it, Jimmy thought, that's the one I'll take.

Brian stirred as though starting to wake up, then fell back asleep. Drowsily, he decided that he must have been dreaming, but he thought he had heard his name.

18

Al Rhodes saw the haunted look on the face of Catherine Dornan when she realized the implications of Brian being with Jimmy Siddons. He watched as she closed her eyes, ready to catch her if she fainted.

But then she opened her eyes quickly and reached out to put her arms around her older son. "We mustn't forget that Brian has the St. Christopher medal," she said softly.

The mask of adult bravado that Michael had managed to maintain throughout the evening's ordeal began to crumble. "I don't want anything to happen to Brian," he sobbed.

Catherine stroked his head. "Nothing is going to happen to him," she said calmly. "Believe that, and hold on to it"

Rhodes could see the effort it took for her to talk. Who the hell leaked to the media that Brian Dornan was with Jimmy Siddons? he wondered angrily. Rhodes could feel his fist itching to connect with the louse who had so thoughtlessly jeopardized the kid's life. His anger was further fed by the realization that if Siddons was listening to the radio, the first thing he'd do was get rid of the boy.

Catherine was saying, "Mother, remember how Dad used to tell us about the Christmas Eve when he was only twenty-two years old and in the thick of the Battle of the Bulge, and he took a couple of soldiers in his company into one of the towns on the fringe of the battle line? Why don't you tell Michael about it?"

Her mother took up the story. "There'd been a report of enemy activity there but it turned out not to be true. On the way back to their battalion, they passed the village church. Midnight Mass had just started. They could see that the church was packed. In the midst of all that fear and danger, everyone had left their homes for the service. Their voices singing 'Silent Night' drifted out into the square. Dad said it was the most beautiful sound he'd ever heard."

Barbara Cavanaugh smiled at her grandson. "Grandpa and the other soldiers went into the church. Grandpa used to tell me how scared all of them had been until they saw the faith and courage of those villagers. Here these people were, surrounded by fierce fighting. They had almost no food. Yet those villagers believed that somehow they'd make it through that terrible time."

Her lower lip quivered, but her voice was steady as she continued. "Grandpa said that was when he *knew* he was going to come home to me. And it was an hour later that the St. Christopher medal kept the bullet from going through his heart."

Catherine looked over Michael's head to Officer Ortiz. "Would you take us to the cathedral now? I want to go to midnight Mass. We'd need to be in a seat where you could find me quickly if you have any news."

"I know the head usher. Ray Hickey," Ortiz said. "I'll take care of it."

She looked at Detective Rhodes. "I will be notified immediately if you have any word at all ... ?"

"Absolutely." He could not resist adding, "You're very brave, Mrs. Dornan. And I can tell you this for sure: every law enforcement officer in the northeast is dedicated to getting Brian back safely."

"I believe that, and the only way I can help is to pray."

"The leak didn't come from our guys," Mort Levy reported tersely to Chief of Detectives Folney. Apparently some hotshot kid from WYME was watching Cally's apartment and saw us go in, knew something was up, and followed Aika Banks home. He told her he was a cop and pumped her. His name is Pete Cruise."

"Damn good thing it wasn't one of ours. When all this is over, we'll hang Cruise out to dry for impersonating an officer," Folney said. "In the meantime we've got plenty to do here."

He was standing in front of an enlarged map of the north-east that had been attached to the wall of his office. It was crisscrossed with routes outlined in different colors. Folney picked up a pointer. "Here's where we're at, Mort. We've got to assume that Siddons had a car waiting when he left his sister's place. According to her, he left shortly after six. If we're right, and he got in a car immediately, he's been on the road about five and a half hours."

The pointer moved. "The light snow band extends from the city to about Herkimer, exit 30 on the Thruway. It's heavier throughout New England. But even so, Siddons probably isn't more than four to six hours from the border."

Folney gave a decisive thump to the map. "Amounts to looking for a needle in a haystack."

Mort waited. He knew the boss didn't want comments.

"We've got a special alert along the border," Folney continued. "But with the heavy traffic, he could still be missed, and we all know that someone like Siddons probably knows how to get into Canada without going through a checkpoint." Now he waited for comments.

"How about staging an accident on the major roads to force a one-laner about twenty miles before the border?" Mort suggested.

"I wouldn't rule that out. But on the same principle as erecting a barrier, traffic would build up in two minutes, and Siddons might just try to get off at the nearest exit. If we go ahead with that plan we'll have to put barriers at all the exits, as well."

"And if Siddons feels trapped ... ?" Mort Levy hesitated.

"Siddons has a screw loose, sir. Cally Hunter believes her

brother is capable of killing both Brian and himself rather than get captured. I think she knows what she's talking about."

"And if she had had the guts to call us the minute Jimmy left her house with that boy, he wouldn't have gotten out of Manhattan."

Both men turned. Jack Shore was in the doorway. He looked past Mort Levy to Bud Folney. "A new development, sir. A state trooper, Chris McNally, got a hamburger about twenty minutes ago at the travel plaza between Syracuse, exit 39, and Weedsport, exit 40, on the Thruway. He didn't pay much attention at the time, but the woman at the pickup station, a Miss Deidre Lenihan, was talking about a St. Christopher medal that some kid was wearing."

Bud Folney snapped, "Where is the Lenihan woman now?"

"Her shift ended at eleven. Her mother said her boyfriend was picking her up. They're trying to track them down now. But if Cally Hunter had called us earlier none of this would have happened, we could have been at every travel plaza between here and ..."

Bud Folney almost never raised his voice. But his increasing frustration over the agonizing twists in the manhunt for Jimmy Siddons made him suddenly shout, "Shut up, Jack! 'If only's don't help now. Do something useful. Get the radio stations in that area to broadcast a plea to Deidre Lenihan to call her mother. Say she's needed at home or something. And for God's sake, don't let anyone connect her to Siddons or that child. Got it?"

19

From his perch just off the road, Chris McNally kept a watchful eye on the cars passing before him. The snow had finally ended, but the roadway remained icy. At least the drivers were being careful, he thought, although they were all probably frustrated at having to crawl along at thirty-five miles an hour. Since he'd picked up his hamburger, he had only ticketed one driver, a hotshot in a sports car.

Although he was focused on the flow of traffic on the highway, he still could not get his mind off the report of the missing child. The minute the alert had come in about the little boy who was being held hostage by an escaped cop killer, a little boy wearing a St. Christopher medal, Chris had phoned the McDonald's he had just visited and had asked to speak to Deidre Lenihan, the woman who had waited on him. Even though he hadn't really been paying any attention, he remembered that she had been going on about just such a medal and a little boy. Now he was sorry he hadn't been more in the mood to gab with her, especially since they told him she had just left for the evening with her boyfriend.

Despite the tenuous nature of the tip, he nonetheless had reported the possible lead to his supervisor, who had passed it along to One Police Plaza. They had decided it was worth acting on and had asked the local radio station to broadcast an appeal that Deidre call in to police headquarters. From Deidre's mother they had even gotten a description of the boyfriend's car, then they had gotten his license number and put out an all-points call to try and find them.

Deidre's mother had also told them, however, that she thought tonight was going to be special for her daughter, that the boyfriend had let her know his Christmas present was going to be an engagement ring. Chances were they wouldn't be out on the road now, but someplace a little more romantic.

But even if Deidre did hear the radio appeal and did call in, what could she tell them? That she had seen a kid wearing a St. Christopher medal? They knew that already. Did she know the make and model of the car? Had she seen the license plate? From what Chris knew of Deidre, good-hearted as she was, she was not too alert and was observant only when something struck her fancy. No, it was unlikely that she could provide any more significant information.

All of which made Chris even more frustrated. I might have been around that kid myself, he thought. I might have been in line behind them at McDonald's—why didn't I notice anything more?

The thought of having possibly been close to the kidnapped child practically drove him wild. My kids are home in bed right now, he thought. That little boy should be with his family, too. The problem was, he realized, thinking back over his conversation with Deidre, the car with the little boy could have come through there anywhere between a few minutes and an hour before she told him about it. Still, it was the only lead they had, so they had to treat it seriously.

His radio went on. It was headquarters. "Chris," the dispatcher said, "the boss wants to talk to you."

"Sure."

When the captain got on, his voice was urgent. "Chris, the New York City police think your tip is the closest thing they have to a chance of saving that kid's life. We're going to keep on beating the bushes looking for the Lenihan woman, but in the meantime, rack your brain. Try to remember if there was anything else she might have said, anything that might be of some help . . ."

"I'm trying, sir. I'm on the Thruway now. If it's all right with you, I'd like to start driving west. If the guy was on the McDonald's line about the same time as I was, he's got about a ten to fifteen minute lead on me at this point. If I can pick up a little time on him, I'd sure like to be in the vicinity when word does come through from Deidre. I'd like to be there when we get him."

"Okay, go ahead. And, Chris, for God's sake, *think*. Are you sure that she didn't say anything more specific about either the kid with the St Christopher medal or maybe about the car he was in?"

Just.

The word jumped into Chris's mind. Was it his imagination, or had Deidre said, "*I just saw a kid wearing a St. Christopher medal*"?

He shook his head. He couldn't remember for sure. He did know that the car ahead of him in the line at McDonald's had been a brown Toyota with New York plates.

But there hadn't been a kid in the car, or at least not that he could see. That much he *was* sure of.

Even so ... if Deidre had said "*just*," maybe she did mean the Toyota. What had been the license number on that car? He couldn't remember. But he had noticed something about it. What was it?

"Chris?" The supervisor's voice was sharp, effectively breaking his reverie.

"I'm sorry, sir, I was trying to remember. I think Deidre said she had '*just*' seen the kid wearing the medal. If she meant that literally, then it could have been the car directly in front of me on line. That was a brown Toyota with New York plates."

"Do you remember any part of the number?"

"No, I'm just getting a blank. My mind was probably a million miles away."

"And the car, was there definitely a little boy in it?"

"I didn't see one."

"That's not much help. Every third car on the road is probably a Toyota, and tonight they're all so dirty you can't tell one color from another. They probably all look brown."

"No, this one was definitely brown. That much is for sure. I just wish I could remember Deidre's exact words."

"Well, don't drive yourself crazy. Let's hope we hear from the Lenihan woman, and in the meantime I'll send one of the other cars to cover your station. Head west. We'll check in later."

At least it feels as if I'm doing something, Chris thought as he signed off, turned the key and pressed his foot on the gas.

The squad car leaped forward. One thing I do know is how to drive, he thought grimly as he steered the vehicle onto the breakdown lane and began passing the cautious motorists along the way.

And as he drove, he continued to try to remember what exactly he had seen in front of him. It was there, imprinted in his mind, he was sure of that. If only he could call it up. As he strained, he felt as though his subconscious were trying to shout out the information. If only he could hear it.

In the meantime, every inch of his six-foot-four-inch being was warning him that time was running out for the missing boy.

Jimmy was seething. What with all the cars going like old ladies were driving them, it had taken him half an hour to get to the nearest exit. Jimmy knew he had to get off the Thruway *now* so he could get rid of the kid. A sign told him he was within a half mile of exit 41 and a town named Waterloo. Waterloo for the kid, he thought with grim satisfaction.

The snow had stopped, but he wasn't sure that was good for him. The slush was turning to ice, and that slowed him up more. Plus, without the snow, it was easier for any cops who might be driving by to get a look at him.

He switched to the right lane. In a minute he'd be able to get off the Thruway. Suddenly the brake lights flashed on the car ahead of him, and Jimmy watched with increasing anger and frustration as the rear of that car fishtailed. "Jerk!" Jimmy screamed. "Jerk! Jerk! Jerk!"

Brian sat up straight, eyes wide open, fully alert. Jimmy began to curse, a steady stream of invective flowing as he realized what had happened. A snowplow four or five cars in front had just switched into the exit lane. Instinctively, he steered the Toyota into the middle lane and barely managed to avoid the fishtailing car. As he pulled abreast of the snow-plow, they were just passing the exit.

He slammed the wheel with his fist. Now he'd have to wait till exit 42 to get off the Thruway. How far was that? he wondered.

But as he glanced back at the exit he'd just missed, he realized he actually had been lucky. There was a pileup on the ramp. It must have just happened. That was why the plow had switched lanes. If he had tried to get off there, he could have been stuck for hours.

Finally he saw a sign that informed him the next exit was in six miles. Even at this pace, it shouldn't take more than fifteen minutes. The wheels were gripping the road better. This stretch must have been sanded. Jimmy felt for the gun under his jacket. Should he take it out and hide it under the seat?

No, he decided. If a cop tried to stop him, he needed it just where it was. He glanced at the odometer on the dashboard. He'd set it when he and the kid started driving. It showed that they had gone just over three hundred miles.

There was still a long way to go, but just knowing that he was this close to the Canadian border and Paige was so exciting a sensation he could almost taste it. This time he'd make it work, and whatever he did, this time he wouldn't be dumb enough to be caught by the cops.

Jimmy felt the kid stirring beside him, trying to settle back into sleep. What a mistake! he thought. I should have dumped him five minutes after I took him. I had the car and the money. Why did I think I needed him?

He ached for the moment when he could be rid of the kid and be safe.

20

Officer Ortiz escorted Catherine, her mother, and Michael to the Fiftieth Street entrance to St. Patrick's Cathedral. A security guard stationed outside was waiting for them. "We have seats for you in the reserved section, ma'am," he told Catherine as he pushed the heavy door open.

The magnificent sound of the orchestra led by the organ and accompanied by the choir filled the great cathedral, which was already packed with worshipers.

"*Joyful, joyful,*" the choir was singing.

Joyful, joyful, Catherine thought. Please God, yes, let this night end like that.

They passed the crèche where the life-sized figures of the Virgin, Joseph, and the shepherds were gathered around the empty pile of hay that was the crib. She knew that the statue of the infant Christ child would be placed there during the Mass.

The security guard showed them to their seats in the second row on the middle aisle. Catherine indicated that her mother should go in first. Then she whispered, "You go between us, Michael." She wanted to be on the outside, at the end of the row, so she could be aware the minute the door opened.

Officer Ortiz leaned over. "Mrs. Dornan, if we hear anything, I'll come in for you. Otherwise when Mass is over, the guard will lead you out first, and I'll be waiting outside in the car."

"Thank you," Catherine said, then immediately sank to her knees. The music changed to a swirling paean of triumph as the procession began—the choir, the acolytes, deacon, priests, and bishops, preceding the cardinal, who was carrying the crook of the shepherd in his hand. *Lamb of God*, Catherine prayed, *please, please save my lamb.*

Chief of Detectives Folney, his gaze still riveted to the map of the Thruway on the wall of his office, knew that with each passing minute, the chances of finding Brian Dornan alive grew slimmer. Mort Levy and Jack Shore were across the desk from him.

"Canada," he said emphatically. "He's on his way to Canada, and he's getting close to the border."

They had just received further word from Michigan. Paige Laronde had closed all her bank accounts the day she left Detroit. And in a burst of confidence, she had told another dancer that she had been in touch with a guy who was a genius at creating fake IDs.

It was reported that she had said, "Let me tell you, with the kind of papers I got for my boyfriend and me, we can both just *disappear*."

"If Siddons makes it over the border . . ." Bud Folney muttered more to himself than to the others.

"Nothing from the Thruway guys?" he asked for the third time in fifteen minutes.

"Nothing, sir," Mort said quietly.

"Call them again. I want to talk to them myself."

When he got through to Chris McNally's supervisor and heard for himself that absolutely nothing was new, he decided he wanted to speak to Trooper McNally himself.

"A lot of good that'll do," Jack Shore muttered to Mort Levy.

But before Folney could be connected with McNally, another call came in. "Hot lead," an assistant said, rushing into Folney's office. "Siddons and the kid were seen by a trooper about an hour ago at a rest area on Route 91 in Vermont near White River Junction. He said the man matches Siddons's description to a T, and the boy was wearing some kind of medal."

"Forget McNally," Folney said crisply. "I want to talk to the trooper who saw them. And right now, call the Vermont police and have them put up barriers at all the exits north of the sighting. For all we know, the girlfriend may be holed up waiting for him in a farmhouse on this side of the border."

While Folney waited, he looked over at Mort. "Call Caly Hunter and tell her what we've just learned. Ask her if she knows if Jimmy has ever been to Vermont and if so, where did he go? There might be some place in particular he could be headed."

21

Brian could tell that the car was going faster. He opened his eyes, then shut them as fast as he could. It was easier to stay lying down, curled up on the seat, pretending to be asleep, instead of having to try not to act scared when Jimmy looked at him.

He also had been listening to the radio. Even though the volume was turned way down, he could hear what they were saying, that cop killer Jimmy Siddons, who had shot a prison guard, had kidnapped Brian Dornan.

His mother had been reading a book named *Kidnapped* to him and Michael. Brian liked the story a lot, but when they went to bed, Michael told him he thought it was dumb. He had said that if anyone tried to kidnap him, he'd kick the guy and punch him and run away.

Well, I can't run away, Brian thought. And he was sure that trying to hurt Jimmy by punching him wouldn't work. He wished that he'd been able to open the car door earlier and roll out like he had planned to. He'd have curled up in a ball just like they taught the kids to do in gym class. He would have been okay.

But now the car door near him was locked, and he knew that before be could even pull up the lock and open the door, Jimmy would grab him.

Brian was almost crying. He could feel his nose filling up and his eyes getting watery. He tried to think about how Michael might call him a crybaby. Sometimes that helped him when he was trying not to cry.

It didn't help now, though. Even Michael would probably cry if he was scared and he had to go to the bathroom again. And it said right on the radio that Jimmy was dangerous.

But even though he was crying, Brian made sure he didn't make a sound. He felt the tears on his cheeks, but he didn't move to brush them away. If he moved his hand, Jimmy would notice and know he was awake, and for now he had to keep pretending.

Instead, he clasped the St. Christopher medal even tighter and made himself think about how when Dad was able to go back home, they were going to put up their own Christmas tree and open the presents. Just before they had left for New York, Mrs. Emerson who lived next door had come in to say good-bye, and he had heard her say to his mom, "Catherine, no matter when it is, the night you put up your tree, we're all going to come and sing Christmas carols under your window."

Then she'd hugged Brian and said, "I *know* your favorite carol."

"Silent Night." He'd sung it all by himself in the first-grade Christmas pageant at school last year.

Brian tried to sing it to himself now, in his mind ... but he couldn't get past "Silent night." He knew if he kept thinking about it, he wouldn't be able to keep Jimmy from knowing that he was crying.

Then he almost jumped. Someone on the radio was talking about Jimmy and him again. The man was saying that a state trooper in Vermont was sure he had seen Jimmy Siddons and a young boy in an old Dodge or Chevrolet at a rest stop on Route 91 in Vermont, and the search was being concentrated there.

Jimmy's grim smile vanished as quickly as it had come. The first surge of relief at hearing the news bulletin was followed by instant caution. *Had* some fool claimed he'd spotted them in Vermont? he wondered. It was possible, he decided. When he had been hiding out in Michigan, some two-bit drifter swore he'd seen Jimmy in Delaware. After he got caught at the gas-station job and was taken back to New York, he had found out that the marshals had kept the heat on in Delaware for months.

Even so, being on the Thruway was really beginning to spook him. The road was good and he could make time, but the nearer you got to the border, the more troopers there might be on the road. He decided that when he got off at the next exit, and got rid of the kid, he'd swing over to Route 20. Now that it wasn't snowing, he should be able to make okay time there.

Follow your hunch, Jimmy reminded himself. The only time

he hadn't was when he had tried to hold up that gas station. He still remembered that at the time something had warned him there was a problem.

Well, after this, there'll be no more problems, he thought, looking down at Brian. Then when he looked up, he grinned. The sign looming before him read EXIT 42, GENEVA, ONE MILE AHEAD.

Chris McNally had passed the fender-bender on the exit 41 ramp. Two police cars were on the scene already, so he decided there was no need for him to stop. He had traveled fast, and he hoped that by now he had caught up to any cars that had been ahead of him on line at McDonald's.

Provided, of course, they hadn't taken one of the earlier exits.

A brown Toyota. That's what he kept looking for. Finding it was the one chance. He knew it. What was it about the license plate? He clenched his teeth, again trying hard to remember. There had been something about it . . . Think, damn it, he told himself, *think*.

He didn't for one minute believe the report that Siddons and the kid had been spotted in Vermont. Every gut instinct kept telling Chris that they were nearby.

Exit 42 to Geneva was coming up. That meant the border was only another hundred miles or so away. Most of the cars were doing fifty to sixty miles an hour now. If Jimmy Siddons was in this vicinity, he could look forward to being out of the country in less than two hours.

What was there about the license plate of the Toyota? he asked himself once more.

Chris's eyes narrowed. He could see a dark Toyota in the passing lane that was moving fast. He switched lanes and drove up beside it, then glanced in. He prayed that it held a single man or a man with a young boy. Just a chance to find that child. Give me a chance, he prayed.

Without turning on his siren or dome light, Chris continued past the Toyota. He had been able to see a young couple inside. The guy was driving with his arm around the girl, not a good idea on an icy road. Another time he'd have pulled him over.

Chris stepped on the gas. The road was clearer, the traffic was better spaced. But everything was moving faster and faster, and closer and closer to Canada.

His radio was on low when a call came in for him. "Officer McNally?"

"Yes,"

"New York City Chief of Detectives Bud Folney calling you from One Police Plaza. I just spoke to your supervisor again. The Vermont sighting is a washout. The Lenihan woman can't be found. Tell me what you reported earlier about a brown Toyota."

Knowing his boss had dismissed that, Chris realized that this Folney must be really pressing him.

He explained that if Deidre had been talking about the car directly ahead of him in the McDonald's line, she was talking about a brown Toyota with New York plates.

"And you can't remember the license."

"No, sir." Chris wanted to strangle the words in his throat. "But there was something unusual about it."

He was almost at exit 42. As he watched, a vehicle two cars ahead switched into the exit lane. His casual glance became a stare. "My God," he said.

"Officer? What is it?" In New York, Bud Folney instinctively knew that something was happening.

"*That's it.*" Chris said. "It wasn't the license plate I noticed. It was the bumper sticker. There's just a piece of it left and it says *inheritance.* Sir, I'm following that Toyota down the exit ramp right now. Can you check out the license?"

"Don't lose that car," Bud snapped "And hang on."

Three minutes later the phone rang in apartment 8C, in 10 Stuyvesant Oval, in lower Manhattan. A sleepy and anxious Edward Hillson picked it up. "Hello," he said. He felt his wife's nervous grasp on his arm.

"What? My car? I parked it around the corner at five or so. No, I didn't lend it to anyone. Yes. It's a brown Toyota. What are you telling me?"

Bud Folney got back to Chris. "I think you have him, but for God's sake remember, he's threatened to kill the child before he lets himself get captured. So be careful."

22

Michael was so sleepy. All he wanted to do was lean against Gran and close his eyes. But he couldn't do that yet, not until he was sure that Brian was okay. Michael struggled to suppress his growing fear. *Why didn't he grab me if he saw that lady pick up Mom's wallet? I could have run after her and helped him when he got caught by that guy.*

The cardinal was at the altar now. But when the music stopped, instead of starting to offer Mass, he began to speak. "On this night of joy and hope . . ."

Off to the right, Michael could see the television cameras. He had always thought it would be cool to be on television, but whenever he had thought about it, the circumstances he envisioned had to do with winning something or with witnessing some great event. That would be fun. Tonight, when he and Mom were on together, it wasn't fun.

It was awful to hear Mom begging people to help them find Brian.

"... in a year that has brought so much violence to the innocent..."

Michael straightened up. The cardinal was talking about them, about Dad being sick and Brian being missing and believed to be with that escaped killer. He was saying, "Brian Dornan's mother, grandmother, and ten-year-old brother are with us at this Mass. Let our special prayer be that Dr. Thomas Dornan will recover fully and that Brian will be found unharmed."

Michael could see that Mom and Gran were both crying. Their lips were moving, and he knew they were praying. His prayer was the advice he would have given Brian if he could hear him: *Run, Brian, run.*

Now that he was off the Thruway, Jimmy felt somewhat relieved, despite a gnawing sense that things were closing in on him.

He was running low on gas but was afraid to risk stopping at a station with the kid in the car. He was on Route 14 south. That connected with Route 20 in about six miles. Route 20 led to the border.

There was a lot less traffic here than on the Thruway. Most people were home by now anyway, asleep or getting ready for Christmas morning. It was unlikely that anyone would be looking for him here. Still, he reasoned, the best thing to do was to get on some of the local streets in Geneva, find someplace like a school where there'd be a parking lot, or find a wooded area, somewhere he could stop without being noticed and do what he had to do.

As he took the next right-hand turn, he glanced in the rear-view mirror. His antennae went up. He thought he had seen headlights reflected there as he made the turn, but now he didn't see them anymore.

I'm getting too jumpy, he thought.

A block later it suddenly was like they'd sailed off the edge of the earth. As far as he could see, there were no cars ahead. They were in a residential area, quiet and dark. The houses were mostly unlit, except some of them still had Christmas-tree lights glowing from bushes and evergreens on the snow-covered lawns.

He couldn't be sure if the kid was really asleep or faking it. Not that it mattered. This was the sort of place he needed. He drove six blocks and then saw what he was looking for: a school, with a long driveway that had to lead to a parking area.

His eyes missed nothing as he carefully searched the area for any sign of an approaching car or someone out walking. Then he stopped the car and opened the window halfway, listening intently for any hint of trouble. The cold instantly turned his breath to steam. He could hear nothing but the hum of the Toyota's engine. It was quiet out there. Silent.

Still, he decided to drive around the block one more time, just to be sure he wasn't being followed.

As he put his foot on the accelerator, and as the car slowly moved forward, he kept his gaze glued to the rearview mirror. Damn. He'd been right. There *was* a car behind him, running without lights. Now it was moving, too. The lights from a brilliantly lit tree reflected on its rooftop dome.

A squad car. Cops! Damn them, Jimmy swore under his breath. Damn them! Damn them! He tromped on the gas pedal. It might be his last ride, but he'd make it a good one.

He looked down at Brian. "Quit pretending. I know you're awake," he shouted. "Sit up, damn you. I shoulda ditched you as soon as I was out of the city. Lousy kid."

Jimmy floored the accelerator. A quick look in the rear-view mirror confirmed that the pursuing car had also speeded up and was now openly following him. But so far there seemed to be only one of them.

Clearly Cally had told the cops he had the kid, he reasoned. She'd probably also told them that he said he'd kill the kid first if they tried to close in on him. If that cop behind him knew that, it explained why he wasn't trying to pull him over right now.

He glanced at the speedometer: fifty ... sixty ... seventy. Damn this car! Jimmy thought, suddenly wishing he had something more powerful than a Toyota. He hunched over the wheel. He couldn't outrun them, but he still might have a chance to get away.

The guy chasing him didn't have backup yet. What would he do if he saw the kid had been shot and pushed out of the car?

He'd stop to try to help him, Jimmy reasoned. I'd better do it right away, he thought, before he has time to call in help.

He reached inside his jacket for his gun. Just then the car hit a patch of ice and began to skid. Jimmy dropped the gun in his lap, turned the wheels in the direction of the skid, then managed to straighten the car just inches away from crashing into a tree at the edge of the sidewalk.

Nobody can drive like I can, he thought grimly. Then he picked up the gun again and released the safety catch. If the cop stops for the kid, I'll make it to Canada, he promised himself. He released the lock on the passenger door and reached across the terrified boy to open it.

23

Cally knew she had to call police headquarters to see if there was any word about little Brian. She had told Detective Levy she didn't think Jimmy would try to reach Canada through Vermont. "He got in trouble up there when he was about fifteen," she'd said. "He never did time there, but I think some sheriff really scared Jimmy. He told him he had a long memory and warned him never to show up in Vermont again. Even though that was at least ten years ago, Jimmy is superstitious. I think he'd stick to the Thruway. I know he went to Canada a couple of times when he was a teenager, and both times he went that way."

Levy had listened to her. She knew he wanted to trust her, and she prayed that this time he had. She also prayed that she was right and they got the boy back safely, so she could know that in some small way she had helped.

Someone other than Levy answered his phone, and she was told to wait. Then Levy came on, "What is it, Cally?"

"I just had to know if there's been any word ... I've been praying that what I told you about Jimmy taking the Thruway helped."

Levy's voice softened even though he still spoke quickly. "Cally, it did help, and we're very grateful. I can't talk now, but whatever prayers you know, keep saying them."

That means they must have located Jimmy, she thought. But what was happening to Brian?

Cally sank to her knees. *It doesn't matter what happens to me*, she prayed. *Stop Jimmy before he hurts that child.*

Chris McNally had known it the minute Jimmy spotted him. The radio was open between him and headquarters and was tied in to One Police Plaza in Manhattan. "He knows he's being followed," Chris reported tersely. "He's taking off like a bat out of hell."

"Don't lose him," Bud Folney said quietly.

"We've got a dozen cars on the way, Chris," the dispatcher snapped. "They're running silent and on dim lights. They'll surround you. We're bringing in a chopper, too."

"Keep them out of sight!" Chris pressed his foot on the accelerator. "He's going seventy. There's not many cars out, but these streets aren't completely cleared. This is getting dangerous."

As Siddons raced across an intersection, Chris watched in horror as he barely missed slamming into another car. Siddons was driving like a maniac. There was going to be an accident, he knew it. "Passing Lakewood Avenue," he reported. Two blocks later he saw the Toyota skid and almost hit a tree. A minute after that, he yelled, "The boy!"

"What is it?" Folney demanded.

"The passenger door of the Toyota just opened. The inside light's on, so I can see the kid struggling. Oh God ... Siddons has his gun out. It looks like he's going to shoot him."

24

"*Kyrie Eleison,*" the choir sang.

Lord have mercy, Barbara Cavanaugh prayed.

Save my lamb, Catherine begged

Run, Dork, run, get away from him, Michael shouted in his mind.

Jimmy Siddons was crazy. Brian had never been in a car before that was going so fast He wasn't sure what was going on, but there must be someone following them.

Brian looked away from the road for a moment and glanced at Jimmy. He had his gun out. He felt Jimmy tugging at his seat belt, releasing it. Then he reached across Brian and opened the door beside him. He could feel the cold air rushing in.

For a moment he was paralyzed with fear. Then he sat up very straight. He realized what was about to happen. That Jimmy was going to shoot him and push him out of the car.

He had to get away. He was still clutching the medal in his

right hand. He felt Jimmy poke him in the side with the gun, pushing him toward the open door and the roadway rushing beneath them. Holding onto the seat-belt buckle with his left hand, he swung out blindly with his right. The medal arced and slammed into Jimmy's face, catching him in his left eye.

Jimmy yelled and took his hand off the wheel, instinctively slamming his foot on the brake. As he grabbed his eye, the gun went off. The bullet whistled past Brian's ear as the out-of-control car began to spin around. It jumped the curb, went up into a corner lawn, and caught on a bush. Still spinning, it slowed as it dragged the bush back across the lawn and out onto the edge of the road.

Jimmy was swearing now, one hand again on the wheel, the other aiming the gun. Blood dripped into his eye from a gash across his forehead and cheek.

Get out. Get out. Brian heard the command in his head as though someone were shouting it at him. Brian dove for the door and rolled out onto the snow-covered lawn just as a second bullet passed over his shoulder.

"Jesus Christ, the kid's out of the car," Chris yelled. He jammed on the brakes and skidded to a stop behind the Toyota. "He's getting up. Oh my God."

Bud Folney shouted, "Is he hurt?" but Chris didn't hear him. He was already out of his car and running toward the boy. Siddons was in control of the Toyota again and had turned it, clearly planning to run over Brian. In what seemed like an eternity but was actually only seconds, Chris had crossed the space between him and Brian and gathered the boy in his arms.

The car was racing toward them, its passenger door still open and its interior still illuminated so that the maniacal anger in Jimmy Siddons's face was clearly visible. Clutching Brian tightly against him, Chris dove to the side and rolled down a snowy incline just as the wheels of the Toyota passed inches from their heads. An instant later, with a sickening sound of metal crashing and glass breaking, the vehicle careened off the porch of the house and flipped over.

For a moment there was silence, and then the quiet was shattered as sirens screamed and wailed. Lights from a dozen squad cars brightened the night as swarms of troopers raced to surround the overturned vehicle. Chris lay in the snow for a few seconds, hugging Brian to him, listening to the convergence of sounds. Then he heard a small relieved voice ask, "Are you St. Christopher?"

"No, but right now I feel like him, Brian," Chris said heartily. "Merry Christmas, son."

25

Officer Manuel Ortiz slipped noiselessly through the side door of the cathedral and instantly caught Catherine's eye. He smiled and nodded his head. She jumped up and ran to meet him.

"Is he ..."

"He's fine. They're sending him back in a police helicopter. He'll be here by the time Mass is over."

Noticing that one of the television cameras was trained on them, Ortiz raised his hand and made a circle of his thumb and forefinger, a symbol that for this moment, on this most special of days, everything was A-OK.

Those seated nearby witnessed the exchange and began to clap softly. As others turned, they stood, and applause began to slowly rumble through the giant cathedral. It was a full five minutes before the deacon could begin to read the Christmas Gospel, "'And it came to pass ...'"

*

"I'm going to let Cally know what's happened," Mort Levy told Bud Folney. "Sir, I know she should have called us earlier, but I hope ..."

"Don't worry. I'm not going to play Scrooge tonight. She worked with us. She deserves a break," Folney said crisply. "Besides, the Dornan woman has already said she's not going to press charges against her." He paused for a moment, thinking. "Listen, there's got to be some toys left in the station houses. Tell the guys to get busy and round some up for that little girl of Cally's. Have them meet us at Cally's building in forty-five minutes. Mort, you and I are going to give them to her. Shore, you go home."

It was Brian's first helicopter ride, and even though he was incredibly tired, he was too excited to even think about closing his eyes. He was sorry Officer McNally—Chris, as he had said he should call him—hadn't been able to come with him. But he had been with Brian when they took Jimmy Siddons away, and he had told him not to worry, that this was one guy who would never get out of prison again. And then he'd gotten the St. Christopher medal out of the car for Brian.

As the helicopter came down it looked like it was almost landing on the river. He recognized the Fifty-ninth Street Bridge and the Roosevelt Island tramway. His dad had taken him for a ride on that. He wondered suddenly if his father knew what had happened to him.

He turned to one of the officers. "My dad's in a hospital near here. I have to go see him. He might be worried."

The officer, who was by now familiar with the story of the whole Dornan family, said, "You'll see him soon, son. But now, your mother's watting for you. She's at midnight Mass at St. Patrick's Cathedral."

When the buzzer sounded at Cally's Avenue B apartment, she answered it with the resigned belief that she was going to be arrested. Detective Levy had called to say only that he and another officer were coming by. But it was two beaming, self-appointed Santa Clauses who arrived at her door, laden with' dolls and games and a sparkling white wicker doll's carriage.

As she watched, unbelieving, they placed the gifts under and around the Christmas tree.

"Your information about your brother was a tremendous help," Bud Folney said. "The Dornan boy is okay and on his way back to the city. Jimmy is on his way back to prison; he's our responsibility once again, and I promise we won't let him get away this time. From now on I hope it gets a lot better for you."

Cally felt as though a giant weight had been lifted from her. She could only whisper, "Thank you ... thank you ..."

Folney and Levy chorused, "Merry Christmas, Cally," and were gone.

When they left, Cally at last knew she could go to bed and

sleep. Gigi's even breathing was an answered prayer. From now on, she'd be able to hear it every night, and listen without fear that her little girl would be taken away from her again. Everything *will* get better, she thought. I know it now.

As she fell asleep, her last thought was that when Gigi saw that the big package with Santa's present was missing from under the Christmas tree, she could honestly tell her that Santa Claus had come and taken it away.

The recessional was about to start when once again the side door of the cathedral opened and Officer Ortiz entered. This time he was not alone. He bent down to the small boy beside him and pointed. Before Catherine could get to her feet, Brian was in her arms, the St. Christopher medal he was wearing pressed against her heart.

As she held him close, she said nothing, but felt the silent tears of relief and joy course down her cheeks, knowing that he once again was safe, and firm in her belief now that Tom was going to make it, too.

Barbara also did not speak, but leaned over and laid her hand on her grandson's head.

It was Michael who broke the silence with whispered words of welcome. "Hi, Dork," he said with a grin.

Christmas Day

Christmas morning dawned cold and clear. At ten o'clock, Catherine, Brian, and Michael arrived at the hospital.

Dr. Crowley was waiting for them when they got off the elevator on the fifth floor. "My God, Catherine," he said, "are you okay? I hadn't heard about what happened until I got here this morning. You must be exhausted."

"Thanks, Spence, but I'm fine." She looked at her sons. "We're all fine. But how is Tom? When I called this morning, all they would say was that he had a good night."

"And he did. It's an excellent sign. He had a very good night. A lot better than yours, that's for sure. I hope you don't mind, but I decided it was best if I told Tom about Brian. The press have been calling here all morning, and I didn't want to risk his hearing about it from an outsider. When I told him, I started with the happy ending, of course."

Catherine felt relief rush through her. "I'm glad he knows, Spence. I didn't know how to tell him. I couldn't be sure how he'd take it."

"He took it very well, Catherine. He's a lot stronger than you might think." Crowley looked at the medal around Brian's neck. "I understand you went through a lot to make sure you'd be able to give that medal to your dad. I promise all of you that between St. Christopher and me, we'll make sure he gets well."

The boys tugged at Catherine's hands.

"He's waiting for you," Spence said, smiling.

The door of Tom's room was partly open. Catherine pushed it the rest of the way and stood looking at her husband.

The head of the bed was elevated. When Tom saw them, his face brightened with that familiar smile.

The boys ran to him, then carefully stopped just inches from the bed. They both reached out and grasped his hand. Catherine watched his eyes fill with tears when he looked at Brian.

He's so pale, she thought I can tell that he hurts. But he *is* going to get better. She did not need to force the radiant smile that her lips formed as Michael lifted the chain with the St. Christopher medal from Brian's neck and together they put it on Tom. "Merry Christmas, Dad," they chorused.

As her husband looked over their sons' heads and his lips formed the words *I love you*, other words sang through Catherine's being.

All is calm . . . all is bright.

THE
DARK
PAGES

Visit The Dark Pages to discover a community of like-minded readers and crime fiction fans.

If you would like more news, exclusive content and the chance to receive advance reading copies of our books before they are published, find us on Facebook, Twitter (**@dark_pages**) or at **www.thedarkpages.co.uk**